THE PATH OF DEEDS

Jason Worrell

ISBN: 0692552200
ISBN 13: 9780692552209
Library of Congress Control Number: 2015917031
Jason Worrell, San Francisco, CA

There's a difference between being violent and being driven to violence. I am not a violent man.

Jack Hammond in
The Chase
Played by
Charlie Sheen

CHAPTER ONE

"That can't be him," Shane Deeds said to no one in his empty truck. "Am I really that lucky?" Deeds slowed the truck down, and as he got closer, the hopeful anticipation became unbearable.

Deeds was squinting to make an identification. When he confirmed who the young man was, Deeds's eyes widened and a subdued smile appeared on his face. He was astounded at this fortunate development but had to suppress his elation and get ready. Deeds spoke with pleasure: "Your luck has run out, you little fucker."

It was unfortunate for the young man standing on the side of the highway. Deeds could tell he was eager for a ride, and when Deeds slowed the truck down, the hitchhiker was positively happy.

The hitchhiker had no idea what was going to happen. He was grateful now, and soon he would be terrified. Deeds looked at the young man and said, "No one can stop what's coming."

The big pickup truck came to a stop in the emergency lane of the highway. Beyond the emergency lane was a vast field that gave way to foothills and grand mountains, all covered in snow. It was a majestic scene whose beauty and power could not be captured with words, paint, or film. You simply had to be present in this frozen land to experience its emotional wonder.

The engine's rumble was strong, and the exhaust, visible. It was a very cold and clear day. The morning sun was shining, and the sky was a perfect dark blue. The ground was a pristine white that led to a gray horizon.

Your breath could be seen as the vapor danced for many moments after it left your mouth. The empty highway was frozen as if in a dreamscape.

Deeds pulled his mesh cap low and put on sunglasses and gloves. He reached over and struggled momentarily to unlock the passenger door and open it, but then he quickly locked it again and fully swung it outward in an inviting manner.

"Thanks for stopping, man! I've been here a long-ass time." The hitchhiker was out of breath after he ran the distance from his former post to Deeds's truck.

Deeds somewhat turned toward the hitchhiker and asked, "Where ya headed?"

The hitchhiker's answer was irrelevant. No matter the destination spewed from his mouth, he was going to where Deeds decided to take him. Indeed, no one could stop what was coming.

"Anywhere but Old Falls. I need to get the hell out of there. You know how it is. Can I ride with you till you get to where you're going? I can catch another ride, I'm sure. Is that cool?" The hitchhiker could not make true eye contact with the driver through the driver's reflective sunglasses. He only saw himself.

"Yes."

"Cool, man; thanks."

The hitchhiker had ratty hair, pale skin, a missing front tooth, and a diamond earring, and he did not smell too good. He threw his old military-surplus duffel bag in the truck's bed. The hitchhiker had to swing his bag a couple of times to gain momentum to reach the height of the big truck's bed. He also had to bounce once or twice to climb in. It was a big truck, and the hitchhiker was short. He climbed in and shut the door.

The door could not be opened from the inside unless your hand had a strong grip to pull up and twist the old rusted lock. The hitchhiker did not know this. Deeds did. The door was quite locked.

Deeds accelerated onto the highway. They were about half an hour away from anywhere, not that it mattered to the passenger. Deeds kept the truck's speed at a normal sixty-five miles per hour.

The young man blew into his hands and said, "Nice and warm in here."

Deeds said nothing.

A minute or two went by. "Yeah, man, shit went down—gotta split," the passenger said, chuckling. "Had problems with the woman—with the boss, too." The young man looked at Deeds for a follow-up question, but none came. The passenger continued. "Yeah, my boss, the higher-ups—they could make things difficult." Again, he awaited a follow-up question from the driver. Silence. Not even a glance in his direction.

Deeds could tell he was fishing for a follow-up question about his boss, job, and woman. Deeds stared at the road.

The passenger, not deterred, asked, "Do you party?" He was reaching into his pocket.

Deeds knew he was going to pull out drugs of some flavor. "I'm not buying," he said to the small-time drug dealer, their paths having crossed many a night.

The passenger smiled. "Hey, it's all good, bro. This is a freebie for picking me up, my man. This one's on me!"

The passenger did not recognize Deeds and did not know that Deeds wanted him dead in the name of all that was fair and just. Deeds abruptly answered no, stared at the open road, and increased the speed of the truck to seventy miles per hour.

Somewhat startled by this unfriendly response, the young man stuffed whatever was half out of his pocket right back in. "Right. Right, OK. I got it. No worries. Got to pay attention to the road. Got it. Maybe later?" The passenger was trying to lighten the tension.

"There is no later." The statement hung in the air and added to the tension.

The hitchhiker was a little put off. "Hey, uh, it's cool, man. It's cool. No worries. We good?"

Deeds said nothing. A minute passed. Then another. Then another. The truck was cruising at seventy-five miles per hour now.

The hitchhiker was looking out the passenger window and windshield but ceased his gazing before it reached the peculiar driver. He looked up, at the dash, at his feet, and throughout most of the truck's interior. He quickly glanced at the big man driving the truck and nervously asked, "Do I know you?"

The young man checked the side-view mirror and leaned forward and looked into the air vents. "Are you a cop? You have to tell me if you are."

Deeds said nothing.

"Well?"

More silence.

"Look, man, it's cool. I'm just looking for a ride. OK? Last dude could only take me a little ways, so I appreciate you helping me out, bro. We cool?"

Deeds said nothing and kicked it up to eighty miles per hour.

The hitchhiker was uncomfortable, but his tough-guy pride was making it worse. After a few more minutes, the apprehensive yet angry passenger declared, "Hey, asshole, I'm not looking for trouble. All right? I got a lotta friends. Motherfuckers you don't wanna fuck with. We got each other's backs, man. You feel me?"

The old truck was loudly storming down the frozen highway, like an angry tank, at eighty-five miles per hour. The rampaging behemoth was on a path, and anyone who crossed that path would be hurt.

The young man acted angry and asked, "You know who you're fucking with?"

The very sentence made Deeds snicker. The desperate statement of a wannabe tough guy too stupid to know the end was near.

In a very calm, quiet, almost pleading way, the hitchhiker said, "Bro, just pull over. I'll catch another ride. OK, man? Can you just pull over?"

Deeds finally spoke. "You don't recognize me?"

The young man was frightened and puzzled. "I don't know. No. I...I don't know. Can you just pull over?"

Deeds reached for something under his seat. When he found it, he gripped hard and said, "I was hoping to find you. I'm a very lucky man."

The hitchhiker was confused and stunned to see the large, fixed serrated-blade survival knife and remained so as he watched it pierce his leg above the knee. The terror and pain caused a silent reaction. The young man was in shock-based suspended animation. This was broken as Deeds pushed and pulled the knife, violently increasing the size of the puncture wound. There was a lot of blood.

In a desperate and agonizing fight-or-flight reaction, the hitchhiker batted at Deeds's face and arm while letting loose a series of effeminate screams. Deeds felt good.

The howling continued but then abruptly ceased after Deeds let go of the buried knife, curled his arm, rotated toward the driver's-side door, and with speed and power threw a vicious elbow right at the hitchhiker's nose. The break was loud, and the brutal blow overcame the helpless passenger, allowing Deeds to slow the truck and pull over, once again, to the emergency lane.

After Deeds put the truck in park, he unfastened his seat belt and turned and faced the incoherent passenger. Deeds grabbed the knife handle with his left hand and propped himself up.

In this elevated position, with his big right hand and his strong arm, Deeds held the hitchhiker in a strangling grip, forcing him up against the passenger's window, and then continued to drive the knife back and forth. This brought Deeds pleasure.

The hitchhiker, through instinct and not a well-thought-out cognizant strategy, resisted and tried to strike Deeds and hit his arms but to no avail. After a couple of moments, Deeds withdrew his right hand and threw a vicious haymaker at the hitchhiker's jaw, knocking him out.

After all reactionary convulsions, flailing limbs, and muffled yells, the hitchhiker was subdued, and any potential retaliation, neutralized.

The hitchhiker was slumped forward. He was drooling, and it mixed with the torrent of blood from his newly crooked nose. He made mumbling and gurgling sounds as his airways were compromised due to his broken nose and broken jaw.

Deeds had a couple of bungee cords under his seat where the knife had been. He grabbed them and attached the first cord's hook to a peg on the gun rack. With as much tension as he could create, Deeds looped it around the young man's neck many times ceasing the airflow.

Deeds then slowly, as he was fighting the cord's tension, reached a peg on the driver's side of the cab with the other hook, where his own head would be when he continued driving. Deeds took the other cord and repeated the process except he attached both hooks on the passenger's side.

One bungee cord was wrapped around the hitchhiker's neck and fastened to the opposite side of the cab. The other bungee cord was wrapped around the hitchhiker's neck and fastened to his side of the cab. The bloodied hitchhiker was arranged rigidly upright.

Deeds grabbed some napkins from the glove compartment and wiped the hitchhiker's face. He held the wad there until the blood flow slowed. Then Deeds stuffed the wad in the unconscious man's mouth.

Deeds then placed his big gloved hand over the broken nose and stuffed mouth and used his strength to immobilize the victim as his central nervous system reacted to the lack of air.

After a few more moments, the passenger appeared to be sitting normally: upright, conscious, and facing the open road. The hitchhiker was dead. Deeds looked at him and said, "You deserved this, you little fucker."

CHAPTER TWO

Engel Falls in previous generations was a town full of people who worked hard and took care of their families and each other. They had pride in their well-maintained and modest homes, their domestic trucks, and the companies they worked for.

There were factories. There were stores and services, and there was commerce, production, and an economy that was plentiful. There were schools, fairs, taverns, and restaurants, and there was a movie house. There were many things to do for the whole family.

There was nothing to indicate that the town of Engel Falls had anything but a bright and prosperous future. However, things got bad.

A once-fruitful economy had taken a nose dive. Companies left, and smaller businesses closed. Anything lucrative vanished. Prosperity ceased. There was no buckling down and riding it out. Life became hard in Engel Falls.

After this collapse, most of Engel Falls had become rundown. The sense of community faded away. In some areas it looked not as bad as a war zone but like a waste zone—an area designated for discarded matter.

Buildings decayed over the years. Places of work were now fading relics of a happier era. What were once busy businesses devolved into silent tombs with broken windows, graffiti, and piles of garbage. What were once well-maintained, hard-earned homes gave way to lawns full of broken-down cars, dead grass, and piles of garbage.

Desperation brought out the weakness in people. While the majority of the hardworking people moved to find work, some—under the guise of stoicism, brave or foolhardy—remained in their town.

Unfortunately, over time these once-strong people died off or begat weak people and fell into traps of cyclical despair with crime and drugs and their subsequent downward spirals.

Other towns and cities in the area were feeling the same harmful economic effects but not to the degree of Engel Falls. This once-strong city, which had often been looked up to by its neighboring sister towns, was hit especially hard. The highest fell the furthest. It seemed that bad luck and hard times were to remain.

Then, about two decades later, things began to improve. There was hope as a tech boom began. It appeared this was the much-needed and long-awaited remedy for Engel Falls's hardship. There was work. There was growth. There was life.

Businesses needed land, pure and simple. Due to the destitute conditions, land in Engel Falls was cheap.

The neglected, faded, and obsolete structures would not suffice. The faded relics of a distant past were demolished to make way for the future of the new and improved and profitable Engel Falls. The boom was on.

The demand exploded for demolition and construction workers; electricians; plumbers; landscapers; road workers; engineers; designers; architects; manufacturers, sellers, and transporters of materials for a new age of office environments and homes; managers for commercial properties; and remodeling contractors.

The supply was low, so people made fortunes in owning, managing, and working these trades. Supplies, transportation, and all subsequent necessary aspects and facets flourished.

There was work to be done. A new wave of population had to be housed. The run-down houses had to be remodeled, rebuilt, or, in many cases, razed. Well, maybe not razed, but the decrepit symbols of hardship needed improvement to fit the upcoming prosperity.

The broken-down people also had to be remodeled, rebuilt, or razed. Well, maybe not razed. After the waste zones of buildings were systematically erased and the run-down houses were cleared, their former inhabitants were paid off and moved elsewhere, since they couldn't really afford anything in the "New" Engel Falls.

The old section of Engel Falls never really did experience the same rebirth. "Old Falls" was where the trailer parks and affordable housing were.

The purveyors of New Falls did what they could to make sure the former waste zones never reappeared in their section of town, and they made sure the decay of Old Falls was contained in Old Falls.

Many attempts were made to transform and let the old sections catch up with the new sections, but it did not happen. Old Falls became the location for industrial and wholesale businesses—the kind of businesses that had yards that were behind fences adorned with razor wire.

Truckers picked up and dropped off materials. Trains did the same. There was a small airport. There were salvage yards and lumberyards. The businesses Old Falls had were where construction workers, contractors, and others came in at first light to buy building materials and then left to rebuild New Falls.

When the working day was done, the workers went home to New Falls. Old Falls was where the successful were not present past the end of the workday.

Here the people were lower class. There were drugs and crime. Things were not as bad as before, not even close. In fact, many in the real-estate game bought land here and waited for gentrification to expand. So far it had not taken off as it had in New Falls.

CHAPTER THREE

Shane Deeds lived and worked in New Falls. At six feet four and over 260 pounds, he was recognized as a big dude. His features were not of comic-book status or something from a movie. He was just simply a big dude, and most people's instincts told them to not piss him off. Yet there always seemed to be a contingent who liked to antagonize him.

In Engel Falls there were lots of big, burly types—tall men with solid bone structures and accompanying girth. New Falls was home to the construction workers, contractors, electricians, truckers, and others who had rebuilt and were rebuilding New Falls. Many of these residents were ex-military. Many (including Deeds, his senior year) had played high-school football.

And since Engel Falls had a colder mountainous climate, the guys often wore their thick jackets and parkas and other thermal wear, augmenting their appearance. Many had beards or longer hair and were outdoorsmen sporting flannel shirts, steel-toed work boots, or shit-kicker cowboy boots.

Most wore sheathed knives on their belts and usually had a dip, a plug of chew, a cigarette, or a cigar handy. And while lots of tough-looking big dudes were around town, Deeds was taller or stronger than most of them.

As these guys rebuilt New Falls, the in-demand builders and workers could afford nice houses, and their kids could attend the affluent schools that New Falls now had.

The techies lived in the same nice neighborhoods. Those who made their nut lived in the hills in their spacious mansions, but everywhere else, successful blue-collar people and white-collar techies lived contently in New Falls, forgetting or unaware of the previous decades' destitution.

Assumptions may have been made about Deeds when people saw him. Maybe he'd played football in school, at which point he started and continued to lift weights. Perhaps he was a man of the outdoors. He probably was a builder of some trade, taking advantage of the boom sweeping New Falls, as was evident by his address, which was in a nice, new apartment complex on the top floor with a great view of the Devil Mountains to the north.

From all appearances Shane Deeds was a hardworking big man like all the other hardworking men around town. Deeds appeared to be a regular guy and was in many aspects.

Deeds was quiet but not one to shy away from a polite conversation. If you needed help, Deeds was there to oblige. Deeds wanted to be known as a nice guy, and he was a nice guy. He had a big heart, and he wanted to be liked.

Deeds's only downfall was that he was emotional. If someone was nice to him, he or she was the greatest person living. If someone was rude to him, he took it personally.

Deeds would get upset and wonder, *Why would they do this?* Many sleepless nights were spent trying to find an answer. Other people could forget and forget easily. For Deeds it was a struggle to let go.

CHAPTER FOUR

Deeds's abode was a typical man's apartment. Nothing flashy, but an obvious effort had been made to make it look nice. Deeds liked a clean place. He was neither obsessive nor compulsive (trendy neuroses to possess, in his opinion) about the cleanliness of his place. Deeds just thought it should look nice in case anyone ever came over. No one ever really did though.

Deeds had been in his place for a few years since the big sale, and visitors were quite rare. Once or twice upon a time, Deeds may have had a neighbor come over and use the phone if they got locked out of their apartment.

One afternoon there was a knock at the door. Deeds opened his door and saw that it was his neighbor.

Deeds greeted him politely, but unfortunately, the curt executive-associate-sales-representative-project-manager-team-leader-looking guy, without delay or even looking up from his phone, asked Deeds if he had signed for a package that he was eagerly awaiting.

"No, I haven't. Sorry."

Frustrated, the man placed the tips of his index finger and thumb at the base of his nose between his closed eyes and stood silently.

Deeds then suggested to the rude neighbor, "Post a bulletin on the bulletin board. Maybe the delivery guy screwed up the apartment number—"

"Yeah, OK, thanks," the impolite man interrupted, returning his gaze to his phone and turning to head elsewhere.

"Well, fuck off, then," said Deeds not so under his breath.

"What was that?" replied the neighbor, finally making eye contact.

Deeds stood up tall in the middle of the doorway to show the rude neighbor that he indeed took up the entire width of the entryway, almost. Diplomatically, Deeds stated that he was only trying to help by making that suggestion.

The tense neighbor asked, "You don't think someone hasn't suggested that? You don't think I could have come up with that brilliant idea myself?"

Deeds thought, *My neighbor is a prick.*

Not to be put down by someone whose arrogance assumed that he was an unintelligent man, Deeds yielded as a response, "I'm sorry I suggested something that someone else already had. I'm supposed to know that others have said the same thing? I'm not clairvoyant. No one is. Regardless, you are to hear people's entire statements and then respond politely, not impatiently wait to speak and interrupt them all the while looking at your fucking phone. I hope the locating process for your absent parcel is swift and effortless. Now, walk the fuck away."

Deeds felt great as he closed the door. Donning a big smile, he went back to writing checks, placing them in envelopes, and placing stamps in the corner. *Christ, it costs a lot to exist.*

Moments later there was a knock at the door. Deeds opened up and saw the same man, now humbled.

"I'm sorry. I was an asshole. You were trying to help me, and I appreciate it. I'm gonna get a marker and a piece of paper and put up a note by the mailboxes. Thank you for the suggestion, Shane."

The man passed Deeds a cold bottle of beer, which Deeds happily took, even though he didn't drink and was pretty sure he'd mentioned it to the neighbor the last time he brought over a beer as a reward for something he could not remember.

Deeds appreciated the gesture, though. "I hope you find it. Thanks for the cold one."

"Cheers," the neighbor said and extended his hand.

They're not all pricks. Some can change.

Deeds and the now-nice neighbor shook hands. The neighbor departed, and Deeds walked into his kitchen and opened the fridge. He placed the bottle on the top shelf next to the others he had acquired through various neighborly gestures and subsequent sudsy rewards.

It would stay there in that exact location until someone came over and wanted a beer. Well, in case anyone ever came over.

The rest of Deeds's place was pretty normal. The bathroom was always clean. The bed was always made. The couch faced the good-sized flat-screen TV. There were random black-and-white pictures of mountains and forests hanging from nails in the wall. All the dishes were put away. The only things on the kitchen countertop were a coffeemaker, a set of knives, a paper-towel holder, and a toaster.

There was a small desk that he used for writing checks. There was a nice dining table that could seat six. There was a bookshelf displaying many different texts: hunting books (he would never harm an animal), murder mysteries, true crime, the classics, George Gordon Byron poetry, Nietzsche philosophies, and biographies of historical people of an odd or dubious nature.

There were CDs and DVDs on another bookshelf. The CDs were organized by preference, and the movies were alphabetized. Deeds loved heavy metal. Deeds loved movies.

The bedroom had a bed without a headboard, a dresser with an American flag over it, and a hamper that was rarely full. His clothes were neatly stored in his closet or dresser as were his boots and sneakers.

The night after Deeds corrected his neighbor's rude behavior, Deeds was home flipping through the channels when there was a knock at the door. Deeds thought it was his neighbor again with news of the found parcel. Gloriously, it was not.

Deeds with confidence opened the door and was about to inquire if the bulletin had worked. However, once he saw who was at the door, he was taken aback. It was the "Busty Broad" from three apartments down, and he was nearly rendered speechless. If she only knew the power she had over him.

The first time Deeds had viewed this woman, Deeds was lost in what he saw. Deeds stole a very long gaze at her and took in her beauty. At the time, Deeds was helping someone move some furniture but instantly stopped and viewed the woman who turned out to be his neighbor.

It was not warm that afternoon, but that did not stop this beautiful lady from getting her mail in a skimpy little dress. Deeds loved it. She was very tall, approaching six feet. She had golden-brown hair and a sensual smile. She also had a pair of lovely and massive breasts. *Sweet fucking Christ*, he mused, *the Busty Broad is amazing.* And now, months later, she was at his door. *Be cool, and don't fuck it up.*

"Hey there," he said, trying to sound relaxed and casual. "What's going on?"

She smiled and said, "Hey, Shane. May I come in?"

She remembers my name? Wow! "Absolutely."

"Thanks."

The pretty neighbor walked in. As Deeds held the door open for her, she smiled and walked very close to him. He inhaled and smelled her glorious hair. Deeds could not quite identify the aroma: exotic fruits, spring in the desert, fields of lavender, a Parisian garden in the afternoon, berries from a Spanish orchard, a meadow at dawn, an alpine creek at dusk, or mountain rain at night? Whatever it was, it smelled fucking awesome.

Deeds dreamed of embracing her, leaning in and inhaling the enchanting, exhilarating aroma of her golden-brown mane. He also thought about how this scenario mimicked a lot of the scenarios that were on the videotapes he'd hid under his mattress as a teenager. *I'd kill to be so lucky!*

As he closed the door, he viewed her as she looked around. She wore very short shorts and a low-cut top. *Do you not know it's freezing out? Shut up and take it all in, damn you!*

She turned around and placed her hands in her front pockets, and as she did that, her breasts jiggled a little as they were squeezed together, also indicating she was braless. *I'd kill to be with you!*

"You have a real nice place, Shane. I'm impressed," she said and continued to look around.

"Thank you. I appreciate that," Deeds replied as he saw her notice the vacuum lines in the carpet. "I just try to be neat and clean."

"It's that, too, but I like the way you have things arranged. I have my couch on this side and my TV on that side," she said and made motions with her hands, the left ring finger bereft of a wedding band or an engagement ring.

"I just try to make things flow," he stated.

She walked over to a couple of the prints. "Your pictures—they're really cool."

"Thanks. Just things I like looking at."

The neighbor smiled and said, "I'll have to hire you to do me." Her jaw dropped and exposed a tongue stud. "Mine! Do mine! Sorry! I mean, to do my place."

She shook her head, and Deeds was enthralled. Vulnerability shows a tangible quality. *Attainable*, he deemed his neighbor.

"I'm so sorry. I didn't mean that," she stated, wide-eyed.

"It's OK—it's OK," Deeds said, putting up his hands. "I knew what you meant."

She placed her hands on her gorgeous face and said, "I can't believe I just said that," now crossing her arms, pushing her lovely breasts forward. "Quite the first impression." *Are we in a romantic comedy?*

To assuage any embarrassment, Deeds said, "You made me laugh, and I thank you. My rates for either are reasonable."

It worked. She began to relax. She laughed a little as her face developed a reddish hue. He did not want her to feel uncomrfortable, so he tried to lessen her embarrassment. *Change the subject.*

"So besides decorating tips and your lustful offer, to what do I owe the honor of your lovely presence?" Deeds said it with authority and confidence. He felt like a new man.

"Well, the reason I stopped by, before I put my foot in my mouth, was I wanted to ask you if the assholes next to me ever bothered you."

Deeds was a little surprised by the question but relieved that she wasn't feeling embarrassed anymore. "Um, no. They're bothering you?" *If I massacre them, will you hug me? If I gut them, will you let me smell your hair again?*

Deeds had seen a younger couple move into that apartment some weeks before. He knew instantly they were Old Falls trash.

Deeds knew that the Busty Broad probably heard rap music or young country all night. Rather, she heard the bass of rap music or young country all night. She probably smelled weed and heard arguing as well.

"Yeah, they're pissing me off," she began. "All I hear is their music and fighting, and they constantly smoke weed—which is fine, but my whole place reeks. Open an effing window! I mean, I've asked them to do so, many times, very politely."

When she said "politely," she put both hands up, and her glorious breasts moved quite a bit, giving Deeds a wonderful burning feeling in his chest.

She continued. "It'll be quiet for a night or two, but then they start it up again. And last night they were sooo loud."

The couple had probably went out to the bars, got loaded, came home, blasted music, got high, fought, fucked, and passed out with the music blasting. Deeds was a bouncer and knew the drill. Deeds wanted to help.

"Have you ever complained to the landlord before? Or the leasing office, I should say," she asked.

"Yeah, I have actually. Lots of times. I've gotten a few people kicked out of here."

"Really? You have?"

"Oh yeah."

"That can happen?"

"Of course. This isn't some trailer park where anything goes. People work here. They need their sleep. Complain to the manager's office every time. Don't speak to the couple anymore. It'll antagonize them, and that may cause an ugly situation, and I'll have to barbarically slay them in your honor."

The gorgeous neighbor laughed and put her hands to her mouth. After a few seconds, she cleared her throat and said, "Well, it's nice to know you've got my back, Shane." She tilted her head to the side, which was a great sign.

Deeds was playing it cool and realized less was more. "Always."

They shared a glance. Deeds could have looked into her eyes forever, but he did not want to freak her out, so he continued with the advice.

"Go speak to the lady with the bad wig, and she'll record the complaint in an official manner. When the complaints are numerous and bad for business, they're outta here."

The voluptuous neighbor's jaw dropped. "I knew that was a wig!"

"Oh yeah. She still has the price tag on it, for Christ's sake."

She laughed again, placing one hand on the kitchen counter and the other to her mouth again. She leaned down, displaying a beautiful curve.

The Busty Broad had such a happy look on her attractive face. "Well, with you behind me and the wig lady's power, I could take over this place."

"Oh yeah. A few days, it's all yours."

She smiled and laughed again. "Well, that's good to know."

Deeds smiled. He loved what was happening, but he knew that if there was an opening for an exit, he should take it. *Always leave them wanting more.* Alas, it was she who was not finished and kept the conversation going.

"So you and Wiggy have done this before and got people kicked out for noise?"

"Oh sure. Lots of noise complaints. Parties with the windows open. Loud shitty music. Threats—"

"Threats?" She looked surprised as she interrupted with concern. "People have threatened you, big man? No effing way!" She was dishing out the compliments, and Deeds ate them up.

"Oh yeah. Given enough liquid courage, everyone's a tough guy."

Deeds had been threatened and an attempt was made to intimidate him once. On a rainy night the previous spring, Deeds was walking home from the grocery store—he needed coffee—and a party on a second-floor balcony facing the quad had caught his attention as he walked by.

Deeds also had caught the attention of the party. The ex–frat boys, post graduation by a year or two, all of a sudden quieted down to whispers after shushing, and they proceeded to stare Deeds down.

Deeds walked and stared back. He knew they were cowards. No one spoke, but several raised their arms in a confrontational way. From the back a lit cigarette was flung. Deeds watched as the trajectory took the cigarette from the second-floor balcony to right in front of him and hit the ground. He never broke stride as he kept the death stare. It was pure luck he stepped on the cigarette, but it looked badass just the same.

Deeds kept the pace, kept the stare, turned the corner, and went up to his apartment. Once inside, Deeds took off his jacket and his boots and put the coffee away. He sat at his table and focused on his breathing. He was trying to calm down but could not shake the feeling that he should teach those pussies a lesson. *Yep.*

Deeds, without his boots, jacket, or wallet, left his apartment very quietly and did not lock the door. In his socks, jeans, and T-shirt, he stealthily walked toward the antagonistic apartment.

He crept silently till he was viewing their front door from behind a pillar in the corridor. After a moment, Deeds walked right up to the door. He viewed what presented itself, assessed the situation, hypothesized reactions and possible scenarios, and made a plan.

Deeds went back to his apartment, grabbed a couple bottles of beer various neighbors had given him, and quietly walked back to the offending apartment. He walked right up to the door. He looked into the window of the apartment but could not really see past the blinds. He guessed most of the partygoers were on the patio or in the living-room area. Even if they weren't, it would not matter. They couldn't hear any activity at their front door due to the loud pounding bass.

He opened the beers and poured them on the ground near the front door. The aroma spread. He then picked up their heavy flower pot and threw it over the railing, down to the first floor. It made a loud crash. He threw one empty bottle down the corridor of the floor he was on. He took a few steps in the direction he was going to flee and threw the last bottle toward the concrete walkway on the first level. The walkway connected to the front entrance where the gates were. More than likely, the cops responding to the noise would park there and step on broken glass as they followed the noise to the offending apartment.

The other neighbors heard the commotion, but the partygoers did not. This bought Deeds time. He walked back to the door and picked up the welcome mat. He held it up to the front window and threw a solid haymaker to the mat.

The glass shattered loudly and startled the party people inside the apartment. He quickly placed the mat back on the ground and quietly sprinted back to his hiding spot behind a corner.

Seconds later Deeds heard the angered yells from the first- and second-floor neighbors. Soon after, the third-floor and fourth-floor neighbors joined in. Then the partygoers finally joined in. Discord and hostility ensued. Deeds felt satisfaction having pulled the strings of these puppets.

Threats were shouted as well as declarations of calling the police. Deeds then spied some female partygoers fleeing quickly.

The male partygoers, wanting to stand their ground, remained near the beer-soaked ground and continued to shout and make threats. The police wouldn't be there for several minutes. *Good.*

Deeds heard three female voices say three female names. He peeked out and saw three young females dressed like party sluts. All were holding their shoes in their hands as they deliberated for a few seconds, and finally Sienna and Sierra went toward the main entrance. Deeds smiled. *Hopefully, they see the broken glass.*

Tracy came toward him. *What to do? What to do?* As Deeds heard Tracy take her little distressed steps toward him, he realized something fun could occur. *Why not?*

Tracy passed by in a skimpy little dress. Tracy was obviously drunk as she worked hard to maintain her balance and accurately press the elevator button. Tracy had not seen Deeds call the elevator moments before and send it to the top floor.

Tracy put one hand on the wall and slowly raised a leg to put her shoe on but stopped and turned around when she heard the pained yells of Sienna and Sierra as they apparently found the broken glass.

Peripherally, Tracy saw Deeds and turned around completely and took in the embodiment of intimidation. She gasped at the sight of Deeds and dropped her shoes. Deeds was an imposing and fearful statue forged from displeased ire.

"Hello, hello."

Tracy was very scared, but Deeds couldn't let her scream, so he charged her, turned her around, and effortlessly put her in a sleeper's hold. Tracy let out a muffled gasp or two but was soon lifeless in Deeds's arms.

Deeds picked her up, carried her to a small area that housed the recycling and garbage containers for the second floor, gently laid her down, and turned her over.

Deeds was pissed at the loud pricks who had tried to intimidate him and thrown a lit cigarette at him. Tracy may have had nothing to do with their actions. Yet Tracy would be made an example of.

"What did I ever do to you, Tracy? Huh? I was just walking home, you perfect little twat! Your boys can't save you now." Deeds looked at the passed-out Tracy, the very perfect and preppie Tracy. Tracy, who thought she was untouchable and would never give Deeds the time of day.

Deeds breathed in three deep breaths and came to the conclusion that Tracy should not be punished for something she did not do. But Deeds was curious.

Deeds pushed up her miniskirt and took off her thong panties. Deeds momentarily saw Tracy's perfect-looking womanhood.

Deeds placed Tracy's underwear in his pocket as she lay faceup under the bright industrial lights.

Deeds felt a little guilty, but he would not dwell on it. *This shouldn't have happened. You're lucky I'm a nice person. This could have been a hell for you, Tracy.* Deeds shrugged it off and surreptitiously crept back to his apartment after throwing Tracy's underwear on the floor of the hallway.

Deeds quietly entered his place, locked the door, and kept the lights off. He heard some loud talking. He heard some radio chatter, which meant the cops had shown up. After a while, everything got quiet again. He then went to sleep and slept well.

The next morning, he woke up and walked down to the leasing office and made a complaint about the previous night's noise. The property director, "Wiggy," as the Busty Broad so knighted her, then regaled Deeds with tales of loud music, broken glass, injuries, drunk people, and sexual deviants "getting crazy" in the halls. Deeds smiled and said, "Damn those deviants," and laughed.

Deeds resumed his surprised expression as his joke was not well received by Wiggy. Deeds shook his head and lamented the actions of his neighbors while beaming with pride as he knew he had gotten even.

An eviction notice was placed on their apartment door, and they were gone within seventy-two hours.

⟨⊱ ⊰⟩

"Yeah." He stared into the eyes of his gorgeous neighbor. "I've made some complaints."

"That's so cool. They should know not to mess with you, big guy," she mocked and punched him in the stomach.

Bashfully, Deeds replied, "Yeah, well."

She smiled and tilted her head, again. *Wow!* "OK, Shane. Thanks a bunch. I'll leave you alone now." She slowly headed for the door. "Hopefully next time, I won't embarrass myself."

Deeds placed a big hand on her shoulder. This was a bold move, but he felt confident. "It's OK. It was a funny thing. You cracked me up."

"Thanks, Shane." She walked by Deeds again but even closer.

He inhaled her aroma and viewed her from behind. *Gorgeous.*

She opened the door, turned around, and said, "By the way, I'm Jessie Caine. You can call me 'Jess.' G'night." The door closed.

"Good night, Jess." Deeds breathed in one very deep breath and exhaled. "What a great night," he said to no one in his empty apartment.

CHAPTER FIVE

After Deeds graduated high school, he spent five years at a nearby state college. He made a few acquaintances and one friend. The degrees Deeds and his friend Josh graduated with did not help them become contractors and eventual co-owners of a contracting business, but that is what happened.

One autumn morning, the first day of school of their last year, Deeds and Josh found themselves seated next to each other in a class. Everyone else in the classroom, while waiting for the tardy professor to show up, had begun discussing the usual college things—namely, happiness and parties. The only two people not engaged in ultrahappy "everything in my life has turned out better than I could have imagined and I can't wait for the future" conversation were in fact Deeds and Josh.

A few weeks later, after a lecture had ended, Deeds was walking in a corridor past the pool to where he parked. As he tried to catch a glimpse of any chick in a swimsuit, he saw Josh walking right behind him. Deeds, who was usually quiet, casually asked, "How's it going, dude?"

Deeds and Josh introduced themselves and continued walking to the parking lot. They talked about how the class they shared was tough and they were curious as to why they were forced to listen to lectures if the midterm and final were based off the reading. Deeds admitted he just wanted to be done with school and start life.

"Cs get degrees, friend." Josh spat as he often enjoyed a dip after, before, and during lecture.

Deeds really liked that phrase, having never heard it before. "Nice! Never heard that one before." Deeds continued, "I just want a degree. To me, it's kind of like a big middle finger to everyone who thinks I couldn't do it."

Josh stopped at his truck, shook Deeds's hand again, and said, "Get it done, and get outta here. See you Thursday."

Over the course of the quarter, they often met before class in a little break room that had vending machines. The shitty coffee was not that bad, and with their small cups filled, they trudged up to the classroom.

During the break they happily and briskly walked downstairs to the break room for a second round of shitty coffee, which was again not that bad and by now necessary. They talked again, and once again they trudged up the stairs.

One day after the lecture, which was increasing in its intolerableness, Deeds gave Josh a container of dip he had bought and tried and did not care for. It made Deeds's head spin. *Never going to do this again!* Instead of wasting an entire can, he gave it to Josh.

"Thanks, friend. Just not a fan? Would you like to try some of mine?"

Deeds's memory made him feel nauseated. "No, I'm good."

Josh put a dip in and asked, "Hey, are you looking for work?"

"What kinda work, weirdo? I mean, yeah, if it's tasteful, I'm in."

Josh shook his head, pointed to Deeds, and said to no one on either side of him, "Funny guy, right here." Josh spat and continued, "Nah, man, I need some help building a fence. Easy work. She pays well. I've done shit for her in the past. Interested?"

"Yeah, sure. I just quit my deli job. But I'm doing a full load of classes this year, so I can be done. How many days is the job?"

Josh spat. "Three days. Afternoons only. A five-foot-high fence for her dog. Easy work, man."

Deeds said, "I'm not much of a handyman."

Josh spat again. "Don't have to be. I'll do the measuring and cutting. You show up, help me demo, help me haul, help me hammer, help me get paid. You're good to go." Josh handed Deeds a piece of paper with a name and an address on it. "Be there after two. We work till sundown."

Deeds and Josh worked past sundown and used tiki torches and numerous older lamps they found in the garage to finish the job in two days. The older woman, who lived alone and had a yapping dog, was very impressed with the speed and the quality of the work. She paid them handsomely and gave them a generous gratuity.

"Well," the nice older woman said, "you finished in two days, but I have some other things that need to be done around here, if you didn't have anything planned for tomorrow afternoon."

Over the next several afternoons, Deeds and Josh showed up when they did not have class and did lots of little jobs for the nice elderly woman. Between the two of them, Deeds and Josh assembled a new bed frame, and when the mattress and box spring were delivered, they hauled them up to the spare bedroom. They finished painting the spare bedroom's bathroom, drilled in the towel racks, and hung up a picture or two.

Josh, with Deeds's help, put up a chandelier over the dining-room table, and they hauled all the garbage out, stored the old chandelier, washed the floor, waxed the table, and put everything back as it was, now improved.

When everything was completed, Deeds and Josh had made some very decent cash.

"Well," the generous older woman said with a smile, "I wish I had more for you to do, but you did everything."

Having a mouthful of spit, Josh was hoping Deeds would be the rep today. Deeds obliged with, "Yes, ma'am. Anything else you need, just call him"—Deeds nodded toward Josh—"and we'll take care of it."

As the nice older lady held and petted her dog, she said, "I also told several friends of mine about the work you've done, so when you're not busy with school"—the lady pointed at both of them with authority to remind them that education was first—"there's work to be done."

"Well, we appreciate it. Thank you very much."

The nice older lady said, "You guys should go into business. You'll become millionaires!"

Deeds laughed and asked, "Is that a guarantee?"

Both parties laughed and said good night. Josh finally spat, and Deeds playfully punched him in the stomach.

Two days later, Josh called Deeds. "Bad news, friend. That nice old lady passed away."

Deeds was saddened by this. "What? We just saw her. Like two days ago. She seemed fine to me."

"I know. She seemed fine to me, too. It was just her time."

Deeds exhaled and said, "She was very nice to us."

"Oh, she was extremely nice. And generous."

"Yeah, she paid very well. I made more there in a week than I did at the fucking deli in a month."

"That, too." Deeds could hear him spit into a cup, and his voice became clearer. "I got three calls for other jobs. Friends and neighbors of hers. That's how I found out. She kept her promise. So let's become millionaires."

"Yeah, let's become millionaires."

CHAPTER SIX

After graduation, Deeds and his friend Josh completed all the bureaucratic paperwork one needs to complete in order to become a licensed contractor and began working throughout Engel Falls.

Even though these were preboom times, there was still work to be done in and around Engel Falls.

Over the next few years, they were able to take on several other employees. These guys were all licensed and hardworking. They worked at a professional pace with professional results. Long hours with care and precision were profitable. Then it became quite profitable as the boom hit.

One of the craftsmen had his wife come into the new office they leased and do the books and answer phones. Pretty soon, they needed someone to be a sales rep and discuss the jobs and deal with the clients.

There was no time for Deeds or Josh to do these things. They were busy working and getting handsomely paid.

The employees, who were already troopers, were needed to work twenty-five hours a day eight days a week. They doubled their workforce. The large paychecks were coming in. They got contracts from the city, county, and state to do multiple projects.

They expanded their business to include landscaping, electrical, and painting. These were very successful ventures as well. Deeds, Josh, and everyone else were reaping the rewards of hard work, smart decisions, and fortunate timing.

This was when an owner of a rival contracting business in a neighboring town made them an offer they simply could not refuse. Everyone in the business that Deeds and Josh started, Precision Contracting, made a sizeable amount of money.

Many started their own ventures in related fields while some continued on with the new company. Deeds and Josh, however, were set for life, almost.

Josh decided to move away and join a business his family had started. They needed someone to help manage the sales reps of their contracting company, and he was happy to oblige. Josh's magic was still present, and his success continued.

Josh worked from home. He was spending time with his family, receiving pay and benefits, depositing to his two sons' college funds, and letting the money he made work for him in sound investments. Josh did not have to work, but he was a born worker and couldn't retire just yet.

Deeds, however, was sans wife and kids. He wasn't interested in growing old and living off the substanial amount of money he made nor was he interested in busting his hump with grunt work again.

Deeds made some inquiries to former clients he had worked for (rich people whose business was knowing what to do with money) and met with investment specialists and wealth-management advisors. With much research, he made his moves and relaxed as they paid off.

Deeds did not spend lavishly. He kept the same huge truck he used for work and he rented a nice one-bedroom apartment.

During this postsale time, Deeds finally acknowledged his whole body had aches and pains so he took care of these physical ailments via physical therapy and chiropractic visits.

Now feeling well healthwise, and with a nicely filled bank account, he was able to dedicate himself to lifting weights like he used to.

Without backbreaking labor Deeds was able to bust his ass in the weight room. The mass collected, and Deeds went from a big guy to an "Oh, wow, don't fuck with that dude" guy.

Deeds had had a tough time growing up, and the antidote to mental suffering had been lifting weights. Over time he and his close friends' physical alterations were noticed by the football coach, and they all played football their senior year.

Life was ideal but Deeds felt he needed more and he was waiting for the next turning point.

One night while Josh was back visiting, he and Deeds went out to a steakhouse. They had fun catching up and reminiscing. As they ate and discussed their financial moves, a fight broke out near them.

Apparently some tough guys were acting hard in the bar, and a shoving match began.

The two small (small compared to Deeds) combatants let their wild punches displace them, and they both lost their balance and fell onto Deeds and Josh's table. Deeds was having a nice time and took the interruption personally. He stood up and threw one punch to both of them and knocked them out. While they were lying on the ground, he picked them up one at a time and dragged them to the emergency exit.

Deeds kicked the door open, and the alarm wailed, but Deeds just concentrated on the task at hand. He threw the first interrupting asshole into the parking lot. As he bent down to pick up the other interrupting asshole, the alarm was silenced, and then Deeds threw him out as well. Deeds closed the door and turned to face applause from the diners.

Deeds was shocked that he had reacted so quickly. He hadn't overanalyzed the situation. He'd just been pissed off and felt victimized by those who acted like they were better than him. So he'd ended the unpleasant situation before it'd affected him further.

Josh had both his hands up in a touchdown motion as he stood up to welcome Deeds back to their disheveled table. Deeds had a sheepish expression as he sat down.

Deeds felt compelled to explain his actions. "Sorry that happened, everyone," he stated to his patrons. He felt as if he was awaiting punishment as the manager made his way over to their table.

"Gentlemen, your dinners will be replaced and are on the house tonight," the manager said.

Josh was surprised. "Sir, this wasn't your fault. Those assholes were the cause. That's not your responsibility."

"I will not hear of it. Dinner's on us, gentlemen." He faced Deeds and shook his hand. "Thank you, sir. The police are on their way, and those creeps will not be welcome here anymore."

Deeds nodded. "I'm just glad no one of importance was hurt. Thanks again."

"Our pleasure, gentlemen."

The waitress came over and made chitchat with them for a few minutes after she confirmed the reorder.

Josh asked, "Does crazy shit like this happen to you often?"

Deeds shook his head. "Uh, no. Hopefully this is the end of anybody getting in my way of trying to have a nice time."

Their new dinners came, and as they dined, again, many fellow diners thanked and praised Deeds on their way out.

When Deeds and Josh left, Deeds was again thanked by the manager. Deeds was happy to help. Everyone there was trying to have a nice time. Those two selfish pricks almost ruined everyone's night and worse—they'd thought they were entitled to act however they wanted.

Deeds walked with Josh to his rented car.

"Well, friend," Josh said and beamed, "you sure know how to show a lady a good time." He threw a fake punch or two.

"Anything for you, sweetheart," Deeds said as he drew his big arm back and was met with, "No no no, don't do that. Don't do that," by Josh.

They shook hands and threw a hug around each other and parted. Josh said, "Can't wait till the next date!"

Deeds shook his head. "Yeah, yeah, get outta here."

When Deeds reached his truck, he heard a "Sir?" and turned around to see the manager jogging over to him. The manager had a card in his hand and said, "We're always hiring new bouncers and security guys to help out on weekends. If you're interested, we'd love to have you."

Deeds politely and with the mannerisms one would have if one was correcting someone said, "I'm not a bouncer, sir. Sorry. I'm just a retired contractor. I have no experience in…stuff like that."

The manager looked surprised. "Are you kidding me? You looked like a seasoned pro."

Deeds smiled, shook his head, and said, "My first time eighty-sixing people, as you would say." He let the statement hang there for a moment and then continued, "Yeah, I've never done that before. Guess I reached a breaking point when they ruined my dinner."

"Well, you mentioned you were retired, but if you want work, we'll pay standard security fees. Give us a call. Sooner, the better. We're having live music this weekend, and I've been procrastinating on getting help. Up to you."

The manager shook Deeds's hand and walked back into the restaurant. Deeds pondered. *Could I be a bouncer? Do I have the ability to turn off my emotions and not take things so personal when some asshole gets out of line? Am I big enough? Would they pay attention to me?*

Deeds had low self esteem and was not aware of how big and intimidating he was.

There was something else. Deeds had a certain je ne sais quoi that separated him from the rest. He had the thousand-yard stare. His opponents could detect, via mammalian brain-based observation, that Deeds possessed the berserker gene.

A berserker was a Norse warrior whose fury was the basis of myths and legends back in Viking times.

The berserker could be counted on to be the last man standing. Furious. Relentless. Remorseless in defending the village or his life. Willing to commit any atrocity in the name of Odin.

Surely in present times, this trait was thought to be associated with sociopaths or those who had antisocial disorder—not people who said they were "gonna be antisocial and skip the party" but people who did not recognize the suffering of others. Remorseless.

Yet here lay the dichotomy: Deeds cared. He was a sensitive man. He hated those who made him feel bad or got in his way of trying to find happiness. Yet he felt compassion. He felt sorrow. He had a big heart.

Maybe this'll be therapeutic. I can help people. I stay up late anyway. Now I'll stay up late, get paid, and, more importantly, help people. I will lift weights, eat a lot, help people, and—who knows?—maybe make some friends and meet some interesting people.

"Guess I'll be a bouncer," Deeds said to no one in an empty parking lot.

CHAPTER SEVEN

One evening Deeds was out for a walk. It was a very cold and crisp night in New Falls. There was a bright, waning gibbous moon casting nocturnal shadows further darkening what already lay cloaked.

Sleep was eluding Deeds, and he was wide awake. Somewhere someone had said or written that attempting to sleep when you were not tired would only further the detrimental effect that sleeplessness possesses. Deeds could not recall having viewed results from any scientific studies, but the sentiment made sense to him.

So he put on his parka and boots and grabbed a few things and headed out.

Earlier that evening Deeds worked a few hours doing security for the local bowling alley and the bar—the 11th Frame—located inside. There were no scheduled events, and the night had ended early as there were not a lot of customers. The owner, Bill McKenna, kept one or two guys on, but he did not need the rest of the crew. Deeds did not need the money, so he volunteered to leave early.

Deeds went home. He watched some TV, but nothing really interested him. It was just on to combat silence. He made himself a simple dinner. A lot of meat. A lot of vegetables. A lot of milk. A big glass of water. Unlike a lot of other people, Deeds ended his dinner with a cup of the morning's brewed coffee, microwaved.

Most people would be afraid the caffeine would keep them awake till all hours of the night, but not Deeds. Deeds usually drank the warm beverage and a soothing calm came over him. It was counterintuitive to consume coffee at night, especially with his history of sleeplessness.

Deeds figured his sleep problems had their bases in psychology rather than diet. It was the repetitive analysis of the day's events that he pored over as he tried to sleep. If an event occurred that upset him, embarrassed him, or made him sad, he thought about it ad nauseam, and it kept him awake. *Not the caffeine.*

Things were supposed to be good now. He was in a very desirable position in life. But the nights were sometimes problematic. The silence and the emotions in the dark could easily keep him awake late into the night. When one lies in a bed surrounded by darkness and silence and is ensconced in emotion, the sight of the sun can devastate that person.

After he sold his company, there was a period of time when he would try to go to sleep at a normal time. For years he awoke very early as contractors do. After being retired a while, he sometimes would be up at that hour but only because he had not fallen asleep yet.

This was a devastating occurrence that would feed into itself and cause more emotional and psychological duress. You just assume that you are indeed a worthless person. Everyone else has been asleep for hours and is waking up to contribute to society.

They are waking up to create, to build, and to accomplish. *I did that!* You, well, you've been up all night. What good are you? The simplest of basic function—next to breathing, pissing, shitting, and fucking—is to sleep when you are tired. If you cannot achieve this, something is wrong with you.

Deeds's thoughts only reinforced this thought. *Go to sleep. It's easy. Why can't you just go to sleep? It's easy to do. Just go to sleep. What the hell is wrong with you? Just go to sleep!*

All this was annoying and furthered the sleeplessness. *Not the caffeine!*

Deeds also felt that drinking coffee at night was the equivalent to prescribing Ritalin to a hyperactive child. Technically, Ritalin was a stimulant, but it indeed calmed the hyperactive kid due to the balancing of the hyperactive chemicals in the child's brain.

If there was too much hyperactive chemical being created and the hyperactive child received more, the body stopped making the chemical, and the child calmed down.

The warm coffee calmed Deeds down and soothed his copious nocturnal analyses. Maybe the caffeine had the same effect that Ritalin had on a hyperactive child's chemicals. Maybe the caffeine increased blood flow, allowing the blood to return to the heart for oxygenation, which indeed produced a calming and relaxing tendency due to vasodilation.

Maybe Deeds liked coffee and he hated wasting things, and the warmness soothed him. *Oh well.*

Deeds was winding his way through New Falls. No real destination in mind—just killing time. Deeds was wondering about certain traits he had. *Why do certain things just bother me so much? Am I too sensitive? Are people not that bad? Is it all my fault?*

When good fortune came his way, it really seemed as if people went out of their way to make sure he was less happy than he should have been, when he should have been at his happiest.

Deeds felt forced to feel guilty over his success. *Why?* He felt as if he had to acknowledge that he did not deserve it and that he had to justify himself, his hard work, and his prosperity even though he'd earned it.

Deeds just assumed all people were resentful and jealous and, therefore, were angry with him. So he stayed away from people. *Is it in my head?*

As his numerous chiropractic and physical-therapy sessions aided in curing his injuries, and with the knowledge he gained, he dedicated more of his life to pumping iron again.

Instead of maintaining, he could move forward and build. The injuries were gone. Deeds felt he was a very lucky man, until people started to make comments about how if they were rich like he was, they'd love to just work out all day.

This infuriated Deeds. No matter what he did, no matter how he spent his time, someone was always going to shit on him. Everything he had, he'd earned. He was sick and tired of justifying himself, his actions, and his existence. Like before, when he'd sold his business and people had been jealous, as he now got bigger, he seemed to attract more mean-spirited people. *Fuck the world. Also, I don't work out. I lift.*

While he ignored the world, Deeds made gains in mass and in willful disconnection. He really did not talk to many people. Why should he? *They'll just put me down.*

It seemed Deeds had tried to be a part of a society that he would rather observe from afar. His immersion in that society brought sadness, pain, sleepless nights, and, ironically, feelings of loneliness. Now he tried to put distance between him and them.

The incident at the restaurant some years back was his baptism by fire and entry into the profession of security and bouncing. He worked a few nights a week, but not for money. Even though his willful disconnection was helpful, he knew he could not be a troglodyte for the rest of his life. He did the job as a form of therapy. He knew he should be among people but not necessarily have personal interaction with them. Deeds believed that an insecure person would not give him shit if there were several other guys the size of Deeds behind him.

Deeds had some positive interactions with people. His bosses were nice. The employees were always thankful for his work, as were his fellow bouncers when they needed assistance.

Deeds was alone for a while and gradually began to feel better. Then he became aware he felt lonely, which marked how he was progressing emotionally. Then he began to seek human connection. He wanted to make a personal connection, like a normal person.

Deeds walked by a lot of houses and apartments, making the assumption everyone was asleep, so he headed to the night-owl places. Deeds was aware that his unknown destination was a populated one.

Deeds had walked by some twenty-four-hour businesses. There were some gas stations with attendants inside the warm minimarkets. He walked by a diner that had a few people in it. He saw some cleaning crews in closed offices. Deeds walked on. He steered clear of the bowling alley he'd been excused from earlier.

Deeds ended up near a bar, Garee's Place, which was untouched by the gentrification that had taken place in New Falls. It had not been remodeled, but the patrons had been replaced by the new populace. Deeds had done some bouncing there in the past but had not been there recently.

Garee's Place was nothing fancy, but it was a safe bar where almost everyone was welcome. As long as everyone behaved, especially the Old Falls patrons, they were welcome.

Deeds stood outside near Garee's Place. Deeds viewed the parking lot. *Not a packed house but a decent late-night crowd.*

There was one lady outside smoking. One guy opened the door, said, "Thank you," loudly over the music, and went to his car. Another guy got out of his truck and walked by a guy who was tilting a little and waiting for a cab to take him home.

Deeds stayed put across the street and a block away. He leaned against the front door of some storefront that was closed for the night. He saw an unilluminated neon sign but did not read what words the tubes that carried the gas formed. He saw another sign with numbers on it but did not know what the business hours were. His hands were thrust into his pockets, and the vapor from his breath held for seconds in the cold, still air of the night.

Deeds thought, *I walked all the way here, but I'm still far. Why can't I walk into that bar and have a fun night? Why can't I go over to those people? Why should they have all the fun? Will they resent me? Will they take the time to get to know me? Probably not. It might be cool for a little while, but someone will ask, "What do you do?" It'll get out that I sold my business, then they'll resent me. I'm not covered in gold or jewelry, guys. I don't go on trips. I don't own a house. I'm just a normal guy. Sick of justifying myself.*

Deeds imagined the patrons inside, drinks in hand, laughing, telling jokes, and sharing stories during a fun night out. In this vision Deeds viewed no stress, anxiety, or resentment—just a fun time for people.

Deeds pictured an older couple holding hands, listening to the funny man of the group tell a story, smiles on all their faces. He pictured a group of guys exchanging stories of married life or what it's like being a father but being thankful for every moment. He pictured a father and a son arguing over the designated-hitter rule. He pictured a guy breaking peanut shells while watching sports highlights, and the cute waitress silently damning his mess. He pictured two younger guys with glazed-over eyes, wondering why they chose dark stouts. And he pictured the guy at the jukebox who had been standing there for fifteen minutes perfecting the next ten-song playlist that everyone in the bar would love and, therefore, praise him for.

Such camaraderie. Such fun revelry. What a great time. Why can't I join them?

You can.

Can I? I feel as if I can't.

Why?

They'll resent me.

You don't know that for certain. Others have, sure, but that's not proven true with these people. And if they do resent you, then turn your back on them.

Deeds thought he recognized a few people heading into the bar from when he and Josh first started out.

Good people, Deeds thought. *Not all of them will resent you. Just go up to them and say, "Hey there. My name is Shane. We used to do whatever at this place, or we used to work at that place. How ya been? Can I buy you a beer?"*

Deeds stood in the dark for quite a while contemplating his next move. Deeds felt like he needed someone to guide him. Like a social wingman, not for hitting on women but for dismissing thoughts of impending insolence.

Deeds could not dismiss these feelings of potential resentment and justifying things. Feeling defeated, Deeds turned around and walked away from the scene.

Deeds was down on himself as he slowly walked back home possessing a defeatist's demeanor. He was feeling lonely and depressed. He was frustrated at not being able to do such a simple thing due to something that might or might not happen. This was the reason why he was out to begin with.

Deeds realized that he was overanalyzing and making too big a deal out of it. *So you didn't go in. Who cares? You can make the choice to try again. Until they give you shit, make no assumptions.* Deeds slowed his walk until he stopped completely. He reasoned it out for a moment. *Until they say something rude, live your life like you want to.*

Deeds stood in the same spot for a while and really focused on his next moves. He closed his eyes yet appeared to be gazing up at the nearly full moon. He took three slow, deep breaths, inhaling through his nose and exhaling through his mouth. The cold crisp air decreased the tension as his lungs felt awakened by the boreal night air.

Deeds turned around and headed back to Garee's Place. Deeds promised himself that he would at least walk into the bar.

Deeds would then ask the bartender for an NA (nonalcoholic) beer, and he would buy a round for whoever remembered him. *Simple. It happens all the time. Be a part of it.*

Deeds felt happy. He was excited. There was a reserved smile on his face, and he was eager to walk in and carry on like a normal person. The anticipation grew, and he walked with a purpose.

On the way toward the bar, a huge, muscular black man with a subdued grin on his face walked toward Deeds. Deeds guessed he must have had a few and had probably gotten a phone number or even better. It was probably better. *This massive man probably gets more ass than a toilet seat.*

Deeds was a big man, but this guy had three inches and forty pounds on him, which was very impressive. Solidly built, big fucking dude. Deeds wondered if anyone messes with him. *Probably not.* Deeds was jealous. *Why not me?*

Deeds thought how this guy would have made one hell of a bouncer. Separating people and intimidating the hell out of them would be easier with his size. Deeds wondered if this behemoth of a man would be his ally.

As the man drew closer, Deeds nodded and in a friendly manner said, "Evening."

The man looked up and said, "Hey, how's it going, big man?" He slapped Deeds on the back of his shoulder.

Deeds replied, "Good, thanks. Have a good night."

"Yeah, you, too, big man."

It was so simple. I'm nice to them. They should be nice to me. That was a nice act from a nice guy. I hope I see that man again. Maybe at the gym? He has to lift somewhere. Maybe I'll ask around. Maybe I can run into him again and offer him a job in bouncing. Maybe we can be friends. Deeds felt good at the prospect of having a friend. He smiled and continued toward the bar.

Deeds could see the bar a few blocks away. He could hear laughter. He could hear music. As he continued to walk, he saw where he'd been standing earlier, observing.

Deeds looked across the street at the front door of the closed storefront and shook his head. *Why were you so scared?* He turned his head and continued walking. He almost felt disgust, but he was in too good a mood, and the impending fun times were too important to taint with any negativity. *Forget it and move on.*

There were still several buildings between him and the old brick building that housed Garee's Place. Past one building and before another, there was a dark, cluttered alley.

From out of that darkness walked a strange-looking woman. The woman looked confused and taken aback but not necessarily by Deeds's impromptu appearance. The woman had dark red hair, looked like she lived a hard life, and was naked from the waist down. The woman then vomited all over Deeds.

CHAPTER EIGHT

Deeds looked down at himself and with nauseous comprehension came to grips with the fact that he was covered in some lady's vomit. *Did that just happen?* The lower half of his parka, pants, and boots were covered in oddly colored chunks that steamed in the cold air. The smell was enough for him to dry heave once or twice, but he managed to keep his dinner down.

This repugnant reality was caused by an unabashed woman of soiled appearance—soiled as in recently used. It also appeared that other graceless events had taken place.

The lady's pants were at her ankles. An unmistakable fluid reflected in the moon's light, displaying that it had dribbled down her legs after being shot onto and into her unmentionables. Some vomit debris appeared on her hands with Deeds having received the majority of the unfortunate and ill-timed purge.

A crumpled newspaper had been used as a paper towel. Deeds also saw a big pile of steaming shit a few steps away with a steaming piss puddle accompanying it.

Deeds watched her for several moments. She wiped her fingers and her mouth and spat a few times. Eventually, the woman looked up and made eye contact. She also gazed at the mess on his clothes and realized she'd caused it.

In a raspy voice, she matter-of-factly stated, "Sorry." Without emotion, and as if it was a normal occurrence, she also offered, "You gotta go. You gotta go."

Redheaded, filthy degenerate just ruined my evening, an evening that had not even happened yet. I was looking forward to having fun.

Deeds took off his parka and placed it on the ground, double-checking the ground for other foul fluids, not that it mattered at this point. The parka would have to be professionally laundered. He just wasn't going to wear it home, despite the night's coldness. The cold air had a sudden effect on him. *Better get used to it.*

In his T-shirt, worn over his long-sleeved thermal, Deeds stood there looking in the dark and then located and grabbed some newspaper. He attempted to mimic the discourteous woman's attempt to clean herself, and with slow and elongated breathing, he crumpled the newspaper as best he could and wiped the big chunks of vomit from his jeans and steel-toed work boots.

Deeds grabbed some more newspaper and crumpled it and picked up some remaining snow from the sidewalk. He mushed the two together and got a makeshift wet rag and attempted to clean himself. Deeds did not have good luck with this attempt. The newspaper shredded and left pieces on his clothes and boots.

Fashioning a small snowball, Deeds scrubbed his boots by hand. *Not working too well either.* He would have to buy some new ones. This realization was one of relief and annoyance. No matter how much he cleaned them, on an unseen molecular level, the vomit would be present in the leather and the laces.

Deeds saw a nozzle coming from the wall. *Maybe this'll do it.* He walked over, turned it on, and let the water rinse the vomit off his boots. Wearing only his shirts, Deeds grew colder, sad, and increasingly frustrated with the bitch that had caused it. He grabbed some more newspaper, crumpled it, got it wet, and scrubbed his pants. Again, it was not too effective.

During these attempts to clean himself, Deeds remained silent. All he could hear was his own breathing, the muffled sounds of the bar, and the water hitting the asphalt. The dark alley was quiet, and the bar seemed distant.

As the filthy woman struggled with balance, she slowly attempted to get dressed. As Deeds watched her, still trying to comprehend what had happened, he noticed she was wearing a scarf. He casually and with authority walked over to her and took the scarf from around her neck.

"Hey," she protested. "That's mine."

Deeds said nothing. He walked back to the nozzle and drenched her scarf in water, wrung it out, folded it, and proceeded to give a final pseudowash to his pants and boots. The parka was probably a lost cause, like his boots, and even though he would get it cleaned, he wanted to do what he could and at the very least lessen the stench.

As the water from the nozzle continued to run and splatter on the asphalt, Deeds used his index finger and thumb to pick up the parka and toss it onto the ground under the flowing nozzle.

Soak the thing for a while. Wring it out as best you can. Wash your hands. Grab a cardboard box or a bag or something and take it home. Leave it outside! Get it cleaned tomorrow, or buy a new one when you buy new boots.

While Deeds did this, he continued to look over at the dirty woman. As if disturbed and annoyed by his presence, she rolled her eyes, made a face, and turned around. Her pants were still at her ankles, and when she bent down to pick them up, she gave Deeds a full view of her ass. She took her time standing up. It appeared she was doing this on purpose. *Is she trying to entice me?*

"You trying to turn me on?"

The woman of questionable character turned her head and half smiled. "Doing anything for you, big man?" The lady's curvy ass acted as a barrier for her pants. As each attempt to pull them up made her buttocks bounce and jiggle, she asked, "See anything you want?"

Deeds saw some smears that were caused by a couple of natural or biological activities. *That's fucking disgusting. Still a decent ass though—just needs some soap.*

Under different circumstances Deeds would be thrilled as she was not bad looking. Unrefined and in desperate need of charm school, but not bad looking. Unfortunately, the reality of the situation and its repellant details were mental obstacles that made it impossible to overcome.

But then it dawned on Deeds. *She must be a hooker. She's not just some drunken chick. She's a drunken amateur hooker. I'm pretty sure she's not attracted to me. She's a drunken hooker looking to make more money. That explains why she's naked from the waist down in an alley, dripping some random dude's cum. For a minute there, I thought she was some disgusting drunken broad who may have had a thing for me, but no. She's just a fucking drunken hooker. What an awful night!*

"If you want it, you can have it." She slowly pulled her pants up, and her ass bunched up one last time before it disappeared behind the denim.

It was a good-looking ass, Deeds admitted. Thick, curvy, and healthy. *Very nice.* Unfortunately, reality reared its ugly head again as Deeds asked himself, *Where was the toilet paper she used?* This detail grossed Deeds out.

"No," Deeds replied. "No, I fucking don't."

"Oh, come on. You know you want it," she said.

Deeds was confused. Bewildered, he said, "You just threw up on me. Moments before that, you took a shit. And you obviously got fucked before that—hopefully before that, or I feel sorry for the guy. I mean you had a shit skid mark on your ass, as TP was probably a diffi-cult item to find in this fucking alley, and there was... some...blood...So you're on your fucking period as well. No. In every way, no. I want nothing from you." *Just be quiet and leave me alone.*

As if this lady was facing a fun challenge, she turned around and started to caress herself. "Oh, come on, baby. Let me make things right. I'll suck your cock. I feel bad for throwing up on you. I do. I'm fine now. Puke and rally, right? Come on. I'll take care of you. Go to the bar and buy us a couple of beers. Put them on my tab. I'm Sandra, by the way, and I'll take care of you right here, baby."

The dark-red-haired lady named Sandra kept her pants unbuttoned. She undid a few buttons on her shirt. Her piercingly sharp nipples were either an in-dication of the coldness or her desire to be further fucked and paid.

Sandra caressed herself. "You can fuck my mouth, baby. You can cum all over my face. I'll call you 'Daddy.'

Don't be too rough with me, OK, Daddy? This is my first time. I hope I do it right. Like licking a lollipop, right? I hope Mama doesn't find out."

I wonder what happened to her when she was a kid.

"Oh, and by the way," she said, dropping any tantalizing tone, "I ain't on my period, and I won't be getting my period for another six months or so, if you know what I mean—if I keep it."

Deeds's jaw must have dropped at this latest bit of information. *Sweet fucking Christ.*

She continued. "The last guy had a big ol' black cock, and that's tough on my ass, or in my ass." Sandra laughed and continued. "Whatever. Tore me the fuck up. So that's why there's blood."

Deeds was astonished as to the cause of the bleeding and surprised at who'd caused it. *That's why that huge, muscular black man had a peculiar smile on his face.* "So you let that huge dude fuck you in the ass, let him cum all over your…your stuff there, you take a shit, and then you vomit on me—all the while you're fucking pregnant and drunk? Wow. Quite a series of good life decisions."

"Fuck you!" On a dime she turned angry.

"No, I think you're plenty fucked. One more ain't gonna help you," Deeds retorted.

In a hollowed, falsely dignified way, Sandra walked over to his soaked parka and picked it up.

"Hey, what are you doing? Keep away? I gotta chase you now?"

"Nope." Sandra threw the parka over the pile of her feces and the puddle of her urine and stepped on the jacket, mashing the waste into it, making it forever soiled and unwearable.

Deeds was shocked, further saddened, and angered. It took a few moments to sink in. Defeated, he said, "That's my jacket. Why did you do that?"

Sandra very calmly picked up the shit-, urine-, and vomit-covered parka and threw it at him.

"The fuck?" Deeds yelled through clenched jaws.

Luckily, Deeds lunged out of the way, but he slipped on some unseen ice that had amassed from the still-running nozzle. Deeds fell down but was unhurt. Some empty boxes broke his fall. It may have looked theatrical, and it was really nothing more than that. With the surprise of falling subsiding, Deeds moved his fingers, arms, toes, legs, and neck a little to determine if anything was broken, strained, or sprained. Deeds was physically uninjured.

Deeds lay on the cold, uncompassionate, and unforgiving ground, exhaling deeply. As his breath billowed above him, dissipating into the dark cold air, illuminated by the light of the moon, he began to ponder and contemplate his current unwarranted misfortune.

Deeds wondered what this scene must look like. If this moment in time was frozen, what would it look like to an outside party? If observers were recording the events that had taken place in this alley into written word, what would they relate? If an artist painted this scene and it was deemed a masterpiece, and a hundred years later it hung on the wall of a grand museum, what would the viewers interpret as they gazed upon the image?

Deeds also wondered what this scene must look like from above. Like if there was a God in the sky viewing this alley with Deeds in a Jesus Christ pose among garbage and human waste with a mean and vile woman looking at Deeds while he looked into the night sky. This scene brought forth what conclusions? *Fuck their conclusions.* The anger and sadness were rising.

Fuck the world, Deeds declared. *This is fucking absurd. Why did any of this happen to me? I was just trying to do something that would make me happy. I was trying to step outside my lonely comfort zone. I was trying something different. I was trying to better myself, so I could smile. This is my reward? This is what happens? Why would someone or something up there want me to feel bad all the time? Fuck that, and fuck those who look to that.* Deeds lay there for several moments. *Time to get up.*

CHAPTER NINE

Deeds was downtrodden and fed up. He just wanted this goddamned night to end. He had had it. Deeds smelled foul garbage as he tried to get up. It was not as bad as Sandra's vomit or the smell of her shit, but enough to be tired of the olfactory assaults. Deeds wanted desperately to leave. *The show is over. Just get up, dust yourself off as they say, and walk the fuck away.*

Deeds was somewhat proud of himself for not reacting with immediate anger as many others would. If he acted on the anger he was feeling, he would have regretted it. *Get up. Go home. Throw away all that has been compromised by the gross shit, buy new items, and forget this night ever happened.*

His thoughts turned to Sandra. *Her life is awful, and I'm not going to add to it. Be the bigger man. My stuff can be replaced, and I will forget this episode, and she won't remember. It's as if it never happened. I can buy new clothes tomorrow. She'll still be worthless.*

As these thoughts were occurring and as Deeds was about to stand, he noticed Sandra had started to laugh. It began as a little childish chuckle or two and grew to a clamorous fit of laughter. Vociferous laughing from a white-trash societal burden cruelly mocked Deeds as he was down. *You're not making this easy, Sandra.*

Even though it was just Sandra and Deeds, as there were no observers writing down the events or painters capturing the essence, and there was no supernatural being gazing upon the cold, dark alley, Deeds was the center of negative attention, and he was done feeling bad.

Deeds was the focus of cruel taunting, and he hated that. Sandra laughed and laughed and pointed at Deeds, who was on the ground because of her mean-spirited actions.

Earlier in the evening, Deeds was at point A and was simply attempting to get to point B. Deeds had become anxious and headed home but was stopped by self-awareness of his foolishness. He'd then decided to turn around and continue on the path to where he wanted to go.

Point fucking A to point fucking B. The path, however, had been compromised. Someone had crossed into his path and made it unnavigable. *All I wanted to do was get to that bar where I might have been happy. But you could not let happen, could you, Sandra? You just had to cross my fucking path, didn't you, Sandra? You made an awful situation worse in every way. Fuck you!*

In an instant Deeds knew he was going to quickly complete the task of getting up and putting Sandra on the ground. Not to cause injury, but just to make sure she knew that was where she needed to be. *Making me feel bad is not too original.*

Deeds wouldn't feel guilt. It was like escorting a belligerently hostile eighty-sixed drunk from a bar and holding him or her till the police showed up to make an arrest. Well within his capabilities, both emotional and physical. *You will hear my words. You need to know. I need you to know.*

Deeds ceased posing like Jesus Christ and cautiously rolled over and attempted to get up. As Deeds tried to avoid falling again, Sandra's laughing had segued into a coughing fit. Big hacks of phlegm and remaining vomit began to come out of her filthy mouth as snot came out of her nose. It sounded as if she were choking. *Good*, Deeds thought. *Choke and suffer for laughing at me. Choke and suffer for exposing me to your waste. Choke and suffer for crossing into my path. Choke and die, you bitch.*

Sandra did not die and did not appear to suffer. She took a clumsy step toward Deeds and ungraciously threw up on him again. Deeds, by this time, was on all fours trying to balance and stand up on icy, foul ground as Sandra's vomit coated his shirt and the back of his head, drenching his ponytail.

Are you fucking kidding me? Again? Steam—more steam since it was colder now—radiated from his muscular back. *Jesus fucking Christ, she did it again!* There was not as much surprise and shock or anger this time, just restrained astonishment as repulsive lightning struck twice.

Deeds acted nonplussed as she wiped her mouth on the back of her hand and bent down to wipe it on Deeds's shirt.

"Thanks, big man." Sandra laughed.

Deeds turned his head and looked up at her. She looked down. Their eyes met. She must have sensed something. She stopped laughing. She just stood there looking in Deeds's eyes and contemplated their message. Deeds's glance conveyed a message: *Enough is enough. The time has come.*

Deeds reached and grabbed Sandra's ankle and pulled with all his strength. The dirty woman fell and hit the ground hard. Deeds quickly and carefully stood up and loomed over her.

"There was no reason for this," he calmly stated as he bent down and grabbed her oily red hair and dragged her over to the still-running nozzle. Her filthy hands immediately went up and grabbed his hand, just like the stunt professional wrestlers act out.

Deeds placed Sandra's face directly underneath the cold water, and it rained an unbearable burning freeze onto her. Deeds's hand was gripped tightly around her neck. The frigid water was attempting to compromise his grip strength, but the hatred over-powered and persevered.

Sandra was not going anywhere. The frigid hell not allowing her to breathe was causing life-clinging panic. The foul stenches were being cleansed, but the stench of fear was present.

Sandra tried to scream as the water shot in her mouth. Sandra was choking and could not catch her breath. Deeds could instinctually sense her panic and knew she would fight to survive if he decided to kill her. The power and the presence of that thought hit Deeds very hard, and the guilt followed. *Don't kill her.*

The water's near-freezing temperature stung as it went up Sandra's nose. She could manage to rotate her face a few degrees to the left and to the right, but the searing cold water stung the insides of her ears.

Sandra fought valiantly, but Deeds's grip was too strong. She lashed out at his face. She attempted to claw his eyes. The cold water and freezing tempera-ture severely handicapped her dexterity.

Deeds pulled her from underneath the nozzle and flipped her over.

Instantly, Sandra mentally prepared to be raped. *Fine*, she thought. *At least I can breathe again. I've been raped before, but at least I can breathe.* Sandra was thank-ful for that.

Deeds ripped off Sandra's clothes, exposing a nice voluptuous body. The flesh glistened in the moonlight. The fair-skinned redhead was shivering and naked under the full moon, in the freezing cold, in an alley. Sandra instinctually contracted her arms and placed them under her body as she waited to be raped. She had been in this hell before.

When Sandra was a young girl about the age of nine, she was walking home from a friend's house one hot summer afternoon. She was supposed to be home for dinner every night at six sharp. Engel Falls was experiencing a heat wave, and that particular afternoon left Sandra and her friend very lethargic.

Not much was happening, and they didn't feel like making an effort to do anything. So Sandra said good-bye a little before four. Both girls hoped their parents would let them play again after dinner, when it was cooler.

As Sandra slowly strolled home, she would rest in the shade of any tree near the sidewalk. She made sure not to go in anyone's yard. Sandra couldn't believe how hot it was. She longed for a big glass of ice-cold root beer and wanted to take a cold bath. With these thoughts, she set out after a few moments' rest.

As Sandra came upon her street, she quickened the pace but not too much. Walking west, into the blinding sun, she made her way to her house. But then Sandra heard the unwelcome sounds of the Kaenick brothers.

They lived a few streets over, so their appearance was odd. Sandra wondered why they were here, on her street, at this time of day when it was so hot out. Sandra stopped. She was hoping to identify their location, so she could avoid them. "Where are they?" she asked no one on the empty street.

Out of nowhere the three brothers emerged from behind an abandoned house. Lots of bad kids did bad things in that abandoned house. The police were frequently getting calls from angry neighbors about trespassing teens causing trouble. The Kaenick brothers had apparently discovered it as well.

The Kaenick brothers were bad people from bad parents but from a family that really controlled Engel Falls. As the boys grew up, they got into trouble. It started out with petty hooligan stuff—destruction of private property, vandalism, minor thefts—that was all categorized as "boys being boys." One of their uncles was a respected minister at the Eternal Salvation Church. His widespread influence, no doubt, helped his nephews, as their punishments were nonexistent.

Later the good Reverend Kaenick was suspected of many bad deeds unbecoming of a man of the cloth. Somewhere there was a file on him and his criminal acts. A lot of his acts just became town lore, never really believed, never fully dismissed, and then just forgotten.

On this hot afternoon, the three Kaenick brothers walked to the front of the abandoned house, picked up their bikes, and mounted them.

The middle brother, Jason, spotted young Sandra and yelled, "Am I glad to see you!"

All three laughed and rode their bikes toward her as she walked faster, hoping to make it home. "Leave me alone," she demanded.

Sandra tried to run toward her house, but one of the brothers cut her off. She tried to break left or right many times, but the same thing happened. Sandra's annoyance gave way to fear as she realized she was trapped.

These self-righteous punks had picked on her many times before, but she was especially afraid this time. As they got closer and closer with every lap, they began to pull her hair and pull at her new yellow summer dress.

The dress was a gift from her mother. She was a talented seamstress and made her daughter a lovely yellow dress with light blue flowers on it. Sandra loved it and wore it as often as she could.

Jason yelled, "Let's cool this bitch off." He hocked a loogie on Sandra's dress.

"Gross! Cut it out! My mom made this for me!"

They repeated what she had said in a mocking tone. A few more loogies made their way to her dress, hair, and face.

Sandra kept yelling, "Stop!"

They made obscene statements that Sandra didn't fully comprehend. They made strange motions with their hips, made peace signs with their fingers, and stuck their tounges through them. Sandra was scared and alone. She crossed her arms and stood still. She was afraid.

After a few more laps, the Kaenicks got off their bikes and threw them to the ground. They surrounded her. Jason was in front of her. He was the middle brother, yet he was the leader. Sandra almost recoiled at his appearance. He was very short with dirty greasy hair and beady eyes. His face was covered in acne, he had disgusting yellow teeth, and he reeked of body odor. The heat wave was not helping his aroma.

Behind Sandra, on her left, was Michael. He was the older brother and the fattest. He had a stutter and a shrill, distinct, choppy laugh. He also had big teeth and no chin. Behind Sandra, on her right, was Davis. He was the youngest and did what his two older brothers told him to do, except not to drool. He had a gorilla walk and breathed through his mouth. He wasn't as fat as Michael, but he did have a learning disability. However, those things weren't really known about back then. He was just thought to be stupid.

Sandra did not know their exact ages. She knew they were older, but they were all held back in school, so their ages did not match their grades. They intimidated her.

Sandra held herself and did not move. After a moment Jason got closer to her. She could not stand his stench, and his breath was worse.

Very calmly he asked, "What's your problem? We was just teasing."

Sandra tilted her head down and toward Michael as Jason's breath was terrible. "Please...just leave me alone," she pleaded.

"Hey, uh, Sandra, right? Sandra, we're not gonna be mean to you. I promise. We was just kidding. We're sorry. OK?"

Sandra didn't move. She was hoping they were just trying to scare her and would leave her alone.

"Whaddya say? Put 'er there. Shake."

Slowly, Sandra opened her eyes and, keeping her gaze down, turned toward Jason, expecting to see an extended hand. Instead she saw a very tiny and erect penis.

Sandra was revolted and yelled, "Eww! Gross!"

Jason grabbed Sandra's head with both hands and forced her face to his small erection. Sandra screamed as the three Kaenick brothers laughed hysterically.

Jason smeared his sweaty foul-smelling penis all over her face, covering her with his smelly, fleshy slime. She resisted with all her might as the weird, smelly, bad-tasting flesh and soiled, matted hairs rubbed her face.

Behind a closed mouth she dared not to open, Sandra screamed, and with her hands she batted at Jason's skinny legs, trying to punch herself free.

Jason, fearing further resistance and injury, moved her head back to her normal standing position, spit on her face, and yelled, "You want more?"

Unbeknownst to Sandra, Michael was on all fours right behind her. Jason pushed her, and she lost balance and fell backward on the sidewalk, knocking the wind out of her. Sandra felt horrible pain on her tailbone and instinctively grabbed it and moaned.

The sight of young Sandra grabbing her tailbone in reaction to the pain Jason had caused, whose hand was already on his erect penis as he was stuffing it back into his filthy jeans, sealed young Sandra's fate.

Jason looked around and spotted no one. Most of the adults on this block were still at work. "Mike, Davis, pick her up and follow me."

The two ugly brothers obeyed and picked her up, following their uglier leader as he casually walked to the backyard of the abandoned house where they were earlier smoking cigarettes, urinating on each other when they weren't looking, mooning each other, and defecating in front of each other.

Jason penetrated Sandra after he had his two brothers throw her in the dirt. The sun cooked the entire yard, only adding to the hell that was present.

Sandra felt excruciating pain in her privates as Jason moaned. With his foul-smelling body on top of hers, she cried and tried to claw and slap his sweaty back.

Sandra was unaware she had vacated her bladder out of fear. Jason stopped for a moment as he felt the urine's warmth. "What the fuck? You pissed on me?"

Michael and Davis laughed.

Jason took a handful of mud the dirt and Sandra's urine had created and spread it on her face. Sandra threw up and was now shivering from shock. Jason turned her over and penetrated her again. Eventually, he let out a long moan and a few grunts, and she felt something warm on her lower back. Sandra felt Jason's hand moving on her lower back and then he smeared his hand on her face and said, "Ta-da!"

Sandra lay there shaking. She was face-down in the dirt, covered in Jason's disgusting fluids. She had contracted her arms and just shook. Jason must have taken in the gravity of the situation. He became silent. Michael and Davis looked at each other and continued to laugh. When they both looked at Jason, who was staring down at Sandra, their laughter died down.

There was near silence in the backyard of that abandoned house. Jason breathed slowly. His two brothers breathed through their mouths. Sandra was crying. She tried to control the sobbing as she called for her mom between fits of crying. Sandra prayed for God to take her away.

Jason, Michael, and Davis all heard her. Jason was not his normal self. He was quiet instead of making jokes or rude comments. Michael and Davis were used to being ordered around, so they just stood in silence, awaiting further instructions.

Jason thought about apologizing. He felt like kneeling and saying he was sorry. He wanted to help her up and walk her home. He couldn't do that though. In fact, the compassion he felt was foreign and scary to him.

Jason stood over her and said, "If you tell anyone, I'll kill you. It was your fault anyways." He knelt down but didn't touch her, and with an almost compassionate tone, he said, "Look, just don't tell anyone. OK? Don't get yourself into trouble, OK?"

Jason stood back up. Still gazing at Sandra, he said, "Let's go."

The two other Kaenick brothers followed Jason as they walked out of the backyard, both complaining about how they had not gotten their turn.

"Why didn't me and Mike get a turn?" Davis asked.

Jason was about to turn around and punch Davis in his chubby face, but he caught sight of two police cars driving toward them.

Without hearing an order from Jason, Davis and Michael took off running. Jason yelled, "Hey! Hey! Don't run! We didn't—"

But the sirens from the police cars interrupted him. Jason figured a neighbor had seen him and his brothers and called the police.

The cars sped up. One skidded to a halt in front of the abandoned house. The police officer in that car got out as the other police car sped after Michael and Davis, who had not split up and were running in the same direction.

Jason silently damned them for he knew they would continue running together and unfortunately toward home.

The officer in the first car was brandishing his baton. In a booming voice, the officer yelled, "Put your hands in the air, Kaenick. Now!"

Jason complied, as he was afraid. The first officer was one of the first black officers on the Engel Falls Police Department. He was big, scary, and severe. His presence demanded obedience.

"Turn around!"

Jason complied.

The big cop grabbed his arms by the wrists and moved him to the hood of the car and kicked his legs wide. Jason felt the searing heat but said nothing as he heard the baton go back into the ringed holder.

"Your no-good brothers running for home?"

"I dunno."

"You don't know, what?"

"I dunno, sir."

"What did you do?"

"Nothing."

"Nothing, what?"

"Nothing, sir."

"You and your brothers aren't trespassing again, are you?"

"No, uh, sir. Never been here before."

"You coming from inside the house?"

Jason realized someone had called, but they weren't aware of what happened in the backyard. "No, sir. Just in the driveway."

"Yeah, I bet. Were you inside the house? Huh? Vandalizing in addition to trespassing?"

The cops did not know. "No, sir."

"Yeah, we'll see." The big cop opened up the back-door of his car, placed his big hand on the top of Jason's head, and shoved Jason in. "Sit tight." He shut the door. He rubbed his palms on his uniform pants as they were covered in Jason's filth. He sat down in the front seat and grabbed the radio mic.

Jason heard a few plastic-sounding clicks and nothing else.

The officer then uttered, "What the hell?"

The other cop returned to the abandoned house right after he figured out his radio was not working. The car skidded to a stop. Michael and Davis were both in the backseat.

Michael and Davis had been visibly crying as their faces were flushed and tearstained. This meant they'd confessed what they had done to Sandra.

The other officer got out at the same time as the big officer and yelled and pointed, "Backyard," as he was running toward the big officer and the yard.

"Say again," yelled the scary officer.

The officer who'd caught Michael and Davis yelled, "Your radio's down. Backyard! Hurry! I already called an ambulance."

The big scary officer and the other officer sprinted into the backyard.

Jason looked over again at Michael and Davis as they continued to cry. It was a pathetic sight. Jason stared and shook his head. He knew he was in trouble.

The officer who'd apprehended Michael and Davis returned with a thousand-yard stare, opened the door, grabbed Jason with one hand out of the backseat, and slammed him across the trunk.

Jason's feet dangled off the ground as he was being searched. The cop was yelling furiously that Jason was under arrest, what the charges were, how he knew Jason would fuck up, how he was gonna lock him up, and so on.

As the cop was yelling, all Jason could focus on was the sight of the big scary cop, with tears in his eyes, carrying Sandra in his arms. The big scary cop, without pausing, found a shady spot in the yard and sat down Indian style.

With his right hand, he removed a handkerchief and wiped her face. He kept repeating, "You'll be OK, honey. You're gonna be OK. You're all right, sweetie." The big cop looked up. "Where's her ambulance?"

The other officer stated, "On its way!"

Thirty seconds later, Jason heard the ambulance sirens. Jason took in the sights and sounds of the big scary cop holding Sandra as his own child and the other cop telling his brothers, "Be calm. We know it wasn't you; it was Jason."

The cop walked over to Jason and said, "Even your uncle can't get you out of this, you no-good piece of shit. Wish we could hang you."

Jason began to cry. Jason knew—he just knew—he was in serious trouble.

Sandra was taken by ambulance to the hospital where she stayed for quite some time. Unfortunately, and to the surprise and the horror of the entire police department, Reverend Kaenick did indeed manage to finagle a deal and get reduced sentences, most charges dismissed, and community service as the worst of the punishments. His three nephews got away with their crimes.

The police officers were furious, as were many residents, but the majority of the town took the side of Reverend Kaenick and viewed Sandra as a hysterical and dramatic troublemaker.

All three Kaenick brothers, over time, graduated to felonies and were charged and convicted as adults for various criminal acts. They lived the rest of their lives in and out of jail. Rumors persisted that one, two, or all three were killed or died in prison. Small-town lore.

As for Sandra, the psychological scars were forever present during her adolescence and adulthood. The damage had taken its toll and would affect her as she attempted to live her life, always being falsely labeled and receiving no sympathy till time just forgot her tragedy.

Never fully trusting, never fully living without fear, never sleeping a whole night, never escaping the shadow of terror, and never really living, she suffered crushing depression and post-traumatic stress. Sandra could not undue the horrific damage she was victim to on that day.

Now, on this night two decades later, under the light of the moon, freezing in this alley, Sandra tried to catch her breath as she was flipped over. She knew what was coming and immediately accepted the fact that she was going to be violated again.

Deeds had no intention of raping her. His revenge was to humiliate her and make her feel as bad as he felt. Deeds wanted to put her on display and embarrass her.

Deeds shoved Sandra until she was parallel to the wall. He put his knee on her back as her arms were pinned underneath her.

Deeds bathed her in the frigid water. It felt like she was being burned alive. Her screaming emanated from a clenched jaw. Sandra still expected to be raped and just cowered in fear, waiting.

Her heart was beating rapidly, and she was very cold. The booze was wearing off, and so was her high. She could barely move. The weight of Deeds and the impending doom were heavy.

Deeds angrily stroked her body. At first he was utilizing very rough hand movements as he asked, "Why, Sandra? Why did you fuck with me? Everyone loves to fuck with me. Oh, they fucking love it. Well, I fucking hate it! I didn't do a goddamned thing to anyone! Why can't all you bully motherfuckers just leave me the fuck alone!" As Deeds dished out his revenge, it dawned on him that what he was doing was wrong.

As it began to set in, Deeds stood back and saw what he was doing and who he was doing it to. He felt like a monster. This was why he did not fight back. He always felt guilt.

He began to cry. He felt regret for losing his temper and was truly sorry. He was sick of pain, his pain and the pain he was causing Sandra. He was furious at her for making him feel bad, but now he was just repeating the delivery of suffering.

Deeds could wash his stuff or buy new things. Sandra's life was awful. Adding this much suffering did not accomplish what Deeds wanted. It was redundant. He wanted an apology, but more importantly, he wanted to know why—why people liked to make him feel bad. Sandra wouldn't know—she'd probably asked herself that very question many, many times.

Deeds lifted his knee from her and picked up the parka and placed it on her. He turned off the water. The dirty parka was still soiled but hopefully provided some warmth even though it was soaked.

Deeds sat there Indian style on the cold, wet floor of the alley and just took in the horrible scene in front of him and cried. After a few moments, Sandra tried to move but only made little motions. Deeds moved toward her and rotated her. Sandra was shivering very hard, and she did not sound good.

Deeds and Sandra made eye contact.

Through chattering teeth Sandra said, "I...hate...you...Jason. I...hate you."

Deeds thought she was hallucinating. Deeds quickly put two and two together and realized "Jason" was the reason for her horrible life. Deeds wanted to help with this catharsis.

"Why do you hate me? What did I do to you?"

Shivering more violently, Sandra managed to say, "You...raped...me...Jason. You...raped...me."

Deeds guessed right. She had been violated. Probably at a young age. Deeds wanted to find out the details. Maybe if she told him who Jason was, he could do something. Deeds was desperate to help Sandra.

"Who's Jason? Where is he, Sandra?"

Sandra broke eye contact and simply said, "Dead."

Deeds wanted to ask how old she was. When had it happened? What had happened? Did they catch Jason? Do you blame yourself? Could he help? But it didn't matter. Sandra's eyes began to slowly close and open over and over again.

Deeds crawled over to Sandra and grabbed her frigid hand and said, "Sandra. Sandra, open your eyes, honey. You're gonna be OK, sweetie. You're gonna be OK."

She smiled and whispered, "I'm...tired."

Deeds was well aware of the fact that he could not do anything. He could not risk calling an ambulance, or she might survive and ID him. It was a rotten decision but necessary, unfortunately. *Chances are she wasn't going to keep the baby anyway.*

Deeds took the parka off Sandra, picked her up, and held her in his arms. The trauma of tonight, the collective impact of past traumas, the drugs, the alcohol, the exposure now, the depression were not going to allow Sandra to live, let alone to live happily.

Deeds did not care about the future. Deeds cared about only one thing right now—making Sandra feel comfortable and cared for.

Deeds held Sandra and whispered, "You'll be OK, honey. You're gonna be OK. You're all right, sweetie." Deeds stroked her wet hair. *What chance did she ever have? What chance did she ever have in this life? She had no shot. Why did bad things happen to her? She didn't deserve this.*

Sandra for the first time in a long while felt cared for and was grateful. She melted into the strong arms that held her. She closed her eyes and remembered the nice cop who'd held her on that hot summer afternoon. Sandra felt safe.

Sandra felt at ease, and that was pleasurable. As she drifted through memories, comforting warmth spread across her being. Sandra found herself walking toward the hot unbearable sun once more. She stopped and decided to turn the other way and go back to her friend's house. Sandra felt relieved and smiled as she walked away from the sadness to the happiness.

Deeds looked down at Sandra as she whispered, "I always...wanted...to go back." Sandra took her last breath and simply drifted away from the struggle that was her life.

Deeds kissed Sandra's forehead and held her for a while. Eventually and reluctantly, he gently laid her down on the cold ground. He stood over her for a moment. When his last tear was shed, he decided to do one last act of kindness.

He squatted down and picked up Sandra and placed her under the nozzle. He cupped his hands and splashed water all over Sandra's body and caressed her. Sandra was to be pristine when she was discovered. Deeds didn't think too much about the impending discovery. He didn't want to think about that. He wanted Sandra, right now, to be clean.

Deeds stood up and looked at Sandra. Her flesh glistened under the light of the waning gibbous moon in that freezing, dark alley. Sandra was beautiful. This sight was a memory he wanted to keep forever.

He wished a painter could replicate this image of a beautiful Sandra. Deeds wished he was a writer, so he could write and communicate every detail of this haunting and enchanting image of beautiful Sandra.

Deeds said nothing as he gazed upon Sandra one last time. She glowed in the moonlight. *Good-bye, Sandra.* Deeds grabbed his parka, turned around, and walked into the darkness in a better state of mind since he indeed had made a connection.

CHAPTER TEN

Kenny and Brian were best friends. The two fif-teen-year-old freshmen were from Old Falls, but both had earned the right to go to school in New Falls. Through a social program, they were sponsored through a foundation's scholarship. As long as their grades were excellent and there was no trouble, they could go to the better school, receive transportation aid, and even receive financial aid for college.

For these two awkward, smart, shy, goofy, happy-go-lucky youths, this was a very fortunate situation since their families (what was left of them) could not afford the tuition to send these bright kids to college.

Both Brian and Kenny had suffered the hardships of life in Old Falls. Yet they were able to avoid those pitfalls and were on their way to making a better life for themselves.

Out of friendship and necessity, they were nearly inseparable. Most students didn't care about their situation. However, some were always there to remind them that they were not supposed to be in New Falls. It was this small minority of young people who went out of their way to make life difficult for them, as if it was not difficult enough already.

Both had endured hardship. While Kenny had suffered physical abuse by his parents on a regular basis while growing up, Brian's abuse was similar until one unfortunate tragedy furthered his sad existence.

Years before, Brian's father while in a drunken rage started randomly firing his pistol in the house late one night. At one point a round was fired up through the ceiling. Brian, clever at survival, had been hiding in his closet, and the round went through the ceiling and closet floor and pierced Brian's leg. Brian yelled in pain and instinctually grabbed the wound.

Brian took a sleeve of a sweatshirt and wrapped it around the wound. Brian was near unconsciousness yet still clutched the wound, slowing the blood loss. The hollow-point bullet had shredded the flesh and shattered the bone.

Brian lay there in the dark for a long time. Eventually, the police showed up after receiving numerous calls of gunshots. Brian's dad opened the door, and the responding police officers immediately wrestled him to the ground and seized the pistol.

Brian's dad was handcuffed and placed on his stained couch with flattened cushions. He was tilted to the side in case he vomited. The police were actually hoping he would throw up now in his home, rather than in the back of a squad car.

Once Brian's dad was neutralized, some officers began to make a perfunctory sweep of the house. Guessing that Brian's dad was currently unmarried, they made a medium-paced effort to clear every room.

They checked under beds. They checked behind shower curtains. And when they finally got to Brian's room, they found him near dead in the closet with a heinous leg wound. An ambulance was immediately called. Brian was rushed to the hospital. Unfortunately, Brian's leg could not be saved and was amputated above the left knee.

As news of this tragedy passed through Engel Falls, many donations were made for the multiple surgeries, therapies, and state-of-the-art prosthesis. That was also when the scholarship was created by the heads of many thriving New Falls businesses.

As soon as Brian was well enough to attend school again, he was able to transfer to a nicer school, and through social services, he moved in with a foster family. The following year, Kenny transferred schools as well, taking advantage of the service's offer.

Soon many other kids received financial aid as well as geographical leniency in dictating which schools they could attend. Talent should not be wasted. The talentless should.

Brian's prosthesis worked well, but a limp was noticeable, rather his limp was noticed by some mean-spirited older teenagers. For the most part, he was usually left alone. Even though most of them could not relate, they were sympathetic to Brian's tragedy.

However, some nasty teens saw Brian and Kenny as targets. Interestingly enough, it was young ladies who made fun of the newcomers most. Brian and Kenny usually just flipped them off and walked away in silence. If their boyfriends were around, they just took it and walked away in silence.

What could they do? They were Old Falls trash lucky to be in New Falls. "Take a little, and become better than them" was the mantra. Maybe not specifically the collected mantra, but the transfers had to undergo some tough verbal abuse from some peers.

It was a school night but the next day was a half day, and Kenny and Brian had caught a movie and were exiting the theater. Most theatergoers headed for their cars as all the businesses were closed for the night.

As they walked through the town center, where the closed shops and restaurants were, they laughed and recited lines of the movie they'd just seen. They quizzed each other on the actors' previous films, recited more lines, and were having a fun time.

Brian liked his foster family, despite their religious ways, but every once in a while, he just needed to get out. Kenny was living with an odd and unique collection of relatives.

The great aunt who was granted legal custody of Kenny had a large house, and related derelicts or low-life relatives found their way to it. They were typical for Old Falls, but he was never assaulted, for which he was grateful.

On this cold night, as they strode through the town center, they were happy. They didn't have to get up early, they liked being out, no one was around to make fun of them, and it was always fun to stay up late. It was one of those significant yet simple occasions that two close friends enjoy and later look back on fondly.

They walked and continued to have fun. They talked of girls they thought were "hotties," who was going to score first, which teachers had the worse breath, which teachers were pervs and put the big-breasted girls in the first row, how fractions and the Pythagorean theorem were going to help them achieve their life goals, what their first cars were going to be, and which teacher they would bang for an A. General teenage stuff.

During times like these, Kenny forgot about his past, and Brian forgot about his limp. They forgot all about the suffering and were able to enjoy life. That was all they wanted. They didn't need popularity or recognition. They wanted a chance to enjoy life. They didn't want to be afraid. Unfortunately, there are those who cannot let that happen. Sadly for Brian and Kenny, their great night was about to end.

As they walked through town, in a closed strip mall, their fun conversation was interrupted by shouted epithets. They had heard these insults during previous negative episodes and knew the perpetrators. They, however, did not know where they came from.

As Brian and Kenny stood together, they looked around and could not see anybody. The shouted insults seemed to come from somewhere close, but there was no one around to be seen.

"Do you see anyone?" Kenny asked, as if confused rather than afraid.

Brian was more afraid than confused and just pleaded, "Let's go. OK? Let's just go home."

They walked a moment or two, and then some things began to crash around them. Both were startled, but Brian was more afraid than before. Several rocks were thrown, some hitting them with direct shots or ricochets.

Then came the empty bottles. The shards of glass blanketed the street, and the loud noises caused the boys to flinch. They'd hear a crash and turn to look.

Then more insults came. After numerous epithets, which included "peg-leg faggot" and "white-trash pieces of shit," were delivered, Brian and Kenny were frightened.

Brian, now more emphatic, said, "Let's get outta here."

Kenny asked, "Where are they?" Fed up, he yelled, "Fuck off, assholes. Just leave us alone."

They walked a little farther, picking up the pace, and they heard laughter above them and looked up. There were two people, a girl and a guy, on the roof of a building. It was common knowledge that scoring on the roof of a closed building was a hip thing to do. During business hours or on a cold night, it got you points from peers. Sometimes the couple got too drunk and crashed down to the ground. Unfortunately, this couple had not fallen to the ground, and they were harassing Brian and Kenny.

Brian and Kenny recognized them instantly. It was Ryan and Lindsay, an older couple from high school who were particularly rotten to them. They went out of their way to be rude, insolent, and hurtful to Brian and Kenny. Verbal assaults and public embarrassment, it appeared, had graduated to near physical abuse and harassment. Lindsay laughed and threw more garbage at them.

Kenny yelled, "Fuck you, bitch!"

Ryan looked at the girl and laughed. Ryan then unzipped his fly, and Lindsay came over and grabbed his exposed penis. They kissed for just a brief second, and with her hand still on Ryan's penis, she aimed it and asked, "You fags need a shower?"

Ryan's urine arced down toward Kenny and Brian. Kenny dodged the urine and backed away. Brian moved too fast and fell as his prosthesis failed him. Brian was struggling to stand. He was helpless and being drenched.

Kenny saw that Brian had fallen and went to help his best friend as the urine rained down. Kenny desperately tried to pick up Brian. It was slippery, and the whole situation was an incomprehensible, shocking scenario, and they just could not coordinate a swift exit.

It was a cold night, so the warm urine steamed off the two victimized youths. Kenny cried a little, and Brian cried a lot. When would the suffering end? They were helpless.

Brian was on the ground, drenched, and Kenny was kneeling above him, trying to shield the piss as he became drenched. The laughs continued. A moment or two later, Ryan's bladder was empty. The laughter dissipated to chuckles.

Lindsay, the heartless bitch, said, "See you at school."

Kenny and Brian watched them disappear from sight and assumed they had walked to the other side of the roof where there was a ladder or fire escape to climb down and hopefully head away from them…or fall down and break their necks. They prepared for another attack, but silence indicated the mean couple was done with this evening's round of torment.

Kenny and Brian took their time and finally stood up. Brian fixed his leg, and they both shed some layers and tried to wring out their clothes.

"I fucking hate them," Brian said.

"I know, man. I know," said Kenny.

"Can we call the cops?" Brian asked.

"And say what? That we received a golden shower? An illegal golden shower? Like they would do anything to them."

Brian screamed through a clenched jaw, "It's not fucking fair!" He threw his urine-soaked sweatshirt to the ground. "We didn't do any thing to those assholes. Nothing! Why do they get to do whatever they want to us? I'm sick of it! I was just trying to have fun. And they get to ruin it. Why?"

Kenny calmly stated, "I don't know." Kenny didn't attempt to make Brian feel better with any clichés. He just stood there while Brian had his moment of sadness and questioning.

The few moments of silence were broken up by Kenny wringing the urine out of his clothes. As the sound of the urine trickled onto the pavement, Kenny looked at Brian and said, "They'll get theirs." Kenny squeezed again.

"Somewhere, sometime, they'll get theirs, man. They'll make fun of the wrong person, and they'll get theirs. It'll happen." The now-cold urine continued to splash the pavement. "It has to."

CHAPTER ELEVEN

Deeds felt pent up in his apartment. He wanted to get out for a while but did not want to attempt to try his luck with another bar. Then a slight ping of sadness resurfaced over Sandra.

Sandra is gone. Something bad happened, but you helped Sandra in a way no one else had in a very long time. Remember her, but do not let her memory become an anchor pulling you away from possible happiness. Then a slight different ping of worry resurfaced over Sandra's death.

Deeds had worried that he had made some mistake that would catch up to him. He left no fingerprints. No one saw him. There was no trace of him. There was no evidence that he had left his apartment.

There was that huge, muscular black man who could place Deeds near the alley a little while before the unfortunate episode. But this man might have to admit to the police he'd paid to have sex with Sandra, whose body was found under odd circumstances (i.e., naked, dead, and frozen in an alley). It would not be favorable to admit to having sex with a prostitute moments before she died, or was killed. Chances were he would avoid it.

The police could not tie the huge, muscular black man to Sandra either. Deeds was extremely thorough in the cleansing of Sandra. Any of the man's fingerprints or other DNA clues were washed away or, frankly speaking, shitted or vomited out since Sandra admitted they had engaged in anal and oral sex. That shit was spread around the frozen and icy alley ground or wound up mushed into Deed's parka, which he had taken care of. That vomit was washed out of Deeds's hair and clothes.

Any traces of Deeds and the huge, muscular black man were wiped and washed away or lost their identifying characteristics as the snow fell later that evening. *Wow, frozen Sandra in the snow...haunting and angelic.*

Deeds had soaked his parka and boots in hot water, laundry detergent from a free sample he received in the mail, and bleach. He let the items dry and thoroughly cleaned his bathtub.

He woke up a short while later and placed the now-odd-colored parka and boots in a garbage bag and knotted it. He then took the bag and tossed it into the bed of his truck and drove across the street to another apartment complex.

The garbage Dumpsters were in the rear of the complex. Not too many people were around at that early hour, and even if they were, would they remember Deeds and his truck? Would they go investigate a man driving? Not likely.

The apartment units were not close to the Dumpsters. This way tenants would not have to be near garbage or hear the loud trucks collect the refuse.

Deeds put the truck in park, got out, and tossed the bag into a Dumpster. He looked; there was no one was around. He got back in and drove. As he exited the complex, he saw the lumbering garbage truck a half mile down the street.

In minutes the items would be in a garbage truck with many other full bags of garbage. Within hours that bag would be in a landfill covered by tons of garbage bags. The parka and boots were not an issue anymore.

The other clothes he wore that night were laundered and placed back in the dresser. Deeds would not wear them again. In time he would throw them out as well, but he did not want to be seen or caught throwing out a whole outfit just after a death had occurred.

Deeds could not be identified. Deeds was not on any suspect list.

The huge dude may be, but I doubt he was the only guy to talk to Sandra that night. I'm sure that Sandra wasn't the only woman to talk to the huge dude as well. Deeds let reason take over.

Many guys talked to Sandra. Many girls talked to the huge dude, who, by the way, would not admit to fucking Sandra. Why would he? The police cannot physically tie him to Sandra. No prints. No semen. Even if the huge dude somehow was in a position to say he saw someone (me), what possible identification could he make? How viable could that identification be after a night of drinking, and in the dark, no less? A big dude in a winter coat with long hair and a beard. Ha! Get real.

There was nothing to worry about. The only thing to worry about was a strategy with Jess. But Deeds was not even worried. Deeds grabbed his new parka, his clean new boots, and a can of dip and headed out for a walk.

CHAPTER TWELVE

Deeds was always trying to not be a pessimist, but he was never an optimist. Deeds was not a leader, nor was he a follower. He was *el solo lobo*, and he tried to react to what he knew. He did not hope for the best. He did not expect the worst. Those expectations (Deeds hated that word since it was so ridiculously overused during his childhood) were a waste of time. When something happened, he would deal with it.

Of course he wanted something to happen between himself and his lovely neighbor, Jess. He did not expect it, nor did he just give up. He did not want to overthink it. Yet he did not want to remain neutral.

The old adage "Don't shit where you live" kept recurring to him, but he ignored it. *But what if it doesn't work out, and I see her around, let alone with other dudes?*

Relax and don't assume the negative outcome. Know something. Know something, and then react.

Deeds contemplated his "Jess strategy" as he walked around. He obviously did not head toward Garee's Place. Deeds thought it would be better just to go out for a quick walk, clear his head, think things over, and enjoy a dip.

Being outside did not require a spitter, the empty container to spit in when one dips or chews tobacco. Cowboys used spittoons back in the Wild West days. Deeds did not want a spitter, let alone a spittoon, in his apartment. Even if the bottle had a secure top screwed tightly on, he did not want it inside his apartment.

So Deeds likened "going out for a dip" to "going out for a smoke." And he did not have to carry a bottle full of brown spit. If a cop ever asked him why he was out, this detailed explanation would be his answer.

Deeds would be loquacious, slow, and detailed in his explanation and his reasoning. The cop would hopefully just quickly end the interaction as he or she sensed impending boredom. *Appear simple, and people will expect less from you.*

Deeds walked around and enjoyed the cold night air as he thought things through. After a while, Deeds headed back home. The walk was helpful and allowed him to think without distraction. Deeds was going to ask Jess out on a date, which would then hopefully progress to the next level.

Deeds figured he would see her around the apartment complex. Instead of asking the rote "How are you?" he would inquire specifically about her unfortunate loud-neighbor situation.

Within a short period of time, he would need to elevate his status from friend to someone who is interested, and ask her out on a proper date.

It was a tightrope walk, though. *Be clear with your intentions. Yet do not appear desperate. Be confident but not overbearing.* Deeds concluded that in the next one or two run-ins with the lovely Jess, he would ask her to dinner. *Done.*

Deeds felt confident. His reasoning dictated that her answer would be a positive one. And as Deeds read people very well, he would observe her true reaction and subsequent feelings—a helpful talent that Deeds possessed.

Deeds was walking home through a little shopping area. It had recently been dusted with a light snow that had already melted. The ground mirrored the businesses' neon "Closed" signs.

Deeds had heard a couple of distant laughs and then spotted a couple walking toward him. The girl had her arms wrapped around the good-sized young man who had just finished a beer and threw the empty bottle to the ground, shattering it. *Litterbug.*

They appeared to be in their mid- to late teens. *Oh, duh,* Deeds thought as he noticed his letterman jacket denoting he was in high school. From afar she was a real looker, and Deeds wished he'd had more confidence while he was growing up or in college, or now.

The couple shared some laughs and were a little tipsy as they walked toward Deeds. They didn't appear to be crossing into Deeds's path and wanting to cause trouble. *Were they just leaving a party? On a school night? Whatever.*

As they got closer, Deeds realized he was being too nice in his conclusions. They were those who'd made fun of him growing up. These were the people who'd looked down on him when he was younger.

No, you don't know for certain that this couple puts people down. They look like that type. Preppie, uppity, popular, and cliché, but you can't make that assumption. They could be the nice ones. He looks like a typical douche, though. Blond. Tan. No hardship in his life. Everyone kisses his ass. No depth. Nothing earned. The kind of guy who hangs out in front of 7-Eleven and looks for a fight but never really has to fight. He likes to intimidate. He gets off on it. And her, don't get me started on her. Bitch.

The couple looked up, and Deeds politely said, "Evening."

The girl made a scoffing, mocking sound of exhaling and laughter. Just the attempt of Deeds greeting them was unwanted and bothersome apparently.

Her beau, seeking confirmation as a man, simply put both his arms up and asked, "What'd you say, faggot?"

It took two or three more steps for that question to sink in. Deeds stopped, turned around, and faced the couple. The young lady put up both middle fingers and made a "ha-ha" sound.

The young man, with his arms up even higher, asked, "What's up, bro?"

Are you fucking kidding me? What the fuck are you doing? Why do you think this is a good idea? I know you're not aware of what I am capable of, but is your common sense so fucked you can't see who you are antagonizing? Are you that fucking stupid? Where'd you get your balls? You're big for your age, and you're big for whatever stupid silly team sport you base your identity and self-worth on, but I'm bigger. Who the fuck do you think you are? Because you're not. I didn't do anything to you. Why did you insult me? Why? Why do you want me to feel bad? Why? All this was thought in a fraction of a second.

Deeds's thousand-yard stare was in full effect as he stated, "When you have a few, it's easy to think you're a tough guy. Then when you meet a real tough guy and piss him off, you'll find out who you really are. Walk away from me."

Deeds gave him a chance. However, the preppie fucker was boosted by liquid courage. His sense of superiority that he got from his coaches and his girlfriend's presence forced him to make a bad decision. "Fuck you, faggot! You want some? What's up?"

Deeds pleaded, "This won't end pretty. Go home." Deeds did not want to inflict more pain. *Please, make*

*the right decision. I'm just trying to go home. I was not caus-
ing a problem. I was just trying to go home. You chose to
insult me. You chose to try and make me feel bad. Why? Why
couldn't you just leave me be? I have caused pain. I have suffered. I am tired of it all.*

Arms still up, the young man asked, "You wanna
go, faggot?"

The young lady laughed and said, "Fuck him up,
baby."

Deeds looked at her and thought she was one of
those ultrapretty tan prom queens who thought she
was royalty. *Another fucking Tracy.* She was gorgeous,
but that personality made her hideous.

"Knock this loser homo out, baby, and I'll give you
a blow job."

The young man looked at her, snickered, looked at
Deeds, and said, "Let's do this!"

The overconfident punk took off his letterman
jacket, displaying several months of bench pressing,
curling, and triceps exercises. The "bar muscles" as
they were called by veteran weight lifters.

They benched and they curled, and they did triceps
on Monday or Tuesday. They then took Wednesday
and Thursday off and returned Friday and got a "preparty pump" and did chest, biceps, and triceps again
in anticipation for the weekend's festivities, where they
donned "extra-medium" trendy T-shirts.

They neglected everything else, thus exposing major weakness: weakness of discipline, weakness of work

ethic, weakness of dedication, and weakness of character. This also resulted in an elevated and unsubstantiated sense of self-worth and invincibility.

Deeds instantly saw this and offered reprieve once
more. "I know who you are, what you are, and what
you're going to be without having met you. And I know
what's going to happen if you don't walk away from
me." Deeds paused and decided he was going to be
the bigger man. The thought of more pain was not
appealing at all. "I don't have time for this bullshit."
Deeds turned around and started to walk away.

While this potentially lethal exchange had seemed
to subside, Deeds had amassed a puddle of spit on the
ground to his side from the dip he was enjoying. This
puddle apparently influenced the young punk's next
move as he hocked a big loogie on Deeds as he walked
in the opposite direction.

This loogie landed right on Deeds's new jacket.
Right on his new fucking jacket that he just fucking
bought because his other jacket was Sandra's death
shroud.

This new jacket represented a new beginning
for Deeds. It was a reminder of something bad that
had happened, but it was also a symbol of a new era.
Hopefully a new era of nonshitty occurrences. Now,
it was covered in a big loogie from a little punk who
needed to be taught a lesson—a lesson the young
punk demanded Deeds teach him. Deeds would
oblige.

Deeds, facing away from the couple, slowly took off his jacket and placed it on the ground. *Déjà fucking vu all over again.* He reached into his mouth and pulled out the dip and flung it into a planter box holding dead flowers. The flowers had frozen to death. Deeds spat one more time and wiped his finger and thumb on his jeans.

Deeds breathed in a deep, slow breath and exhaled, and the vapor was present in the cold air. He stared over his shoulder at the punk who would not walk away. "You shouldn't have done that."

Deeds then rotated back his head in the opposite direction. By now, the young punk was in a martial-arts stance. The girl laughed at Deeds and sang, "He's gonna kick your aaa-ass," like when a child taunts another child. *Childish cunt.*

Deeds turned his head again and watched over his shoulder as the young punk did some shadow-boxing mixed-martial-arts (MMA) bullshit. With every punch thrown, the young punk made a very sharp "shh" exhalation sound before he ducked and weaved to imaginary punches thrown from a nonexistent opponent. It was laughable.

This is going to be funny. I was regretting it, but now this'll be fucking funny. No regrets. This was not my choice. No remorse. This was his decision. I am calm. I'm not emotional. I feel no guilt. I will feel no guilt. If by chance this wannabe tough guy won this fight, he'd go on to pick many others and hurt people. I'll stop him now. Too much rap

*music? No father figure? Fuck off. This impending distribu-
tion of pain is righteous.*

Deeds turned back and faced the other way as the
young punk continued to throw air punches. Little by
little, he got closer and kept inquiring, "What's up,
bitch?" while his girlfriend encouraged him with, "Get
him, baby. Get him!"

Deeds took his time. *Let him come to you,* Deeds
concluded.

As the little punk got closer, Deeds pictured his
height compared to himself. When he got up close
enough, the sound was synonymous with a tolling bell
of impending misery and agony. This barbaric onslaught would be precision based, not rage based. Rage
clouded the execution of brutal and severe strikes.

When a step was taken, and Deeds's instinct calcu-
lated it as perfect for executing his plan, he rotated his
entire body with a speed that was only matched by the
power and accuracy of the savage haymaker delivered
to the side of the punk's face.

The punch landed on a spot that boxers and
hockey enforcers called "the button." It disrupted consciousness and simply turned the opponent "off." Old-
timers would hit "the button" and send the opponent
to "Queer Street" (i.e., a grade-two or grade-three concussion) as consciousness was lost.

There was a very loud crack when Deeds's hoof-
like fist made contact with the neophyte's face. It was
a sound that let everyone know that, physiologically,

something was very, very wrong. The young punk was in la-la land as he fell to the asphalt where his skull made a sickening thud—a horrific and meaty thud.

In that very instant, the young lady knew her boyfriend's jaw was broken and that he now had a traumatic brain injury. Her eyes were wide with shock and pure horror at what had just transpired.

Deeds viewed favorably the scene before him, a scene he had not started but had finished. He had no desire to go overboard and create further carnage. It was not necessary. The message was sent. The message was received. The message was understood. His work was done.

Deeds saw a hurt little boy on the ground. Deeds was not proud of what had happened but understood that he'd had to take care of this situation or else this punk might have indeed caused harm and pain to someone who did not deserve it.

No one deserved to feel bad about himself or herself thanks to these sadistic pieces of shit who chose to cause pain. Fire had to be fought with fire. Hopefully this punk learned not to pick on anyone anymore.

The girlfriend could not grasp what had happened. How could her badass, tough-guy, varsity-football-player boyfriend lose a fight? How could this have happened? How was she gonna get him home? What were people gonna say? Would he lose his scholarship?

She walked near the pile that was her soon-to-be former boyfriend. Defeat was a major turnoff for her.

She did not bend down to help him. She just looked at him, shook her head, and then placed her face in her hands. After a moment she looked up at Deeds and said, "That was a cheap shot. He…He wasn't ready. That wasn't a fair fight. This isn't over. OK? I'll remember you. We'll fucking find you!"

Snickering and with confidence, Deeds said, "I'll be waiting for you, hon."

Frustrated at her loss, not with the anguish her boyfriend was in, she angrily yelled, "Fuck you. We'll find you, and my boyfriend will kick your ass with one arm tied behind his back! You'll see!"

Deeds got annoyed and lost his cool. "Listen, you little fucking princess cunt! I didn't want this. He wouldn't walk away. I asked him to. Remember? I tried to walk away myself, and he fucking spit on me! Are you fucking kidding me? That was his decision. This was his fault. Fucking get over it, prom queen!"

With stoic pride she placed both hands on her hips and stated matter-of-factly, "That was me, asshole."

No fucking way! Deeds was taken aback. "No shit?" he asked, surprised and in an almost friendly conversational tone. She simply nodded, crossed her arms, and with a very sardonic, shrewish tone made a "mmm-hmm" sound.

Wow. That loogie drove me overboard. It was a game of brinkmanship, and I incorrectly guessed he spat on me, and, therefore, we together made the choice to cross the Rubicon. It was her though. Well, what are you gonna do about it? Leave her alone. It wasn't Sandra's fault. This bitch, however—it was her fault. I'm not going to assault her. I'll continue the lesson via his pain. Consequences for me be damned.

Deeds looked at the punk on the ground and then looked back at the prideful high-school girl and asked, "You said your little man here could kick my ass with one arm tied around his back?"

She haughtily nodded and said, "That's right, asshole!"

Deeds walked over to her, placed his big left hand between her folded arms and her body, and with a downward motion, forcefully unfolded her arms. He then quickly brought up his left hand and placed it on her breast and gently squeezed. Her eyes went wide. Then he shoved her to the ground. Like a child, she fell on her rear end with a surprised sound of air exiting her beautiful mouth. "Hey," she let slip in a breathy, throaty tone.

Deeds walked over and grabbed the right arm of her unconscious boyfriend and dragged him over several feet to where the concrete they were standing on ended and the curb abruptly gave way to the parking lot's asphalt.

The young punk's wrist and hand were on the lowered ground of the parking lot while the rest of him remained on the curb's elevated height. The forearm was diagonal to where the curb's concrete and the parking lot's asphalt met.

Deeds looked at her while she sat on the ground and asked, "One arm?" Deeds pointed to the young punk's arranged arm. "This arm?"

Deeds raised his leg, and with immense power his size 13 boot came crashing down and snapped the young punk's radius and ulna like they were fucking twigs.

The girl almost vomited. Her tan face lost color and went pale. She shuddered at the sight and horrid sound. She was in a catatonic state of disbelief. This memory might haunt her, but in all likelihood her shallow ways would probably force her to forget she witnessed this brutality. The shallow ways would also aid in her forgetting that she'd helped cause it.

Deeds looked at what he'd created and thought how arms should not look like this. The prick's arm had an unnatural and catastrophic angle in it. This night was not over.

Deeds walked over to her and without effort pulled her up by her shoulders. He looked around. They were very alone. Deeds placed his big right hand on the side of her face and stared into her very pretty eyes.

"I didn't want this to happen. OK? I hate pain. I've suffered plenty of it." For some reason Deeds felt as if he had to explain or justify himself to her. He did not want her to have the wrong idea about him.

"I'm not going to tell you my life's story, but I fucking hate pain."

She closed her mouth and swallowed and then asked, "Then why did you...do this?"

Deeds answered angrily, "You! You made me feel bad. You put me down."

She closed her eyes and bowed her head.

"No doubt you made others feel bad," Deeds said.

She began to cry as the guilty do.

"This had to happen. You two needed to learn. You needed to learn that you can't pull this shit. If you didn't cross my path, you would have continued being pricks to people, wouldn't you? That, I cannot abide."

At that moment a lot of sadness and emotion that was just under her surface began to violently erupt. What had been building for a very long time could no longer be contained. The storm could no longer be ignored, and the levee broke.

An emotional and pivotal moment in her life was going to take place. Clarity, anger, resentment, lashing out, freedom, and ceasing the burden that conformity and compliance and expectational obedience carried were going to be present in this catharsis. Deeds was there for it.

The teenage girl let go a torrent of tears. This release, fueled by the shock of witnessing the justifiable assault, and the freeing effects of alcohol made her true feelings come out.

The sobbing affected her breathing. It was as if she had just finished a high-altitude long-distance run in record time. Her face was now flushed. She was dizzy. Her legs were wobbly. Sweat began to pour down her forehead. It steamed in the cold air. Her eyesight was compromised by her tears and squinting.

In this state of panic and shock, the body withdrew the blood from her limbs and extremities and pooled it in her torso to protect her main organs. Her central nervous system thought she was in a life-or-death struggle and acted accordingly.

Her hands were like claws that possessed a strong grip on Deeds's shirt. Her face had an odd and peculiar grimace on it. If Deeds had not been holding her up, she, no doubt, would have added to the piled collection of lessons taught in this empty parking lot.

Deeds had heard of panic attacks but did not know if this was one. "Are you a diabetic? Do you have seizures or anything like that?" Deeds was concerned but could not really make a huge effort to save her life, if that became necessary. "Do you need to sit down?" Deeds looked around for two things: witnesses and a place for her to die. *Christ, another Sandra.*

"I'm…I'm sorry," she said through short gasps.

Deeds was surprised as he looked down at her again. "What?" Deeds was confused.

Still crying and with shortened breaths, she said, "I'm…really…sorry."

The panic was still there, but it had not increased. Deeds was certain this was an emotional episode and not a medical emergency that required a shot of insulin or anything like that.

Out of nowhere, Deeds picked her up and carried her to the planter box with the dead flowers and sat her down. He sat next to her and put an arm around her and recited lines he'd heard from movies or TV or read in books: "Calm down...Take a deep breath... Follow my breathing...It's OK; it's OK...You're gonna be oooh-kaaay...Shhhh, it's all right..."

Despite all the anger toward those who'd attempted to make Deeds feel like shit, he was a very nurturing man. If you were respectful to him, he'd do anything within his power to help you. He'd give you the big shirt off his back. The number of people in this group was small though. The other group—well, there were a lot of people in that group.

After a good ten minutes, she began to breathe normally. It was a very touching scene really. She was huddled up with a tearstained face while Deeds's big arm was wrapped around her in a very protective position.

Her tears had collected on his jeans in a darkened blotchy stain. He tried to lighten the mood by making a joke. "I, uh, I got to be honest. If anyone looks at your tear stains and makes fun of me for pissing my pants, I'm gonna be upset." It worked.

She laughed and snorted as snot came out of her nose and landed on the stain. She gasped and said, "Oh my god, I'm so sorry."

Deeds replied, "No, no, now everyone will know it's not piss with your snot rocket. You did me a favor."

The girl laughed as she used her sleeve and wiped it up as best she could. "I'm sorry."

"No, don't worry. It's OK."

"No. I'm sorry. I'm…truly sorry for everything."

Deeds silently nodded. It was a lovely bonding moment, but it was unfortunate where this night had had to go. "I am, too."

Deeds looked up and viewed all around him. He saw no one. He did not think these mom-and-pop stores would spring for security cameras facing their front entrances—the cash registers and maybe the backdoors, but not a scanning panoramic view of the front entrance and parking lot. Deeds and the girl were alone.

Her cleaning skills were good as the snot was no longer visible. She then just placed her hand on where the tears collected. She did not rub provocatively. She was not attempting to be seductive. She simply placed her hand on the tears, which happened to be on Deeds's muscular quad. It was as if she was taking ownership. It was if she was acknowledging the emotions.

The girl started to move her thumb across the tears once or twice and then simply turned her hand over. Deeds knew what she wanted, and he placed his big hand in hers.

Through a stuffed nose, she asked, "What happens now?"

Deeds did not want the bonding to end or the connection to be severed, so he did not answer. He simply stated, "Why don't we just sit awhile?"

She nodded and said, "OK," through an even stuffier nose.

Deeds let go of her hand and reached into his back pocket and pulled out a handkerchief. He handed it to her and said, "Here."

She shook her head and said, "No, I don't want to get it dirty."

Deeds made the motion again and said, "That's what they're there for. Please."

She took it and sat up straight and faced away from Deeds. He was saddened as he thought the connection was lost. She would probably freak out and run away and be a liability to his liberty.

She blew her nose a couple of times after she wiped her face. To Deeds's amazement, she held on to the handkerchief and leaned back into Deeds. Deeds was relieved and very happy.

Yet while he was happy, there was a gnawing truth rearing its ugly head. Her question of "What happens now?" was a problem. He felt emotions for this high-school girl. These were emotions similar to those he'd felt for Sandra.

As connected as he'd been to Sandra, Deeds felt his emotions had not been as recognized by her as she'd been unable to be mentally present in his care and concern. He wanted more with this girl.

Already his emotions had run the gamut. Rage, anger, and vengeance had led to consoling and care. He'd tried to be there and make Sandra's exit a very nurturing and loving transition. Whether she'd been aware or not would never be known. Deeds had done his best and took comfort in knowing that he'd done what he could with all his effort for Sandra.

Deeds wanted to get closer to this girl. Her vulnerability was a huge attraction. The attraction was not in a sexual way, but more of a platonic admiring and extolling recognition of the redeeming qualities someone has.

Of course it was obvious that her gender was a factor. He could not make this emotional connection with a dude. He'd wanted to comfort Sandra. He wanted to comfort this young lady.

"A lot of things happened tonight. Some of them"—Deeds motioned with his head to the pile—"weren't about you, but, well, given the information at the time, this night has brought many things up to the surface that are about you."

She nodded while still in his embrace. "Talk to me." The girl sniffled and whispered, "What's the point?"

With caring authority Deeds stated, "Hey. I wanna know. Please." He could hear her, and she sounded more congested, meaning the emotions were probably coming out again. *Good. I want to hold onto this moment. I want to be there for you. I am here for you.*

"I didn't see you as a person, ya know? You were something that was there. I wasn't thinking about how you felt. I wasn't acknowledging you or your feelings." She started to cry again. "I'm so sorry. I blocked out the fact that you were a person. And now..." She was crying in a sorrowful way, and her voice went up an octave. "I see how nice you are to me, and I feel so bad." She cleared her throat and took a deep breath and said, "I feel so bad for all the shit I've caused you and everybody." She really had Deeds in a strong embrace.

Deeds leaned in, kissed the top of her head, and stroked her hair. "You obviously feel bad. That means you have a heart and you feel guilt. I don't know you, but from what I've seen tonight, except for that one part, I'd say you have a kind heart."

She cried and shook her head and said no.

Deeds disagreed and continued. "Yes, yes you do. You just have to let yourself be that person: the lovely girl with a big heart. But you won't. You choose to be someone else. Why?"

"I don't know."

"Come on; yes, you do. Why do you go against who you are? To impress friends?"

"I guess."

"Does it make sense to be friends with people you can't be yourself with?"

She suddenly sat up and with anger said, "You don't know anything about me! You don't know my friends! You don't get it! Fuck you!"

Deeds gave her the thousand-yard stare inches from her face and said, "Being that person, the one you're not but act like—that person is as cliché as one can get. That bitch is ubiquitous! That unoriginal cunt is all over the place. I see that fucking broad everywhere. OK? In any part of her life, I've dealt with that bitch. High-school twats who are rude to the regular people just trying to get by. The uppity mommy with the snot-nosed brats who do whatever they want. You're gonna end up just like that."

The girl's eyes teared up as she said, "You think I don't know that?"

Deeds nodded and asked, "Then why did you insult me? Why did you spit on my new jacket?"

"I'm sorry. I'd like to buy you—"

"That's not the fucking point. What would've happened if you two ran into someone your own age or smaller than that jerk-off boyfriend of yours, huh? How far would you and Mr. Forearm have taken this shit?"

With that, the young lady began to cry again, but this time there was anger in her statements that were released in an avalanche of resentment-based animosity.

"I'm sorry! I'm sorry for causing all this shit, but don't you think I have my own shit to deal with? You know what I go through? I fucking hate it! I fucking hate all of it! I fucking hate all of them!" With that she bolted toward the still-unconscious pile on the ground and began to kick him.

With every field-goal kick, she would yell, "I hate you, Ryan! I fucking hate you!" She got about three or four good kicks to Ryan's face before Deeds picked her up and took her into a darkened corridor.

Ryan's girlfriend put her hands to her face and cried some more. Deeds asked, "What the fuck was that about? Where did—"

"Ryan raped me."

Deeds was astonished. His facial expression must have communicated that. She knew to keep explaining.

"It's your typical story, I guess. He invited me to a party. You don't say no to that. He picked me up. There was something weird with him that night. I think he knew he would do...that...to me." She took in a deep breath and tried to remain calm.

"We got there, and he kept giving me drinks. No one was really talking to me. I tried not to drink so fast." She paused and took more breaths. "Anyways, I was pretty hammered. I remember him taking me upstairs to his friend's room. It reeked of weed. He had this little pipe, and he lit up. He asked if I wanted some. I said no, but he wouldn't give up. So I smoked some. My head felt so heavy. I just remember lying down on the bed. I woke up hours later. The sky was lighter, which freaked me out. My...My clothes were off. They were in a pile on the floor. Then the pain hit me. I hurt so bad, down there. There was dried blood."

It was a heartbreaking moment. Now Deeds was full of sadness and rage. He felt bad that something so vile had happened to this girl he felt connected with. A protective feeling arose within Deeds, supplementing the comforting feeling.

"Long story short, I slowly walked back home and snuck in. My parents had been out that night and were oblivious to my hour-long shower at five o'clock on a Sunday morning. I just lay in bed and said I was sick. I felt like killing someone. I felt like killing myself. I hated me. I still fucking do. Anyways, that night I got a text from Ryan. He said—"

Deeds interrupted to correct her. "Texted—he texted." Deeds felt bad for being a know-it-all. "Sorry, please continue."

"Yeah." She had a confused look on her face, but it disappeared. "Well, he texted how much fun he had and how everyone at the party liked me. I was about to call the cops, but what was I gonna say, ya know? I was drunk and stoned and got into a bed with him? I was a fucking idiot, and I didn't want to deal with everyone's bullshit. He was nice to me after that. It was a real relationship. But since then I just started being a real bitch to everyone. Then I found out he was cheating on me with his whore cousin, Amanda. Can you believe that?"

Deeds placed the tips of his index finger and thumb at the base of his nose between his closed eyes and shook his head a bit. "What?"

"It's OK," the young lady said, realizing what she had just shared was quite shocking.

"No, no. Just…Give me a second." Deeds took a deep breath. He towered over her in that darkened corridor and placed a hand on her shoulder and said, "Do you want me to break his other arm?"

She smiled. "No, I'm over it."

"You don't get over being…ya know…It doesn't work like that."

"Well, it's been a year of it, so whatever."

"His own cousin?"

"Yeah, she's so ridiculously pretty, but like the biggest whore ever!"

"Cousin. His cousin." Deeds couldn't get over that.

"Yeah. His cousin."

The weight of the admission hung in the air but was dismissed as she stepped toward Deeds and hugged him for a very long time in that darkened corridor.

After a few moments, a car drove by. Once they established the location and travel path of the interrupting car, they were relieved to know that the car's occupants could not view Ryan on the ground. The precious moments were over, and Deeds placed a hand on the knife in his pocket.

"Look," he began.

He did not want to kill her. Maybe he could intimidate her. Either way, he needed her to be silent. He also needed Ryan's silence. He didn't want to go to jail. Killing Ryan would be easy. Her silence—this was going to be awful. He tried to reason it out. He wanted her silence. He wanted more of a connection with her. He would love it if he could wait for her to turn eighteen, but there was no fucking way. *What are you thinking? It can't be like that!*

"Look," he said again.

She said, "Lindsay."

Deeds smiled. "That's a very pretty name. Lindsay… Anyway, Lindsay, I—"

"Don't worry about it. I'll say some scumbag or scumbags from Old Falls jumped us."

A huge wave of relief pleasantly crashed over Deeds. He was surprised at himself, at how coolly and quickly he was calculating actions of elimination. Lindsay's story was a relief, but he was still uncertain.

"Lindsay, I—"

"I know. I don't want to die. So I'll call the cops and say they jumped us. I got knocked out. And Ryan fought back but got fucked up. He sooo has brain damage, so I'm sure he won't give a description. If he doesn't have amnesia, I'll remind him that he raped me. He won't say shit."

Deeds absolutely loved her and loved what he heard from her, but at the same time, he was not 100 percent trusting. He really wanted to be, though.

"You still don't trust me?"

Deeds was silent for two seconds. "I do. It's just that—"

"Lindsay Powell. One thirty-eight Doyle Street. It won't get back to you. I promise. If Ryan remembers or says anything, he goes to jail for rape, statutory; I'm still seventeen. And I tell everyone he fucks his cousin. He and his parents would be destroyed."

Deeds let go of his knife. He trusted Lindsay. "I'm sorry for all your pain. I hope you become the person we know you can be."

She leaned in again for a final embrace—a different, more favorable final embrace than the one shared with Sandra. "Thank you." She grabbed his big hand and kissed it and left the darkened corridor, alive.

She took out her phone, walked to Ryan, and sat down next to him on the ground. Within several moments Deeds heard parts of her statements to the 911 operator: "There were two or three of them...One had a shaved head maybe...I don't know; they knocked me out...My boyfriend's unconscious and really hurt, too..." Lindsay then slapped and roughly rubbed the side of her face to make a red area and a bruise. *Smart girl.*

Lindsay put the handkerchief in her purse in a little zippered pocket. Everything else she dumped out and spread around. She didn't carry any cash usually, so she could claim they'd robbed her but hadn't taken the credit cards. She stretched her clothes out to make them appear disheveled. She lay down on the wet ground and let the cold dirty puddles soak into her clothes.

She checked Ryan, who was still unconscious. If he lived, it would be a miracle. If he lived and recovered and remembered this night, that would be the miracle of all miracles.

Lindsay wished him agony and death. "I hope you suffer and die, you piece of shit," she whispered to Ryan, who did not react.

Lindsay regretted calling so soon. She should have waited to make sure the "big guy" had enough time to get home.

Deeds walked home knowing he was not going to have his liberty compromised. He loved Lindsay. He wanted to be there for her the rest of her life, but he knew he could not.

Deeds was not saddened by this. He knew he had allowed Lindsay, in a way, to be reborn. He would always have that knowledge. He knew what he meant to her and what he and his presence had allowed her to become: herself.

Walking back to his apartment, Deeds was really thankful for all he had, and he had a lot.

CHAPTER THIRTEEN

The veteran detective viewed the body first. It was not an in-depth or thorough examination. He quickly noticed that there were no apparent lethal wounds (like a slit throat, bullet holes, head gash, or decapitation), so he decided to let the medical examiner and investigators do their thing. The body had some bruising, but from looking at her, it could probably be explained from the life she'd led.

The detective started the interviews. This part of the job was tedious but necessary. You'd interview ten witnesses and get ten differing accounts of what had happened, and usually less than one actually helped in an investigation.

That less-than-one, however, put criminals away. His work and the examiner's and the investigators' work put criminals away. The examiner's and investigators' work was more helpful, but the human element was necessary.

The science was crucial, not a citizen who was completely incorrect in what he or she had witnessed. Some people were too eager to help because they wanted to be heard and to feel important. All of this unsubstantiated testimony was worthless if the forensics were not present.

What lay hidden from sight told a more informative story. This story was already a little odd to begin with because she should not have been in this bar in New Falls. She would look more at home in an Old Falls trailer park.

So the detective went into Garee's Place and asked the proprietors and employees for statements, which did not take very long. They had seen her before but didn't know her name. They gave approximate times of when she came in and when they didn't remember her presence anymore. The detective knew they were not being 100 percent truthful.

He asked the usual questions. "Was she social? Did anything stick out? Any records?"

The bar employees' responses essentially boiled down to the following: "It's a cash bar, Detective… People talk here…a lot of different people…I'm sorry I can't remember more details."

They suggested that the detective come back during regular hours, and they could point out customers and staff who maybe could help in the investigation.

This was a ploy. The veteran detective knew that when word got out about the body, the regulars would not be returning for a while. They weren't necessarily guilty; they just thought it'd be smart to minimize any negative association.

"That's a good idea. Thank you," he said. It was a lie, but it was always better to be polite.

Returning outside, Detective Joseph Duran looked for clues in and around the alley. Stopping for a moment, he got his cigarettes and lighter out. He realized how long this pack had indeed lasted and was pleased. *I gotta quit though,* he mused as he gazed into the pack of his recently less present vice.

"Hey, Joe," the quiet voice said. "Between the smoking and the stress of the ex-wives, I'd say we'll be toe tagging your ass by this afternoon," the short-and-not-sweet crime photographer said.

Joe lit one and coughed. "No, I've cut back. And we don't get paid till next week."

Detective Joseph Duran, or "Joe" as he was known, was a twenty-five-year veteran who'd seen what people were capable of doing to each other. Not so much in New Falls, but in Old Falls and in the bad old days of Engel Falls, he had seen his share of chalk outlines.

Joe was a working man and a true Engel Falls lifer. His suits were usually wrinkled. He had thick gray hair combed back that the higher-ups kept warning him to trim to code and a thick goatee discolored by years of chain-smoking.

Joe was well above six feet tall and over two hundred pounds. Many coworkers were surprised when he chased down suspects and caught them. He was in decent shape despite only drinking coffee or beer and eating fast food for most of his quick meals.

Joe was a tough guy and a hard-ass. He was difficult to get along with sometimes. If you were a worker and helped Joe close a case, he respected you and was friendly, to a point.

Joe had two ex-wives and a grown child from each; he barely saw either but talked to them frequently. Joe would often leave a meeting or a crime scene to politely explain to his offspring, after confirming an emergency was not the reason for the call to him, that he would call back later, and he always did.

Joe was glad to see the metamorphosis of Engel Falls; rather he was glad to see the end result—the progress of New Falls. His job kept him in and around Old Falls, which was fine.

Joe felt Old Falls was a "containment zone." He was well aware that people were going to do drugs, commit crimes, and kill each other. There was nothing he could do about it. There was nothing anyone could do about it. His job was to find out who did what and put their asses in jail. The Outreach Puppies for Prisoners Hugs Not Drugs Rehabilitation programs, or whatever such nonsense they were calling it these days, was bullshit in his eyes. Shit bags commit crimes, and Joe puts them in jail. End of story.

A recent argument he'd had with a New Age detective with a master's degree in criminal psychology had resulted in Joe's following rebuttal before the rookie stormed away: "Hey, Moon Beam. Shit bags are gonna kill each other. Get it? That's the way it is. Accept it, or you're gonna be very fucking disappointed every time you get a call."

The rookie replied, "All I am saying is if you look at recent statistics—"

"Fuck you, and fuck your statistics! A shit bag kills another shit bag. It's just another one eighty-seven. We do not mourn the shit bag's demise. We find the shit bag who committed said one eighty-seven, and we put his fucking ass in jail. Old Falls is a containment zone. Got it? Kill each other there, and stay there! And don't come near my fucking neighborhood. End of fucking story."

The detective searched his pockets and reluctantly said, "I need a cigarette." The crowd that had assembled laughed as Joe lit up in the station. The rookie stormed off. The rookie requested a transfer. The rookie was transferred. Joe went back to work.

Now, in an alley in New Falls, a frozen unidentified female was naked and still and covered in melting snow. Joe smoked and looked calm.

"Got anything, Joe?" Detective Wilde walked up with a cup of coffee in one hand and a pack of cigarettes in the other, with one extended in offering to his unofficial superior.

Joe awoke suddenly from a deep concentration and took a cigarette. He lit it from the half-smoked one he already had going and said, "It's not too normal for an Old Falls murder to be in New Falls." Joe took a long drag as Detective Wilde lit up. Joe had a cigarette in each hand.

"You know her?" Detective Wilde asked.

Joe shook his head. "No, but look at her. This isn't a New Falls housewife who got locked outside her home getting the cat inside, slipped and fell on some ice, and froze to death."

Joe put out the older cigarette on the sole of his shoe and said, "Hey," signaling a uniformed officer to take it and dispose of it and not contaminate his crime scene. Then Joe snapped his fingers, but the pack of cigarettes with a new one extended was already present in Detective Wilde's hand. Joe took one and lit it up with the second cigarette and again had two cigarettes going, one in either hand.

Detective Wilde asked, "So Old Falls lady here makes the trek and goes out for a few at Garee's Place—great jukebox, by the way—and what? Decides to streak alone at...When do you place time of death, Dr. Hansen?"

Dr. Susan Hansen was a doll. Everyone in the department loved and adored her. She was nice. She was supportive. She listened. She was a sweetheart in a morbid and gory profession. And she was gorgeous. Long dark brown hair, dark eyes, great body, beautiful smile—she really had it all.

Dr. Hansen walked up, having examined the body minutes before Detective Wilde showed up. Joe had arrived minutes after him.

"With maximum lividity being present, I'd place time of death before closing time."

Detective Wilde nodded. "Well, I guess exiting patrons did not notice a hidden naked dead woman."

Joe, who was not paying attention to Detective Wilde, smiled an immature smile and asked, "Hey, Doc, how's business?" Joe loved bad jokes. He was hoping Dr. Hansen would say, *Not too good,* so he could say, *Oh yeah? Business has been dead?* No dice.

"Not falling for it. Get some new material, would ya please?"

Joe continued to smile. "I missed you, too."

With a restrained smile, she whispered, "Dipshit," and pulled out her phone and stepped away.

Joe stood there and knew what was coming. The smile disappeared. "Don't say it, Wilde," Joe demanded as he put out the second cigarette on the sole of his shoe and signaled the still-present uniformed officer to take it. Joe only had one cigarette going.

"What?" asked Detective Wilde.

"You fucking know. I don't wanna hear it, all right?"

With calmness that exemplified a full comprehension of what Joe was alluding to, Detective Wilde said, "No idea what you're talking about."

Joe counted backward from five in his head. He got to three—

"I'm just saying you should ask her to dinner," Wilde said.

Joe displayed three fingers and said, "Almost made it to two."

Detective Wilde took an assertive stance and used his hands as he said, "Keep it casual, but dinner makes your intentions known."

"What intentions?"

"You know what I'm talking about. Take a shot, old man."

Joe leaned in and with a raised voice said, "Mind your own fucking business. Too many things could go wrong. It's easier this way."

Wilde put up both hands, "Oh, you mean being a fucking coward?"

Joe pointed at Wilde and said, "I'm not a fucking coward. I know it won't work."

"OK, Kreskin," said Wilde as he turned away.

"I really want to pistol-whip you like Ray Liotta did in *Goodfellas*," Joe said through clenched teeth.

"Well, if you kill me, you get to see Susan again. I'm just saying—"

"I know you're 'just saying.' Why do people say they're 'just saying'? I know. I fucking know. When you talk, you are 'saying' something. I fucking know. I can fucking hear it. I know you're not fucking singing. I know you're not fucking signing." Joe mimicked sign language and continued. "And I know you're not fucking yodeling."

Wide-eyed, Wilde asked, "What the fuck is your point, you old babbling incoherent fuck?"

Joe's voice was now severe and calm as he leaned in and invaded Wilde's personal space. "When you're already speaking, you're saying something. To tell me you're 'just saying' even though you're fucking already saying something is fucking redundant, annoying, and the mark of an *asshole*!"

"Listen to me, fuck face," Wilde demanded as he got closer to Joe's face. "How 'bout I fist your fucking ass and make you my puppet?"

Joe leaned in even closer. "That's funny because your mom is coming over tonight, and she requested the same fucking thing, you fucking assho—"

Joe did not complete the epithet as they both turned and saw Dr. Hansen standing there silently shaking her head. She wore a tired expression on her pretty face.

With a confused expression, Susan asked, "Joe, clear something up? Is it your fist up her ass, or does his mother have her fist up your—"

Joe quickly and humbly interrupted. "My hand is up Mother Wilde's ass"—Joe was about to take a drag but stopped—"ma'am." Joe tried to end all of his statements with correct grammar.

Susan said, "Well, tonight you're busy with Mother Wilde. Tomorrow's no good for me. How about the night after that, you take me to dinner?"

Joe was silent.

Detective Wilde nodded his head, looked at Joe, raised his eyebrows in anticipation, closed his eyes in disgust, and shook his head. Detective Wilde turned to Susan and asked, "What time do you want him to pick you up?"

Susan took in a breath, contemplating. "How about we meet…at…You like Italian?"

Before Joe could answer, Detective Wilde answered, "He loves it."

"Great," Susan said with a smile. "How about we meet at Mazzeo's Ristorante at, say, eight?"

Joe didn't even try. He just looked at Detective Wilde and nodded.

"He's looking forward to it."

Susan laughed, shook her head, and simply said, "Dipshits," as she walked to her county-issued vehicle.

Detective Wilde turned and faced Joe and put up his arms as if awaiting a response. After a few moments of Joe just looking at him with a smile on his face, Detective Wilde asked, "Is there anything you'd like to say to me?"

Joe put out his cigarette on the sole of his shoe, said "Hey," to the still-present uniformed officer, and turned to Detective Wilde and said, "Just give me a cigarette, Chuck Woolery."

CHAPTER FOURTEEN

In a shitty double-wide trailer in Old Falls, a guy "coming down" was regaining awareness, feeling nauseated, and feeling shitty. Not a lot, but just enough to want to be left alone. He had lost his high and had been taking a few sips of Old Crow to ease the discomfort of reentering a harsh reality.

He had smoked some shit in the afternoon, and it was only several hours later. In his youth he could remember, rather he was told of, being awake and raging for days at a time.

For the last year or so, only once in a while, he'd have some fun, crash and go to sleep, and wait weeks or months to rage again. Coming down got harder as he got older. Plus, he got richer selling it. Booze was safer.

Still, coming down was not a picnic. He really just wanted to drift off to sleep when his...What was she to him? Girlfriend? Fuck buddy? His buddy's on-again-off-again girlfriend or fuck buddy? A distant cousin? A mother of two kids the state had, one of them being his? All of these were correct.

Anyway, that lady started bitching about the bills, the garbage on the floor, the lack of money, and the niggers who got more welfare than she did. He was not in the mood for this.

"What the fuck happened to this country when a white woman gets overlooked for a fuckin' nigger? Could you explain that to me? This is my fuckin' country! They should go back to fuckin' Africa...Are you listening to me?"

He was not.

"Hey! Are you fuckin' listening to me?"

"Hmm?" Randy was in a haze. He assumed earlier he had been very enthusiastically engaging, conversationally speaking. Now he just wanted some quiet. Unfortunately, Randy was not able to articulate that he was unable to reply succinctly.

Randy did not feel well. He had a headache, and his fingers kept fidgeting. He concentrated and was able to focus, control his breathing, and attempt to partake in an interaction.

He opened his eyes even wider, but the lights were uncomfortable, so he asked for them to be dimmed.

Then he stretched, rubbed his palms on his face, and cracked his knuckles.

He was sweaty and felt tingly. He took another swig of Old Crow and felt better. His jeans were dirty, his tattoos were faded, his fingernails were blackened, and the perspiration made his yellow-stained wife-beater cling to his sinewy body.

Randy was on the floor of Joy's trailer. Propping himself up against the wall, he realized she was in a bitchy mood and regretted being there when she was angrily complaining.

When he was horny, she was down. When he wanted to get high every once in a while, she was down. When he wanted to be close and love and feel loved, she was down. He would love it if he could just come over, get drunk, fuck, and spend hours holding each other.

But she was probably still messing around with her old boyfriend who happened to be his friend and business partner in their drug trade. They both were using less and less, and making more money even though they never seemed to have any.

"The Elf," as he was known, was Randy's friend and Joy's old boyfriend. The Elf had a good connection and was a good business partner, as was evident by Randy making a decent living.

All these details were complicated, and the Old Falls way of life made things even more difficult thanks to Child Protection Services, warrants, custody battles, court appearances, lawyer fees, parole officers, drug tests, unwarranted hatred, blame, and so on.

Life in Old Falls was hard. Now Randy was listening to Joy run her mouth. Disappointment woke him up fully. "Fuuuck," Randy slowly mumbled.

"What the fuck did you mumble?"

Randy shook his head and said, "Nothing, nothing. What about the niggers?"

Joy was upset to say the least. "You can at least listen to me, you sack of shit. I know I ain't gonna get any fuckin' support from you in any fuckin' way, but you can at least fuckin' listen."

Joy was thankful for all the support she received from Randy but did not want him to know.

"I'm listening, goddamn it! And I support you plenty, too, so quit yer bitchin' 'bout that shit!" Randy slapped his face a couple times and looked up at Joy. "The niggers on welfare. Continue with the story," Randy eloquently said as he motioned with his arms dramatically.

Joy shook her head and was about to retort but then realized it was better to continue. Better as in, if you anger your man too much, you may get a fat lip.

"I'm gonna lose my trailer. I'm gonna lose my trailer 'cause I ain't as eligible as some nigger bitch with a shitload of kids."

Randy was pretty sure the trailer was taken care of by the Elf's bosses. "They tell you that?"

"They might as well have, those Jew sons uh bitches!"

Randy was confused. "They tell you they was Jewish? That's a weird thing to bring up to a stranger."

Joy picked up a pack of cigarettes and threw them at Randy's head. "That ain't the fuckin' point!"

They hit Randy in the face, startling him. "Relax, babe!" Randy saw what was thrown at him and immediately forgave Joy. *Oh, cool,* he thought as he slid one out, grabbed a pack of matches, and lit up. *Hmm.* These were cigarettes black guys usually smoked. "Speaking of niggers, baby, where did these come from? You fuckin' a nigger?" Randy asked jealousy.

"Fuck you!" She threw a motorcycle magazine at Randy's head. "I'll fuck who I wanna fuck, just like you."

The magazine hit Randy in the face, startling him. "Babe, fucking relax!" Randy saw what was thrown at him and immediately forgave Joy. *Oh, cool,* he thought as he gazed at the attractive topless brunette leaning on a motorcycle. Long brown hair, no smile, just a solemn-looking, gorgeous girl leaning on a bike in the desert under a blue sky. *Paradise.*

"Baby, I ain't seeing anyone else. Just you, baby. I promise." Lies. He had a batting order of low-life girls, some above eighteen, he'd partied and raged with. A couple of them were even known to stay in Joy's trailer park. If the identity of one particular chick he'd messed around with became known to Joy, he'd be in deep shit. It was all based on lust, as his heart was with Joy.

"Bullshit. And I ain't fucking no one else but you. Especially no fuckin' nigger." Lies. Joy and her stepsister Sandra had recently and jointly blown a huge, muscular black man whom Sandra eventually had anal sex with for cash. They'd seen him around the local bars over the years and agreed how hot he was.

Sandra let him fuck her in her ass in an alley near a bar the night before last. Joy didn't want to run the risk of getting pregnant, again, nor did she feel up for anal sex at the time, so she just blew him and made out with her stepsister so the huge, muscular handsome black man would cum quicker. Joy's mind was elsewhere as she went through the motions, hoping it would be over soon. She got twenty bucks for it. Sandra got forty.

Joy felt guilty because she felt like she betrayed Randy. She tried to dismiss this feeling, but it lingered.

"I found those cigarettes at the bar. If a nigger, excuse me, if a black man forgets his shit, it's up for grabs, far as I'm concerned." Joy placed the tips of her index finger and thumb at the base of her nose between her closed eyes and took several deep breaths.

Joy, in a calmed voice, said, "Give me one, please."

Randy put down the magazine, grabbed the pack, took out a cigarette, grabbed the matchbook, and handed the two items to Joy.

Joy put the cigarette in her mouth. With her right hand only, she opened the matchbook with her thumb and bent down a match from the row of matches but did not tear it off. She flipped the matchbook, bent the match all the way over, swiped the match along the rough igniting surface, and lit the cigarette.

Joy took a long drag as her left hand took the cigarette from her mouth. She exhaled a bluish plume of smoke on the lit match still attached to the matchbook that she held in her right hand. The momentary fire was extinguished.

The plume of smoke increased in width as it left her mouth, but decreased in integrity as it dissipated in the meager light of the trailer. Joy felt calmer as she inhaled deeply the soothing effects the cigarette possessed.

For a few moments, the trailer was quiet, and Randy was grateful. But he knew better. This was the eye of the storm. The diatribes continued.

"Speaking of fuckin'," Joy began in a temporarily quiet voice, "I ain't gonna get the fuckin' babies back if you ain't gonna work and get me my money like you said you was."

"I'm working, baby. I got money saved up," Randy claimed as he sat casually on the dirty floor and smoked some other man's cigarette and looked at the same topless brunette in the magazine. "If you need more, I can get money from the Elf. We'll get you a lawyer and get most of the babies back. I promise." Randy's eyes opened wide.

Before Joy could get mad or sad, he said quickly and with sincerity, "I'm sorry. I didn't mean that."

Randy did not like referring to the period in Joy's life when she dated the Elf. Unbeknownst to Randy, they were still in contact until a while ago. It had been an unfulfilling cycle.

Joy would call the Elf, and they would meet, fuck, get high, and make plans on how they would be boyfriend and girlfriend again. Nothing ever happened though.

Joy lied and told the Elf she wasn't with anyone else, let alone his friend Randy. That would have caused trouble. Yet she continued to see both guys anyway. Maybe deep down she knew not to be with the Elf, especially since he'd hurt her very, very bad. But the Elf just had power over her.

When she first started seeing Randy, Joy thought it was just a temporary thing. She denied her true feelings for Randy as they developed, still thinking she and the Elf would end up together.

Joy was lying to herself. She had feelings for Randy. He was there for her. He was around discussing how they would get the kids back. The Elf had fathered two of her kids, and Randy was the father of the youngest. Both Randy and the Elf were at the hospital for the birth of the youngest one.

During the pregnancy, prior to the pregnancy, and after the state took the kids away, Joy had to sneak around with the Elf so Randy would not catch them, and Joy and Randy had to sneak around, so the Elf would not catch them. Gradually, it became Joy and Randy sneaking around the Elf most of the time.

It soon became an almost normal relationship. The Elf was rarely present, so sneaking around ceased to be an issue. A couple of times, Randy had walked in while the Elf and Joy were hanging out.

"Oh, hey, you two. Uh, it's been a while. Just checking the stash. Did you need some more?" Randy assumed they were still an item even though Joy denied it.

The Elf had no clue and just thought Randy was good at keeping the stash supplied for Joy to retain and distribute. Joy helped in the operation. She got free room and board as she housed the stash and was in charge of distribution (i.e., she handed baggies out to people).

Joy would receive a phone call from Randy or the Elf on who was coming over to the trailer and what amount of product they were due. These calls were always made on burner cell phones.

The customers were not strangers. They, their character, and their financial capability were known before business was carried out. The "higher-ups" took care of that, and they provided protection through intimidation, follow through, and notoriety. Joy was never scared for her safety or the kids' safety.

Joy never handled the money; that was a prior and separate transaction the guys would carry out. She just held the product while the guys handled and kept the money and then handed it over to the higher-ups. She received a decent wage and amount of product, which she simply sold, against the wishes of the higher-ups, but she had not been caught yet.

As time passed, Joy was simply not feeling it for the Elf anymore. Randy was there for her in every way. Randy was light-years ahead of the Elf in terms of sexual knowledge.

The Elf made Joy orgasm every once in a while, while Randy drove Joy insane with pleasure. Randy was a possible and plausible future, and she liked that. *Can it be like this all the time?* Her suspicions and insecurities and past betrayals made it difficult to trust though.

Joy did treat Randy poorly and regretted it. It was misguided and misdirected anger. Joy was trying to get over the Elf and took it out on Randy. Now Joy was frustrated because she wanted Randy all to herself. Yet she did not know how to ask for this or if he would want it, so she took out her anger and frustration on Randy.

In the past Joy would think of the Elf when he wasn't around, and she would get wet. Now Joy would think of Randy when he wasn't around, and she would get wet and play with herself and then call him to come over and finish the job to levels she never knew existed. The signs were clear. But Joy wanted Randy and wanted Randy to want to be exclusive. But Randy was not exclusive. Joy knew. She really knew.

As Joy finished the cigarette, she remembered how she'd acquired the pack. She remembered watching her stepsister have anal sex as she made out with her. When the huge, muscular handsome black man finished and came all over her stepsister's ass, Joy couldn't wait anymore.

As the man gave them both cash, offered his half a pack of cigarettes when Sandra asked for one, and walked away smirking, Joy, fueled by alcohol, abruptly asked Sandra, "Could you please stop fucking my man? Could ya? You can fuck anyone in this fucking town. Leave Randy alone, goddamn it!"

Joy only suspected they were having sex behind her back.

"Well, sis, I don't know what to tell ya. I thought you were cool with it. Aren't you still fucking the Elf?"

Joy was heartbroken. In a way she knew, but hearing made it real, and Joy was sad. Joy wanted to scream how she had not been with the Elf in a very long time and was in love with Randy, but she knew there was no point.

Sandra then rubbed her palm where her anus was and pulled out a crimson-stained hand. "Goddamn, that brotha tore my ass up!"

Joy knew the secret and was going to let Randy know she knew. "Sandra hasn't gotten back to me since we went out drinkin' the other night," Joy calmly stated.

"You serious? What happened?" Randy asked too eagerly.

"I knew you'd be concerned about her."

"Of course I am. She's your sister...stepsister... whatever. She's family." This was part of the reason.

"No, I think it's 'cause you're fucking her. Don't deny it! She told me."

"Oh please! I ain't fucking Sandra," Randy stated as he put the finished cigarette in an empty bottle. "Goddamn it, baby! You think I'm fucking the whole town!"

"No. Just my stepsister and the twats down the way." She pointed down the row of trailers. "And all the little twats you sell shit to. I know they can't all have cash on them."

All of that was true, with the stepsister being a point of pride. Sandra was a dirty girl. Dirty, real hot, and amazing at sex. Joy was usually mean to Randy, so what better way to get back at a girl you're sorta seeing than to fuck her sister, or stepsister. Even though Sandra was hot and amazing, she was not Joy. Randy wanted Joy.

Randy figured Joy would end what they had soon and get back with the Elf. Randy did not want this, but he felt he could not do anything about it. Fucking other girls was cool, but he wanted to be with Joy. Randy was certain Joy did not want this. So he got back at her without knowing what the truth was.

"Every time you come over here to fuck me, I taste who you were just fucking," Joy angrily stated. "Take a fucking shower, Randy! I taste pussy juices all over your mouth. I taste shit on your cock, which means you've been fucking girls in the ass, without rubbers! How many babies do you have, huh? How many pregnant girlfriends on the side do you have, huh?"

Coolly, Randy replied, "You can't get a bitch pregnant fucking her in the ass, baby. Everyone knows that." He regretted it as soon as the statement left his mouth. "Oh shit."

In a scene out of an animal documentary, Joy screamed and flew across the trailer with an onslaught of punches, slaps, jabs, kicks, knees to the head, hair pulling, and nails slashing.

Whatever coming-down sluggishness remained in Randy was now gone. He was trying desperately to block the attack but was failing. He felt cuts appear, and he could taste blood. All he needed to do was to stand up and push her away, and then he could control this crazy woman he loved.

Randy brought up his leg and kicked straight out at her knee without thinking. He heard a nasty pop. Joy screamed and fell to the floor. She was clutching her knee and crying.

Crying from the pain, crying from the shock of who had caused it, crying from the frustration at not being able to express her feelings, and crying from the realization that this predicament was indeed her life.

Randy looked at Joy and felt awful for what he'd done. He was just trying to defend himself. Maybe he let his anger get the best of him. He could have just tripped her or just rolled away or opened the door and took off, never looking back.

He wanted this fight to stop. He wanted all the fights to stop. He wanted her pain to stop. He wanted his pain to stop. Randy just wanted to tell Joy he loved her.

Randy got to his feet. He was riddled with guilt as he viewed her on the dirty trailer floor. She was crying, and her eyes were closed. She was in pain. He caused it. He just stood there and looked down at her. It shamed Randy because this was something the Elf would have done, and he knew he was better than that.

Through the tears and sobs, she opened her eyes and looked up at him. She removed one hand from her knee and extended it toward him and said, "Help me, baby," and it broke his heart.

Randy reached down, put his arm around her, and asked, "Can you stand?"

"Yeah, I think so," Joy answered and then stood up and put her weight on the unhurt leg.

They stood side hugging each other, hoping their mutual embrace would convey the emotional heartfelt messages they were afraid to express. Randy kissed the top of her head. Joy felt his heartbeat as she embraced him.

When she was ready and with Randy's help, Joy limped to the couch and sat down. Randy went and found a paper napkin and wiped her tears away. Joy was thankful and cried more. She laughed and apologized, and Randy laughed too.

Randy walked over to where he had just been sitting, picked up the bottle of Old Crow, and took a swig. He walked to the couch and sat down, took another swig, and gave the bottle to her.

After she took a long swig (Joy could always drink Randy under the table), she sheepishly smiled. "I shouldn't drink too much." She emptied the bottle in a gulp. "It ain't good for the baby," she said, rubbing her stomach.

CHAPTER FIFTEEN

A couple of nights a week, the local bowling alley, Open Lanes, where Deeds bounced at the 11th Frame, had "Dollar-a-Game Night." The owner, Bill McKenna, had hoped and was proven correct that by having dollar games and dollar shoe rentals, a younger crowd with rich parents would come in and bowl, buy food, play arcade games, and increase Bill's profit. It was a successful venture.

Between league nights and Dollar-a-Game Nights, Bill was doing very well, and wealth trickled down as he hired many people to work the front desk, cook, tend bar, serve, do maintenance, and, of course, provide security.

The first Thursday night of every month was costume night. Themes included favorite movie characters, superheroes, or cowboys and Indians.

Anyone with a costume got a free drink and prizes were awarded for the best costume, usually the most revealing. Basically, a big-breasted young lady, big-breasted MILF, or big-breasted cougar always won. There were no complaints.

On other nights Open Lanes might play disco, techno, eighties one-hit wonders, or classic rock, and had light effects and strobe lights. Regardless, the kids that didn't want to go to the movies, didn't want to stay home, or couldn't score beers went to Open Lanes, much to Bill's delight.

The high-school kids came in, spent money, and left a few hours later, depending on their curfews. The young adults who were not in high school anymore showed up later than the high-school kids and stayed much later, depending on when their first class was or when they had to be at work.

Parents were mostly in favor of the alley's events except for the revealing costume contest in the 11th Frame, but you had to show proper ID to Deeds or another bouncer to get in. These kids were not out and about and up to no good. They were someplace relatively safe with plenty of security to hamper any attempts to do stupid teenager shit.

The owners, aware that they lived in a litigious society, hired a bunch of big dudes to maintain civility. The big guys were paid handsomely, and so far it had worked out very well for everyone.

These big guys were local guys making a few extra bucks. The big dudes mostly knew each other, trusted each other, and knew the kids or knew of the kids because they knew their parents or knew of their parents. The situation seemed to work out for everyone, especially Deeds, who enjoyed working there.

Why wouldn't he enjoy working there? He was paid (not that he needed it), it felt like he was contributing, and it was giving him something to do. There were no real threats to his safety. It was ideal. He was usually in the dark when he worked inside. When the bright light effects were on, he worked outside.

Sometimes a situation got out of hand. Problems started with both New Falls or Old Falls people. Security was good in terms of quelling fights or preventing them before the first punch was thrown.

The bouncers just split people up and intimidated them until order was restored. The troublemakers were then escorted out. If any trouble happened outside, the police were called. The process was very simple and effective.

There was a small contingent that quickly made the shit lists of the security crew and the owner, Bill. A few small-time drug-dealer pests were around here and there. Bill did not want them inside. Most of the time, there had to be a problem before you were escorted out. But if you kept the deals hidden, you could stay and make a living. Word got around, mistakes were made, and dealers became known. And they weren't let in. What were they going to do? Call the cops?

These little pests were annoying, but they were dealt with. There was one individual who was a repeat offender. A short, combative, scummy guy with a missing front tooth, ratty hair, pale skin, and a diamond earring kept getting hammered and becoming a nuisance. He was constantly thrown out. He'd return after some time had passed and pull the same shit. He always had a lot of cash and always bought a lot, tipped a lot, and then started shoving matches.

"Little Fucker," as he was called by the security guys, was not a physical threat to the bouncers, hence his other nickname: the Elf. Little Fucker to LF to the Elf was validated by his short stature. Many nights the phrase was ordered or directed to "throw the Little Fucker out," or "eighty-six the Elf." The nicknames had caught on and evolved. The Elf was annoying, but not too much of a hassle for a seasoned bouncer.

However, it was soon discovered that the Elf was indeed selling in the 11th Frame. That was when the owners permanently eighty-sixed him. They didn't need that potential risk for lawsuits or being shut down.

The Elf would attempt to enter the bar but was refused every time. A few times Deeds himself silently towered above him in the near dark, and without words or physical movements, he refused the Elf entry.

The Elf was embarrassed every time but cunningly figured out an alternative plan to make a living.

Knowing that this was his place to sell (it was territory claimed by the higher-ups—the Elf's bosses), he set up shop across the street in a strip-mall parking lot.

People figured out where he was and crossed the street to buy. It became tricky for Bill though. You couldn't search your customers. What people did outside of the 11th Frame was their concern. When people caused problems inside the 11th Frame, they were escorted out. So the patrons knew that if you couldn't handle your shit, the cops would be called. For the most part, things went smoothly. Sometimes, they did not.

One particular night, the costume theme was cowboys and Indians. It was packed. Many had joined the party and were dressed up in shitkickers and Stetsons or headbands and feathers.

Deeds was drifting inside and outside of the establishment, making his rounds and trying to keep an eye out for trouble. As reserved as he was in social situations, he did OK at work.

Deeds was not expected to mingle. He did not have to worry about interactions. He did not have to defend his financial fortuity. He did not have these annoyances thrust upon him, these burdens unleashed by those who were jealous. He did not have to defend himself or downplay his affluence through hard work and good timing. He was not put down and did not receive unjustified resentment. Deeds could just exist and do the job he was hired to do. He was just another big dude on the lookout for trouble.

Toward closing time Deeds was standing outside in the cold during a break. He was aware of the Elf's presence across the street. *Fuck him.*

As he stood outside, Deeds's presence in the dark was a deterrent for the Elf. Lots of people were drinking inside and gawking at the sexy cowgirls. The Elf could make a lot tonight, but he'd have to cross Deeds's path. The Elf had remained across the street.

Fuck off and get killed, Deeds mused as he stared at the Elf. He was not dressed for the cold, and no one was walking across the street, so Deeds thought he would be leaving soon. *Keep smoking your cigarette and view me. You are not more than me. I can bring you suffering.* Deeds's inner monologue had a flair for the grandiose.

As he thought this, the front door opened, and Bill's wife stuck her head out. It was the face of a beauty. Deeds was always grateful when he saw her. She was of average height and had the body of a farm girl: voluptuous and curvy. Big natural breasts bounced with every step. Her long hair was auburn.

As his hate-based gaze turned to the beauty, he was taken aback for just a moment. Deeds did not comprehend her message by hearing her as much as he focused on the vapor from her pretty mouth and deduced from its shapes that she had declared there was a fight in progress.

Deeds said nothing as he moved quickly past her beautiful aura, noticing the relief and gratefulness in her eyes, and entered the warm bowling alley. Instantaneously, he scanned the scene in front of him and located the trivial commotion.

As he got there, he assessed the situation and knew exactly what had happened but did not care. *Cliché bastards influenced by rap, representin', and not backing down but not marching forward. Cowards.*

Deeds thundered up from behind and placed his big forearm across the sternum of the closer guy. Reaching out with his long arm, he placed his palm on the opponent's sternum and stood between the two in perpendicular fashion. He remained flexed and rigid. Deeds stared at the ground and waited for another security guy or two or three or four to join him in separating the two parties.

With all the people and the loud young-country music, it took just a slight moment longer to rally the troops. Deeds was not worried. These kids were skinny, young, and fearful of Deeds's strength and thousand-yard stare.

The situation ended as a few big guys came and separated the youths. Deeds was praised for his speed and effectiveness by his fellow bouncers. Deeds just nodded, said thanks, and shook hands to demonstrate his appreciation of what he felt.

Out of all the glances, the glance that interested him the most was the one from the owner's wife from twenty feet away. Their eyes met. The glance was not broken, and it became a look. This look lasted a few seconds. Thoughts of familiarity were present in his brain. It was as if they were already close. She tilted her head and silently mouthed, *Thanks, Shane,* and then smiled. It seemed familiar.

Surprisingly, he walked up to her without hesitation and stuck out his hand. "We haven't been formerly introduced...uh...*formally* introduced. Sorry. I'm Shane Deeds."

The owner's wife laughed and said, "Hi. I'm Sarah Caine." They shook hands.

"Caine. That's funny. I have a neighbor named Jess Caine, or Jessie Caine."

Sarah laughed. "Funny, I have a sister named Jessie, or Jess, Caine, and she's your neighbor."

"Small world, huh?" Deeds smiled.

"Small world, Shane."

Did your sister mention that I love her? "So how long have you been married to Bill?" *Just be cool, ask questions, and then get to Jess.*

Shocked, Sarah was taken aback and gasped. "What are you talking about? Bill's my stepdad!"

Way to go, genius. "I'm sorry." Deeds was nervous. "I guess I remember seeing another similar-looking lady a while back. Sorry, you do look a little young."

She smiled. "That was my mom. Bill and my mom are separated."

"Oh, I'm sorry to hear that. That can be very hard for the children."

"I'm twenty-eight, Shane."

"Shit."

"Don't sweat it. My mom can be a cunt."

Wow. "So you don't get along?" *Dude?*

"Uh, yeah, not especially." Sarah laughed. "She doesn't approve of my lifestyle. Bill and Jess are my family. Technically, Jess is my half sister. Kinda complicated. I can draw you a map if you want."

Oh, Sarah's a lesbian. Instantly, Deeds felt relief wash away the anxiety. "That might help, thank you."

They both laughed.

"Well, at least Bill is around for you. Sorry about your mom, but that's her loss. I'm sure you're a lovely daughter."

"Thank you." Sarah tilted her head. "That was sweet."

"Well, tell your sister—"

Sarah's expression was that of slight confusion.

"I mean, tell your sister, um, your half sister, we met, and say hello from me." *Good save.* "You two will have to stop by next time you're at her place." Deeds extended his hand for a friendly shake good-bye.

Sarah rolled her eyes and wrapped her arms around Deeds's thick frame for a pleasant hug. She ended the embrace and gently pulled the side of his head toward her mouth and with a tantalizing whisper said, "You tell Jess hello from me."

Deeds felt like he just got great news. Sarah lightly patted his chest and walked into the 11th Frame.

CHAPTER SIXTEEN

Deeds was really looking forward to going on a date with Jess. He thought she was gorgeous and felt extremely grateful she'd chosen him. He felt fortunate that she would even acknowledge him, let alone go out on a date with him. She was a knockout. Her body, her hair, her smile—everything was perfect. *You're a lucky bastard, Shane Deeds!*

Deeds had awoken early still disturbed by the events from the previous evening after he met Sarah. But then he had run into Jess in the hallway and he'd felt better.

"Hi, Shane," she eagerly said with much happiness.

"Hey, Jess. How are you?"

"Awesome! And very relieved. I took your advice and spoke to Wiggy."

Deeds nodded. "Oh, good. Are they"—Deeds pointed to the offending neighbors and lowered his voice—"behaving now?"

"Oh my God, it's so nice not listening to their bass all effing night. Thank you, thank you, thank you." She launched herself at Deeds and gave him a very pleasant bear hug.

Deeds laughed a little, but he wanted to propose right then and there. She smelled wonderful, and her breasts felt amazing pressed against him.

She let go and said, "Sorry, I'm a hugger."

"No, that was awesome! You made my day." Before he could propose marriage, he should take her out on a date. "I, uh, I think I should take you out to celebrate."

She leaned in and grabbed both his hands. "Shane, you wanna take me out on a date?"

"I do."

Jess played with his hands a little bit and said, "I'd love to." She gave him a wonderful smile.

I'd love to kiss you right now in this hallway.

Deeds and Jess talked about where they should go to dinner. Deeds made one or two suggestions, but then Jess asked if he liked Italian. Deeds loved food, so they agreed to her suggestion of Mazzeo's Ristorante.

"I've never been there but always wanted to go."

"It's so good! You'll love it."

"Perfect."

Still smiling, she said, "I'll see you tonight."

"Whenever you're ready, just come knock."

With a seductive grin, Jess said, "I'll come...over at seven."

She went in for the hug, and Jess kissed Deeds on the cheek. "Till then." She turned around, walked into her apartment, and shut the door.

"Till then," Deeds said to no one in an empty hallway.

That night he was quite excited, but he knew he needed to relax and just be himself. Getting all worked up and nervous would display a weakness, and there was no way Jess was going to be turned on by a guy who showed weakness (i.e., a nonstrong subservient man who kissed her ass).

Deeds had made that mistake, as many young guys do, when he was younger. After he reached a certain age, he realized that the older guys he worked with were somewhat correct in their claims that if you treat a woman poorly, they'll dig you more.

Deeds did not completely believe this nor did he subscribe wholly to this train of thought. However, he did know not to be a pushover and to just be himself.

No acting, no bullshit, and no obsequious behavior would be tolerated because no one (especially a woman, Deeds thought) respects that guy. Do nice

things and help people out, but do not be a compla-
cent little peon.

Deeds came back from the gym and did some
chores around his place. He cleaned the bathroom
and the kitchen. He did the dishes and vacuumed.
When he thought his place looked nice enough for
a certain hot neighbor to want to come over and continue the evening—

No, no, don't jinx it!

Deeds put on a nice pair of dark jeans, a dark gray
sweater, and his formal pair of Doc Martens. He then
found a watch he never wore and put it on. He found
his smaller pocket knife and put it in his front right
pocket. Then he put on a black leather belt.

With his trimmed beard, hair pulled back, nails cut,
and clothes that usually came out once a year, and with
a bouquet of (thirteen) roses he'd bought at the grocery store, he was set and confident. Now he only had to
wait a half hour before she would come over. *That's OK,*
he thought. *I'll be calm, cool, unflustered, and ready to go.*

With fifteen minutes to go, he was taking a half-
full bag of garbage to the trash chute when he ran
into Jess. Jess was not on her way over to Deeds's apartment as she clearly was not ready for their date, a date
Deeds was eager to have.

Jess appeared to be coming home from the gym as
she donned track pants and a hoodie and held a refill-
able water bottle. She also had the facial expression of
being flustered and overwhelmed.

Jess was dramatically speaking into her phone, defending herself to someone as she said with restraint, "I can do whatever I want. You obviously do...You have no right to say that." She simply waved to Deeds, mouthed, "Hi," went into her apartment, and shut the door loudly.

Deeds was confused. She'd barely acknowledged him. Every other time, she'd been very flirty, friendly, and personable. Now he felt like any other neighbor. *In agreeing to go out with me, did she feel like she crossed the line and now regretted it and resented me?* He almost wanted to go over to her place and remind her that they had a date because she'd acted like he was just another goddamned neighbor.

Hoping it's not a sign of things to come. No, she's just having a bad day. I'm sure the date will be wonderful. Christ, what if it's not? What if she regrets agreeing to go out with me? Relax! If you don't know something, do not engage in frivolous thoughts based on assumptions.

An hour later there was a knock at Deeds's door. *Forty-five minutes late for the first date is not the most auspicious way to begin a relationship, but oh well.*

Deeds opened the door and saw a frazzled Jess. She was stunning despite her demeanor, which conveyed she was annoyed and fatigued.

She opened her eyes wide and said, "Hi," in a breathy almost uninterested tone.

Well, this is gonna suck. "Hey there. How are you?"

"Good. Ready?" Jess was leaning away.

"Sure, hang on." He stepped inside to the counter and grabbed the roses. "Wanted to give these to you." He handed her thirteen dark red roses.

Jess nodded her head once or twice. "Thanks." She did not smell them. "I'll just drop these off real quick," she said as she headed back to her apartment. Finding her keys in her purse was distressing for her, even though she'd just left her place. She hastily went into her apartment, let the door close, and was out by the time Deeds walked up.

Who is this person? "They'll be fine without water for a little while, I'm sure."

Jess replied, with heavy breath, "I know. Ready?"

This will be awful. Deeds opened the door to his newly washed truck with the nice-smelling tree hanging from the rearview mirror. He tried to help her up, but she got in without any assistance.

As Deeds walked around the front of the truck, he looked at her, and she already had her phone out and was texting. *Is she fucking texting her friend and asking her to text back in X amount of minutes with a fake emergency? Are you fucking kidding me? Why did you agree to go out with me? You don't know that. Just be cool. Maybe she's turning her phone off.*

Jess's phone remained on, and she was still on it as he started up the truck. He did not say a word. He knew that if he tried to compete for her, against the phone, he'd lose. *Plus, who the fuck are you to make me compete for you anyway?*

Deeds had some random classic-rock station on low volume as he pulled out of the parking space in the complex's garage. He was about to try and start a conversation when Jess, all of a sudden, was looking out the passenger window very intently. Deeds looked too and saw nothing but cars. The point of interest kept her attention as she rotated her head until the object was out of sight.

Silence and your inattentiveness be damned. "You OK?"

Jess looked forward through the windshield. "Yeah."

What's with her? "Did you see someone? You want me to stop? They owe you money?" Deeds's attempt at humor and levity fell to the unacknowledging and unentertained.

"No. Let's just go."

Deeds had a very deep moment in which he contemplated just turning the truck around and saying politely, "This will not work out," or saying with disdain, "You're fucking rude as hell, and I'm not taking you to dinner despite your wondrous breasts."

All right, time to get a little deeper. "Jess, is everything OK?"

"It will be." Almost as if she was awakened from a nap, she looked at him, faced forward again, placed the tips of her index finger and thumb at the base of her nose between her closed eyes, and said, "Yes, sorry. God, you must think I'm a total weirdo."

And rude and hurtful. "No, not at all. I'm just a little concerned. Wanna make sure you're OK, is all."

"I'm sorry, Shane. I…I'll be fine." Jess took a deep breath and asked, "So where we headed?"

CHAPTER SEVENTEEN

The good detective had not been on a date in years. Frankly, he did not think he would ever go on a date again. Luckily, his partner was good at facilitating what Joe wanted but would never see to fruition.

His two marriages ended with reserved anger as both his ex-wives did not gouge him financially but, indeed, were displeased with the fact that Joe was married to the job first, to them second. A lot of his paycheck had gone to them.

Both ex-wives felt isolated, abandoned, and unfulfilled. It was a cliché to think you should never get involved with a cop, but it had been proven true twice in the case of Joe.

With the divorces long settled, with Joe's exes remarried, and with one son in college and another starting chiropractic school, both his sons required money, and Joe was happy to pay.

Joe tried to have the strongest relationship possible with his sons. As far as he could tell, they were straight shooters and never got into trouble. He tried as often as possible to call and e-mail them. If they were busy, it didn't matter. Just as long as they both knew he was there for them, regardless of how busy everyone was.

Joe worked a lot of hours so his sons could achieve whatever they wanted. He was proud of them. Joe put bad guys in jail because that's what he did, and his sons benefitted as a result. He'd continue to put bad guys in jail. That's all he knew how to do. For many years he had dedicated his time to doing that.

The money accumulated, and his investments were savvy. His house was paid off, and there was money in the accounts for college tuition, start-up capital for a practice, and a nest egg for retirement, not that he ever envisioned himself retired.

But tonight was a different night. Late in the work day, Joe was unable to concentrate on solving crimes. Frankly, he did not care. He was just pushing papers around and checking the time every few minutes. He'd grab a file and start reading, and a sentence or two later, he'd lose interest and check the time. He'd then reread what he'd skimmed over, and the same thing would happen.

So he'd grab another file and view crime-scene photos, but the carnage put him in a sour mood even though very little shocked him anymore. Nothing was being accomplished. Time was being wasted. He wanted to get the hell out of there, so he did.

Joe grabbed his things and left the office early. Joe was expecting some looks of confusion, and he felt as if he was going to have to defend himself. He was already resenting people as he was sure they would pry and invade his privacy. They had no right to know what his plans were and whom they were with. That was his concern. They should just mind their goddamned business.

No one said anything. Not even one coworker made eye contact. They just assumed Joe was going out on a case or to interview someone or to the lab or to do something related to an investigation. Relieved, Joe exited the building and went to run some errands in preparation for his date.

First, he went to his barber, who squeezed him in for a haircut, a beard trim, and an old-timey shave. Joe still had a big goatee, which was good, but he felt he was more approachable when it was neatly trimmed but still met his standards, which was important in regards to honesty and self-contentment.

From there he went to the mall. He parked and went into the men's section of a department store. After a lap he went back to where he'd mentally marked items he thought looked OK.

After a few minutes of looking, he picked out a couple shirts and sweaters, a couple pairs of slacks, some new casual but nice shoes, and a belt that would never hold a pistol. He left the department store and headed back to his car in what he felt was an efficient use of time with strong results to show for it.

From there he drove a short distance to his drug store. He walked in and was greeted by a young punk with a douche-bag haircut who, through a barely open mouth, squeezed out, "Hey," with minimal effort. Joe thought how he'd be arresting the future shit bag within six months.

Joe passed the condom aisle, winked at the boxes, and thought *soon* as he made his way to his destination. He realized he would be buying several things, so he hustled back to the entrance and grabbed a shopping basket.

The young punk with the douche-bag haircut delivered the same, "Hey," with even less of an effort. Joe just looked at the kid, smiled, and shook his head. The kid's eyes communicated that he remembered Joe but could not place where.

"Busy night?" Joe asked.

The kid just stared and said, "Huh?"

Joe said, "Wow," and went back to the aisle he'd just visited. Once there, he grabbed some shower gel, a loofah, nicer shampoo and conditioner, a new toothbrush, floss, some fancier deodorant, an aftershave that was inexpensive but smelled nice, and mouthwash.

Not that he did not have these already back at home, but he wanted brand-new items for his fresh start to, hopefully, a new chapter.

Joe waited in line at the checkout and hoped that the young punk with the douche-bag haircut would not be summoned to open a register. Luckily, the young teenage girl working an after-school job because she wanted the money, not because it was due to parole terms, was efficient and friendly.

After going wide-eyed as the total was rung up, he dropped the bag off in his passenger seat and then headed to the grocery store next door for the finishing touch: a nice bouquet. He did not buy roses, thinking that would come across too strong. He bought a lovely arrangement of yellow and orange and light purple...flowers.

From there he went home. He left everything on the table except the bags with the clothes in them, which he took upstairs. With a Swiss Army knife, he cut off all the plastic thingies and removed all the tags and stickers.

Joe then took the new clothes and placed them in the dryer with a dryer sheet, on low heat, for just a few moments to freshen them up. He pulled them out moments later and put them on hangers and decided on the outfit.

For the special occasion, he chose a nice white collared shirt, a dark gray sweater, and black slacks. *Traditional, not fake-fancy Euro fashionable, and not too young or too old, with an air of casual and confident famil-iarity.* "This'll do it," he declared to the clothes as they hung.

Joe then flossed and did not like the reminder of his infrequency pertaining to oral hygiene as he saw blood in the sink. He used some mouthwash and then brushed his teeth for a few extra minutes. He rinsed with mouthwash again right before he trimmed his fingernails and toenails.

He turned on the shower and utilized hotter-than-normal water. He took five minutes and used the loo-fah and scrubbed the hell out of his right index and middle finger in an attempt to at least somewhat de-crease the yellow stains from years of smoking and not caring.

He loofahed every bit of himself, including his feet with their freshly trimmed toenails. He scrubbed his hair with shampoo and let the conditioner do its thing as he let the hot water rain down on his neck and up-per back.

He dried himself off with the fancy towels that he never used and got dressed. Strangely enough, he did not have to promise himself not to smoke because he had not really thought about it. He wanted to smell nice for his date.

With the application of aftershave and with flow-ers in hand, he looked at himself in the mirror. He thought he cleaned up nice. He took in a deep breath and said to his reflection, "Just be cool, and just be you. You can do this. You're an HK Terminator, and you got this." He took in another deep breath and said, "Go get 'em!"

CHAPTER EIGHTEEN

Deeds regretted turning the truck off when the DJ said Rush was next after the break but he did it anyway as he still wanted to focus on Jess. He really wanted to show how gentlemanly he was and open the door for her (it was already unlocked), but she was already out of the truck. He was hoping she would side hug him or put her arm around his as they walked into the restaurant, but no. She rummaged through her purse after she had checked her phone. Deeds could see that she had some texts and a couple of missed calls and two new voice mails.

The smartass in Deeds wanted to say, "Well, you go ahead and check your phone. I'm gonna head in and have a nice dinner. Maybe there's a nicer broad in there who'll talk to me." The air smelled wonderful, and in some other circumstance, he would be looking forward to the upcoming dining experience.

Deeds and Jess walked together, yet alone, to the front door, which Deeds opened. "Thanks," Jess said with little emotion. Deeds didn't respond. As was his habit, he looked behind him as he held the door open and saw a very pretty lady walking toward him.

Holding the door open for her gave Deeds the excuse to gaze at her. She had long and very pretty dark hair, looked well dressed, had a nice body (yoga, Pilates, or barre probably), tan skin, and a very warm smile.

As she walked up, Deeds politely motioned for her to go in. The nice-looking lady said, "Thank you!"

Deeds answered, "You're welcome."

She kept it going. "That was very nice of you. Thank you. Someone raised you right."

Deeds smiled and said, "Thank you for saying that. Common courtesy is not so common anymore."

"Well, as long as there are a few gentlemen out there, we'll be OK." This pleasant woman gave Deeds a wink.

"We try."

This lady made Deeds feel good about himself, unlike his date. Deeds wanted to join this nice lady for dinner, but he was going to try and salvage the date with Jess, wherever she was. *Where the hell is she?*

Deeds looked around the entry area and did not see her. He looked into the restaurant in case she'd been seated quickly. No sign of her. *Maybe she's in the restroom.* Deeds looked into the short hallway where the restrooms were and saw Jess texting on her phone. *You fucking kidding me?*

The nice and pretty lady who'd been so pleasant to him was seated. As the hostess made her way back, she smiled warmly and said, "Hi there. How may I help you?"

Deeds smiled back and said, "Hello, I...We'll be just a second," as he motioned toward the restroom.

The young hostess said, "Whenever you're ready, sir."

"Thank you."

Deeds stepped out of the main path. After two minutes went by, he checked his seldom-donned watch and walked over to the restrooms. Jess was not there. Assuming Jess was now using the restroom, Deeds headed back to the hostess's area, when he noticed Jess had snuck outside and was talking on her phone. *Ah, for Christ's sake!*

Jess was animated as she was talking. She was talking a lot, and the cold turned her angry words to vapor. Deeds was close to getting a table for two, and if she showed up, fine. If not, fine. He was hungry and ready to have a nice dinner regardless of the company. He looked at her and thought how gorgeous she was but how rude she was. *Does she know that her rudeness is upsetting me? I know I'm overly sensitive, but this is the behavior of an asshole.*

After a few moments he summoned up the courage to walk outside and say something to the affect that their table was ready. As he took his third step toward the door, Jess entered in a huff.

She looked at him and asked casually, "Table ready?" The question was asked with minimal, if any, interest.

"Yes, it is." They followed the hostess to their table.

Deeds pulled the chair out for her, and she surprisingly said, "Thank you," and meant it. *Hope?* As she scooted her chair forward, her lovely breasts bounced in a way that made Deeds feel something in his chest. *She's being distant and rude, but, Christ, she looks gorgeous!*

Deeds sat down and saw the pretty lady from earlier with her lucky date. His back was toward Deeds. *What a lucky guy.* The lady was smiling and giving all her attention to him. There was a nice bouquet on the table. Deeds looked at his date and saw Jess with her hands on the table.

"Shane?"

He quickly looked away from that couple and turned to his gorgeous and neglectful date. "Yes?"

"I'm really sorry for acting like a total bitch."

"No, you're not acting like a—"

"Yes, I am. I'm really sorry. It's just been a crazy day. Some shit has gone down from out of nowhere. It's just really bad timing."

Deeds leaned in and asked, "He?"

She looked surprised. "What?"

Deeds said again, "He. He has bad timing."

Jess said nothing.

Deeds said, "I never asked if you had a boyfriend. I assumed you didn't, but that may have been wrong. I mean, look at you!"

"Shane, thank you. No, I don't. It's just…"

Don't fucking say it's complicated.

"We were together for a while, and then, you know, he—"

Deeds put up his hands. "Hey, it's OK. We don't have to talk about it if you don't want to. I just want to make sure you're OK and you want to be here with me and have a nice dinner." *Ball's in your court, lady.*

"That's all I want, Shane."

This surprised him.

"I was so happy you asked me out. I even called my sister and talked to her about it. 'He finally asked me out! He finally asked me out!' She must've thought I was in high school again."

Deeds smiled, was about to mention he met Sarah but then something occurred to him. "Wait a minute. Finally?"

"Well, yeah, Shane. Remember when we first met each other at the grocery store and I asked if you played football for State?"

"Of course. We talked for a minute or two and said good-bye. Then we waved to each other in the parking lot." He told her his name but she did not say her's.

Jess smiled. "Yes, and I saw you get into your truck."

"I remember that." Deeds saw her up close and was enraptured. "Glad I went out for coffee."

Jess smiled. "Me, too." Jess took a sip of water that the busboy had served them. "Well, I was psyched when I saw your truck in my parking garage later. Then you ended up being my neighbor. Yay!"

This was all news to Deeds. "Really? You were psyched?"

"Oh yeah. I wanted to leave a note on your truck. I actually did."

Confused, surprised, and a little sad, Deeds said with urgency, "I never saw it."

Jess nodded. "I know. I chickened out and took it back."

With his mouth open, Deeds shook his head. "This is unbelievable, Jess. I don't know what to say."

With devastatingly bad timing, the waiter appeared and took forever in explaining the specials. *Never in my life have I or anyone I've dined with ordered the goddamned specials, so hurry up and take our fucking drink order and disappear, asshole.*

"I'll be right back with your drinks."

"Thank you," Deeds said graciously. *Beat it!* Deeds turned and faced the lovely Jess. "What did the note read? The one I never got."

With a sheepish grin, Jess said, "Oh, I just wrote something about how I was looking for the recycling bin on that side of the complex even though I knew it was on the other side, and I wrote my number and drew a winking face."

Un-fucking-believable! "Are you kidding me?"

"No. Kinda cheesy, huh?"

"Kinda awesome, you mean."

"I didn't know if you were married or had a girl-friend or whatever. And if she saw the note, I didn't want you to get into trouble or anything. So I took it back and was planning on running into you in the hallway."

"I'm speechless, Jess." With that he put his big hand into hers. "Thank you."

"No, Shane. Thank you for putting up with my rude behavior tonight. I'm sorry. You don't deserve that."

Deeds realized that whatever—rather, whoever—the problem was, and it was probably a former boy-friend, it was an obstacle that in all likelihood would not go away. And that problematic obstacle would in-deed interfere with anything he would try to create. Jess was not over her ex.

Even though she acted affectionate toward Deeds, and he did think she was attracted to him, she needed closure with the ex.

Deeds felt very lucky that Jess had feelings for him and never would have guessed that would be possible. However, she simply was not over the other guy. It was probably a fresh breakup, and confusing feelings were present if she was acting like this.

A few years back, Deeds himself was in a similar situation with a gorgeous fitness model named Alyssa, whom he'd met at the gym. She was not over her ex-boyfriend, and she was not over her ex-husband, and for some odd reason that Deeds could not for the life of him fathom, she kept in close contact with both, among others.

The fitness model would talk, e-mail, and text with the former lovers on a regular basis, often in front of Deeds. "Oh we're just close," was the excuse for why she would still be in contact with multiple exes. She was also in contact with a lot of "guy friends," which basically meant she would flirt with a lot of guys she was attracted to but would not date them.

"They talk about their girl problems with me, and I talk about my guy problems with them. That's all. No big deal. OK?"

"Uh-huh. Sure. Um, have they suggested that maybe...I don't know...in five years, that if you both aren't married, that you guys do indeed get married? Has that come up?"

"Well, yeah, but I'm sure they were just kidding."

"Right. Right. I'm sure they were. Your other guy friends, the little body-building posse, the 'roid guys, do they ever suggest to mate and create a 'superbaby,' you know, since you all have great genetics? Ever come up?"

"What's your point, Shane?"

"My point, Alyssa, is that these guys are after you and they're being led on. Cut the ties."

"I can be friends with whomever I want!"

If her "friends" went elsewhere for a relationship, she would turn on the flirting and bring them back around until they wanted her again. At this point she would cruelly distance herself.

Alyssa surrounded herself with what she did not want and went after what she could not have. This had hurt him. When Deeds attempted to date or meet other ladies, she was all over him. When he was single, she was distant.

It was a hard lesson, and it caused him a lot of pain, but Deeds had learned from it. So now he knew what the signs were and recognized them in Jess. She simply was not over her ex. Even though she had feelings for Deeds, she was not over the ex.

Jess could not move forward until she cut the anchor that was the ex. So for right now, Deeds and Jess were going to have dinner and talk things over like friends do because that's all they were going to be.

CHAPTER NINETEEN

Joe could smell the enchanting aroma of delicious, authentic Italian food as he got out of his car. The stimulating paean of Rush's "Tom Sawyer" added to the excitement he already had.

Joe was giddy. Joe was happy. Joe was not nervous. Joe felt confident and was eager to see Susan and have a wonderful night.

With unwavering and eager determination, Joe walked into Mazzeo's Ristorante and was greeted by a lovely hostess.

"Good evening," said the nice young lady who was light-years ahead of that young punk with the douche-bag haircut at the drug store.

"Hi there. I'm..." Joe saw beyond the pretty hostess and took in Susan with that gorgeous smile, looking quite lovely. Joe felt very fortunate because he knew that smile was for him. "Having dinner with that lovely lady right over there." He waved to his date.

"Well, lucky you! You have a wonderful time tonight."

Joe replied, "Thank you, I think we will."

"Enjoy!"

⟢ ⟢

By the time the entrées arrived, Susan and Joe were on one of the all-time great first dates. They agreed when their drinks arrived that there was to be no shop talk.

"Here's to getting to know you," Joe stated with a raised glass of red wine.

Susan smiled her million-dollar smile. "I like that. Cheers."

As the night progressed, they had really gotten to know each other on a deeper level. They discussed their childhoods and what each's family life had been like, their grown-up kids (she had college-aged sons as well), their lives at this stage, and brief mentions of their previous marriages. They really communicated, understood each other, and bonded. It was a lovely evening of good food, good wine, and extremely pleasant company.

Susan was looking at Joe with a cute little reserved half smile with a hint of apprehension. Joe picked up on it and was hoping the conversation would get even deeper.

"Something on your mind?" Joe asked and then took a bite of delicious cheese tortellini with prosciutto and peas sans mushrooms.

"Yeah, there is, Joe. I, uh…I'm having just a wonderful time. I thought I would. I mean, I knew I would, and it's nice being proven correct."

Joe wiped his mouth, took a sip of water, placed his hand on Susan's shoulder, and said, "This has been a lovely evening, Susan, and I will always cherish tonight."

Susan really liked what Joe said. She put her hand on top of his and leaned her face on their shared grasp for several wonderful moments.

"Joe, can I ask you something?"

"Please."

"Well, I see that, you know, you got a haircut today—"

"No good?"

"No! No, you look great. It's just—"

"What?"

"It's just…Did you do that for me?"

"What do you mean?"

"Well, you got a haircut; you bought some nice new clothes and put them in the dryer for a few minutes."

Joe laughed.

"You smell like a man should, and you haven't smoked once tonight."

"Yeah?"

"Did you do that for me?"

Joe again put his fork down, wiped his mouth with his napkin, and took a sip of water. "Well, yes and no. I mean, I knew we had a date tonight, and I wanted to look my best."

"Well, I very much appreciate it, Joe. I do. But I want to know what motivated you."

Joe was familiar with a woman's psychology and was not in any way bothered or disturbed by the questions because his answers were going to be honest and his own.

"When I got ready tonight," Joe began, "and did all the things I did this afternoon, I did them because I wanted to be at my best because anyone who is nice enough to go on a date with me deserves the best effort I can make."

"Oh, Joe, good answer!" Susan said as she reached again for his hand.

Joe and Susan held hands for several moments before he continued. "I didn't go out and do a bunch of stuff just to try to impress you. I did things to…better myself…not to alter who I am but to better myself, so you could see me at my best and, therefore, go on another date with me."

Susan had a *duh* look on her face. "Well, of course we're going out again."

They squeezed each other's hands.

"I just wanted to make sure that you weren't trying to, you know—"

"Be something I'm not in hopes of impressing you?"

"Exactly."

"No, I'm too old to start being someone else. This is me, Suze."

"Susan."

"Yes, ma'am."

Susan smiled.

Joe continued. "You know me. I'm not one to make an effort that's not genuine. Of all the things I am, I am honest."

"Of course you are. That goes without saying."

"Thank you. That was a good line of questioning. I mean, you know my paycheck goes to my sons and the bank, so I don't spend too much on clothes, plus I really don't date, Susan. I just wanted to look my best. In fact—keep this a secret—I've been cutting back on the cigarettes a lot."

Susan looked pleasantly surprised. "Really?"

"Oh yeah. Compared to my old three-and-half-pack-a-day habit, I'm down to less than a pack every two to three days. Plus, I joined a gym."

"That, I did notice. You've definitely lost some weight."

"Thanks. I just lift a little and do some jogging on the treadmill."

"Very commendable, Joe."

"Thank you." Joe took another sip of water and said, "Basically, my point is that I did those things a while ago, so I can improve myself. A point came where I needed to make some adjustments, and I did.

If you never asked me out, I still would be improving myself. Sure, I might not buy new clothes, but I am trying to better myself. Not much point in living if you're not bettering yourself."

Susan reached into her purse and pulled out her phone. Joe was taken aback by this act. She looked at it for a few seconds, pressed a few buttons, and then asked Joe, "Can you read this text, please?"

Joe wiped his mouth on his napkin, scooted his chair closer to Susan, leaned in, and looked toward the phone. The phone was not on. She then placed her left hand on the side of his face and planted a very passionate kiss. They parted, and Susan smiled.

Joe said, "What a wonderful night."

CHAPTER TWENTY

With the pressures of the date off, and with Jess's damn phone off, Deeds and Jess had a nice time. They were two friends who were attracted to each other, and they were having a lovely dinner. She opened up about her ex named Erik and the power he had over her. *Fucking asshole. Yeah, I'm a little jealous.*

Apparently, this guy came from money, which explained how he was able to buy a brand-new silver Corvette every year. *I've seen that car! What a fucking asshole.*

Apparently, this guy was just not motivated. He did not really work because he did not have to. He basically lived off his parents while Jess worked hard in her various jobs.

Jess loved him but was not happy with his lackluster existence. Jess did not like what this lackluster existence turned her into—a nagging girlfriend. She was upset that he did not have any desire at all to create or contribute, in any way.

So, eventually, he got a random office job. Still, she was unhappy because she resented the fact that it took many fights and arguments for him to do this. Jess wanted to be with someone who was motivated. He was not. And recently she had abruptly ended the relationship. For him it was out of the blue, but for her it was a long time coming.

Deeds had a sneaking suspicion that she'd ended the relationship the evening she came over to discuss the loud neighbors. Whether she'd been afraid of being alone, wanted to test the waters, or simply wanted to feel wanted, she'd come over and had an impact on Deeds, which was not fair to him.

"I was just sick of the same old shit from him. Nothing changed. Even when it did, it wasn't the change I wanted. I wanted him to grow. It didn't happen. I didn't think it ever would. So I ended it. He was pretty upset. I felt relieved though. I want more. I want to see what else is out there. I mean, I care for him, but I wish he had the desire to change for himself. He got a job, yeah, but not because he wanted it; he did it to get me off his back. It's like it meant nothing. I don't know. Was I too harsh?"

Entrenched in the friend zone. It's OK. At the very minimum, I can sneak a peek at glorious cleavage and maybe get some hugs.

"No. Your instinct was telling you something. For some reason, people—smart people like you—ignore their instinct. I don't get it. If you're not happy, you're not happy. It's as simple as that. Sacrificing your smiles will make you happy? Get outta here."

"Oh my God, Shane." Jess stared as if something remarkable occurred to her. "You put things into such a clear perspective."

"I just clear-cut the bullshit until the brass tacks remain. Life and life's decisions are easier that way."

"Thank you, Shane. You've really helped me." She caressed his arm.

"Oh, this counsel is not pro bono. You're getting a bill."

Jess laughed, set her fork down, and brought her napkin to her face. "Oh my God! I almost choked!"

"Wait till you see my bill."

She continued to laugh in an adorable fashion. It was a very sweet and bonding moment between Deeds and Jess. In any other circumstance, he would predict future dates and a relationship, but under these circumstances, the outcome did not appear to be favorable.

Deeds was not being pessimistic. He hoped he was wrong and that his analysis would be corrected. But until then, he would just enjoy the evening.

Right now, things were good, and he was having dinner with someone he was very attracted to. There were other recent nights where connections were made but under grossly different circumstances.

"I'm gonna go powder my nose and leave my phone here."

Deeds nodded. "Smart move." Deeds did not stand up completely as that would draw unwanted attention to the fact that the lady he was having dinner with was going to take a piss. So he half stood and sat back down.

When he looked up, she ducked down and whispered into his ear, "Thank you, Shane." She kissed him sensually (as sensual as a kiss on the cheek could be).

When she removed her lips from his cheek, she hovered there for a moment or two, and her breath tantalized him to the point where he was glad he was seated. *Oh wow, Jess!*

"Be right back, hon."

Whoa! What the hell was that? That was wonderful! Maybe there is a chance. Maybe I've shown her what a real man is. Maybe she sees in me everything that other loser was not. "I'll be here," Deeds said casually.

Deeds was certain there was lipstick on his cheek. He left it there, brandishing it to any passerby. It was a trophy that he had earned. He wanted to take a picture of it and hang it on his wall.

All right. It's official. Jess has you. You've dug her for a long time, and she just made you feel amazing. She said she's

been thinking about you for a long time, too. This could hap-
pen. But…you need to keep cool.

Deeds looked up to see Jess coming back from the
restroom. She was smiling at him. It was not a generic
smile. It was a smile that you share with someone you
have feelings for. *All the signs are pointing to hell yeah!*

Deeds stood up all the way and placed his hand in
hers as she sat down. Jess was beautiful, and if looks
could kill, there was genocide in Deeds's heart.

"Miss me?" Jess asked with a look that tantalized
Deeds.

He saw a shot, and he took it. He leaned down to
her and whispered into her ear, "Yes." He kissed her
cheek and sat down. Jess placed her hand in his and
made an "aww" sound.

"Well," she said, "I'm glad you stuck it out with me
'cause this was so nice. Thank you, Shane."

"More where that came from." *Maybe I shouldn't*
have said that.

"Hope so."

I'm glad I said that!

As Deeds and Jess left the restaurant, their arms
were interlocked with Jess placing her other hand on
his biceps, which he kept flexed. He helped her into
his big truck, and as he walked around, he saw what he
wanted to see—Jess reaching over to unlock his door.
Deeds shook his fist in victory.

Deeds and Jess left the parking lot and were heading home.

Surprisingly, Jess asked, "Where we going now?"

Deeds was taken aback. "Oh. I was just gonna head home. Whatcha thinking?"

"It's early. Let's keep it going."

"What did you have in mind?"

"Umm, how about another round somewhere?"

"Let's do it. Where were you thinking?"

"How about that British pub place? It's not rowdy. Shouldn't be too crowded."

"Perfect."

"Do you know where it is?"

"Oh yeah. I worked there for a little while." Deeds was not a fan of this place.

"Oh, OK. I guess you would know where all the bars are."

Shane parked his truck in the parking lot. As he shut his rig down, he turned and faced Jess and said sternly, "Don't move."

Jess was confused. He exited the vehicle and walked over to Jess's door. As he rounded the front, her expression turned to a smile. Deeds opened the door and Jess said, "Chivalry's not dead in New Falls, is it?"

Deeds extended his hand, which she took. "No, ma'am."

"Thank you, kind sir."

They walked into the establishment, which could not be classified as a bar. It was a restaurant with a few shamrocks hung around a little area where an inexperienced, fake-titted broad might eventually serve them a drink.

"Why would an English pub"—Deeds did air quotes when he said "pub," which women love—"brandish a shamrock?" Deeds didn't get it.

Jess looked at him, and her eyes matched her clueless response: "Huh?" Jess didn't get it.

"Never mind. How about you grab us a table, and I'll get us a round. What would you like?"

"Oh, uh, whatever amber they have on tap."

"Coming up."

Deeds saw the usual jabroni douche bags from his gym all decked out in their trendy extra medium-sized attire, all a size too tight, showing off their "bar" muscles and their "preparty pumps." *Fuck off! Look who I'm with!* Deeds got to the bar as the fake-titted bartender walked away from him. *Par for the course.*

Deeds waited and glanced at Jess as she just got settled. A little shit-eating twat douche bag walked up and sat down. *That was fast. Frat boy's wasting no time.*

By the time he got his nonalcoholic beer and a random amber on tap, the jabroni douche bag was still there. And Jess was smiling and tilting her head. *What the fuck?*

Deeds felt like dumping both beers over the two of them. He did not know what to make of Jess's actions. *Why is he here? Why are you allowing this? Not to sound like royalty, but how fucking dare you?*

Deeds caught a little bit of their soon-to-be-ending conversation.

"Yeah, so we all party there. It's a sick apartment. Shit gets crazy. I'm a DJ. You should come over since you live in the same building."

Oh, wonderful. I've had to deal with assholes like you before, and I'll fucking do it again.

"Evening." Deeds stood looming over the uninvited guest.

"What's up, bro?"

Deeds set the beers down. "Two beers, two seats, and three people?" Deeds shook his head. "Have a good night."

The frat-boy shithead knew he could not win but wanted to end the exchange on his own terms. "Yeah, whatever, bro." He got up, stood about equal to Deeds's shoulder, and turned to Jess again. "So come by the apartment whenever. You'll find it. You'll totally hear my sick beats." He extended his hand, and Jess shook it. "Later, bro," he said to Deeds, who smiled, calmly said, "Fuck off," and sat down.

Not lowering the volume of his voice, Deeds asked, "Friend of yours? I'll have to buy you some douche-bag repellant."

Deeds was aware that the previous sitter of his seat was still behind him. Jess was looking at the former sitter but not in a friendly way. It was more of an observational way. Deeds guessed the young man, out of Deeds's eyesight, eventually left the immediate area.

"That was—" Jess began to disclose his name but was interrupted.

"Doesn't matter. Friend of yours?"

"Nope. Just met him. Why?"

Deeds had taken a few sips. Jess had not yet drunk her beer and as of now had not thanked him.

Deeds asked, "Well, did he inquire if this seat was occupied?"

"Yeah," she casually answered.

"What did you tell him?"

Jess's expression displayed attitude. "He didn't give me the opportunity. He asked and just sat down before I answered. Is there a problem?"

Deeds was calm but possessed severity in his outward appearance. "No. I would never just go up to a gorgeous woman who was sitting alone at a bar because there's a one hundred percent chance she's with someone."

Jess asked, "What if I was alone?"

Deeds shook his head. "In my experience ladies enter together, or the lady enters with a guy. That's all."

With a scoffing smirk on her beautiful face, Jess asked, "Is this two guys in the school yard seeing who's the toughest?" Jess's attempt at levity failed.

"No. I am. And he knows that. That's why he left."

Growing weary and annoyed, Jess said, "Look, it was typical guy shit. That's all. Happens all the time. Get over it."

"Not with me." Shane took a sip and looked around the establishment.

To her credit Jess tried again to defuse the situation, which allowed Deeds to calm down because it actually validated what he felt. "Look, Shane, I'm sorry he sat down. He was just some guy who lives in our building—"

"I'll be sure to stop by and say hello."

Jess, now annoyed, said, "Look, he didn't do anything."

"Neither did you."

Jess was confused. "What?"

"You just let him sit here, in my seat. I find that... odd."

Jess was not expecting to be questioned like this. "Well, what did you want me to do?"

"Say something along the lines of 'Sorry, my date will be sitting there.' Something like that."

Confused again, Jess asked, "Date?"

Deeds felt heat and churning in his gut. Deeds, with some semblance of vulnerable emotion, asked, "This...isn't a date?"

With a wary quizzical look, Jess responded, "No. It was just dinner, Shane."

All the kisses, all the tantalizing embraces, the fact that she'd acknowledged in the hall the night before that he was asking her out on a date, the confessions of long-standing attraction, all the hand-holding, arm-in-arm walking, and so on—had Deeds misinterpreted that?

Deeds looked at Jess. "I thought this was a date. I was actually pretty positive this was a date."

Jess shook her head. "No. You asked me to dinner, so I said yes. That's all."

Deeds was confused. "I'm confused. All the hand-holding, the little kisses, you admitting you put a note on my truck, you know, giving me your number, the looks, the in-depth conversations, the nice kisses— that's not indicative of a date or at least feelings?"

Jess shrugged her shoulders. "I mean, I did those things, yeah. I wanted to. I mean, yeah, I did them 'cause I wanted to, but, yeah, no, we're not out on a date." Jess took a sip and then another. She looked to her left, where Deeds was guessing the little shit-eating twat jabroni frat-boy douche bag was.

"This isn't a date. We're just having, you know—"

"Dinner. Drinks. Physical and intimate connections." Deeds paused. "I guess I thought that meant more."

Suddenly, Jess got a puzzled expression upon her now not-so-attractive face. "We haven't been intimate!"

Deeds knew that. He did not mean sexual intimacy but meant a soulful connection had been made. "I know." He placed the tips of his index finger and thumb at the base of his nose between his closed eyes. "I know."

Jess took another sip and asked, "How much do I owe you for the beer?"

CHAPTER TWENTY-ONE

The nondate continued. Deeds assumed that the distance between them would grow. Her unexplainable change of heart and callous disregard caused him hurt and confusion.

The intimacy established at dinner was no longer present, yet she joked and smiled a lot. Deeds did not know how to perceive this and thought Jess was certifiably schizophrenic.

After two more rounds, they headed home. Jess's phone had made its reappearance but not in the form of trying to surreptitiously communicate with an ex but to show off pictures of whatever and to look up things that came up in conversation. There was a causal vibe shadowed with indifference due to lack of intimate interest.

When they were a few minutes from the shared apartment building, Jess unbuckled her seat belt and scooted over to Deeds and placed her head on his shoulder. *What the fuck?* He did not know what to say. He was confused and mentally exhausted.

To connect and then disconnect and act blasé and nonchalant and then make a move (and this was a move!) were the acts of a person who did not know what she wanted or was not aware of the effect she had on the innocent. These moves were confusing, but Deeds hid it well.

"Hey there. How we doing?" He did hope the evening would return to what it had reached.

"Thank you for a wonderful night, Shane. Sorry about the phone. Sorry about that fucking asshole who sat in your chair. He's lucky you didn't beat the shit out of him."

Aha! So you admit that it was wrong of that motherfucker to do that! It was also wrong of you to let him sit there! "I had a great time, Jess."

Jess giggled. "My friend texted me to not sleep with you tonight."

What the fuck? "Is that right?" Deeds was utterly confused. He was clueless as to how someone could make such a lovely connection and then just dismiss it as if it was nothing—to dismiss the evening as a casual, meaningless encounter and then make this move and mention sleeping together. *What's with this broad?*

Deeds never thought he would be so lucky to be in a position to have sex with Jess. Now the idea of the two of them having sex was an anecdote mentioned in humorous passing? *What the fuck is with this broad?*

"Tell her to mind her own fucking business!" Deeds was severe, but it was taken as a joke by Jess.

She laughed and said, "Oh, I will definitely tell him to mind his own fucking business!" Jess began to text someone.

Don't tell me..."You, uh, you have a guy friend, do ya?" Deeds asked, trying to mask the exhaustion of yet another weird twist.

"Yeah. He's an ex, but we're friends. We didn't work as a couple, but we're good friends. You know, he tells me about the girls he's seeing, and I tell him about the guys I'm seeing."

Reach over and unlock the door and push this broad out of the truck!

Jess continued texting, and Deeds felt pain in his gut and started to sweat a little. He was hurting. This night with all of its wonderful highs and bad lows was not fair.

With clenched teeth, Deeds parked his truck, helped Jess out of the truck, and walked her to her apartment.

As they reached her door, Jess turned around and said, "I had a blast, Shane! Thanks!" Jess hugged him in an upbeat yet unfamiliar way. If a sales rep were to hug him, this is what it would feel like—nothing.

Deeds wanted to invite Jess over to his place and spend time together. No distractions. No phones. Just the two of them and their feelings. He wanted to appreciate her voice and listen to her all night. He wanted to open up and express who he was and what he could offer her in terms of a relationship. He wanted to sit on the couch till the wee hours of the morning. He wanted Jess to fall asleep in his arms, and he wanted to hold her and listen to her breathe as he stroked her pretty hair. He wanted Jess to not want to say good-bye to him. He wanted Jess to want the night to last forever and despise the eventual exchange of good nights.

"Good night," she said cheerfully; then she turned around, unlocked her door, went inside, and let the door close behind her.

No dice. "Good night," Deeds said to no one in an empty hallway.

CHAPTER TWENTY-TWO

The Elf had to stay in sight for his customers, but he also had to hide from the bouncers who would call the cops. Every once in a while, a big bouncer would leer at him, so he had to duck behind a few bushes next to a flickering lamppost.

The night before, he was at a bar, and he apparently got shitfaced, blackout drunk because he awoke this afternoon on his entryway floor. He felt terrible. His lip was swollen, he had a few bruises, and his sides ached. "What the fuck happened?" he asked no one in his empty apartment.

Over his morning sodas and vomiting, he tried to piece together the previous night's events but came up blank. He eventually looked down, and something puzzled him. Then it became a dire situation once full awareness was achieved.

Now realizing the weight of the situation, he panicked as he stared at the chain that should have been attached to his wallet. His bosses were due money, and there were lethal consequences for not paying. *Why did you take that phat stack out last night?* The Elf had indeed placed a thick stack of cash in his wallet last night. That wallet's location was not known.

"Fuck me running," he lamented as he emptied his pockets onto the kitchen table. He looked around his place, in his car, but there was no sign of his wallet.

He needed this money. He had little cash in his place. His bank accounts did not have enough to cash out and cover what was due. The Elf was really mad at himself for not coming home after selling last night.

He'd taken all the money he had with him and stupidly gone to a bar where he knew he did not have the willpower to be conservative. To be fair he did not even know if he'd spent it all. He would know if he found the wallet. *But where the fuck is it?*

The Elf reflected on which bars he frequented, and one, in particular, hazily stood out, so he decided to go there to look for his wallet. He was hoping most people were honest and that one of these stand-up citizens found it and turned it in to the bar's lost and found. *It could happen.*

With slow, hampered movements, he cleaned up and got dressed. The alcohol in the mouthwash made him vomit again. So he had to just sit on the dirty bathroom floor and breathe.

The Elf was sweating and shivering. He could not decide whether it was the hangover or the fear. After a short while, he cleaned up again. Cursing the profuse sweating, he splashed cold water on his face as opposed to showering again; he toweled off, brushed his teeth again, and got dressed again—in dry clothes, the others being soaked in perspiration.

He realized how fucked he would be with his "employers" if he could not find his wallet. He remembered there was a few grand of their money that needed to be accounted for in two nights. He started to get nervous and sweat, but he did not want to change clothes again, so he just had to deal with it.

"Fuck, fuck, fuck, *fuck!*" The Elf was aware of what his bosses did to those who did not pay exactly what was due. You just disappeared. "Not good," he said and wiped the sweat from his brow on a pair of dirty boxers from the hamper.

The Elf was set to leave. All he needed was his coat, the cold having literally taken his breath away when he stepped outside earlier and checked his car. The sweat made the cold piercing and almost personal. He searched and could not find his coat. "Fucking great. Just gets better and better."

He looked all over his place to no avail. But then he realized he hadn't been wearing it when he woke up. It did not make sense to think he would have taken it off and put it somewhere in his place and then gone back to the entryway to pass out. And it was not in his car. So, unfortunately, he must've left it at the bar. "Fuck!"

The Elf searched his closet, got a thinner jacket and a thermal long-sleeved shirt to help against the cold. They did not. He shivered as he walked to his lowered car with rims and little gas in the tank. He got in and cranked up the heat after the car eventually started, and he drove to the bar.

The Elf heard the door unlock several moments after he banged on it several times with his fist. A huge, muscular black man opened it. Just the sight of this man was awe-inspiring to everyone, especially the Elf, his moniker being accurate.

The Elf instantaneously remembered being in a headlock by this man.

"Get the fuck outta here!" boomed his voice, making the Elf flinch. Then the man thunderously slammed the door.

Perplexed but fearing for his life, knowing the bouncer would not be as severe as his bosses, the Elf knocked again. Luck was on his side. An older biker-looking guy opened the door.

He opened the door just a little, and he was obviously keeping the huge, muscular black man at arm's length. The older guy was big too. He was covered in faded tattoos, with a big gray beard and long gray hair pulled back.

"What do you want, you little asshole?"

The Elf thought, *Hey! That's "Little Fucker," thank you!* The Elf did not risk a smartass remark.

From behind the door, the angry giant boomed, "Fuck that muthafucka! Let me take care of him! Let me do this."

"Relax, Phil! I got it." He turned to the Elf. "What do you want?"

With humility derived from fear, the Elf asked if they had seen or knew of the location of his wallet or jacket and if they could check the lost and found.

The big biker-looking guy calmly replied, despite the fact that he was holding back a three-hundred-pound-plus angry bouncer, "I just checked the lost and found when I got here, and there ain't any wallets, pal. And the only jacket left behind would be a fucking tent on you."

From behind the door, he heard great bellows saying the Elf had thrown his wallet as well as his jacket into the creek behind the bar as he was screaming repeatedly, "I don't need this shit. I don't fucking need this shit!"

I did that? Fuck. I did. Fuck!

The door shut on him again. He slowly, through a haze, pieced together what had happened. He had been in a headlock, thanks to the obsidian behemoth named Phil. He had been launched into the cold night. People were laughing and clapping their hands. *Why were they clapping? Was it funny? Was the distance of the toss impressive? Were they glad to be rid of me? Was I pissing people off? Probably yes to all.*

The Elf remembered his ramblings about his money not being good enough or too good, for these people, and how he did not need it because he could make more very easily.

As he was dragged outside, kicking and yelling and knocking shit over the whole way in defiance, and then thrown to the ground, another bouncer threw his coat to him. Inebriated, he could not catch it, and it fell to the asphalt. He didn't need it. He could buy a thousand coats. That's how much he was worth.

So he picked it up and wildly threw it. He also ripped his wallet from the chain and let loose a Hail Mary.

"Fuck," he mumbled as he stood there and realized what he had to do. With shame he walked behind the bar and searched. The freeway was thirty yards up the steep hill, and the noise was intolerable, especially with a hangover.

Feeling nauseated, he kept looking around the dry ground, hoping his wallet had not gone into the slow-moving, scummy, frigid, light brown water or the swampy mushy puddles near the nasty creek.

The Elf was miserable. The sun pierced his retinas. The sweat stung his eyes. The nausea could come back at any moment if he did not stop to close his eyes, wipe his brow, and calmly breathe several deep breaths.

He found his jacket covered in mud, next to the slow-flowing murky water. It was soaked with dirty sludge. He picked it up and assessed that it was unsalvageable.

"Fuck," the Elf mumbled as he checked the pockets and came up with a lighter and some wet cigarettes in the zipped, sealed liner pocket. He searched and searched the outlying area and came up with nothing—just used condoms, pieces of hopefully not human shit, and garbage. The sun was getting lower in the sky, and the breeze was making the frigid air colder.

Walking over to the filthy creek, he realized that if the wallet floated, the moderate current would have taken it far away by now. In case it sank, he looked into the water only to realize that it was so dirty and dark, he couldn't see anything. He wasn't even sure how deep it was. If it was shallow, he might walk into it, seeing if his feet could feel for it on the creek's floor. But what were the odds that it would be shallow enough that he could find it with frozen feet, or that it did not float? He looked for a long branch or something to check the depth. He found an unfolded wire hanger but hesitated as he reviewed his plan.

The cop car that drove by put an end to the review. "Fuck." He hustled back to his lowered car with rims, which he'd parked farther down the road from the bar.

Covered in sweat and muddy feet, he drove off with his teeth chattering from the cold and from the fear of knowing that he had to move a bunch of product and ask people for money before it was due, or he was dead. "Fuck!"

CHAPTER
TWENTY-THREE

The Elf was down. After walking away from the muddy creek, he got in his car and just drove. He was trying to formulate a plan but was unable to. He then tried to come up with viable options. None made sense to him. It grew dark.

After fifteen minutes or so, the "Low Fuel" warning light came on. He hated spending money now, but it was necessary. He had some cash in his car somewhere.

Maybe he could hit up Joy for some money; maybe Randy, too. The Elf had not seen Randy in a while, but he was sure he could count on him in an emergency. And this was an emergency!

With these possibilities, the Elf breathed a little easier. He wouldn't be able to borrow their product because they would be taking on his troubles, which was not fair to Joy or Randy. But if he could borrow money from them, and if all the numbers and quotas were correct, then he would not end up dead and buried in a field near the freeway.

With these new strategies, he felt much more at ease and was able to concentrate on the important things, such as his horrible headache and awful nausea. "Hair of the dog," he said as he saw a gas station and minimart and pulled into the parking lot.

The Elf found a twenty in the glove compartment and walked in. He got a couple of stares as he realized he was sweaty with the color drained from his face. He felt embarrassed because he usually dressed very nicely and was never in such a disheveled state.

The Elf bought a tall boy and a pack of cigarettes, put the rest toward gas, and went back to his car. After he fueled, he drove a few yards and parked in the small minimart lot. As he drained a third of the beer, he felt better but almost threw up again at the taste. He lit a cigarette and decided to call Joy.

The Elf dialed the memorized number on his burner cell phone and waited. After several rings Joy picked up.

"Hey," Joy said, not recognizing the random number but correctly assuming who the caller was.

"Hey, yourself. It's been a while."

Without enthusiasm Joy replied, "Sure has."

The Elf asked, "Why did it take so long to pick up?"

"My knee is hurt."

"You hurt your knee?"

"Yeah. I was resting on the couch, and it's still a little sore. Took an extra sec to get up."

"Oh boy, what did you do now?" The Elf asked in a perfunctory manner as he was eager to ask if she had any cash, but he knew it was better to act interested and caring to get what he wanted.

"Nothing. I was just carrying something out, and I missed a step. I heard a pop."

Randy was making a cutting motion across his throat and silently mouthed, *Wrap it up.*

Joy shook her head because that was not the correct signal to *wrap it up.* She not-so-quietly whispered, "That's you're dead. This is wrap it up." She stuck her index finger out and rotated her whole hand.

Furiously, Randy put his index finger to his lips. This signal was clearly communicated as Joy went wide-eyed.

"What was that?" the Elf innocently asked. He did not hear the not-so-clandestine exchange between Randy and Joy because an eighteen-wheeler drove by the parking lot of the minimart. "I didn't hear ya."

"Uh, nothing!"

"No, baby, you heard a pop. I didn't catch anything after that. Stupid truck drove by."

Joy got loud when she was nervous. "I didn't say anything!"

The Elf knew this. "Baby, you're loud, so you're hidin' something. After the pop, what happened?"

The Elf listened and recognized a song playing on the radio in the background, which diverted his attention. "Hey, it's your song! You love that dumb fucking song. Well, listen, can I come over in—"

"My knee is hurt, and I can't have visitors."

"Visitors? It's me, baby. Just relax. I got a few things to do, and I'd like to come over in a little while. I know it's been a long time, and I am sorry about that, but I got some shit to talk to you about. I need a favor, or I'm in deep shit. OK?"

"Well, I don't know what you want me to do about it. I don't know how I can help you or why I should."

Randy nodded and patted her leg as he soundlessly mouthed, *Smart.* The simple contact aroused him, and he slowly got turgid.

The Elf, not dissuaded, simply said, "Baby, I'm coming over. I need a little help, OK?" The Elf then saw this situation from her perspective. "Look, I know it's been a while. Too long and I'm sorry. I know we've made plans. We'll get the babies back. OK? Maybe we can start a new chapter between us. I really want to. We've been through too much, and I want a new start with you. I really do, but I'm in a sticky situation right now. Help me get out of it, and after we'll focus on us. OK? Can I come over?"

The Elf being in this present scary situation had realized that he had been taking Joy for granted and wanted to show appreciation for her. Fear had a way of cutting away the superfluous matters, and things became clearer. He had feelings for Joy. And he wanted to admit that to her. And he wanted the happiness that a relationship with her could provide. He regretted the wasted time.

As if she had not heard a single heartfelt word from the Elf, Joy replied, "I can't have any visitors. My knee is hurt."

"What's with the 'visitors' shit?" The Elf was curious as to why she was acting peculiar. "Why can't I come over?"

"There's no one here."

Randy's erection went down instantly. He slapped his palm to his forehead.

Oblivious, the Elf muttered, "I understand that, baby. I'm not gonna have a party. I need to borrow some money. That's all, baby." The Elf braced for the argument and got ready for the rebuttal.

"Fine. Come over in two hours. I'm gonna—" She lifted up her sweatshirt and exposed a big stretch-marked breast to Randy who immediately started to lick the nipple. Joy breathed in heavy.

The Elf thought the cell phone was cutting out. "What, baby?"

Joy was barely present in the conversation with the Elf. "I'm gonna take a quick nap. Come over in..." Joy's voice disappeared.

The Elf hit the phone on his steering wheel and mumbled, "Fucking piece of shit."

"What, baby?" the Elf asked again.

"I'm gonna take a quick nap. Come over in two... uh, two...oh God, two hours. OK?"

The Elf felt guilty bothering Joy when she was in pain. It had been a very long time since he'd seen her. Randy usually volunteered for the job and kept her supplied with product.

The Elf asked with much concern in his voice, "Your knee hurting that much?"

"Yeah. No. Uh, yeah! I'm fine. Let me take a nap, and come over in two hours. OK?"

"Two hours is a quick nap?"

"Yeah! Two hours!" With that, the conversation ended.

"What the fuck was that all about?" The Elf threw his cigarette out the window into the cold night air. He took another big swig of beer. He was feeling better. Mentally he was at ease, and physically he was not as hungover.

The Elf lit another cigarette and decided to call Randy. The Elf had memorized his burner cell number, too. Hopefully Randy still used that phone. He basically prepared to have the exact same conversation.

After several rings Randy picked up. "Hey."

"Hey, yourself. What's going on, man?"

"Nothing much, man. Where are you?"

The Elf was confused. "What? I'm at...dude, whatever. I need to come and see you."

"I ain't gonna be home for a coupla hours."

Perplexed, the Elf asked, "Why is everyone busy for two hours right now? Look, I need to talk to you about a few things. I need to borrow some cash, man. I'm in a bad situation, and I—"

"Yeah, fine. I'll be home in—"

"A coupla hours. Got it. Are you OK?"

"Yeah, uh, yeah I'm good. How are you?"

"Not so good, man. Like I said, I'm in a bad spot, and I need some help."

"Yeah, fine. Be at my place in two hours."

The Elf could not figure out why these two people were acting so strangely. Then he heard the same song on the radio that Joy was listening to.

"Uh-oh. Whatcha listening to? Huh? That's a real faggy song you got on, queer! Ha-ha. Only chicks like that song, man."

"Oh! I just—it was on the radio. I was looking for something else. It was on a commercial, and then you called, and I couldn't change the station."

Randy slapped the radio off and then sat back on the couch where Joy promptly put all of his large erection back in her mouth, continuing the impassioned oral sex. She was moaning loudly and making slurping sounds. They were loud sounds, but Randy didn't think the Elf could hear it.

"What's that weird sound, dude? You watching porn, man?"

Randy grabbed Joy by the back of her head, thrust her farther down himself, and just held her there. Luckily, her tongue was still moving very serpentlike as she breathed through her nose.

"Yeah, dude, you caught me; I'm watching porn and listening to teenybopper shit. Get a new god-damned phone!"

Even though they were not in front of each other, the Elf still raised a hand and said, "OK, man, relax. Sorry. Can I come by?"

"Yeah, in two hours." Randy hung up.

The Elf chugged the rest of his beer after he damned those two people for being weirdoes. He threw out the second cigarette and lit a third. With all that was happening, he wasn't feeling too safe going anywhere other than Joy's. He wanted to get his hands on some cash and feel the security it possessed.

Maybe he could help with her knee, ice it up, wrap it up, get his fat cock sucked, and head out to the parking lot across from the 11th Frame and sell what product he had left at home. "Fuck it." He left the minimart parking lot and headed to Joy's.

CHAPTER TWENTY-FOUR

The Elf pulled up to the entrance of the Blackhawk Mobile Home Community and parked. Sometimes it was a pain in the ass to find parking near Joy's trailer. It was a one-way path in there, and if your luck was bad, you could be doing some laps for a while. So he usually parked in a "Future Tenants" space at the leasing office if it was past business hours, which it was now.

There were several cars already parked there, so the Elf had to park in a patch of gravel behind the leasing office. The Elf got out, closed and locked his doors, and headed to Joy's on foot. It usually took a little over five minutes to walk there, but he was moving slowly tonight—but not too slow, because it was freezing.

The Elf noted the usual characteristics of a trailer park, as the loud voices and loud music were in abundance. It did get quiet as he approached Joy's trailer though. From the looks of things, most of her neighbors were not home.

The Elf saw a light on in Joy's trailer. Hopefully she was awake despite the two-hour-nap request. He still had her key, and hopefully she hadn't changed the locks.

As he walked closer, he heard the unmistakable sounds of sex. Joy was having sex. The sex was unusual though because Joy was loud. A loudness the Elf had never experienced with Joy. There was no way she was masturbating, so she was enjoying some serious sex with someone else. Joy was having sex with someone else. *What the fuck?*

The Elf saw red but maintained silence as he approached her trailer. The sounds changed and were now different. She was moaning loudly, but then she began to yield strange muffled hums. Then he heard a man moan.

The Elf crept up the stairs silently and peeked in the window. He saw Joy, naked, sitting on the edge of the couch playing with herself, with an ACE bandage on her knee, with a pair of balls in her mouth, with streams of drool running down her breasts, with the balls belonging to his friend Randy.

Astonished, the Elf took in the scene in front of him. Randy was naked—*I never knew he was so muscular*—and had a clump of Joy's hair in his hand while his other hand was jerking his large cock off while his balls were in Joy's mouth while she played with herself.

That's why they were so fucking weird on the phone! That's why I heard the same song! Well, they want to do this for two hours? No fucking way!

After a few moments, Randy stopped jerking off and placed his erection in Joy's mouth. All of it disappeared. The Elf would have had no way of knowing that Joy did not have a gag reflex had he not seen this.

Joy, with much zeal, went back and forth quite vigorously. Finally, she leaned back and exhaled loudly with lots of drool running down to her breasts again and said, "That's so much fun to do to you, baby!"

Randy collected the drool from her breasts, leaned over, and placed his hand on, around, and then in her vagina. After only moments she climaxed. That same hand then went to Joy's mouth where she sucked all of his fingers. Then the hand went to the side of her face, very tenderly, and he declared, "I need your ass, baby!"

Gently and with the kind of great care that you would show an injured grandmother, Randy lifted Joy to her feet and then gently laid her facedown on the floor of the dirty trailer, shoving a few pieces of garbage out of the way.

Randy then grabbed a pillow and gave it to her, so she could prop herself up at the hips and be comfortable. With both hands, Joy spread her ass and said, "Please, baby, bury your cock in my ass. It's yours, baby. Please!"

Randy grabbed her hair again and placed his hand in front of her mouth, so she could spit into it. She obliged. He then put the spit on her anus, rubbed the anal perimeter for a few moments, and eased his erection into Joy's ass.

Joy moaned and moaned and went berserk with pleasure. The Elf felt humiliated because Joy, most of the time, just lay there with him. Now it appeared she was the queen of wild animalistic sex. Now she was fucking his friend. His friend Randy was fucking Joy in her ass. It appeared to be hot as their bodies were covered in sweat.

Joy's ass bounced in an attractive and seductive rhythm as Randy's cock devoured what taboo dictated inappropriate. She took one hand away from spreading and began to rub herself vigorously, increasing her moans. Catching on and being very in tune to Joy's desires, Randy used his thumb to enter Joy's traditional orifice and sent her over the edge.

Joy screamed as if she were a murder victim as copious amounts of fluid squirted out of her. The moans gave way to shudders as she made a fist and began to punch the floor. "Keep going, baby," she demanded. "I can squirt again!"

Increasing the sexual rhythm and thrusting severity, Randy said, "I love you, Joy. I love you so much."

Joy, elated, turned around, placed her hand on his as it rested on her lower back, supporting him, and said, "I love you, Randy. I only want to be with you. Forever."

Their shared look was indicative of true love plus the relief and happiness of being able to express true emotions that were no longer secretive. It was a moment they'd remember for the rest of their lives.

The Elf had had enough. He was in an explosive, savage rage. He'd had no idea they were having sex. He'd had no idea they were in love. He'd had no idea she could squirt. He had to right this wrong. A boulder of hurt and sadness had been heaved upon him, and he could not bear it. This betrayal, this humiliation, this deception had to be corrected.

The Elf squatted down and very slowly, with careful and meticulous precision, put the key in the lock. Slowly and quietly, he unlocked the door. The next movements had to be completed through tearful eyes.

The Elf barged in with a barbaric fury. The no-quarter look in his eyes said one thing; everyone was going to die. There was no plea that could yield salvation. There was not a verse in any psychology textbook that could alter the finale, which was indeed death.

The Elf saw and quickly grabbed an empty Old Crow bottle that was lying on the table, and with all his might, he did what he could do to make sure the bottle went through Randy's head. In an instant Randy went from alive and in love to near dead. *Now, to end Joy.*

CHAPTER TWENTY-FIVE

As best she could, Joy rolled over and backed herself into a corner where the wall met the couch when she heard the shatter of glass and felt Randy vacate her. When she turned around and saw Randy motionless on the ground, bleeding from a horrific gash in his head, she began to cry.

Joy looked up to see the Elf with a fixed death gaze upon her. She always figured this fate was set in stone for her and Randy.

Joy could not stop what was coming. She had hoped and tried to think positively and wished for good things. Yet all this positive thinking and well-wishing was to no avail as was evident by this terrible scene. She knew.

Joy buried her face into her hands and cried at her loss. Sadly, Joy kept repeating "Randy, baby" and "I'm sorry, baby" while never looking up. Distraught did not come close to describing the loss she experienced at this moment in her pained life. This letdown confirmed that thinking positively was a waste of time.

It was always in the back of Joy's mind that their time together was running out and they would get caught. And really caught, unlike the other times when they'd just talked their way out of it.

In a sadistic rage, the Elf kicked Randy in the back of the head and through clenched teeth yelled, "Why?" He kicked him again. "Why? Answer me, bitch! Why?"

After the last kick, Joy yelled, "Stop it! Just leave him alone." She let go a wail of anguish accompanied by a flood of tears. "Leave my baby alone," she pleaded.

The Elf continued to kick and ask the same question. Then the Elf reached into his front pocket and took out a knife. He unfolded the sharp knife, grabbed Randy by his sweaty and bloodied hair, placed the blade to his neck, and yelled, "Look at me, Joy. Hey! Look at us, bitch!"

Joy looked up and saw her unconscious Randy with a knife to his neck and the maniacal eyes of the regretted link between them. Randy's large erection bounced off the floor to the movements caused by the Elf.

Joy whispered, "Don't hurt my baby," as her lips trembled. She was at the pinnacle of fear and despair. "Don't hurt my Randy."

Joy never answered the Elf's question. She was devastated and everything else seemed pointless. She realized the end was near. Joy just looked at Randy in a peaceful manner and said, "I love you, baby. I always did."

As if on cue, the Elf drug the blade across Randy's glistening neck and unleashed a cascade of crimson.

Joy just looked down and muttered, "Oh no, my baby, my baby," but she did not go into hysterics as gurgling sounds came out of Randy. Joy was motionless; she had given up.

The Elf let Randy's body fall to the dirty floor. As comprehension became present, the Elf took in the carnage and despair he'd created. He was fully aware he was going to kill or die in the process of trying to kill Randy, his former friend. But now that he'd actually done it, and done it in such a grizzly manner, he was mentally unattached to the surreal scene.

The Elf had acted out in anger. Almost reflexive in nature, the Elf exacted his unplanned revenge and caused grave injury.

Everyone has lost their temper in the heat of the moment only to have reason come back and, hopefully, prevent a criminal act. Everyone gets close.

But when Randy was not yet dead, the Elf continued causing pain and torment to both Joy and Randy. The taunting of Joy, the watching of Joy having her heart broken, and the grand throat slashing as the final act was not something the Elf was used to. Joy and Randy's feelings and emotions for each other were news to him, and he acted irrationally with lethal and irreparable consequences.

The Elf wanted to apologize for hurting Randy and for hurting Joy. He wanted to justify his anger. He felt betrayed, and he was hurt. His life was full of pain, and he had just caused more pain to people whom at one point he had cared about.

I'm in pain, always. Finding you two hurt me. You hurt me. I wanted to hurt you, but I didn't mean to do this. I just...I was mad. I mean, yeah, you had every right to be with anyone, but why him? I mean, it's OK, I guess. I realize that it's OK, but it's way too late now. It doesn't help Randy. He's fucking dead. I killed him. I killed Randy.

The Elf was well aware of what had to happen. He had to end her life. Vengeance was one thing, but she was witness to something he could get the gas chamber for. The Elf was certain Joy would not keep her mouth shut, not this time.

The Elf went to the back bedroom and grabbed a stained sheet from the bed, and with his bloodied knife, he cut a long strip. He wrapped both ends around his fists, and with one fist pulled away from the other, he increased the tautness. *Do it.*

The Elf unwrapped the sheet from around his small fists, held it bunched in one hand, and walked out front. What he saw broke his heart. Joy had crawled over to Randy and was lying next to him with one arm over his back. This was emotional torture. The guilt was overpowering, and the Elf was on the verge of tears as he realized Joy did not care about life anymore since he'd taken Randy's.

The Elf attempted to act tough as he grabbed Joy by the hair and dragged her to in front of the couch where she lay crying. She was covered in Randy's blood, and the scene made the Elf snap. He began to cry. *What have I done?*

Joy heard the Elf's crying. She was done with this life. She had suffered such tragic loss, loss that every woman fears and loss that every mother fears. She was done with it all. The state had taken her two children, and they were better off. She missed them, but there was nothing she could do for them, especially since she knew the end was near.

Joy's unborn child was better off, too. She looked down at her belly and rubbed it. *I'm sorry, sweetheart. Your brother and sisters and me are very sad we can't meet you. I wish we could, sweetheart. I'm so sorry. Mommy loves you.* She wondered if she would have had a boy or a girl. She had a son and a daughter already—two daughters, actually.

The Elf had killed her firstborn daughter. He'd become a murderer well before this evening. He'd killed their eleven-month-old baby girl.

Joy had asked him to watch the baby for a few hours. The Elf left right after Joy did, but he claimed the baby was fine when he came home an hour later.

Joy did not ask too many questions. She didn't know, nor did she really want to know, how her beautiful daughter met her demise. Knowing the Elf, he probably shook her or hit her or smothered her. A part of Joy died that night, and the rest of her life was incomplete.

That night, the Elf worked furiously to clean the trailer, staying up till dawn. He wanted the trailer to not be suspicious. The stash, the cash, and the alcohol were stored at his place. He then compromised the crib's railing and called the police, saying they had found their daughter, who had apparently fallen in silence to her demise. The Elf and Joy were asleep and heard nothing and were never awakened. The horrific discovery was made that morning. The grief was real. The authorities never questioned their mourning. The authorities were very sympathetic. The authorities were fooled.

Fortunately, or unfortunately, the Elf had gotten away with it. Charges were never filed. Joy felt compelled to remain silent, so she kept quiet and went along with the sad story he created.

After this unbearable trauma, Joy drank and did whatever drugs she could to escape the immense pain she experienced every waking moment from the heinous, traitorous actions of the vile, cruel monster that ended the life of her firstborn.

Joy felt she had to protect him because he was the only one to protect her. So she just went with it. She never mentioned her firstborn. The Elf was the only one who would ever love Joy, so she could not do anything to cause him to abandon her. Joy felt she could always have another child, and she did. Her children made her feel happy, but they reminded her of the unbearable loss.

But now, in this very big moment of awareness with explosions of epiphany, Joy fucking hated the Elf with every ounce of her being.

Fuck him! Fuck him! He murdered my baby girl, and now he just murdered the man I was in love with. Now he feels guilty? Now he feels fucking guilty? Fuck you! Fuck you, you piece of shit. You're an ugly monster. I hate you! I almost wish there was a hell, so you can rot in it, you fucking son of a bitch. And now you're crying? You want me to feel sorry for you? With all my hatred, I want to cause you pain. I don't want this to be easy.

"You gonna kill me, huh? Gonna kill your ex?" Joy asked.

The Elf was still feeling guilt and sorrow over his actions. "You've been fucking my friend. How could you do that to me? How could you do that to us?" In this state the Elf lowered his emotional defensive wall.

Joy sensed weakness and turned it up a notch to bombard the Elf with pain. "I wasn't just fucking him. We was moving heaven and earth. I've never been fucked like that before in my whole life."

The Elf, now with less sorrow, quietly said, "Shut up."

Joy kept going. "What? You don't wanna know how he made my pussy squirt all over my fucking trailer? It was like a sprinkler was turned on in here."

The Elf raised the volume of his voice. "Shut up!"

Not backing down Joy said, "My pussy exploded in every fucking direction, and that was when he was fucking me in my ass. Did you know that? I loved him so much I let him put his huge cock anywhere."

The Elf yelled through tears, "Shut the fuck up, Joy!"

Joy kept going. "He had such a nice body. Muscles. Huge cock. Nice eyes. Tall. He cared about me. We were in love. We were gonna get the kids back and get married and live together and love each other and create a life together."

The Elf, now without sorrow as his tough-guy persona returned, chuckled at Joy's sentimentality and said, "The fuck you were," and laughed. "The fuck you been smoking, bitch? You think I'd let you take my kids away from me? Get real, bitch." The guilt-ridden and sorrowful man who regretted his impulsive actions was gone.

In a very dignified manner, Joy sat up more, pushed her sweat-soaked red hair away from her face, and asked, "Did you not notice how my son looked nothing like you but looked a hell of a lot like Randy?"

The Elf closed his mouth and remained still. *Oh shit!* His son did look like Randy. This was a life-altering surprise from out of nowhere.

"Oh bullshit! You're just trying to piss me off." The Elf knew it was true though. A bomb of surprise and shock detonated in his mind.

Joy continued. "Every once in a while, I would let Randy cum inside me and not just in my ass or my mouth, which he did all the fucking time. One time, he came in my pussy. My God it was so fucking hot. His huge cock made me feel like I was in another world. But it wasn't just Randy's cock that made me feel that way." Joy cried again and longingly looked at Randy.

Joy continued. "That night, I wanted to create a life with him as the father."

The Elf retorted, "You're so full of shit, you know that?"

Joy acted like she did not hear him and continued. "My Randy created a life with me that night. It felt so good and so right." She paused and took in a deep breath and reminisced for a moment or two before continuing.

"And I got pregnant with his son. Finally, in my life, something wonderful happened to me." Her tone took a turn toward the angry. "But I had to let you put your limp small dick in me one last time, so you would think I was pregnant with your child, but no. No no no. It was Randy that gave me such a good-looking son. What do you think of that, loser?"

The Elf shook his head and said, "You're full of shit." He stood there looking down at her, and he knew she was telling the truth.

The Elf instantly remembered coming over one particular evening and having sex with Joy, and she'd been very persistent that he finished in her. Joy had been persistent to the point of weirdness. He'd thought it was a bad idea, but she'd nearly demanded and assured him that she was on the pill. But then she'd gotten pregnant anyway. *That never did make sense.* Everything she said now made complete sense.

"Bullshit. Your two kids are my two kids." The Elf regretted saying that because now she would finally bring it up. This whole time, Joy was quiet about it. Now, there was no reason to hold back.

"Three," Joy screamed. "Three babies, you miserable piece of shit! Three! Did you forget? Huh? Did you forget killing my baby girl? You fucking murdered my baby girl, you fucking monster!"

Joy got herself up on the couch, and the Elf ran over and backhanded her, which had no effect on her. She simply turned toward him again.

"You fucking murderer! You killed my baby girl!"

The Elf then just flat out punched Joy in the face. Her hands gripped the couch cushions for just a moment. Joy made no sound. She spit blood onto the floor and continued.

"Remember my angel? You remember her? You murdered my angel because...Why? Crying? She was crying too much? You fucking monster! You betrayed me and killed my baby girl."

The Elf hit her again and was going to once more but realized it was a waste. Joy needed to say these things, so he just let her. It was to be a final magnanimous act from a murderer to a dying woman.

"My angel was crying, and you killed her. You shook her or hit her or smothered her till she was quiet. I fucking hate you so much. I would give anything to watch you die."

The generosity was over, and he needed to show Joy who the man was. The Elf hit her one last time and then grabbed her hair, threw her to the ground, and forcibly flipped her over.

The Elf took the sheet out, wrapped it around both fists, and circled Joy's neck. He started to choke her. Joy managed to slip some fingers in between the sheet and her neck, thus decreasing the pressure. She coughed a little as she braced herself up on her elbows.

The Elf was hunched on Joy's buttocks as he had the vengeful idea to take what he never had but what Randy was privy to. He unwrapped the sheet from her neck and his left hand and placed his right hand on the back of Joy's neck, pinning her down, even though she could have easily thrown him off.

The Elf quickly undid his pants. He then put one knee on Joy's back and began to play with himself so he would become erect. It was taking a while. Joy noticed and asked, "What's the matter, loser? Can't get it up?"

Instead of yelling at her, he licked his thumb and shoved it in Joy's anus. *This ought to shut her up and show her who I am!*

"Wow, did you get a bigger cock?"

Defeated, the Elf yelled, "Shut up," as he slapped the back of Joy's head with his other hand.

She laughed. She felt no physical pain.

The Elf finally got hard. He then wrapped the sheet around Joy's neck with more tension this time. Her breathing was severely compromised. She was nearing the end, but the Elf did not want her to depart just yet.

The Elf undid the sheet again, and again Joy gasped for air and coughed. While she coughed, he spread her buttocks and spit near her anus and rubbed his penis around it. He slid his manhood in, and it felt glorious. He had wanted this for a very long time, and now he finally had it.

Joy began to laugh. "Are you even in me?"

The Elf vacated her, grabbed her by the hair, picked her up off the floor, and propped her over the couch. He then wrapped the sheet around her neck and completely cut off her breathing. The Elf entered her again and began to violently thrust back and forth.

The Elf knew that choking someone was not a quick endeavor like it was portrayed in the movies. It took more time than the average person thought, and it was taking Joy a while.

The Elf was still feeling nauseated. With everything that had happened today, the mental exhaustion he felt, and the fact that he was out of shape, maintaining a vigorous pace, such as he was, was indeed difficult.

The Elf lost his erection and pulled out of Joy. Joy turned her head a little, but the Elf was not in the mood to be made fun of more. With that, he increased the tension with all his might, and Joy passed away.

The Elf maintained the tension for several moments. After a while he stood up and pulled his pants back up. Exhausted, he sat down next to Joy as she lay propped on the couch. He took several minutes to catch his breath. When he felt better, he felt for a pulse in two locations and checked to see if the body moved. Joy's body did not move. Joy was dead.

CHAPTER TWENTY-SIX

The Elf began to regain a level head. His breathing had slowed, and he began to think clearer. Things had gotten way out of hand. None of this was planned. He had become an unwilling and unplanned graduate to murder. Well, he was already a murderer, but now he was a multiple murderer.

Joy was dead. He had killed her. Randy was dead. He had killed him. He had killed them both with severe brutality. He could not alter what he'd done. He could not go back and undo the killings. What he could do was not get caught for this loss of control.

The Elf had managed to steer clear of the law when he'd previously ended a life, but he did not want to tempt fate again. Justice had a way of emerging and being thorough after multiple homicides. There was no way to manipulate this scene. So he had to remove himself and his presence from this scene.

The Elf figured he had a little while to safely vacate the area. The immediate neighbors were not home. The shades were drawn. The trailer was dark. Still, time was of the essence.

The Elf went into the kitchen and found some rags, paper towels, a bottle of blue liquid glass cleaner, an ancient bottle of bleach, a pair of needle-nose pliers, and two shopping bags.

The Elf needed a pair of gloves, so he went to Joy's closet and found a pair of her cold-weather gloves and put them on. They fit well. While he was there, he moved all the clothes at the bottom of the closet and found an old military ammunition box where she kept her earnings.

Even though Randy and the Elf or the higher-ups handled the cash, Joy did deals on the side.

What she had was neatly stacked and wrapped with rubber bands. He grabbed the money and put it into the first shopping bag. He saw an envelope with more cash in it. On the envelope four names were written: Berman, Burke, Pepper, and Rojas, which the Elf concluded was a law firm. *Wow*, the Elf thought. *She was gonna pay a lawyer to get the babies back. Well, most of them.*

The Elf went to the mattress and moved it, exposing a hole in the box spring where the shoe boxes full of product were. He took the box, put it in the bag, and put the mattress back. *The numbers will be correct. I'll just sell it. Anything missing will be deemed a loss due to the robbery and homicide.*

The Elf came for cash, and now he had some. As a bonus, he also had product, which he would sell. He would also go get Randy's cash and stash, but not all of it as that would point the finger at the Elf doing an inside job. As long as he pounded pavement, the Elf would make his payment and dummy up about Joy and Randy.

He took the bag and walked up front, placing it by the door. Now, it was body detail.

The Elf grabbed the pliers and walked over to where Randy had been having sex with Joy. He knelt down, took his time, and methodically picked up every shard of glass with the pliers and placed them into an empty Big Gulp cup he found on the kitchen counter. After several moments of a very thorough visual inspection of the area, he took the cup full of glass shards, poured some bleach into it, and shook it for a while.

He then used his knife's blade to block the glass from falling out as he poured the cup of bleach into the sink. He poured half out and then flipped the knife over, exposing the other side of the blade, and poured the rest out. He placed the cup of shards on the counter.

The Elf located an old Dixie cup and placed his knife in it and poured bleach into the cup until the knife was submerged. After a few moments, with a gloved hand, he removed the knife, put it under scalding water from the faucet, and then dried it with a rag, thus removing his fingerprints.

He then went to Joy's body and delicately unwrapped the sheet from around her neck and put it in the cup of bleach where the knife had been. He let the sheet soak for a few moments and then removed it and placed it in the sink and let the hot water flush that murder weapon. After several moments, the Elf stopped the water. He then took a rag and poured bleach on it.

With the bleach-soaked rag, the Elf wanted to thoroughly go over every square inch of Randy and Joy. Scrubbing with the bleach-soaked rag would hopefully have two effects: getting rid of any of his DNA and, again, getting rid of fingerprints.

Making sure not to step in the puddle of Randy's blood, with firm pressure he scrubbed Randy's entire body. When he came to Randy's genitals, he picked up the bottle of liquid blue glass cleaner and sprayed a bunch, even though he'd had no contact.

With all of Randy doused in bleach or glass cleaner, especially his hair where the Elf grabbed him, and all the pieces of glass from the whiskey bottle with the Elf's prints on them collected, soaked in bleach, and ready to discard, he felt Randy was clear.

Moving on to Joy, the Elf knew it would take more effort and time. The first area of concern would be

Joy's anus. Even though he had not climaxed, he knew his semen could have leaked out. His precum often stained his pants and left embarrassing spots as he tried to hide them in strip clubs after lap dances. He thought of a funnel but realized he could utilize a makeshift one.

The Elf found an old beer bottle and filled it with bleach and hot water. With Joy lifeless, propped up, and bent over the couch, he did his best to gently spread her anus. Realizing there was no need to be polite, he used his thumb and as best he could, he gaped her orifice and inserted the bottle.

As he got most of the long neck securely into her, the Elf tipped up the bottle pouring the bleach into Joy's anus, thus killing the DNA from him and Randy. As the noxious chemical filled her and compromised any trace, he then painstakingly wiped her whole body with a bleached rag.

Not satisfied and somewhat overcareful to the point of paranoia, the Elf scrubbed her down again with glass cleaner and paper towels.

When done with Joy, the Elf took the second shopping bag and placed the cup of glass shards in it. He took the torn sheet that was soaked in bleach and hot water, wrung it out, and put it in the bag. He took the knife and placed it in the bag.

Everything he touched before putting on the gloves was wiped down. He took a few moments and walked through the events, focusing on everything he'd had physical contact with. Everything was clean.

The Elf decided to go through the closet and dresser drawers and remove any remaining clothing of his. He found a few things and tried to remember if there were other shirts or hoodies or anything else remaining. He could not think of anything.

He reached under the bed, looking for a suitcase. He found an old military-surplus duffel bag that Joy used to say was from a Desert Storm veteran she was going to marry. *It was probably some drifter she fucked.* He would never know for certain. There was not a visible name or ID number on the bag. His guess was that it came from a military-surplus store.

In any event it had no holes, and the owner was long gone, so it became the Elf's property. The sudden image of a drifter with a military-surplus duffel bag was an enlightening visual, and its presence was moving.

The Elf pondered about making this payment a final payment and leaving Engel Falls for good. This bag represented a new beginning. The Elf envisioned throwing a bunch of clothes, money, and a pistol in the faded-green bag and getting the hell out of Old Falls and being done with this lifestyle.

The Elf loved the idea of starting a new life somewhere else. Somewhere warm. A place where he could get a real job and not waste his time selling or taking drugs.

He could picture getting a place somewhere. Buying new clothes, eating right, and taking care of himself. Maybe he could get a job with a union and use the benefits to get healthy. He wanted to better himself.

The idea made sense. What he'd done tonight and what he had gone through today were things he regretted and never wanted to repeat. "Fuck this life, and fuck Old Falls," he said to no one in Joy's empty double-wide trailer.

He grabbed the old military-surplus duffel bag and went to the front. He tied off the other two bags and held them. He would dispose of them in a Dumpster at one of the nearby industrial businesses.

The Elf looked at Randy. Then the Elf looked at Joy. He wanted to hug her and say how sorry he was for not committing to her, for not loving her the way she did him, and for killing their baby. He got emotional and let slip tears of remorse.

In a toddler way, the Elf cried, and through sniffles and broken, fragmented sentences, he tried to apologize to Joy for hurting her. He was a pathetic, snotty, and blubbering mess, as he genuinely bid farewell.

A car drove by, and the Elf squatted down to the floor in a panic. He was relieved as it kept driving down the path, but then panic set in again as he wondered if they were looking for a spot, as he had to walk to the front where he was parked.

Luckily, he heard the car stop and a door open and close. The Elf turned off the light and walked outside. Thankfully, the person had arrived at a trailer on the other side of a turn.

The Elf used his sleeve to wipe the door handles. After several seconds he carefully and quietly began the walk back to his car, hiding behind trees, scared of being seen, and going from dark area to dark area.

CHAPTER
TWENTY-SEVEN

The Elf was freezing, but he needed money. He had Joy's stash and cash and had some of Randy's, which helped, but he still needed to make his nut. He was convinced one good night would save him. If the count was close, he was dead. He needed that exact number.

The Elf kept thinking of the idea of leaving Old Falls as he stood in the parking lot across from the 11th Frame. After a horrible day, a day that had changed his life forever, the Elf wanted to make his payment and be done with this shitty chapter and begin a new one.

Maybe he could act his way out: like, he wasn't going to sell drugs because he'd gotten sober, and he could not be around the drugs and suffer a relapse. *Yeah, I saw the light or whatever.* The Elf liked that idea.

The Elf regretted his time here. He regretted wasting his money on drugs and binge drinking, rounds of free drinks for girls he thought would like him, lap dances, flat-screens, trips to Indian casinos, gold chains, a motorcycle he never learned to ride, and a diamond earring.

He did not buy a house or put money aside. There were no investments. There was no stream of legitimate income, so the IRS would be all over him very soon.

The money he made did not go toward making his life better so he could get out of Old Falls. He threw it away on fleeting momentary senses of worth.

The Elf stood across from Open Lanes and chain-smoked cigarettes and waited. It was slow, and he was not dressed for the cold. The smoking and freezing air felt as if they were cutting his lungs.

Randy was bigger and taller than the Elf, so his jackets did not look right. Plus, he didn't want to have any ties or proof he was in Randy's apartment near the time of his death. Wearing a dead man's clothes may constitute suspect behavior.

It had been an excruciatingly awful day. He awoke with a brutal hangover, which he still had. He got yelled at by bigger and better men. He scrounged like a dog in the mud. He contemplated submerging himself in a freezing, scummy creek and scavenging like an amphibious rodent. He found out his friend was fucking his ex, and he killed them both. He committed the act of rape on someone who at one point cared for him. He stole cash and drugs like a small-time junkie burglar. His day was filled with fear, rage, betrayal, guilt, remorse, and humiliation.

All these events arrived with an apocalyptic nightmarish intrusion, yet he had to forget and focus, or he was dead.

CHAPTER
TWENTY-EIGHT

Amanda was twenty-four years old and perfect, if you were into that sort of thing. She was above average height and had a ridiculously gorgeous, firm, tan, and toned body. Her dark blond hair appeared to have strands of gold cascading down, adding to her angelic beauty. With a little breeze flowing through her golden locks, they were of the sun. Amanda was like a legendary mythical goddess from aeons past.

Amanda's perfect teeth were white and shone often. Her breasts were natural and perfect for her frame. They were firm, but they bounced when she walked braless. No stretch marks or hang lines. The center skin between her breasts was without creases.

No freckles, just clear glowing skin and spectacular pencil-eraser nipples.

Amanda watched a plethora of porn. Her porn viewing rivaled any fifteen-year-old teenaged male in the world times three. Amanda knew all the actors, the lines of dialogue, and the acting characteristics of all the major porn stars by heart.

She recognized the houses and locations regularly used for filming, and she had the addresses of the production companies written down in case she ever decided to pursue a career. This acquired knowledge was not of a devout fan per se but of someone who watched for her own edification and picked up these tidbits from observation.

Amanda observed and memorized the flowing yet choreographed ways of sexual artistry. The grunts, the silent screams—when to grip, when to scratch, when to place her palms on the sides of her head, when to grind her teeth, when to hold her breath and arch her neck to expose the veins, when to be silent and open her mouth and eyes very wide, when to rub her own clit, when to spread her buttocks, and when to put a finger in her own ass.

Amanda practiced fellatio on her dildo. With much practice she became comfortable with most of it down her throat. She wanted to give the best oral sex. Sometimes she would gag a little. Any spit that involuntarily came up was not to be wasted and used as lube.

With the dildo lubed up, she would relax her anus as best she could and insert it. With much practice she became comfortable with most of it in her. If anal sex ever came up again, she would be ready.

What was between Amanda's legs was her most prized possession. Hairless, tan like the rest of her, toned like the rest of her, and very welcoming with perfect-looking lips.

She was told many, many times that she tasted delicious. She had become curious, and during one encounter, Amanda had sucked the guy's fingers that had been in her only to find that she indeed tasted good. Well, maybe not good, but she could tolerate it if it added to her allure. So going down on guys in between positions was never a problem.

Sometimes, she would play with herself and stare at the guy and make little sharp exhalation sounds. This always worked. In a needy and timid voice, like she didn't know what an orgasm was, she would then breathlessly say the name of the guy, if she remembered. It was a greatly appreciated act.

When the guy first entered her, she would always be on her back, so she could use another great move, which was to grab him by the shoulders forcefully and slow him down. She would again use sharp little exhalation sounds as if it were painful, trying to insinuate that the guy was too big for her. They got off on it.

Subconsciously, she knew it made them cum quicker, so it would end sooner. Marathon sex gave her urinary-tract infections that were painful. Amanda would spend a small fortune on antibiotics, cranberry juice, and cranberry supplements. *Oh well, a small price to pay for being the best, most sought-after hottie in town.*

Amanda always swallowed the guy's cum. She did not want it on her face. If it got onto her face, it would get into her hair. She hated that! She would immediately have to shower and shampoo out the sticky substance, and that would dry out her fine hair.

"C'mon, baby. It's good for your skin," was often offered after she declined the facial inquiry.

Fuck off, asshole! My skin is immaculate, you piece of shit! Be thankful I even talked to you, let alone allowed you to fuck me, you ungrateful pig.

Amanda, often against their wishes, forced their erections down her throat when they neared climax, so they had no choice in terms of when or where to finish.

The cum would have shot everywhere because Amanda was so hot and the guys were so horny. It could not be helped.

When Amanda had first started to have sex by her choice, many times the distance covered and the large volume would be astonishing as it was launched onto dashboards, windshields, walls of hallways, headboards, or other people's faces. The impressive volume was often a surprise to the shooter as well as anyone else partaking.

So to avoid all that cum flying everywhere, to avoid drying out her beautiful hair, she had to swallow. For maintaining healthy hair, for easy cleanup, for practicality, and for convenience, Amanda swallowed. There were not too many complaints.

Amanda indeed was phenomenal at sex, and it would only get better. Men would soon have access to her ass, and she would be fine with it. *I have to be.*

Amanda's body and the sex she delivered had to be the best. Everything had to be the best: the best sex, the best body, lots of friends, and a party girl who could go till dawn. *That's what they want, and I can give that to them.*

Amanda had not always made the best decisions. Many times she was disgusted with whom she slept with and why. To get out of speeding tickets, to get better grades, and to piss off her cousin Ryan's girlfriend, Amanda had indeed engaged in bad choices.

It's fine that you hate Lindsay, but why did you fuck your own cousin? Yeah, he's a good-looking guy, but he's your goddamned cousin! Does everyone have to know how good you are?

That rumor may have spread by now, but not having time to regret, she justified her actions as doing what was necessary to ensure that everyone knew she was the sexiest girl ever. This was very important to Amanda, and she could not let herself down. A bad decision could be accepted if it furthered the greatness she sought.

Yet, with all this perfection and pleasing people, Amanda sometimes felt down. Sometimes this depression would cause problems. Amanda knew she had it. Her mother had had it.

Amanda recognized the signs and realized they both had the same ailment. Amanda subconsciously knew that her attempts at perfection resulted in a lack of happiness and fulfillment. *Fuck that! I'm happy!*

Yet there were times when it just weighed her down. It was a devastatingly emotional burden, and its presence was worse than any physical weight. The tension would be considerable and cause headaches.

There were times when certain places around her temples and eyes seemed like they were going to burst and cause a full-blown skull implosion. *Would that be a bad thing? The pain would stop at least.*

In her delirium she would have dreams or hallucinations of taking a needle and piercing certain painful points on her head, letting the pressure leak out, diffusing the strain before her skull burst.

She remembered watching a news show as a kid with her mother one Friday evening when she was allowed to stay up late. Seeing victims of proper migraines just bash their heads against furniture out of pure frustration and desperation was frightening.

The footage of normal people succumbing to the life-altering pain stayed with Amanda as she felt sympathy for the victims. Normal men and women, with families, friends, and jobs, acting as tortured animals saddened Amanda. She wished she could help people. Later in life she learned what it was like to be in such desperation to alleviate pain.

Sometimes the anguish was to the point of taking sleeping pills to sleep the day and the pain away. She even purchased pharmaceuticals from the Elf or exchanged sex with the Elf for the pills once or twice. Amanda felt like every once in a while, she needed to knock herself out for a day and then get back to normal.

Between episodes of pain and depression, there was an underlying presence of worry and anxiety that the pain would return. She could control it, though, and focus on other things and pursuits, but it was never fully forgotten. This anxiety-based fear would sometimes cause nausea or stomachaches and affected her appetite.

Amanda was not going to go down the path of eating disorders. Those girls were weak in her eyes. Amanda was strong. *Right?* Regardless of how she felt, Amanda made sure that she ate three healthy meals a day.

She spent a lot of money on groceries and bragged about all the organic, sustainable, gluten-free, non-dairy, unprocessed, conflict-free food she ate. *But the drugs and alcohol were OK? Shut up!*

Amanda set goals and did what she had to do to reach them. Amanda wanted to be the best and wanted everyone to say she was perfect. *Once this has been achieved, everything that was endured along the way will have been well worth it.*

Amanda did everything correctly. She completely shaved everything, she whitened her teeth, and she tanned. She was an on-again-off-again communications major, and she religiously did spin classes, walked for diseases, and raised awareness for whatever cause was trendy.

She got her nails and hair done and bought new clothes frequently. Amanda flirted with her beautiful green eyes, smiled a lot, and always remembered to reach over and touch a man on the arm when she fake laughed.

Amanda made sure to laugh a lot, and she gave a lot of hugs with an extra amount of embrace accompanied with a subtle but unmistakable caress. She chewed a lot of gum and responded to many statements with, "Oh my God, are you serious?"

Amanda had everything going for her. She was seeking perfection. She was told she was perfect by every dude she went down on. Amanda had it all. Amanda was perfect, if you were in to that sort of thing.

CHAPTER TWENTY-NINE

The 11th Frame was packed. It smelled like sweat and beer. It was wall-to-wall cowboys and cowgirls with a few proud warriors and squaws. Amanda had lost count of what vodka and cranberry juice she was on. Feeling good was fine, but she needed to keep her cool. She switched to just cranberry juice and moved about the bar and socialized.

The bar was big, long, and elliptical, a relic from a former era that could fit dozens of people. This was surrounded by an area of tables and an outer area of booths. There were a few animal heads on the walls. There were lots of old-timey advertisements for chewing tobacco, whiskey, and cigars. There were old-timey movie posters for *The Wild One, The Searchers, Touch of Evil,* and *Paths of Glory*. There was a big jukebox in the corner next to the dart boards and pool table. The 11th Frame had lots of potential to find someone.

It was not a surprise that no girls talked to Amanda. So like every other time, she talked with the guys. Tonight, unfortunately, most of the guys were here with their wives on this Wild West theme night. The preponderance of cowgirls made it difficult to do what she was best at. Amanda despised these bitches invading her territory.

A problem with having a cowboy costume party in New Falls was that there was a decent contingent of real cowboys and "concrete cowboys." They did not have to buy costumes. Even the rest of the guys usually had cowboy paraphernalia. For them it was just another night at the bar. Yet all these cowboys and wannabe cowboys weren't going to buy her drinks and fuck her with their wives around. *What a waste of a night.*

It was too late to go to another place. The local bars would be closing in a while, and she did not want to leave and go outside if she did not have to. It was way too cold as evidenced by Amanda taking a cab to the bar even though it was a short walk.

Amanda was basically not wearing clothes. Her denim miniskirt was very mini. Her beautiful womanly lips would be shown if she pulled a Sharon Stone for a lucky cowboy.

Her low-cut, sleeveless, cowgirl shirt tied at the bottom and exposing her flat stomach did very little to protect her from the elements. Her pigtails and cowboy hat completed her costume as most patrons gazed at her wondrous breasts that gently bounced as she walked.

Amanda and her lack of clothing demanded attention from the 11th Frame clientele. The guys instantly fell for her, and their wives immediately hated her. The other single ladies hated her as well as she crushed their feeble attempts to meet a single guy. There was even a mannish woman or two checking her out. *Gross. I don't want some dyke checking me out.* The thought did not please her, she reminded herself.

Amanda just assumed that lesbians were out of their minds. *Why would any chick be with another chick?* She often wondered about that. She often wondered about that at great length.

For a split second before totally dismissing the idea of being with a woman, Amanda did have questions. At first there were questions about the techniques. *How did they do it?* Yeah, she'd had three-ways but never really did things to the other female. She couldn't do that. *Right? No, lesbos are out of their minds.*

Her porn viewing had started at an early age, when one of her mother's boyfriends used to watch "kissing movies" when they were alone, while her mother took many naps, and she had seen women kissing each other all over and loving each other.

Amanda resented what lesbians did to each other because of the effect it had on her mother's boyfriend's behavior and what he did to Amanda after watching those movies. But that was a long time ago. Lately, Amanda's curiosity had been growing. There were thoughts that gave way to fantasies, but she quickly dismissed them.

Amanda never truthfully asked herself, but that did not mean she did not have an answer—the answer possibly blowing her mind. Maybe she did have an answer.

Amanda had frequently let the thoughts of others be her thoughts. *I never answered for myself. I didn't feel I was allowed to. Things are done a certain way. To deviate from that is to do something wrong, and I can't do something wrong, or I'll get in trouble.*

Goddamn it! Trouble from whom? Who's gonna get mad at me now? Who will hurt me now for disobeying? They can't hurt me anymore. I will not be punished for doing what I want to do. I can ask a question and give my own fucking answer. I can…I can…holy shit…I can do what I want. My God, I can do whatever I want. Wow. It's hard to believe this, but I can do whatever I want!

These thoughts, these epiphanies, these life-altering conclusions hit hard and left Amanda thunderstruck. These realizations sprung from a slight moment's questioning of the same old thought patterns.

An idea presented itself, and for some reason, tonight, right now, right here in this bar, the thought pattern's path traveled askew. It did not go down the same path. It went another direction.

The worn-out, hardened footprints in the snow were no longer the only way. Amanda had stopped, lifted her head, and looked to the left of the path and to the right of the path and saw the untouched fields of pristine white.

Amanda saw this pristine, virginal snow where she had not tread before. The excitement was overwhelming. The lure was enticing. The temptation was not going to be refused.

These instantaneous reactions and conclusions were questioned, mulled over, reasoned out, and eagerly accepted within an instant. Total awareness was regained. Amanda had experienced an internal and heartfelt atomic detonation that resulted in life-altering possibilities.

No one else cared. They didn't even notice, but to be fair there was nothing to notice. Time slowed down for Amanda as she came to these conclusions, but to everyone else who may have been watching, it was just a few steps and a pair of wide eyes on a gorgeous girl.

A new challenge. A new adventure. All of a sudden it hit her as she looked at a few of the ladies in the bar. Amanda had a realization that shattered all her preconceived notions.

Being with a woman may be a better experience. They might be better lovers. I'll just be with a woman. Yeah, why not? They would know my body better than any of these jerks. I would have more of a connection with a woman. There would be more of a bond. I want to be important to someone.

The cowboys could not pick up Amanda with their wives around, and frankly she was tired of the same old bullshit from all the nearly identical-looking guys. They all did the same thing, said the same thing, and acted the same way. It was cliché and tiresome. It would be a burden to continue down that path.

Amanda walked up to a cowboy and smiled. She heard him say, "Hey there, sweet cheeks," and she took his beer and drank from it. He smiled and was about to say something else stupid, and she just walked away. His friends laughed.

"Cockteasing bitch!" he said through clenched teeth.

That asshole was very interested, and then he spat a horrible insult in just an instant. They ultimately don't care. They never did care. Done with them. She spanked her ass and walked away.

Amanda was gorgeous. She wasn't being egocentric. It was just fact. Two plus two equaled four. The sun sets in the west, and Amanda was a knockout.

Tonight Amanda would try something new. She would share her beauty with a woman. No longer would she deny her desires due to a link to a past horror.

CHAPTER THIRTY

For the first time ever, Amanda cruised the bar not for a guy but for a woman. Again, it shouldn't be too difficult. Normal population statistical data dictated that there should be some lesbians in the bar.

It was the twenty-first century, and they didn't have to hide anymore. They've always been a contingent in any population, so hopefully now they're less hidden and in the mood.

In an instant, a glance can evolve into a look that can display attraction. So far the glances were all glances of only being awestruck by Amanda's beauty, irrespective of orientation. None had turned into a legitimate situation where the attraction could lead to an encounter that could progress.

Some girls appeared down for some fun, but Amanda did not want fun. She was not interested in some bullshit spring-break "I kissed a girl for a shot" shenanigans.

Amanda had, over the years, heard about a bar frequented by local gays and lesbians somewhere in Old Falls. She did not know the name or location. She could catch a cab, and the driver would know, maybe. It was near closing time though. It was freezing. It was late. Maybe that was a good thing. Plus, she had no desire to go to Old Falls. She did not care for the people on that side of town.

She should just slow down a little. Baby steps. *Go home and do some soul-searching and think over your decision to seek a woman.* Maybe she was being too spontaneous. Maybe she should watch some lesbian porn and see how she enjoyed it. Then she saw her.

A full-figured lady with long, auburn hair was looking at her as she walked into the bar and sat down. Their eyes met. The glance went from a glance to a look. This look then graduated to a passionate stare with an accompanying self-imposed lip bite and restrained smile.

Amanda was surprised at how attractive and confident this pretty lady was as she sat down at the bar like she owned the place. This lady was truly good-looking. And the more she looked at her, the more attractive she became. A well-built, attractive girl next door was sharing passion with her eyes.

This sensual, natural beauty had a voluptuous body and was somewhere in her twenties. She looked like she was a down-to-earth chick who was comfortable in her own skin. Amanda was instantly drawn to her.

Sure, there may have been younger, taller ladies there with skinnier bodies and trendy tattoos, but this woman was a true knockout. She appeared confident and comfortable as if she had no insecurities. She exchanged a glance with Amanda, clearly indicating that she was attracted to her, and she did not hide it. *Confidence is sexy!*

Amanda felt some butterflies in her stomach. Amanda's confidence was a little disrupted. Instead of assuming this woman wanted her, she really hoped that they would connect and get to know each other.

Amanda hoped this was not just someone who thought Amanda was only sexy, but someone who wanted to be attached to that beauty and, more importantly, recognize her own inner beauty.

Amanda was smiling a genuine smile of happiness when she sat down on the stool next to the attractive woman. "Hi." She extended her hand. "I'm Amanda."

Sarah smiled and simply said, "I know."

CHAPTER THIRTY-ONE

Amanda was puzzled. "I'm sorry, have we met before?"

The beautiful woman placed her hand on Amanda's arm, gently rubbed it back and forth, and said, "No, no, I just know who you are. I'm Sarah. It's nice to meet you." They shook hands.

"Well, I'm a little curious," Amanda stated with a hint of cute worry.

"Oh, it's nothing," Sarah chuckled. "My stepdad has owned this place for a long time is all. I've seen you around. People know your name."

Now Amanda got a little nervous. Her quest for perfection was now a shame. "Oh, um…" Amanda didn't know what to say. She didn't know if she should explain things or get defensive.

The lady appeared to not care as she asked, "What can I get you, Amanda?"

Feeling more confident and relieved, Amanda asked, "Well, um, what are you having?"

"Guinness," she said to the bartender.

"You got it, Sarah. And what can I get you?"

The bartender silently appeared and smiled warmly showing no preconceived notions based on Amanda's past. He was just a nice man eager to serve his customers. Amanda was pleasantly surprised.

Amanda was also surprised by Sarah's order as she too loved Guinness. She was sick to death of low-cal vodka and piss hipster beers. She looked at Sarah and said, "Nice!" She looked at the bartender. "Two please." Turning her attention back to Sarah, she said, "I freaking love Guinness!"

Not expecting that response, Sarah said, "That's awesome. I think we're gonna get along!" Amanda and Sarah smiled warmly at each other.

In a very bad and cheesy Irish accent, the bartender said, "Aye! Two pints of the black stuff for the two lovely lasses. Oh, Sarah, oh Sarah, the pipes, the pipes are calling."

Sarah laughed and said, "You need a little help there, Mr. McBadaccent."

"Well, maybe if your dad paid me more, I could take a trip to County Shillelagh, or whatever, and perfect it."

With no hesitation Sarah replied, "I'll bring it up at the next stockholders meeting."

Amanda laughed.

The bartender looked at both of them, nodded his head, and said, "All righty, two sneezers, coming right up."

Amanda laughed and said, "Hey, I liked your accent."

The bartender smiled proudly and said loudly over his shoulder to no one, "Cancel the two. Make it a single sneezer. Order in!"

Amanda was all smiles. "Well, I'll have to come here more often. This guy's a riot."

Sarah agreed. "Oh, he's hilarious. Everyone here is pretty cool."

"Yeah, I like this place. No fights. Few assholes. Staff is always polite. So your dad owns the bar and the bowling alley?"

"Yep. Bill McKenna. He's actually my stepdad. But I consider him to be my dad."

Amanda tilted her head a little to the side. "Ah, that's sweet. A supportive family helps. Do you work here full time?"

"Mmm, not really. I manage a few properties around town. Doesn't take much effort. So I'll come down here and help out when I can. What do you do besides break hearts?"

Amanda blushed as she said, "Oh, you," and grabbed and played with one of her braided pigtails for just a moment. She let it go and continued. "I'm finishing up school. I'm on the six-year plan—oops."

Sarah patted Amanda's hand and said, "Hey, it doesn't matter how long it takes. It's an accomplishment."

Amanda smiled. "Aw, thanks. Less than a year, I should be done. I hope."

"Then what?"

"No idea." They both laughed.

Amanda turned her head as she saw the bartender walk up with two beautiful pints of black. "Maybe I'll become a bartender's apprentice?"

The bartender acted angered and asked, "What? You think I need help? You don't think I can keep up?"

Amanda said very seductively, "No, no, I hear things. You can definitely keep up." She smiled.

"Ladies, ladies, flattery will get you everywhere," the smiling bartender stated.

Sarah simply replied, "You wish."

The bartender nodded his head once or twice and said, "Yeah, yeah, a little bit. Nice to see you two, and these are on me." He rapped the bar with his knuckles twice and walked toward another customer.

Sarah said, "Thank you. You didn't have to do that."

The bartender bowed his head and then asked a customer if he wanted another.

Amanda, even though she was used to free drinks, took this free pint to heart. It meant a lot to her. "Thank you so much," she said to the bartender, and she turned to Sarah. "Wow! That was so nice of him. We'll have to go out again."

Sarah simply replied, "OK."

They clinked glasses and took very respectable pulls.

CHAPTER THIRTY-TWO

For the next hour or so, Amanda and Sarah talked. It was not the usual chitchat you might witness in a bar nearing closing time. It was a very in-depth and personal conversation.

Amanda instantly trusted Sarah. Amanda's walls came down quickly. She happily took in and cherished every word Sarah spoke. She wanted to know all about her past, her goals, her hardships, and her struggles. Amanda wanted to know what made Sarah *Sarah*.

It was a different type of an attraction Amanda had for Sarah. Of course, she was sexually attracted to her—she was very pretty. But there was something deeper. It was a connection that was as strong as a best friend or someone in an exclusive relationship would have.

All these new feelings made Sarah that much more appealing to Amanda. Also what was appealing was the chance of a future. There was a genuine possibility that this authentic connection could last for more than a night. Amanda felt like she did not have to act like her former self.

Wow! Former self. I don't have to be that person anymore. The more Amanda got to know Sarah, and the more Sarah got to know Amanda, there was a mixture of playful and exciting nervousness and heartfelt emotion.

Amanda was dreading that Sarah would know of her past, be disgusted, and also realize that Amanda was not a tried-and-true traditional lesbian. They had not brought up their sexual orientations yet. Was that something to be confirmed? Did Sarah just assume that Amanda knew? Was Amanda to just assume that Sarah knew that Amanda assumed? Amanda's facial expression gave away her concerns.

"You OK?" Sarah asked.

Amanda wanted to confess everything and unburden herself of all the unpleasant truths. Sarah deserved total honesty. Amanda was afraid Sarah would walk away, but Amanda had to get things off her chest.

"Look," Amanda gazed into her empty pint glass, her third empty pint glass. She felt as if she should try to be quiet. She'd been drinking vodka before she had three pints of Guinness, and maybe she was not in the best state of mind. She reminded herself that she had a high tolerance and continued.

"I don't know if I'm a lesbian. OK? But the thought of it is fucking exciting. I wanna experience it. I wanna experience it with you. But, I don't even know if you're a lesbian. I saw you, and I was instantly attracted to you." Amanda made eye contact with Sarah. "I think you're just unbelievable. After getting to know you, I think you're fucking amazing. I think being with you would make me feel things I've never felt before."

Amanda placed her hand on Sarah's and squeezed. To her wonderful relief and excitement, Sarah squeezed back and said, "I am…a lesbian, sweetie, and I am…ridiculously attracted to you. Have been. But that's nothing new. Everyone is."

Sarah took a deep breath and leaned in. "Amanda, if there was no chance of a relationship or intimacy with you, I still would have gotten to know you, hon."

Amanda felt the relief wash over her, and she instantly felt lighter. Amanda closed her eyes and bowed her head. Sarah placed her left hand on Amanda's face. With no hesitation Amanda kissed her hand, looked into Sarah's eyes, and said, "Thank you."

Sarah stood up and embraced Amanda, and Amanda took in every emotional connective essence of this wonderful embrace.

CHAPTER THIRTY-THREE

"Last call, for alcohol," came from the comedic bartender. This was greeted with a collective booing. It was a customary routine to follow this up with hurling as many insults as you could at the bartender.

Around the 11th Frame, it became a rite of passage for any new server or bartender to announce last call: a little baptism by fire for the newly unknowing hired worker to see how thick his or her skin was, to see if the person could take a joke, and to introduce the new worker to the club, so to speak. Everyone laughed and had a good time with it because it was all in good fun.

"I know, folks. I know. I'm gonna miss you, too."

"Fuck off!"

"But I'll see you tomorrow. C'mon now. Spend some quality times with the kids."

"My kids are asleep, asshole."

"Maybe read a book."

"I'm gonna bang your mom,"

"Wake up early and run some laps."

"Maybe your grandma, too."

"And be all that you can be."

"Fuck off!"

"Hey, hey, hey, I already heard that one. Be original now."

"Oh, sorry, guess I'm tired. Take care. Good night."

"Get home safe, everyone."

As the hoopla died down and people said their good-byes, Amanda got sad. She did not want this night to end. Amanda lost track of time as Sarah gave her the most satisfying embrace of her life.

Amanda felt loved and protected like never before. She felt that she'd been honest for the first time in her life, honest in terms of being able to be herself and admit that she felt emotion for someone else and not just a hollow need to reach a goal.

Sarah was not a vehicle to seek recognition, rather a vehicle to seek happiness. Sure, she'd just met her, but she knew that regardless of what occurred after the embrace ended, Amanda was going to know and love Sarah in any possible way.

Sarah kissed the top of Amanda's head, and they separated. Amanda was dazed and not because of the alcohol. "Sucks that had to end," Amanda said with regret.

"Plenty more where that came from, hon," Sarah stated as she ran her fingers through Amanda's golden locks.

Amanda took a deep breath in and said, "Guess we gotta leave, huh?"

"Yeah, they have some closing to do."

Amanda looked into Sarah's eyes and confessed, "I don't know what happens now." This remark was stated with confidence as she did not know.

"Well," Sarah started as she went to retrieve her jacket, "I'm walking you to your car, and you're gonna wear this."

Amanda put it on, and they said their good-byes to the nice bartender and thanked him again.

"My pleasure, ladies. Get home safe!"

They walked into the night air. It was frigid. It was still. It was almost quiet. The other patrons were in their cars and leaving. Sarah asked, "Which one is yours? Betcha I can guess."

Amanda laughed. "Oh, sorry, I took a cab. I don't drink and drive."

"Oh, good. Neither do I. Do you want to split a cab?" A look of worry came across Sarah's face that made Amanda pensive and sad.

"What?" Amanda asked with some urgency.

"Nothing, sweetie, I just…On second thought, I just think we shouldn't rush into anything. I think we should take our time."

Amanda's pensiveness continued.

Sarah added, "Don't get me wrong. I want to be your first and make love to you all fucking night. I promise! But I see a future with you. Rushing into something can complicate things, you know?"

Amanda smiled.

Sarah continued and held Amanda's face. "I have feelings for you. I think you know that."

Amanda nodded.

Sarah continued. "I want to know you for a long time, hon. We take our time and make this perfect. OK?"

Amanda could not believe what she was about to say. "You're the first person who has denied me, and I love that." Amanda leaned in and kissed Sarah with a loving passion that simply erased Amanda's past conquests in the very instant their lips met. Amanda was reborn.

It was a loving display of a soulful connection between two loving people who had found something they'd been searching for their entire lives. Their passion was only matched by their emotional bond. They were as one. They gently released their lips and ended the wonderful kiss.

Amanda looked into Sarah's eyes and said, "That was the greatest kiss of my life." They hugged each other.

Sarah whispered into Amanda's ear, "Me too, hon." They separated to arm's length and held each other's hands.

"Well, I don't know how much energy you have left, but can I call you? Tonight, I mean. Are you going home, or are you headed somewhere else?"

Amanda smiled because she thought she detected just a hint of Sarah being twitterpated. Amanda was touched.

Amanda got closer and held Sarah's hips and said, "Of course you can call me," and gave Sarah a quick kiss. "That's my second one. Still loving it," she said with some giggling. Amanda reached into her back pocket and pulled out her phone. They exchanged numbers. They kissed for a third time and hugged each other once more.

Sarah said, "OK, hon, I'm really fucking cold. The only two things that could make me walk away now are the fucking cold and the fact that I will talk to you soon, and, uh, hopefully see you tomorrow?"

Another quick kiss on the lips, and Amanda said, "Of course."

With confidence Sarah said, "Keep the jacket if you're walking home. I'm taking a cab." She put two fingers in her mouth and loudly whistled for a cab. Instantly the cab turned a corner into the parking lot and pulled right up next to the two starry-eyed ladies.

"You sure you don't need a ride, hon?"

A long passionate fifth kiss was followed by Amanda saying, "No, thank you. You were right. We'd probably end up at one of our places. Whichever's closer I bet."

They both laughed.

Amanda continued. "Besides, I'm expecting an important call soon." She smiled.

"Oooh, anyone I know?"

"Well, I'm not one to kiss and tell, but so far I'm head-over-heels impressed."

Sarah just smiled and longingly looked into Amada's eyes. "I'm glad I met you, hon."

"Me, too."

"Walk home safe."

"Talk to you real soon."

The cab pulled away. Amanda watched it go until it was completely out of sight. She wrapped Sarah's coat around her tightly and put her hands in the pockets. The cold, which appeared all of a sudden, made her walk fast—that and the call she was expecting. As Amanda quickly walked home, she thought she heard someone whispering.

The cab driver exchanged greetings with his pretty new passenger and asked for an address. Sarah stated where she was going and asked how he was. They chitchatted about the bar and the bowling alley, how her stepdad was the owner, and how he'd met Bill McKenna a few times and liked him.

The driver then mentioned to his new passenger that she "had quite the admirer," referring to the short and shadowed weirdo who was just absolutely engrossed with something that was going on near the entrance of the bar she was just at.

The driver was then interrupted by a radio call from dispatch, which he promptly answered and was engaged in until they pulled up to the address Sarah had given him.

Sarah listened to the driver's last statement and thought he was referring to Amanda and what they'd achieved this evening. Moments later, as the cab pulled up to her place, Sarah breathed in deeply, let it out slowly, put her hands to her face, inhaled the still-present aroma of Amanda's shampoo, and responded to the cab driver's statement, "Yes, quite the admirer."

CHAPTER THIRTY-FOUR

Amanda stopped walking when she heard the strange sound again. She thought it was coming from where the drug dealers hung out but dismissed that idea as it was very late and everyone was gone.

Amanda looked behind her, ahead of her, and back to the where the dealers hung out but did not see anything. After a moment or two, she saw little short arms wave to her.

"Hey! I can't get no love?"

Oh shit! This fucking guy! "Hey. How are ya?" Amanda perfunctorily asked while leaning toward the direction she was walking, indicating very clearly with her body language that this exchange was going no further.

"I'm good, baby. Little cold. Maybe you can warm me up, huh?"

I literally want to throw up and build a time machine and go back and not fuck you, you disgusting ugly piece of shit that means less than nothing to me. "Yeah, not gonna happen. Have a good night."

Perplexed, the Elf said, "Hey! Wait a minute. Where the fuck you going, baby? It's me. You don't remember me? C'mon now!" It was stated in a groveling manner that made Amanda want to leave with more haste.

"Guess I don't. See ya."

Taking it as a personal insult, the Elf hustled up to Amanda as she was quickly walking away, crossed into her path, and asked again, "You really don't remember me?"

"No." She dodged left and right to walk around him and end this unfortunate run-in. "I guess I don't."

"You gotta be kidding me, baby," the Elf stated as he blocked her. "Oh, wait, I know. I know what's up. We were partying hard when we hooked up. Ha, ha, that's it. All my bitches know who the fuck I am."

"Yeah, that must be it. G'night."

Amanda sidestepped the Little Fucker and walked on, but he simply rotated his body and placed his arm on her shoulder as she walked by. "Where we headed, sweet tits?" They looked like they were a couple, for one step.

Amanda erupted in anger. "Get your fucking hands off me!" She spun away from him and kept walking, but the Elf kept at it.

"Baby, what the fuck is up your ass? Besides not my fat dick. Ha-ha!"

"Get the fuck away from me!"

Confused again, he said, "Baby, I just wanna party. C'mon now. Why you gotta do me like this, baby?"

Absolutely livid with a colossal amount of hatred she'd never experienced before, Amanda clenched her teeth and spoke with such violent acrimony that it caused her face to go red.

Amanda was enraptured with the freedom Sarah allowed her to have. Sarah did not grant freedom like a government leader grants clemency, but she aided Amanda in gaining a clearer perspective. Sarah was in the right place at the right time to aid the transition. Her presence in this new chapter of Amanda's life was very fortunate.

Amanda's rebirth and her new course was a gift she loved. However, this piece of shit was a reminder of a past that disgusted her. Amanda wanted to forget the mistakes. Amanda only wanted to hear Sarah's voice and go to sleep and dream about her. This monster would not let her go home.

Amanda's depression had always been present in some degree. The depression was a bastardized offshoot of a rage—rage from a violation at such an early and innocent age.

Amanda was helpless against this early betrayal and its aftermath. The fact that this rage was an obstacle to her success and contentment only festered and created more rage. This rage morphed into an obsession to be perfect and to please. This was the final straw. This rage could no longer be contained. All the regret and sadness and anger and fear and resentment exploded.

"You fucking piece of shit! I fucking hate you, you know that? You ugly short-dicked illiterate piece of shit! It makes me sick what I did, and I only did that for pills, you asshole. If I could, I'd take a scalpel and carve out of my brain that fucking disgusting memory I have. It makes me wanna throw up. It fucking shames me. So just get the fuck out of my way, loser!"

The Elf was tired of being insulted and put down. In his eyes, all the girls he talked to dug him. It wasn't the drugs that he had. They genuinely liked him and were impressed with the way he carried himself—like a G. Like a businessman. Like a playa.

Throughout this day, he'd received a lot of insolence and was humiliated. He was clueless as to why. He used to be respected. He decided to make a stand.

The Elf stared at Amanda with severity in his eyes. "You really don't wanna fuck with me. Not today, you fucking dyke." The Elf was planning to go on and speak more threats but was interrupted.

In a mere fraction of a second, after she heard the epithet *dyke*, Amanda, with her hands in the pockets of Sarah's jacket, spread them, opening up the jacket and allowing her to quickly kick the Elf in the balls with no warning.

Unfortunately, with all the studying of the male anatomy she accomplished in her former life, Amanda was not familiar with the fact that when in a cold environment, the male genitalia has the characteristics of compacting and withdrawing. Plus, the Elf had private parts that were in proportion to the rest of his small features.

What the Elf received was a painful kick to the insides of his legs. Although painful and uncomfortable, it was not as detrimental as a kick to the balls should have been. Amanda was banking on this as she tried to deke around the mildly hurt Elf.

The Elf reflexively grabbed at the jacket, which caused Amanda to rotate and lose her footing. With her next step, her foot landed in a crack in the old road's asphalt. Amanda shrieked at the pop she felt as her ankle severely twisted, and her high boot heel offered no support.

Instantly, she knew she had a broken ankle. She retracted her leg, and while in midair, with no point of her making contact with the ground, she moved her hands and arms to clutch her injured ankle.

As the uninjured ankle made contact with the ground, the ice saw to it that there would be no safe landing. As she slid up, heels over her head, a tremendous velocity had been created, causing a violent impact. Her head made a cruel and devastating landing on the asphalt.

Amanda's skull cracked. It was particularly loud in the still night. Amanda began to convulse. Uncontrollable shaking and the crimson stream on the frozen ground let the Elf know that Amanda was in a dire situation.

The Elf panicked. His inner-leg pain was temporarily forgotten as he walked over to Amanda. He leaned over her with his hands out like he wanted to attempt to hold her down. "Oh no. Oh no," muttered the Elf through heavy breath as he tried to figure out what to do.

"OK, OK, uh, the alley's closed, and they won't let me in. Did I bring..." The Elf made a mad dash to his station. When he got to his standing point, he checked his bag and found his burner cell phone.

"Ahh!" he yelled with relief and dialed 911. The cold had a delaying effect on his dexterity, but he did manage to dial successfully. Just as he stood up, he saw a really big guy run over to Amanda on the street.

The big guy kneeled down, screamed, "Hey!" back toward the alley, waited two seconds, took off his jacket, placed it on top of the still-convulsing Amanda, and ran back to the entrance, where he banged on the front door for a few seconds.

The Elf was on his fourth or fifth ring to 911. He saw someone open the door, and the big guy shouted something and then ran back to Amanda.

"Nine-one-one, what is your emergency? Nine-one-one, what is your emergency? Nine-one-one, emergency, are you able to give a location?"

The Elf ended the call on his burner cell phone, and as silently as possible, he ran away, forgetting his bag.

CHAPTER THIRTY-FIVE

Deeds was just about to leave for the day. He went inside Bill's office to say good night, but he was on the phone. Bill did his patented index finger, thumb trigger, one-eye wink to say good night and then pointed to the envelope on his desk adorned with Deeds's name. Deeds picked up the envelope and rapped his knuckles on the metal desk twice and headed to the break room.

Deeds unplugged the coffeemaker he'd specifically purchased for himself and the staff. He rinsed out and washed the coffee pot and dried it as best he could with the cheap brown paper towels. He opened the little fridge and checked the levels of the milk and the cream. They were half...full. They were half full.

He grabbed his jacket from the peg on the break room's wall and looked at the back and saw no sign of any stain. A loogie had been spat onto it recently, but a thorough washing made the jacket brand-new again, even though it was already brand-new. *I wonder how Lindsay is.*

He made his way to the front door and braced for the impact of the cold air. He took in a lungful of the crisp air, thought about Sarah's mysterious reference to Jess, closed the door behind him, checked that it was locked, and headed toward his truck. He then saw something strange.

Deeds saw someone on the ground shaking. A normal passed-out drunk did not shake like that. Mindful of the ice, Deeds ran over and saw the stream of crimson.

Blood and convulsions. There's not much time. He shouted at the front door, to no avail. Deeds placed his hand on the side of her face and said to the familiar-looking and violently shaking young lady on the ground, "Stay with me." He took off his jacket and placed it on her, hoping the warmth would help increase her chance of survival.

Deeds made a mad dash for the front door and banged on it loudly till someone ran up to unlock it. The nice-guy bartender, whose name Deeds could never remember, ran up, with Bill the owner close behind him.

"Call an ambulance right now! We have a massive head trauma! Go!"

The bartender said nothing and sprinted to the phone by the front desk and dialed.

Bill yelled, "I got a first-aid kit." He ran to his office.

Deeds ran back outside and kneeled by the girl's side. The convulsions had slowed considerably. "Oh no," Deeds said as he felt for a pulse. A very faint one was found on her carotid artery. Deeds was relieved but did not hope for the best. "Stay with me, hon. Stay with me," he said as he took out his handkerchief and placed it on the head wound in an attempt to cease blood flow.

Deeds looked at the gorgeous woman on the floor and kept thinking, *Not again. Not again.* He looked up to see the bartender running and heard him yell, "They're on their way!" Bill was behind him with a first-aid kit.

Bill asked, "How is she?"

Deeds yelled, "Gauze and a survival blanket!"

Bill opened the case and handed the gauze to Deeds who promptly let go of his soaked handkerchief, opened the package, and applied it to the wound while Bill opened the blanket and quickly unfolded it.

Bill stated a couple of times, "She'll be fine. She'll be fine. They'll fix her right up."

The bartender looked at Deeds and asked, "Did you see what happened?"

Deeds replied, "No. I walked out and saw her convulsing. I put my jacket on her, ran back, and got you guys."

No one really knew what to do. It's difficult to be helpless. You know someone's life is in dire straits, but being unable to do anything about it is the embodiment of frustration.

This dying young lady had a big, cold-weather parka on; a survival blanket; thick gauze on her head wound, held in place by Deeds's big hand; the bartender checking her ulnar pulse; and Bill standing up and looking for a few moments and then kneeling down while asking rhetorically, "Where are they?"

Bill then asked, "Was she hit by a car? Was this a hit-and-run? I mean, that's a broken ankle right there."

Deeds had not noticed her ankle was at an angle that was indicative of being broken.

Deeds looked away as this was the second catastrophically broken bone he'd recently seen. The bartender could not take it and turned around to control his nausea. Bill had a very sad look on his face as he viewed the protruding jagged bone for a moment or two and then hung his head and slowly shook it. He was genuinely sorry someone had endured such a horrendous injury.

This compound fracture was a truly awful and saddening sight. Deeds pulled the blanket down to cover it. All three men were frustrated and eager for the ambulance to show up.

Deeds then let his vision focus on all the fissures in the old asphalt. There certainly was a lot of uneven ground to walk on. He wondered about the ice, which could have caused the unfortunate fall. He looked up a few more feet and saw where the drug dealers usually hung out. Then he remembered the Little Fucker standing out there earlier, before Sarah came to him to break up the fight.

Jumping to conclusions is a feature of mob-rule mentality. However, Deeds saw the Little Fucker there earlier, and then he sees a gravely injured woman, and he does not see the Little Fucker there anymore. Deeds knew that it was not coincidence.

Deeds wished he could be like a cop from an eighties action movie and beat a confession out of that Little Fucker. Then he wished he could be like a mobster and choke him with wire.

Deeds knew that Little Fucker had something to do with this, and he wanted to beat that scumbag within an inch of his life.

Bill asked, "Any idea what happened to her?" He knelt down as the bartender shook his head and remained silent. "Any idea at all?"

Deeds heard the sirens a split second before the other two guys did. He continued to look over at the dark area in the parking lot across from the bowling alley's parking lot and then shook his head. "No idea." *God damn you, you Little Fucker!* "I have no idea what happened to her."

CHAPTER THIRTY-SIX

The Elf was fucked, yet again, and even further so. He had fled the parking lot after watching Amanda crack her skull and violently convulse. Three guys, including some big dude, were there, and they, no doubt, called 911.

The Elf really did not do anything to hurt Amanda, but try telling that to the cops while your previous murders were still fresh in a trailer and you were peddling illegal narcotics. *Officer, you're not gonna believe this, but...*

The Elf fled toward his car parked a half mile down the road behind some buildings. As soon as he was in sight of his car, he realized he'd forgotten his bag.

The unfixable and uncorrectable and ruinous revelation hit him like an actual effective kick in the nuts. His eyes went wide, he gasped, and he placed his hands on his knees and just shook his head, repeating, "No, no, no...," over and over.

The bag held the cash he made tonight and the rest of the product that was going to save his life. Now, he did not have it. The Elf was frozen in utter despair. *You gotta be fucking kidding me!*

It was now officially a disaster. He was in a world of shit. Before, he was in a real tight spot, but there was always a chance of climbing out of the hole. Now, he was still short, he was down product, and he could not sell the miniscule remaining product he had in his pockets to make the quota.

The Elf realized there was no way he could sneak back and retrieve the bag. If Amanda ended up dying at the scene, the area may be taped off as a murder scene. If she was still alive by the time the ambulance got there and they transported her to the hospital, the police would still be present.

The Elf could not get over how truly fucked he was. There was nothing he could do. Now he only had one option: leave.

No matter what I do, no matter how badly I fuck up, or any attempts to unfuck myself, I end up fucking myself up even further. What's the point?

The Elf did not have the money nor did he possess the means to make money. He was now indirectly involved in one potential death and directly involved in two, well, three other deaths.

Potential? Amanda's dead. She was convulsing like crazy. She couldn't survive that. But if she did, she could identify me. I have to leave.

The decision was made. The Elf knew he had to lie low and make preparations to get the hell out of Engel Falls.

With what he had in his pockets, he thought he could weasel his way onto the couch of someone for a night or two. He needed to be out of sight, and the Elf was pretty confident that the higher-ups would not know the location of his hideout—the couch of some random druggie from Old Falls.

Another concern the Elf had was that he had called 911 and hung up. He'd heard all 911 hang-ups were investigated, but he did not know if that was bullshit or not. In the old days, it was easy to see the number and address of the household that hung up, but in the cellphone age, who knew?

So he got in his car and did the speed limit to his next location, which was a small independent gas station that closed at nine and still had a working pay phone. He made a few calls and finally found some chick who agreed to let him stay over. He knew he was cool for tonight and tomorrow night, so he'd go home and prepare to leave.

In two nights, when the chick got home, he'd head over to her place. He already forgot her name but memorized her address. He usually dropped off the payment at a bar in Old Falls at ten, so if he didn't show up at the bar in two nights, he figured they'd be at his place first thing the following morning or maybe even later that night.

He thought he'd play it safe and leave his place in the afternoon before the money was due, disappear, and then pull a no-show at the bar at ten. Technically, he could remain at his place till about one minute after, when he was officially late, but why take chances?

The Elf would have a few hours to kill. Maybe he'd go to the movies in a darkened theater. Maybe he'd find some random campground and park. Maybe he'd drive around, so he'd always be moving. Maybe he'd get a motel room for a few hours and then check out and head over to her place when she got home after after the bars close. *Maybe she's hooking. Definitely getting laid, then.*

After he called the girl from the pay phone, he wiped his fingerprints from the receiver. He then looked around on the ground and found a rock the size of a baseball and picked it up.

He took out his burner cell phone and dropped it to the ground. He knelt down and hit the cell with the rock many times, shattering it. He picked up the small pieces, threw them in a trash canister, and rearranged some other garbage, so the pieces were not visible.

No ties to the 911 call that came precisely at the same time the call from the 11th Frame was made and no ID from any of the three guys who went to Amanda's aid. The Elf headed home for quite possibly the last time.

The Elf parked his car in a cul-de-sac a ways away from his place, just in case. He was not late with the payments yet, and he was all but certain the cops could not figure out who called 911 and hung up. Barring any unforeseen circumstance, the cops would not be at his place. *Just being safe.* Paranoia and caution are always on the forefront of the guilty but not yet caught.

The Elf noticed nothing out of the ordinary, so he entered his place with confidence. Once inside, he gathered some clothes and put them in the old military-surplus duffel bag. He organized and packed and prepared to abandon most of his possessions. He packed clothes that were practical and bid farewell to his swagger. Maybe tomorrow he'd go to a thrift store and buy a real winter coat. *Gonna be cold on the road.*

CHAPTER THIRTY-SEVEN

Deeds got up early for the second day in a row. His mind was restless. It had been a very odd week. The highs, the lows, the connections, the detachments, the loss of life, and the violence were taking a toll.

The date with Jess was a distraction but he did not bank on a positive next step. He wanted to be hopeful but thought that would be unhealthy.

This thought made Deeds sad and then he would remember the scene of that pretty girl convulsing. Sadness and anger were present on this morning.

That pretty girl had more than likely been killed by that piece of shit they called the Elf, and Deeds wanted to find him. The act of the search would lift Deeds's spirits. *What if I get lucky and actually find him? Then what?*

Deeds showered, got dressed, ate, and was pouring the remainder of his coffee in a to-go thermos when there was a knock at his door. It was just after eight, and despite the infrequent visitors he had, this was particularly peculiar since it was so early. *Chances are it's not Jess asking me to moisturize her body and to begin a relationship.*

He unlocked the three locks and opened the door to a no-nonsense-looking older man with a brand-new haircut.

Casually, Deeds said, "Good morning."

"Good morning," the gray-haired stranger in a trench coat said and then referred to a pocket-sized notebook, indicating he was more than likely a police detective.

"Are you Shane Deeds?"

"I am."

"Mr. Deeds, I'm—"

"Shane."

"OK, Shane. I am Detective Joe Duran of the Engel Falls Police Department. May I have a word with you?"

"Yes."

Trying to establish familiarity and to assuage concern for the purposes of disarming any resistance the big man in the doorway might possess, Joe asked, "It's a little cold this morning. May I come in please?"

With no hesitation, Deeds said, "Perhaps. What's this about?"

This sent a message to Joe. *He's one of the Good Samaritans from the other night, but he's hiding something. I don't think he did it, but he's hiding something.*

"Well, you gave the officers a statement the other night. You and two other gentlemen. Is that correct?"

"Yes."

"Well, unfortunately, things have changed. The young lady died at the hospital yesterday evening. She was in surgery—the brain trauma, the swelling, and so on…She passed away."

Deeds was saddened by this news, and his demeanor change was of genuine mourning, yet not enough for a familiar status. Joe thought, *He didn't know her.*

"I'm sorry to hear that. How old was she?"

"You didn't know the victim?"

"I did not. I've seen her around the alley and the bar but didn't know her."

"So you've seen her before?"

"Yes."

"But you didn't know her?"

"I did not."

"Can you tell me anything about her?"

"I don't know anything other than what I've recently learned."

"Which is what?"

"That she died from brain trauma, sir."

"Of course."

Joe and Deeds stood staring at each other for a moment or two. Joe could not get a reading on this guy.

"Shane, before you ask, I have witnesses that put you inside the alley. You're not a suspect. I checked the security footage, which had time coding."

Deeds was happy to hear this, but he still did not trust the detective.

"We have statements from a cab driver and another acquaintance of the victim that you were not in sight. The same cab driver said there was a suspicious-looking character in the parking lot across from the 11th. We have statements from Bill McKenna and"—the detective looked at his notes but could not seem to locate the name—"the bartender that you were inside the alley and then left and then came right back to get the authorities alerted. And we have statements saying how you kept her alive. Now"—Joe stood up tall—"may I come in, so my ass can thaw out? Please?"

Shane did not blink. Then he nodded and said as if he knew, "You take it black."

Shane hid the thermos as he poured its contents into two regular mugs. The detective did not need to know that Shane was just about to leave his apartment. Apartment leaving is not a crime, but it would lead to questions, and Deeds did not want to answer questions falsely. Two sugars and cream for Deeds and black for the detective.

Joe asked some "getting to know you" questions: How long have you lived here? What line of work are you in? Where are you from originally? And so on.

Deeds was not rude but not overly friendly. He was not quiet nor was he talkative. You do not show your hand if they do not call, and you do not let the car salesman know that you are interested in the car.

Joe was drawn to this big man he was interviewing. There was something about Deeds that Joe trusted. *Seems like a stand-up guy.*

"So since the victim died—"

"She was a person. Can you refer to her by her name please?" The big man was sincere. *Stand-up guy.*

"I'm sorry. I can't do that till we notify the family. Regulations." The detective made a face that displayed his seeming annoyance with his higher-ups and his seeming regret at not being able to identify the victim.

That may have worked well with other suspects and people being interviewed, but the detective's habitual utilization of this ploy decreased his effort to the point of being ineffective.

"Sir," Deeds began, "your overuse of that facial expression, lo these many years, to demonstrate how you really wish you could divulge that info…'But damn it—my bosses won't let me'…is not an effective strategy with me. You're attempting to make a connection based on how we both hate bosses. Then when I'm comfortable with you, I'll divulge anything I'm hiding. I'm sorry, but I'm not hiding anything." Deeds guessed the Elf was responsible, so he hid that from the detective.

Joe picked up a "tell" and knew that Deeds was hiding something. He was not the one who'd committed the crime, but he was hiding something. Joe underestimated this man. Joe trusted Deeds to be a "good guy," but he picked up a definitive "tell." *What are you hiding?*

"Look, I'm sorry. I didn't mean to belittle your intelligence. You're right. You get into a routine, and you rely on it to the point where you make no effort. And bluntly speaking, dealing with the Old Falls shit bags day in and day out, my act works most of the time."

Deeds respected the detective but still could not trust him. "I don't doubt that, Detective."

Joe drained his coffee. "This is wonderful by the way."

"Thank you. I don't fuck around with my coffee."

Joe was impressed by this man and said, "Obviously not."

Joe took in a deep breath and acted as if he was conflicted over something but then chose a path, a path of forthcoming. "Her name was Amanda. She was twenty-four and a student at State. The last people to see her, according to the bartender, whatever his name is, were a female friend at the bar, whom we've got coming down to make a statement, and a cab driver who says someone was nearby and acting suspiciously.

"Something else we found that was interesting, and you may be able to shed some light on, is a little area across the street from the alley."

Deeds played dumb. "The strip-mall parking lot?"

Joe didn't buy it. "Yeah, the parking lot where"—Joe slightly paused—"fuckers sell dope. I know you've seen them. The cab driver said he saw someone at the empty lot. You've seen them there."

"I never said I didn't."

"Well, what can you tell me?"

"Fuckers sell dope there."

The detective placed the tips of his index finger and thumb at the base of his nose between his closed eyes.

"If you're gonna be a wise ass, we can discuss this at the station."

"If that works better for you, tell me what time. I'll be there."

Joe chuckled. "Look, cut me a break, huh? I'm doing my job. We need some help here."

"I'm trying to do just that, sir."

Joe, feeling the fun of a challenge, said, "I know you've had run-ins with the dealers who sell there. You personally have bounced those small-time"—Joe slightly paused again—"fuckers out of the 11th, and you've seen them across the street."

"Yes."

"Can you give me a name or an alias?"

Deeds said, "No." Deeds shook his head one time too many and then immediately regretted the extraneous motion as it was a tell. Hopefully, it—and the regret for having committed a tell—were not visible. He continued. "I'll see some asshole peddling in the bar, and I escort him outside and call the police. I have seen people across the street. I don't go over there. If they see me or one of the other guys, they think twice about crossing the street."

Joe saw the tell and the subsequent regret. "I don't doubt that."

Deeds gave a slight nod to thank him for the compliment.

"So you think it was one of those small-time"—Deeds slightly paused—"fuckers that may have murdered Amanda?"

Throwing caution to the wind and knowing that this big guy with great coffee was on his side—rather, the side of what's right—Joe proffered much information.

"We found a bag, just a shopping bag, near where dealers have been known to set up shop. We found product and cash." The detective decided to try a tactic to hopefully force a truth out; lying. His lie was to insinuate something, even though it was bullshit, to try to get a nugget of truth about anything. A small-time nickel-and-dime dealer would be accused of a major sale, a major sale to the deceased, which might lead this big quiet guy to admit something—the something he was hiding.

"My experience tells me that the large amount of product is indicative of a major sale that did not happen. Amanda may have had something to do with this big deal."

Deeds held eye contact with the detective for several moments and then spoke. "So Amanda said good-bye, put her friend into a cab, and then tried to do a major deal?" Deeds shook his head. "That doesn't make sense."

"Why else would she happen to be there with a high-volume drug dealer with a large amount of product?"

"I've seen *The Wire,* sir. I'm sure the professionalism of these pieces of shit is quite lacking." Deeds thought for a second and continued. "Why didn't she split the cab with the friend? Where does Amanda live? Rather, was Amanda's place within walking distance?"

"Yes."

"So you think she was going to buy a lot of drugs and then walk home?"

"Maybe she did. Maybe she attempted to, but the dealer stole 'em back."

Deeds thought and shook his head again. "No. The location of Amanda goes against that. I found her a ways away from the sell spot. I don't think she said good-bye to her friend and then crossed the street, bought a bunch, got assaulted down the road, and got stripped of the drugs that were then left behind."

The detective was impressed as Deeds continued. "I saw no purse on her person or thrown away nearby. The dealer did not sell her a large amount of product that she was going to carry by hand out in the open to another destination—and then decide to kill her, take back his product, and manage to then forget it and the cash. Unless you find a purse that this twenty-four-year-old young lady would be seen with, and for other reasons, that story does not make sense."

"Well, you're very analytical. What do you think happened?"

"Well, utilizing the principle of Occam's razor, I think she said good-bye to her friend and, while walking home, got attacked and suffered a lethal brain trauma."

"That's pretty simple, no? Kinda boring and pretty linear, ain't it, Shane?"

"Well, I'm not telling you anything you don't already believe."

The detective shook his head and smiled. Joe's bullshit was not working. "Are you CIA?"

"No, they'd make me cut my hair."

They both laughed.

"Well, humbly, I'd say we're two smart guys who think she was attacked by some fucking shit bag who deals across from your alley. So back to my earlier question: who did you see that night and do you know the names or aliases of any of those pieces of shit?" The detective was pleading and demanding with ESP that Deeds say, *It was the Little Fucker. I saw the Elf assault her.*

Deeds shook his head and answered, "I'm sorry, Detective. I can't give you their names."

They held eye contact for several moments, until Deeds asked, "More coffee?"

CHAPTER THIRTY-EIGHT

Deeds decided not to leave his apartment for a little while even though apartment leaving was still not a crime. The detective left just before eight thirty. He gave Deeds his card in case he remembered anything. He also told Deeds that he would call him in a day or two and maybe he'd like him to come down to the station to go over a few things, but Deeds politely declined.

It would have been less noteworthy if Deeds had just diplomatically agreed. But Deeds did not fancy himself a liar. He was asked a question, and he answered, "No."

Joe was surprised and at the same time not. "Why?" he asked.

Deeds was honest. "The coffee's better here. No offense."

Joe put up his hands in an "I give up" fashion and simply stated, "You're right," and walked away.

It was just about two hours later. Deeds did not go to his windows to check to see if the detective was surveilling the apartment because then the detective would know that Deeds was checking to see if the detective was surveilling the apartment.

So Deeds sat on the couch. He made a snack and watched a little TV. Not used to watching TV this early, he deemed morning TV absolute trite shit. It was full of fake-news talk shows where the man and woman morning team faked interest in the guests' interests and unimportant traffic reports, kid's cartoons, and other garbage.

He turned it off and sat in silence. He was not asleep. His eyes were closed, yet he was upright. Sometimes closing his eyes and breathing slowly could aid in ways sleep could not.

After a few minutes, he heard Jess's lovely voice in the hall. Then he heard another female's voice. There was concern in their tones. He opened his eyes, got up, opened the door, and saw Jess and her half sister Sarah hugging each other. Sarah was crying.

Deeds walked up and with great concern asked, "Hey, Sarah, Jess. What happened?"

Jess was sympathetic to Sarah's emotions but was surprised to see that Deeds and Sarah were so friendly. Jess tilted her head and greeted him. "Hey, Shane. This is my—"

Sarah looked up and said in a sad voice, "Shane!"

With all her might, and it was substantial, Sarah wrapped her arms around Deeds and cried into his big chest. With familiarity that could take years to establish, Deeds and Sarah embraced each other like they were lifelong soul mates.

True, they had just met the other night, but their instincts told them to trust each other since there was a connection. Sometimes people just get along very well in a short amount of time. Deeds loved it and was thrilled that this closeness and trust had been established. Now she was crying, and Deeds needed to help her.

Sarah embraced Deeds while he placed his right hand on her lower back. His left hand caressed the back of her head while he kissed the top of her head in a very loving and protective manner. Deeds simply wanted to comfort Sarah and provide her with an embrace that held the assurance of a safe home. *Guess I should find out what happened.*

After some time Sarah let go and took a small step back with her left hand still touching him.

"What happened, hon?" Deeds thought that maybe Bill McKenna had had a heart attack or something. *The stresses of Amanda's attack perhaps.* "Is Bill OK?"

Sarah wiped her tears away and nodded, confirming Bill was OK, while Deeds's right hand was on her shoulder, massaging away tension.

Jess, surprised by their closeness, said with heartfelt sympathy, "Sarah lost someone close last night."

Deeds immediately opened his eyes wider and said, "Amanda?"

Sarah started to cry again, and they embraced each other for several more moments.

Not impatient, but simply wanting to know, Jess asked, "How'd you know, Shane?"

Before Deeds could answer, Sarah answered for him. "Shane kept her"—she took a breath—"Shane kept her alive till the medics showed up."

Jess exhibited a heartfelt reaction as she placed her hand on her mouth and made an "aw" sound.

Deeds continued to look at Sarah. "I did what I could. We did everything we could. Your stepdad, what's his face...the bartender—we all did everything we could until the ambulance came." Deeds used his big thumb to wipe Sarah's tears away. "I'm sorry, Sarah. I really am."

"Thank you, Shane. I know you are." Sarah side hugged him and said, "They said you kept her alive." She cried again. They embraced.

During the hug he looked at Jess and said, "A detective came over this morning."

"Oh," Jess said and nodded. "Any suspects? Any... leads or anything?"

Deeds shook his head. "I don't know. The guy just asked questions. Didn't say much. He was pretty tight-lipped."

Jess nodded.

Deeds was interested and tried to focus on a more positive aspect of their relationship. "How long were you two together?"

Sarah laughed with an ironic laugh. "That's the crazy part. I just met her the night before."

Deeds was surprised but a second later, not so much anymore.

Sarah continued. "It was really different. We met at the bar, and we hit it off. More so than hitting it off—we made a connection. An instant connection, you know?"

Deeds nodded and said, "People meet, and everything clicks. It happens." He made eye contact with Sarah, and she smiled. Deeds was about to look over at Jess, despite their date being very strange. Even though it was a rough night, he was still very much enthralled with her. Then a man's voice from inside Jess's apartment interrupted the potential for a "moment."

"What are you doing out there?"

With an annoyed look on her face, Jess answered, "We'll be in in a minute."

"What?"

"In a minute, Erik!"

Jess was agitated, but it was not all due to the interruption. A secret was now out, a secret that deemed her weak. Regardless, if she did not end the statement with the dreaded name Erik, it was obvious who was inside.

Shane looked over at Jess. All the feelings he held for her, still, up to this very moment, all the enchanting beauty he saw in her—everything was placed on hold. Jess had a guilty yet resolved look on her face. A face that communicated "I'm not doing anything wrong," but deep down she knew she was making a mistake. The easier step is a convenient one, especially when it has already been taken.

Did you fucking call him after I dropped you off, Jess? No, it was probably earlier. You probably made plans with him during our fucking date. I feel betrayed.

Sarah looked up at her sister and said, "Oh no. You're back with...him?"

"Him" was stated in an exaggerated whisper. Jess started to squirm. Deeds liked to think he had something to do with that. He said nothing, but as he viewed Jess, a completely new person was in his vision.

"Just shut up, OK? We'll talk later. Come inside. It's freezing." This statement from Jess was entirely directed to her sister.

Sarah vehemently shook her head. "I'm not going in there with that asshole! Are you fucking kidding me? He's a total asshole, Jess! What the fuck? All the shit he's put you through over the years. All the shit he's given me. He's such a close-minded asshole. C'mon!"

Jess squirmed even more. Did she feel guilt that Deeds found out this way? Did she feel bad for hurting his feelings? Was she showing remorse?

To her credit Jess looked up at Deeds and held his look for a while. It appeared she might have been about to apologize or say something, but Deeds cut her off.

"Sarah," he said as he looked into his friend's lovely eyes, "would you like some coffee?"

She very affectionately side-embraced him. "Thanks, Shane." They walked toward his apartment.

He opened the door for Sarah, and she said thank you as she walked in. Deeds looked over at Jess with some hurt, confusion, and sadness.

"Jess! What the fuck?" said Erik.

Jess looked down and then went inside her apartment. Deeds felt deceived. Even though he knew it was bound to happen, he had hoped it would not. No dice.

CHAPTER THIRTY-NINE

Deeds made a fresh pot of coffee after he took Sarah's jacket off and placed it on a hook near his front door. His jacket was on an adjacent hook. It was also Amanda's death shroud on that hook. *I am beset with death. Especially my jackets.*

They sat at Deeds's table and drank coffee. Sarah was all atwitter as she recapped her meeting of Amanda. Deeds listened, smiled, and laughed as Sarah poured her heart out. Then things became sad. Deeds got up and knelt in front of Sarah, and they hugged.

After several moments Deeds stood up and his knees cracked. "Sorry," he said in regards to the painful-sounding noise.

"Are you OK?" Sarah asked with concern.

"No, I'm fine. Bad knees."

Sarah stood up. "Here, give me your cup. I'll get refills. You sit on the couch."

Deeds said, "Thank you."

Deeds sat down on the left corner of the couch, sort of catercorner to the rest of the couch to his right. Sarah came by and placed his refilled cup to his left. He leaned that way to retrieve it and to take a quick sip. While Deeds did that, Sarah sat right next to him, grabbed his right arm, and rested her face on his big bicep.

Deeds was touched by the connection and tried to play it cool. He took a sip, put the mug down, and said and asked, "What a surreal experience you've been through. How you holding up?"

Sarah just shook her head slightly and said, "I'm numb."

Deeds leaned over and kissed the top of her head. "You've had quite a shock. You'll run the gamut of emotions. Just acknowledge what you feel and deny nothing. Embrace every emotion with honesty, and let it run its course."

Sarah silently nodded and squeezed his arm. "I don't know," she said moments later. "Is it weird to care so much about someone I just met?"

"No, not at all. Time doesn't dictate how much emotion you feel."

"Case in point, Shane. I'm here with you." She patted his arm. "I met you right before I met Amanda, but

I'm here with you. My idiot sister is down the hall, but I'm here with you. Thank you, Shane. Really."

"My pleasure, Sarah. You're a great person, and I'm sorry this happened."

Sarah caressed Deeds's arm. "Oh my God, am I keeping you from something?"

"No! No, I work nights. You know that."

Deeds leaned to his right and put his feet up on the coffee table, and Sarah leaned to her left, brought her legs up, and curled them beneath her. Her left arm was wrapped around Deeds's right arm, and Deeds's right hand held Sarah's right hand on her thigh.

The smell of fresh coffee permeated the warm apartment. Deeds reached for the remote and turned on the TV to the Classical Masterpiece music channel on a lowered volume. He also leaned forward, turned to the side, and grabbed the blanket that was on the back of the couch behind them and placed it on Sarah. Sarah's priceless response was "aww."

They continued to talk and remained close for over an hour. They enjoyed each other's company as they got to know each other.

They talked about the things that made them get up in the morning, what they wanted out of life, past experiences, past relationships, and the things they went through every day. Deeds very much enjoyed it. He was amused as he thought, *Wow, now this is a great date.*

Sarah eventually turned her head and looked at the clock. "Christ, is that really the time? I've got to go to work." She gave one final squeeze to Deeds's arm, which was asleep, but he'd be damned if he was going to say something to end that pleasant moment.

The blood rushing back into his deprived tissues was a relief as her recognition of the time thwarted acute compartment syndrome and subsequent amputation. "If this isn't an excuse to call in sick, I don't know what is," he said as he opened and closed his hand surreptitiously, trying not to be noticed.

Sarah stood up, folded the blanket, set it on the armrest, and walked over to the table where she had earlier taken off her shoes. "I'm gonna go in for just an hour or two. I'll explain it to the boss, and she'll be OK with it. She may be a little upset, but I want to do this face-to-face." These statements from Sarah had a tension in them. With her shoes on, Sarah stood up.

Deeds was thinking, and his expression communicated that. Deeds had met Sarah's boss many times. He had done numerous jobs on the various properties she then managed. Now she ran the company Sarah worked for.

She was a lesbian, too, and was probably interested in Sarah. Or perhaps she still was interested despite Sarah's attempt to leave the relationship. *One of these.*

"What's on your mind?" Sarah asked.

She was in for an interesting example of observational deduction with subsequent basis for conduct.

"Is the boss not dealing with the relationship ending well, or is she not dealing well with you not wanting to get into a relationship?"

Dumbfounded, she said, "Who the fuck told you that?"

"My observations," he quietly retorted. Deeds smiled and asked, "Which is it?"

"You're unbelievable."

"Thank you. Well?"

Sarah shook her head a few times and said, "Uh, yeah, she wants to date, but I don't. Telling her about Amanda may hopefully let her know there's no chance."

"With respect, I disagree."

"Really?"

"Yes."

"Why?"

With confidence Deeds said, "I think she'll see it as competition being eliminated. She will misconstrue what you say as a guilt-driven confession and think that you're subconsciously asking her for forgiveness and, on a deeper level, want her to know you're single."

A blank and pretty stare from Sarah displayed how blown away she was. Instantly trusting his thought processes, she asked, "So what should I do?"

"Well, say you've lost someone you're close with. She'll ask if it was family. She'll hope it was family, at first. You simply say no. Then explain how you need some time off. She'll casually, but with promptness, revisit and attempt to ascertain the identity, your personal connection, and importance of the departed. You then show some restrained anger, a 'How dare you?' sorta thing, and then walk out."

Sarah shook her head a few times and simply said, "Wow."

Deeds stood up and said, "I could be way wrong, but I think it'll play out that way. So, you know, be prepared. You don't need anything else to be burdensome today."

Deeds walked over to where she was standing and hugged her as if he'd been doing it for years. The confidence he did it with surprised him a little. He took one step back. She had a peculiar look on her pretty face.

Deeds asked, "You OK?"

Sarah took in a deep breath and did not reply.

Deeds's concern grew. "What's the matter? Now you look like something's on your mind."

"Well, it's kinda weird, on every level."

In suspense Deeds asked, "What is it?"

"Well, I don't know how else to say this, Shane, but I want to see you again."

Relieved, Deeds said, "Of course! Man, you scared me. Come over anytime. You know you're always welcome here."

Sarah shook her head while maintaining eye contact. "No. I want more, Shane." Sarah took two steps toward Deeds. "I want to...go on a date with you."

Deeds was silent and did not move. He was surprised and confused. "But I thought you were—"

"I know. I know, but once upon a time, I had a boyfriend or two before, you know, I acknowledged who I am. But I feel something for you, Shane."

"Please excuse my ignorance, and I hope I don't offend you by anything I say or ask—"

Sarah shook her head. "Not at all. Go ahead."

"Are you saying you're not a lesbian?"

Sarah chuckled a little. "I guess this makes me bisexual. For the better part of a decade, I've dated only women, but that doesn't mean I wasn't attracted to men. I just found I was attracted to women more."

Sarah was nervous, and Shane wanted to comfort her, and he would, but he needed further discussion.

"I guess...I mean, I know I've been attracted to men. Like I said, I had boyfriends, and I was attracted to them. But I would meet women and be attracted to them, too. I guess I'm just attracted to whom I'm attracted to. You know?"

Deeds nodded and said nothing.

She continued. "I need a connection. To be with someone, I need a connection. If I have a connection with someone, I'll be with that person regardless of gender. I think we have that, Shane." Sarah's vulnerability was very attractive. "Even my nontraditional ways are traditional, right?"

They both smiled, and Deeds was able to grasp her thoughts as she clearly communicated them.

"We have a connection, Shane."

"Oh, no doubt at all we have a connection. I mean, I am attracted to you, inside and out. But to be honest, when you said you were a lesbian when we first met, which seems like ages ago, I instantly was calm because I knew there was not a chance. I was relaxed, just like that."

Sarah nodded. "So you were able to be you?"

"Yeah."

"So what you're saying, Shane, is that I've gotten to know who you are? The real you?"

"Yeah."

"So what's the problem? If this is who you are, I like what I've experienced."

"Yeah, that's a good point."

But Deeds did not allow himself to get swept up in emotion even though it would have been euphoric. Deeds decided to bring it back down to terra firma. Not to be cruel, but to be real and to be honest.

"Sarah, you've suffered a loss. The sad emotions mixed with me consoling you...Could everything be making you feel vulnerable? I mean, I respect your feelings. I really do. I'd like to embrace them. Even though I just met you, I'm really taken by you."

Sarah smiled and got teary eyed.

"Meeting you the other night and getting to know you this morning have been wonderful, and I'm thankful. But now you're saying it can go further because you're not a lesbian? Being bisexual is now allowing you to feel and express different emotions?"

"They're not different. I'm attracted to you. That's the bottom line."

With concern Deeds said, "I just want to make sure this is a well-thought-out decision made by you and not something clouded by emotional loss. I mean if we... are together...and then you question whether or not you made a brash decision, that'll suck for me. You're, I assume, easy to fall for."

Sarah took another step forward, but Deeds took a step back and said, "I went on a date with your sister. Did she tell you?" *It needed to be said.*

"Oh. You did?"

"Yes."

"No, she didn't tell me. I mean she called and babbled something about you two going out but I didn't know you had already."

A few sad moments went by, and then an astounded Sarah realized what Erik's presence meant for Deeds.

"Oh shit! Honey, I'm so sorry. You found out in a harsh way."

"Yeah, kinda harsh. She's not going forward with me. She went back to him."

Sarah shook her head. "I can't believe she's with that asshole again, and then she just throws it in your face like that. That's just mean."

"Yeah, it hurt a little."

"She mentioned you guys had talked, she liked what she saw, and something about going on a date. She sounded excited. I mean, who wouldn't?"

"Oh, you," Deeds said. "To be honest, the date wasn't too special. Odd at times. She was distracted most of the night, and I think we're gonna be friends, at most, which is great. Even before this morning, I knew it wasn't going to go further."

Deeds talked about how Jess had pretty much only discussed Erik. "I know all about…him and his stupid silver fucking Corvette." They both laughed and Deeds continued. "It seemed like a venting session. But that's OK. I'm glad she trusts me. We spent most of the night discussing how she wouldn't go down that path ever again, why she couldn't get over him, but at the same time, she was over him. She wants to date me, but she has…him, and I'm pining for her—blah, blah, blah."

Sarah looking annoyed. "Not fair to you."

"No, not really, but oh well. I'm done with it. I'm not going to let her lead me on. Been there, done that. It's not fun feeling like you're competing and auditioning all the time."

Deeds took a step closer to Sarah. "Spending time with you today was better than anything I've had within recent memory."

Sarah nodded. "Yeah, but it might get weird."

"That wouldn't matter, Sarah. What matters is if we're good together and have something strong. There's always going to be reasons not to do something. Granted, ours are more…unique. But being close to you is the bottom line, as you said, either as a friend or something more."

"I don't know what to do, Shane."

"Yeah. Well, if I may be bold with you—"

"Please."

"Amanda—"

Sarah got a little sad and looked down at the floor.

"This loss is going to be with you for a long time. And with time, you may be able to make peace with that. But this process may get confusing if you're dating me when I went on a date with your sister, who, by the way, lives right over there and would hear us."

"Hear us what, Shane?" she asked with a smirk.

"Never mind that," he said with subtle pride.

"I just don't know what to do, Shane."

"Well, I think you should briefly talk to your sister. Act like you would if I never walked over this morning. Avoid…him. Then go and deal with your boss. Were you gonna speak with the cops again?"

"Yeah. I said I'd go in."

"OK, I'd say you've got a busy day. After all that, I would go home and lie down and just think things over and let your instinct tell you what to do."

Sarah took in a deep breath and said, "You're right."

"To those who listen."

Sarah nodded. "I'm pretty drained. Emotionally, I think I hit them all."

"Oh, sure. And there's more to look forward to."

Sarah walked over to the desk, picked up a pen, wrote her number on a "Have You Seen Me?" flyer, and set the pen down. "I'm giving you my number; otherwise, I'd call you in like ten minutes and put off everything I need to do. You're a smart guy. You'll know when to call me. I trust that."

"You got it." Sarah walked over to Deeds, and he said, "In any event, regardless of the outcome, I'm so glad we—"

Sarah placed her hands on the sides of his face and planted a lovely kiss filled with loving emotion and gratitude. Sarah pulled back with her hands still on his face and said, "I love you, Shane." She kissed him again and then hugged him very hard. Sarah then let go and walked to the front door.

She took her jacket, which was next to Amanda's death shroud, off the hook and turned around and looked at Deeds. He did not speak and neither did Sarah. What else could be said? She opened the door and left.

"I love you, too," Deeds said to no one in his empty apartment.

CHAPTER FORTY

Deeds was still surprised by the events that had taken place. It was about half past noon. He knew he should at least make a few inquiries and spread the word about the Elf through the local bars and their bouncers.

If anyone were to see the Little Fucker, that person should drop a dime, so Deeds could...*What am I going to do?*

Deeds set out to make a few stops at various places he'd worked over the years. He grabbed his jacket, wallet, phone, knife, keys, handkerchief, and lip therapy and headed out.

As he walked past Jess's apartment, he couldn't help but overhear (he walked right next to the door and leaned in) that an argument was taking place. *Two things Jess: one, way to go down the same path thinking it will bear new results, and, two, ironically, your neighbors will deem you loud and complain to Wiggy.*

With Sarah on his mind more, with Jess on his mind less, with Amanda motivating his actions, and with the freezing temperatures on his flesh, Deeds got in his truck and made a mental checklist of places to go. Garee's Place was not on that list, but that was OK. The Elf wouldn't show his face there. So he set out for other bars.

CHAPTER FORTY-ONE

"Help you?" the big, long-haired, long-bearded biker-looking guy asked when he opened the door.

"Yes, please. I was looking for the owner, Mr. Gray. Is he in, sir?" This gentleman, Deeds guessed, was probably a welcoming father figure, an avuncular figure, a good friend to all he knew, and a fair boss.

"Sorry, big man. He sold the joint to me about a year and a half ago and retired somewhere in the desert. Is there something I can help you with?"

Deeds was proud. Of all the people who said their dreams aloud, Mr. Gray had been the only one to accomplish them. He'd owned a few establishments and sold them all and his house and moved to where it was warm. *Good for him.*

Mr. Gray had always loved the desert. Deeds remembered seeing southwestern prints adorn his office walls, and he had that turquoise ring. "Good for him. That's great news." Deeds was sincere.

Deeds continued as he stood nearly eye to eye with the new owner. "Well, sir, there is something you might be able to help me with. I used to bounce here. I bounce at the 11th now, and I was wondering if I could speak with you about a certain…situation."

The new owner opened the door all the way and waved Deeds inside. "Yeah, sure. Come on in."

Deeds walked in. Even though it was under new management, the bar looked and smelled exactly the same as it had two years ago when he'd worked there.

"Want some coffee?"

Fuck yeah, I do! "Yes, please. Thank you."

The nice, new owner refilled his cup and poured a new cup for Deeds. "Cream and sugar?"

"Please."

He held both cups, came around the bar, set Deeds's down, and took a seat. "So you looking for a job? Bouncers never stay too long in one place," the biker-looking owner was saying when out of nowhere a voice boomed down as if from Mount Olympus, "The fuck I don't!"

Deeds could swear there was an echo.

The new owner put up both hands and said humbly, "With Big Phil being the exception, of course."

Deeds turned around and was very surprised to see the huge, muscular black man. *We meet again!* If the sun was behind him, he would have eclipsed it. Deeds did not think Big Phil recognized him.

"What's up, big man?" Big Phil's gigantic hand engulfed Deeds's big hand like a child's.

Deeds stood up and looked up to make eye contact with this huge man. "Not much. How you doing?"

"Good, baby, always good," he said with a perfect smile. He looked at the biker-looking owner and asked, "You hiring a new sheriff for the territoy?"

The owner nodded and said, "We were just getting to that."

Deeds wanted to correct this before they put him on the schedule. "I'm sorry, let me clarify. I bounce over at the 11th, and I wasn't seeking employment, though I'd like to stay in touch. I wanted to ask you guys about a certain…situation that has caused a big problem at our place."

The biker-looking owner's expression changed as he said, "Oh shit! I heard what happened the other night. One of my son's an EMT. He told me."

"Ah." Deeds studied the owner's face and compared it to one of the EMTs who worked on Amanda. "Yeah, yeah, I see it now. Strong resemblance. I watched him as they tried to keep her, uh, alive."

The new owner's expression turned to a pained one. "Oh no," the new owner said with concern.

"Yeah, unfortunately she didn't make it."

"Oh, that's terrible. It, uh, sounded like it was a pretty brutal attack. I mean, it wasn't no accident."

"Yeah, it wasn't an accident and it was pretty fucking awful."

With much concern, Big Phil asked, "Wait a sec. Fill me in. What the hell happened?"

Deeds, without censorship, said, "Well, I'll tell you what I know, and then I'll tell you what I think." He sipped his coffee and continued. "It was me, the bartender, and the owner, Bill McKenna, closing up for the day. I headed out and saw Amanda—that was her name—convulsing on the asphalt. I ran over and saw that she was bleeding from a nasty head wound. I put my jacket on her and ran back and got the bartender to call nine-one-one, and Bill...You know Bill?"

The new owner was in suspense as he said, "Yeah, I know Bill."

"Good." Deeds continued and made sure he made eye contact with both guys. "Well, he brought the first-aid kit, and the three of us kept her alive till your son and company got there. A homicide detective paid me a visit this morning and informed me of Amanda's passing."

Big Phil, with genuine sadness, said, "That's just awful." He placed the huge tips of his index finger and thumb at the base of his nose between his closed eyes and said, "I'm sorry that happened."

All three guys were quiet for an informal moment of silence. These three large, tough-looking gentlemen cared.

"How old was she?" Big Phil asked after the impromptu moment of remembrance passed.

"Twenty-four," Deeds said with regret.

"Way too young," said Big Phil.

"Agreed."

The biker-looking owner was upset, shook his head, and stated, "My son's twenty-four. I...I couldn't imagine—"

Big Phil vehemently interrupted. "Hey! Don't talk like that."

The owner nodded his head and said, "You're right. You're right."

Big Phil looked back at Deeds and asked, "Well? That's what you know. Tell us what you think."

The new owner, in agreement, asked, "Yeah, what are you thinking?"

"When I heard the sirens," Deeds began, "my attention went to a little dark area across the street from the 11th. It's just a parking lot, but dealers go there to sell. You know how it is. They're not welcome in the bar, but we can't control where they end up."

Both Big Phil and the new owner nodded and grunted in unison as they both knew from experience.

"One dealer, in particular, we've had problems with for a while. He just stands there, across the street, and does his thing. This Little Fucker thinks he's such a badass, and he just—"

"Little Fucker?" an excited and angered Big Phil said. "*The* Little Fucker?"

Deeds nodded, making a mental note to not piss this guy off.

Phil looked at the new owner. "That Little Fucker! Goddamn it! You shoulda let me break that motherfucker in two when he came here the other morning! Goddamn it!"

"Take it easy, Philly. Let's confirm this." He looked at Deeds. "Describe this prick."

"Little. Ratty hair. Pale. Missing tooth. Diamond earring. Walks around like he's a fucking gangster."

Big Phil swung his right fist into is open left hand and then bellowed, "That's him! That's the trouble-making motherfucker!"

The new owner just nodded. "That's him all right."

"So you've had a recent run-in?"

Big Phil was fired up as he said, "Hell yeah! He acted like a major asshole, and I launched his skinny ass outta here. Then he came back, all apologizing and shit. I wanted to beat that motherfucker's ass! Now, you think he killed this girl at your place?"

"That's what my gut's telling me. He's been the only one at that spot for a while. Cops found cash and drugs there. That's what happens when you flee, you know, say, after you kill a twenty-four-year-old girl. You forget your shit."

They all nodded emphatically.

"I think he tried to pull some shit with this girl, and she denied him, and he got revenge. If I'm wrong, I'll fucking apologize to him, but at the very least, he saw what happened."

The new owner responded, "No, you're letting him off too easy. It was him."

Big Phil agreed. "It's him. These small-time fringe guys—they're the ones causing problems. All eager to impress. Make a name for themselves. Earn their stripes. It was him. No motherfucking doubt."

"Question is," the new owner said in a serious tone, "what do you want us to do if we see this little prick? Call the cops, or call you?"

Deeds nodded in contemplation for a moment or two. It was quiet in the bar.

Big Phil asked, "What do you want us to do?"

Depending on what happened after this meeting, this single moment could be a life-altering event. All of their lives might possibly mark this single moment as a moment of regret.

Their individual paths and their collective path were at a crucial and perilous turning point. Deeds could not bear the guilt if anything happened to these two stand-up men, but a wrong had to be righted.

Deeds grabbed a cocktail napkin and a pen and wrote his cell number down. "That's up to you, both of you. Cops or me. I leave it up to you."

Deeds stood up and finished his coffee. "Thank you for the coffee, sir, and if anyone asks, I appreciate you considering me for a security position at your establishment, and I look forward to hearing from you." He placed the napkin on the bar.

Deeds shook hands with the owner. Deeds then shook hands with the huge, muscular black man and thought, *You and Sandra, huh?* "Take care of yourselves, and watch your six." Deeds could tell Big Phil and the owner were ex-military. *They've spilled blood.*

CHAPTER FORTY-TWO

"What do we have here?" Joe entered the squalid double-wide and took it all in. He let the observations flow freely. It smelled moldy and smoky with traces of chemicals, and it looked decrepit.

It was as if Joe had been in this trailer many, many times before. Maybe he had been. *Didn't a kid die in this trailer? Maybe it just looked like it. So much death.*

No doubt he would find old food in the refrigerator and on the countertops. He was certain there were multiple filled ashtrays throughout the trailer. He could smell the weed. He could smell the funk. He could smell the body odor. He could smell the garbage cans filled to capacity, making it seem like they were erecting shrines to a garbage god.

He could picture the yellow and brown stains in the toilet and the rust stains in the shower. There were empty bottles, cans, and crushed cigarette packs strewn about. All this was in addition to the two naked murder victims on the dirty floor. *There's no place like home.*

One second after ceasing his observations, Detective Wilde said, "Angry murders, boss," and handed him a cigarette. "There was some serious barbaric rage here."

Joe held the cigarette and, for the first time ever, declined it by giving it back to Detective Wilde.

Joe said, "I'm cutting back. I'll have one later, when we're done."

Detective Wilde instantly realized that the date with Susan had gone well and that Joe had let himself get whipped and was being forced to quit smoking.

"And no, no," Joe said, preempting Detective Wilde's immediate thought.

Wilde knew not to pursue this until they were alone. He also did not want to be the only one smoking, so he put the cigarettes away and continued with the investigation.

"Well," Wilde stammered, "this was not a quick and quiet assassination. This was a loud, painful, pleasurable, and unplanned revenge…You really don't want a cigarette?"

Joe was looking at the bodies. "No, thanks."

Wilde shook his head. "All righty then."

"So who do we have?" Joe quickly changed the subject.

"Can't find IDs in this mess. His wallet has not been found, and good luck trying to find her purse. The neighbors say their names are Joy and Randy. Some say she is the owner of this quaint abode, and others say she just lives here selling drugs."

"Ah," Joe said. "Someone connected set her up?"

"Probably. She's not gainfully employed according to her neighbors. She might be on welfare, and we'll confirm that soon."

Joe looked around and walked into the kitchen area. After a few moments, he said to anyone listening, "Well, we'll find the stash and know what she was selling. Maybe based on what she sells, we can sweat known peddlers and—"

Wilde knew silence meant something. "What's up, Joe?"

There was urgency and confusion in Joe's voice when he asked, "Joy's a mother?" Joe walked in from the kitchen with a photo in his hand. "Looks like Joy had some kids. Did you check the entire trailer?"

"Of course!" Wilde yelled and continued. "There're no fucking kids here. A neighbor said the state has them."

"OK, OK, relax." Joe paused and, with a smirk on his face, said, "You should date more."

As if on cue, Susan Hansen walked in and said, "Yeah, what's with you?"

Wilde threw up his hands and said, "Oh, here we go."

Susan, without hesitation, like she was a seasoned pro at it, walked up to Joe and gave him a kiss on the cheek. "Hey, there."

Joe looked pleased and surprised. "Hey, yourself."

Wilde shook his head and said, "Ah, for Christ sakes!"

Suddenly, Joe's whole existence of putting shit bags in jail ceased to matter. Everything had changed. When Susan walked up and kissed him, that became all that mattered.

His whole life was death, carnage, tragedy, and sorrow. He was sick of it. No matter what he did, no matter how many criminals he put away, no matter how many murders he solved, it accomplished nothing in the grander scheme of things. Joe did not become happier.

As Wilde was addressing the issues of murder weapons, strangulation, voided bowels, lividity, and times of deaths, and as the stench of death, rot, and defeat hung in the air, all Joe wanted to do was to hold Susan and tell her he loved her and that he wanted to spend the rest of his life with her.

Joe was enthralled by Susan. She was so beautiful and just made him so happy. *Yeah, we only had one date, but so what? Am I not allowed to care for someone I've known for a long time? We've known each other for a very long time, and we finally say what's in our hearts. Time requirements can go to hell!*

As Wilde was informing everyone about the disgusting details from the horrendous crime scene, Joe was thinking of what Susan would look like in a bikini walking on the beach with a drink in her hand at sunset, her dark brown hair flowing in the warm breeze, her tan skin glistening from suntan lotion, and that beautiful smile that was for him.

Joe, with little familiarity, said in an elevated volume, "Dr. Hansen?"

After a couple of seconds, she came in from the back room. "Yes?"

She was very pretty. He pointed to his notebook and walked outside. No one really noticed.

Susan smiled warmly in the cold air, leaned in, and whispered, "I had such a wonderful time on our date."

Joe said nothing. He just looked into her eyes. Susan was enraptured by this look and melted. She realized and knew his feelings for her were the real deal.

She acted cool, stepped closer, and asked, "What's on your mind, Detective?"

Joe dropped his notebook in the snow and placed both his hands on the sides of her face and planted a big, long kiss. When the kiss ended, Susan looked like she had just received good news. She smiled warmly and said, "Wow!" She put her arms around Joe's waist and asked, "What's gotten into you?"

Joe breathed in deeply. "I had a thought," he said.

"Do tell," she eagerly said.

"Well, literally, the thought was of you, in a bathing suit, walking on the beach at sunset with a drink in your hand."

Susan's eyes went wide. "Really? You want to go on a vacation with me?"

"Well," Joe began, "yeah, but more than that."

Even with a confused look on her face, she was smiling. "What do you mean?"

Joe shook his head. "I don't know, Susan. I just loved our date so much. It had an effect on me."

Susan in a soft voice said, "Me, too. I loved it."

Joe placed his hands on her shoulders and said, "Forgive me if I'm too forward, but I see myself with you, on a beach. You know? I just see us together." He emphasized the last word. "Living our lives, someplace warm. Together. Walking in the sand. Holding hands. Making love throughout the day."

Dr. Susan Hansen still had a surprised expression on her face, but the unabashed enthusiasm was present. "Joe," she cutely stammered, "I don't know...I mean, we—"

"Hey," he comfortingly said, "I just had this lovely vision, and I wanted to share it with you. I hope I don't come across as too confident, but I think this"—he motioned with his hand to both of them—"could go wonderful places. I want it to. I'm pretty confident you want this to go to the next level, too."

With a hint of cute anger, Susan said, "Of course I do."

Joe continued. "I just had a nice daydream, and I wanted to share. I mean"—he looked toward the squalid double-wide—"in there is hell. In you are beauty, warmth, and joyous feelings. My imagination broke free. I thought it'd be cool to retire with our pensions and move to a warm beach and be with each other. That's all."

Susan took in a deep breath and exhaled. With that breath came a lovely humming sound, like when someone likes his or her delicious food. "Well," she began, "I'll speak to someone in HR and my financial advisor. See what kind of factor time is. See what's in the accounts and what my pension will allow. Then I'll go bikini shopping."

Joe felt like he'd just won the lottery.

"But before all that, you need to make dinner reservations for a second date. I mean, I'm not that kinda girl where we go on one date, and then we just retire together. Got it?"

Joe smiled.

CHAPTER FORTY-THREE

Deeds had been driving around for a while. His apartment ban on dip extended to his truck as well, but that had been broken today. He walked into a liquor store and bought a can of Copenhagen Long Cut Straight and a bottle of water. He chugged the water and instantly had himself a spitter.

Deeds listened to numerous albums as he drove around Old Falls and then saw a sad image as he drove past a trailer park. He saw multiple cop cars and ambulances. Obviously, there was a murder because the EMT crews were milling around as other people in suits were walking in and out of one particular trailer.

What caught his eye the most was a scene near the trailer but hidden from those milling about. It was a man and a woman embracing each other. *Oh no!* It must have been loved ones consoling each other at the news of the murder victim.

They were a little older, so Deeds assumed that they indeed were the recipients of the dreaded phone call that parents fear. This poor couple had probably watched their beloved child make a series of bad decisions that led him or her to an early demise in a shitty double-wide trailer in Old Falls.

If the son or daughter did not overdose, then maybe they were robbed. Perhaps they were trying to rob someone and they got killed. No. Someone would have been in the back of a cop car, so someone OD'd or got killed. Those poor parents. Their hearts are broken forever.

CHAPTER FORTY-FOUR

Detective Joe Duran had no idea how to continue with his day. His mind was racing. He was excited and eager to take this unpredicted turn onto a new path. The surreality of this developing and, so far, fortuitous new chapter in his predictable life and career was hard to grasp.

Joe had assumed that wives would come and go, and indeed they had. He had assumed that he would be a part of his sons' lives and eventually his grandkids' lives. But he would do this as a homicide detective.

Joe assumed he would die as a cop. He didn't see himself retiring and collecting a pension on the golf course while criminals continued to break the law. He wanted to put away bad guys because that was what he was supposed to do. This duty would never end.

For years he had been ignoring the simple truth that no matter what, there were going to be bad guys doing bad things. Joe was digging a grave while criminals kept kicking dirt back into it. And regardless of the grave's depth, he would end up in it.

There was always going to be another shit bag who deserved twenty-five to life. Joe had amassed a large number of arrests and convictions. He prided himself on that. Yet there it was: another file on his desk, another dead body, another bad guy who'd done a bad thing. It never ended. It never slowed down. Bad guys did bad things, and it was never going to end.

There would be an end to Joe though. He was middle-aged, and he was giving his life as sacrifice for the prosecution of criminals. Joe assumed this burden with the mind-set that it was a righteous thing to do. It did not matter if he wanted to do it or not. It was his duty. Now his goals had shifted.

The thought of sacrifice was never really questioned. Any questioning of the whole process was ignored and replaced with thoughts of duty, honor, and fidelity. That's how and why he got up every day and went to work.

Lately he felt nihilistic about the whole process. He worked hard to put away a bad guy for his bad deed. Usually a bad guy did a bad thing to another bad guy. *The fuck do I care if shit bags kill each other?*

Sometimes good people got hurt, and he felt as if he needed to avenge their undeserved hardship.

That's why he became a cop: to help people. But most cases were bad people hurting bad people.

Someone would go to jail, and yet there was no feeling of victory or satisfaction because right as the investigation and trial ended, like clockwork, another file would appear on his desk.

The cases, the victims, the criminals, the verdicts, the defenses—it all blended together at this stage in his long career. He did not want to be a part of that machine anymore. He wanted to be with Susan.

Joe got out of his car at the police station. He visualized himself walking into his captain's office and simply saying, "I'm retiring, and I'm gonna spend the rest of my life loving Susan."

Joe stood and soaked in what sun the partly cloudy and cold afternoon yielded. He cracked his neck and stretched it for a few moments. He did not want a cigarette. His body, however, was rejecting that stance as it let him know through sweating, strange and unexplainable aches and pains, and a bad headache that he indeed wanted another cigarette.

Joe really wanted to buy a box of cigars and a bottle of champagne and celebrate. He felt his career was coming to a desired end. He could smell the saltwater and feel the grip of Susan's arms around him. Joe smiled and then replaced his expression with his usual scowl.

Joe walked up to his desk, and there it was. Another file. Another bad guy had done another bad thing.

Fuck! He did not even open it. If Wilde was there, or if some random rookie walked by, he would have thrown it to him or her. Joe sat in his chair and silently said good-bye and bid farewell to this demanding chapter of his life.

Joe was nagged by the file though. Its presence meant something had happened. Joe decided to just take a quick look at it. Interestingly enough, it was a series of files on Sandra, the woman they'd found frozen and naked near Garee's Place.

Joe perused all the paperwork. Turned out she'd been raped at an early age by members of an old family of Engel Falls, an old blue-blood family that ran things for a while once upon a time. The Kaenicks had their hands in all of the town's business and were basically the unelected leaders. They also appeared to get away with a lot of white-collar malfeasance.

It had not been the wealthy and powerful Kaenick faction though that had molested the victim. It had been members of a branch of the Kaenick family tree who were indeed white-trash bad-seed hicks who'd committed the atrocity against such a young girl in that abandoned house's backyard all those years ago.

The reports were unfortunately well detailed. Tests, statements, and examinations had concluded that the hymen had recently been punctured. The victim had had multiple abrasions and contusions that were indicative of being held down. She'd been covered in urine and received the perpetrator's ejaculate on the lumbar region of her back. She'd also had a grade-one concussion and suffered from dehydration.

Three low-life scumbag punks of the shit-bag branch of the Kaenick family tree had been arrested at the scene, after they'd turned on each other. Yet nothing had stuck. They'd been pretty much slapped on the wrist, despite the testimony of two furious cops and multiple doctors and nurses and therapists and psychiatrists, the latter of the two specializing in post-traumatic stress and underage victims.

The judge had handed down very convenient sentences: light, playful slaps on the wrists. Things had evened out as they all, later in life, went to prison, with one ending up dead, which was great. But justice had never really been served for the victim. Sandra was her name.

Sandra had had numerous run-ins with the law, including drugs, assault, trespassing, criminal mischief, and prostitution. She'd been the victim of many beatings. Bad guys had made her a victim, and then she'd become the bad guy, and then other bad guys had done bad things to her.

Did she deserve it? Probably not. So what if I arrested her and put her in jail? Is that the help she needed? Would it have saved her life? Should I have killed those three disgusting boys as revenge? Is that justice?

The patriarch of this horrible Kaenick family was a local minister as it turned out. It was widely accepted that he'd gotten his nephews off. It was also widely accepted that he bribed officials, took payments, and did favors for anyone who made donations to the Eternal Salvation Church.

The IRS had been after him for years, and it'd finally gotten its wish granted and audited him. This had only emboldened the good reverend as the good citizens of Engel Falls rallied around him. Then a wonderful thing had happened. Charges of multiple molestations had been filed.

Apparently, the good reverend had a penchant for little girls, just like his scummy nephews. It had been at the end of his trial when Reverend Kaenick lost all hope. He had been able to receive bail, which was quite odd considering the multiple charges, but he'd listened to his lawyers as they told him that he was indeed going to jail. Reverend Kaenick knew that his guilty verdict was all but certain.

At his church, the night before he was to hear the jury's verdict, a devout young lady of eleven years old paid a visit to the soon-to-be-found-guilty reverend. She reported that he was intoxicated and he lurched and grabbed at her rear end and vaginal area. She managed to escape, and she ran home to tell her mother, who called the police.

At this point no one in Engel Falls supported him. His power and authority were gone, and soon his freedom and liberty would be as well.

Reverend Kaenick put a bullet in his head when he heard the sirens. Police found his body, but it was not the same two cops who'd arrested his nephews. They had requested to be relocated to other police forces in the state. They were disgusted at the leniency given to the three monsters.

The church got boarded up. No one attended the funeral for Reverend Kaenick. No one knew what to do with a church where the minister, who'd delivered sermons every Sabbath, molested children, stole money, and committed suicide. Within a year or two, someone had decided to burn it down.

The vacant lot was reclaimed by the earth as some things began to grow there as the memories of the sinister deeds became part of small-town lore. Joe read one last passage on one of the briefs. It read the lot where the church used to stand was later purchased and turned into a trailer park, the same trailer park where Joe professed his vision to Susan not more than a little while ago. Joe laughed to himself at the sick and twisted irony.

Joe closed the file, stood up, and walked into Captain Tertel's office. Joe knocked on the door and was told to come in.

"Hey, Joe," said Captain Tertel with a warm smile on his young face, very atypical for any captain. "How can I help you, bud?"

Joe took a seat. With the thought of Susan in a bikini motivating him, Joe pictured a checklist. On this to-do list were two points: retire and make dinner reservations with Susan.

A long time later, Joe emerged from the good Captain Tertel's office with a smile on his face. His to-do list was half completed as he pulled out his phone to make dinner reservations.

CHAPTER FORTY-FIVE

Deeds had made his way to several other establishments to put the word out. None of these places had personnel as caring or receptive as the first bar he visited, where he'd really felt understood and validated by Big Phil and the new owner, whose name he had not caught.

The other places he'd visited were places he had worked at. Apparently, too much time must have elapsed because he was not remembered nor was he really welcomed. Deeds thought it strange how easily people forgot people.

He would see a member of the staff and instantly recall the person's name, details of the person's life, and an inside joke they used to share. Those days were gone.

In some places the employess that Deeds remembered were simply not there. Also absent was the concern as well as the caring. At these places he would just ask a few questions or instruct them to call the police if they saw the person he sought.

It had been a long day, and tomorrow Deeds planned on having another long day. As long as there was not another visit like the one from the detective this morning, Deeds would spend the day checking in with the same bars. This would let them know he was serious about his inquires.

Deeds was not up for going to the gym tonight, so he would double up tomorrow. Tomorrow should not take as long, technically, since he did not have to tell the same story over and over and over again. All he planned to do was drive around Old Falls and New Falls to the same places he visited today and check in.

Deeds would also be driving around and scouting locations where the piece of shit that hurt Amanda might be hiding.

So Deeds headed home and planned on eating a lot of food and relaxing. Maybe he'd watch a movie or two. They'd be movies he'd seen ad nauseam as Deeds was in a mood to turn off the critical thinking and do next to nothing.

He parked his truck and wasn't too proud to admit he looked for a silver Corvette. Its absence was something that Deeds did not know how to feel about nor did he know what it meant. The possibilities were numerous. *Whatever.*

Deeds had no idea what he was doing or what was going to happen. He had been at one point, perhaps still was, enthralled with Jess. He was so attracted to her, but as a person he was very turned off by her schizophrenic behavior.

But she was so gorgeous. And you know who else was gorgeous? Her fucking sister, and, more importantly, she was gorgeous on the inside. But there was one slight possible obstacle, not even a caveat but an obstacle: she might be a lesbian. *Christ!*

A tidal wave of confusion seemed to drench Deeds. He had love but wanted guilt-free and obstacle-free lust with Sarah but did not think that was possible. He had lust for Jess but did not think love possible. He wanted justice for Amanda. He wanted to hold Sandra one more time. He wanted to connect with Lindsay. He missed his friends from growing up, he missed his mom and dad, and he wanted a brutal and savage death to be visited upon the Little Fucker.

Deeds recognized his symptoms and knew that he was, as he deemed, "in a trench," and if he was not careful, his depression and feelings of abandonment, ostracism, and yearning would lead to sustained pain.

Deeds knew to acknowledge each and every emotion he had. By doing that, he let them pass in a healthy fashion, and he'd able to move on without dismissed feelings lurking beneath the surface, exploding without much provocation.

Deeds was walking toward his apartment, his emotional sanctuary, when he heard Jess's sweet, sexy, and now very affectionate voice. It was odd to him.

"Hey, you," she stated, almost unaware of the emotional unrest she had caused.

Deeds played it distant. He did not have the energy and did not want to further the depths of his very present emotional trench. Not for Jess. So he would have to stand up to her. *Good luck.*

Deeds asked in a bland tone, "How's it going?"

Jess did not waste time and said, "I've been thinking about you."

Christ! Right the fuck back in! "Good things, I hope." Deeds tried to say this without any emotion while trying to still be friendly and not rude.

Deeds walked up to her and stopped with no intentions of exchanging a hug. "Mmm," was the exhaled moan she yielded as she pressed her glorious and braless breasts against Deeds in a time-stopping hug. If she suggested it, Deeds would pleasure her right here, right now in this frigid hallway. So he had to abruptly end the moment.

"How's Erik? He good? You two good?" Not too subtle, but it was necessary.

Jess pulled away, and Deeds maintained eye contact, which was one of the most difficult tasks he'd ever attempted. He failed. Her breasts and her cleavage were of a buxom goddess.

Jess noticed but continued with her sardonic expression. "Why?"

"Didn't see the infamous silver 'Vette." Deeds motioned with his head to the parking lot behind him and said, "You guys not hanging out tonight?"

Jess's gaze went down to below Deeds's belt and came back up. "No. So what?"

Deeds shook his head. "Sew buttons."

"What?"

"Old joke. Bad joke."

"Oh," Jess said as she acknowledged that she did not know it as Deeds acknowledged that her not knowing occurred frequently.

Her demeanor changed. Jess looked at Deeds's shoes and appeared to speak to them. "He's not a bad guy, ya know. I was even gonna ask if you wanted to hang out with us some time."

Deeds smiled and shook his head and asked, "The three of us?" Deeds shook his head again and said, "Thank you, but I'll pass."

With subtle attitude, Jess reminded Deeds, "You don't even know him."

Deeds nodded matter-of-factly. "Correct."

Jess crossed her arms and accentuated her breasts and said, "You don't know what it's like, OK? I've been with him for a long time. You just can't turn it off."

"I know. I never asked you to. I even absolved you of any misleading behavior."

"What does that mean?"

"That means—"

"Look, Shane, I have two great guys pining for me. Do you know what it's like to have that responsibility? And don't tell me you're not after me. I know you like me, Shane."

"Oh yeah?"

"Yes. You like me, and I...I like you, Shane. A lot." Jess continued and, in the throes of vulnerability, said, "I think of you, and I get warm feelings in my chest." She placed her hand on her chest, just above her left breast. "I think of you, and I smile. I smile at what could be between us. I smile because I know how amazing you'd be to me and how you'd treat me. I think of all these things, and I smile. And I smile a lot 'cause you're on my mind a lot. I could fall in love with you so effing easy, right here, right now. You could be in my heart forever."

Deeds wanted to pick Jess up, and with her legs wrapped tightly around him, he wanted to kiss her for hours in the cold hallway, say he loved her, say how he wanted to dedicate his life to her, to them, and sensually connect with her for many more hours. He loved her.

"But—"

Motherfucking, fuck me running, fuck, fuck, fuck! Deeds shook his head. "Always a but and never a break."

"Erik's in my heart, too. I can't just turn it off."

"Yeah," Deeds said as he placed the tips of his index finger and thumb at the base of his nose between his closed eyes, "you said that."

"Well, it's true. Sorry if my feelings are an inconvenience for you."

"This life is an inconvenience."

"Don't say that."

"Why not?"

"It made me nervous when you said that."

"So?"

"Look." She stepped closer and put her hands on his big chest. "Regardless of what happens, I care about you a lot. You're in my heart. I just can't make a decision. I wish I could. I'm sorry, Shane."

With the thought of love and intimacy completely out of his thoughts, he asked, "Would you like to come in for coffee?"

CHAPTER FORTY-SIX

Jess asked, "Is that a good idea?"

Deeds chuckled. "Yeah, I'm not in a place to make a move or anything."

"Well"—Jess leaned in—"I could put on some makeup. Put on something sexy. That might help."

Now was not the time to flirt.

Deeds looked with severity into Jess's eyes and said with profound honesty, "You could be covered in blood and fecal matter, and I'd be with you in any way you'd allow, Jess."

Jess's eyes were wide and filled with disbelief and astonishment.

"Sorry." Deeds brought his hands together. "Should have kept that one to myself." Another awkward moment passed. "Look, I'm gonna go inside and, uh, make a pot of coffee. You're more than welcome to come over, but if you don't, I understand. Might be better if you—"

With a strength that surprised and thrilled Deeds to his very core, Jess grabbed him, rotated his body, shoved him against her door, which then opened, and before he knew it, Deeds was inside Jess's apartment.

Deeds did not really feel the wall but knew he'd been thrown against one as a framed picture fell to the floor. He, out of reflex, glanced at it for just a brief moment and saw an image of Jess and Bill and Sarah standing in front of a Christmas tree. Deeds's gaze went back to Jess as he eagerly awaited what was next and unknown.

Deeds said nothing as Jess came to him as a demon possessed, attacking and absorbing all that was him. She grabbed his shirt and pulled Deeds's mouth to hers, where she began a sensually intimate connection Deeds could not fathom ever being experienced by any mortal. *Oh my fucking god, Jess! I love you, too!*

Jess and Deeds were as one. The explosive, passionate, and dangerous emotions were of hellish tormented love breaking free from all restraint after lying dormant for aeons. All that mattered was Jess. All that existed was Jess. Forever was Jess.

With her hands now under his shirt and her nails tearing at his flesh, she savagely kissed him and moaned as if she was climaxing right then. Jess and Deeds kissed like their ecstasy was an amalgamation of violence, freedom, brutality, and love.

Deeds could not believe what was happening. Her mouth; her serpent-like tongue; her spit; her carnal desires almost completely unbound; her flesh; her body; her wavelike movements; her hands caressing, clawing, drawing blood; her essence exuding, letting Deeds know that Jess was indeed ready were all blessed wanton gifts.

The violent kissing continued as Jess breathed heavily, when she could, and moaned. With the moans becoming more powerful and increasing with frequency, Jess stopped the kissing and placed her left hand on Deeds right below his belt and let go an even louder moan as she felt him. She then placed both hands behind Deeds's head and took out the hair tie and let his hair fall down, and then she moaned even louder.

With a wonderful, "Oh...my god, Shane," she replaced her left hand on him and her right hand on her own precious area and began to rub vigorously. Within moments Jess began a moan that rivaled any victim of a painful murder.

The shuddering, the teeth-clenching death growls, the hurt whimpers, the increasingly strenuous grip upon Deeds, and the look of disbelief all led to a growing moan. Adding to the intimate frenzy was the soulful connection they were sharing.

They maintained eye contact as she neared. Instinct dictated that this release was going to be long and loud. This was something Deeds had not experienced on this level nor did he think he would ever be privy to. A once-in-a-lifetime event was about to take place.

Deeds pulled Jess to him and embraced her firmly. Their bodies were held together by a bond stronger than any connecting matter or device. Deeds kept Jess upon him as the moan continued to grow and signaled an imminent life-altering experience.

For Jess, the universe was about to implode warmly inside her as she reached a peak she never thought possible. And then it happened. Jess let out a wail that the dead could have heard. It was a long orgasmic yell that got louder as it continued and indeed it continued for a very long time.

Jess acted as if she was wounded as her right hand slowed the vigorous rubbing, but it did not stop altogether. The slower pace was maintained but then increased again as Jess's eyes let Deeds know that a second implosion was going to occur. And as if confused and yet triumphant, Jess said with pending urgency, "Oh...Shane...oh my God...Shane...more!"

CHAPTER FORTY-SEVEN

After it was all over, following the third life-altering implosion, Jess just stared into Deeds's eyes
as his eyes communicated that this could happen all
the time, maybe, if she would commit to him. Her eyes
communicated that she was wanting of this.

There, in Jess's apartment, they remained, embracing each other and speaking what was in their hearts
without uttering a single word. It would have been difficult for Deeds to fully express what he felt for Jess, so
he just let his eyes express what he felt.

It was a moment they would share for the rest of
their lives. The height of the connection they just
reached might never be repeated. They stood motionless as one, as time was not a factor.

Their breaths were in sync as they just loved each
other without restraint. As the wondrous moments

passed, he noticed every detail and savored them. Her scents, her essence, her flowing hair, her flesh, her curves, the placement of her hands, her lips, her eyes, and her breath, which slowed down and became deeper and elongated as she descended back to this world—all of it was magical.

"I," Jess began, "I—"

Deeds interrupted her with a long and soulful closed-mouth kiss. They parted, and their eyes connected again. His big left hand went to the side of her face and caressed the lovely flesh that came together in a perfectly created pattern that was her beautiful face.

"This," Deeds began, "could never be topped. Everything came together for one perfect moment of sheer..." Deeds looked down, trying to come up with the perfect word but failed and said, "There's not a word for it."

Jess's eyes began to fill with tears. It had hit her. Deeds knew the dreadful thought was dawning in her mind.

Deeds wiped some tears from her face and hugged her with care and love. "Don't be sad, Jess. Most people never experience what we just shared. You and I— we'll always have...what we just had, forever."

Jess continued to cry as if she was in mourning, but Deeds communicated how she should be happy. "Have you ever experienced anything like this before?"

Jess said nothing as she shook her head.

"Do you think this'll happen again for you? Something so, so..." Deeds could not finish the question, but she knew what he was attempting to communicate and she shook her head again. They embraced each other with vigor.

They both ignored and refused to acknowledge the loud sound of the rumbling engine as it entered the parking garage. The fucking silver Corvette had appeared and ended the moment, but their shared memory would remain eternal.

Deeds grasped Jess's beautiful face and kissed her. He then let go, and as he walked around her, he grasped her hand, not wanting to let go, but he knew he had to. He held on for as long as he could and then let go. Deeds walked to the door and let himself out. In seconds, the moment had ended.

"What a great night," he said to no one in the cold empty hallway.

CHAPTER FORTY-EIGHT

Deeds was staring at the open fridge for a solid two minutes before he closed the door. He had been looking at the accumulated beers and was very tempted to have one or all of them. He knew he wouldn't, but if there was ever a time to grab a cold one for the first time, this night's events almost begged for it. *I can still taste her...*

Deeds took his shirts off, went into his clean bathroom, and turned around to admire, in the clean mirror's reflection, the streaks of blood adorning his back. If the night had ended on a positive note—rather, if by next morning Deeds had been done pleasuring her and they'd started a relationship—he might have thought of having those streaks of blood immortalized with tattoos to remind them of what they'd shared. *The flesh will heal, and so will your heart.*

Deeds did not actually take a cold shower, but it was definitely not hot or warm or even lukewarm. He got out and dried off. He quickly put on a wifebeater and some boxers. There was no way he was going to be able to go to sleep, so he knew he'd be up, and that was OK. He was still enjoying the rush.

Even though he would have to get over it, he wanted to savor what had just happened. *I can't fucking believe that just happened.* Deeds thought he heard yells from a woman. *I wonder what she's doing right now.*

With wet hair and a postshower sweat going, Deeds grabbed some dip, pinched a fifth of the can, placed it in his front lip on the left, grabbed an empty water bottle from his recycling container under the kitchen sink, and went outside on his patio despite the freezing temperature. *Fuck it.*

The piercing chill of the frigid boreal air was a diversion for almost one second, but the thoughts of Jess just came back. Over time, as the bottle accumulated a decent amount of brown spit, the cold air felt cleansing, and its primal effect on Deeds was calming him and physiologically bringing back rationalization as the blood traveled north to his brain.

Jess, she's in lust with you, but if push came to shove, she may not love you. That would crush you. Whether she's with that silver 'Vette fuck or some other dude, she would have reluctance and couldn't give you the heart commitment you want, the heart commitment you deserve. If she truly wanted to be with you, she would, plain and fucking simple. What you had with her tonight, what you shared will never be taint-ed by any relationship bullshit. If she dug you, she would not have been so distant at dinner, regardless of that other guy's cellular presence.

Deeds took in a deep breath that burned his lungs. The exhaled vapor flowed around him as it took several moments to dissipate. He took out the dip, put it in the bottle, spit a few more times into the spitter, and secured the lid.

Deeds got tears in his eyes. He was sad, but he knew it was for the best. He was still going to mourn even though this was one of the best nights he had experienced. He again realized how lucky he was to have such a wonderful connection. Although brief, it would last forever.

"What a great night," Deeds said to no one on his empty patio.

CHAPTER FORTY-NINE

Deeds brushed his teeth and turned on the heat but remained in his XXL boxers and XXL wife-beater. He opened the fridge once again and looked at the beers for just a couple of seconds, shook his head, and grabbed a bottle of water.

Deeds wanted to go over to Jess's. He wanted to experience her body and her love. He wanted to see her. He wanted to hold her. He wanted to talk to her. *Shit.* He realized he was close to becoming dependent on her. That was no good.

Sarah! Deeds saw the "Have You Seen Me?" flyer that Sarah wrote her number on. It seemed like weeks ago, yet it was this morning when they shared that warm comforting experience.

Deeds wanted to call her. He legitimately wanted to see how she was doing and find out how the rest of her day went. *Was that all? Am I torn between two women—two sisters? One of which I helped with life-altering orgasms and the other being a lesbian or at least bisexual, both being the daughters of a boss of a job that I don't need? You struck out with one; you gonna try for the other?* "It's like a fucking Greek tragedy," he said as the nervousness came over him. Deeds felt like he needed to confess.

Deeds paced the room and tried to figure outcomes, likelihood of scenarios, possibilities, and potentials for good and bad situations concerning his disclosure of events. No one would know, and predictions were worthless when the truth could be made known via phone call.

"Hey, Shane!" Sarah had said after he idientified himself.

"Hey there. Sorry, it's late, but I kinda wanted to talk to you."

"Aww," Sarah said, "that's so sweet of you. No, it's not late at all. I was hoping you would call."

Deeds felt relief. He never wanted to interrupt or be a burden. "How did everything go today?"

"You are a genius!"

"Never heard that before. This is Shane Deeds you're talking to."

"Oh, stop it. No, everything you said about my boss came true. It was like a script. I couldn't believe it. She said what you said she would say, and I said what you said I should say, and now…I have bereavement leave!"

"Nice! I'm glad things worked out well."

"You knew it would."

"I got lucky."

"No, you knew."

"Did you go to the police station?"

"Yeah, but the detective guy wasn't there. Hardly anyone was there."

"What do you mean?"

"Well, the receptionist or front-desk lady was absent. So I just walked to where the map guide said his desk was, and he wasn't there. The rest of the office was nearly empty. Anyone there didn't really pay any attention to me. I left a note on his chair. Didn't hear from him. Oh well."

Deeds changed gears. "I have to ask; how are you feeling?"

"Confused as hell. If I can be honest." Deeds was about to say she could, but she did not pause. "I was ready to fuck you for hours."

Deeds was taken aback by that statement and unfortunately aroused again and could not express himself too well as he simply said, "Oh yeah?"

Sarah continued. "Oh God, yeah. I wanted to just fuck you all day!"

Deeds's inability to speak caused the silence. Sarah did not speak for a moment or two. She then simply let out an erotic, exhaled hum. "Hmmm. Yeah. For hours. It would have been a life-altering experience for me—"

Deeds found a word to say: "Us."

"Thank you." Sarah corrected herself. "Us."

Sarah's tone changed as she went on to say, "But it was too soon after wanting to be with someone else. The shock of falling for someone and then having that person be taken away from you and then falling for someone else, not to mention all the new doors being opened or reopened—it was a surreal day. I'm glad I didn't act impulsively. I regret it, too, mind you." Sarah chuckled. "But I'm glad cooler heads prevailed—even though all the head would have been hot and wet."

Deeds could not find a word.

Sarah exhaled another "hmm" sound again and silence followed. "Anyway," she said suddenly, "how are you doing, Shane?"

Deeds was unavailable. He could not communicate with her. He had to be rude and regretted it but knew it was the right thing to do. "I'll call you right back."

Deeds did not wait for a response. He hung up, grabbed some dip, pinched a fifth of the can, placed it in his front lip on the left, grabbed the same spitter from before, and went outside on his patio despite the even now colder temperature. *Fuck it, again.*

Deeds stood there and just could not wrap his mind around the new Sarah situation and the still-new Jess situation. *You can't fuck them both. You can't connect with both. One you connected with, and she goes on about how she wants to fuck. One you do something better than fucking with, but you don't connect with her like you did with her sister. It's a fucking shame.*

With his mind going back and forth from one wonderful lady to the other, he knew nothing could happen. *Fuck,* Deeds lamented, *it's a fucking shame.*

Deeds took out his dip, spit a couple more times into the spitter, and went inside. He brushed his teeth again, picked up his phone, and dialed Sarah's number.

"Shane," Sarah said in an annoyed tone, "if you just rubbed one out, you shoulda stayed on the line. I could've helped you. Wouldn't have taken so long, guaranteed."

"Next time, promise."

Sarah laughed. "Well, now that your...head...is clear...What did you end up doing the rest of the day?"

Deeds was now calmer and could talk but did not know how much to say. He wanted to discuss how he went to a bunch of different places all over town and put the word out that he was looking for the miserable dirt bag.

But that would lead to the question of what Deeds was planning to do. What would Sarah's reaction be? How much would she want to know? Would this make her an accessory? Deeds decided to keep it light and nebulous.

"I just went to a few places I've worked at and asked if they knew him. Asked them to call that detective. That's all." Deeds felt he sold it.

"Wow," Sarah sounded thankful but too impressed, which indicated she was not. "I appreciate that. Hopefully, they'll get him, if he did it."

Deeds was confused. "You don't think he, uh, you know, had anything to do with what happened, anymore?"

"Well," Sarah began and then took a deep breath, "if he did, then I hope they catch him and lock him up. But—"

"But what?"

"Well, we don't know if it was him. Maybe she fell. I don't know. We don't know."

Deeds was a little put off by this and felt he needed to cause a little discomfort to bring back the appropriate emotions. "Can you say her name?"

"Yeah," Sarah said strangely, "of course I can." Sarah did not though. "I didn't really know her, you know? It's weird. I miss her. Don't get me wrong. This was traumatic, but I didn't know her."

I don't understand women at all. None of them. Not a one.

"This is very different from what you were expressing this morning to me and"—Deeds could not say her name—"your sister."

"Are you disappointed?"

"No, just a little surprised." Deeds was very surprised.

Sarah continued. "I've thought about her. I've thought about you, too, Shane, all day."

Deeds said nothing. He said nothing because he did not know what to say. There were three questions rattling around in his brain: *What do I do with the Little*

Fucker if I catch him? What's going to happen with Jess and me? What's going to happen with Sarah and me?

Deeds's instinct dictated that nothing should happen with either Jess or Sarah. There were way too many things that could cause hurt, and Deeds did not want that to occur to anyone. Deeds did not fancy himself to be the kind of guy who could pursue something knowing he was causing pain.

OK, Deeds thought, *I am not going to pursue either of them. But I can get the motherfucker who hurt Amanda. Should I still? Sarah is acting odd. Why is Sarah backing off? Was she just exaggerating this morning? No, keep inquiring.*

"Without being rude," Deeds began, "you were in a lot of anguish this morning. Anguish over losing Amanda. I mean, Amanda died a horrific death, and if I may be so bold, the detective and I both think that drug dealer had something to do with it, either indirectly or directly. That doesn't bother you anymore?"

Deeds went too far, but the coming on to him and the sexual innuendo so soon after the mourning was odd—powerful, but odd.

"Of course it does!" Sarah yelled, and it caused Deeds to remove the phone from the side of his face. "Why would you ask that?"

Calmly Deeds said, "Your words were a little peculiar to me. They seemed opposite from what they were this morning. Healing takes more time than that. I think you're downplaying what you feel as if it's going to help. But it's not."

Deeds could hear sobbing and was glad. "I mean, I've suffered. I've lost people. I've been abandoned. What I said this morning was advice based from experience in loss and dealing with it. I wasn't spouting daytime talk-show horseshit."

Sarah was crying.

"Look," Deeds began but then heard the call end. "Or not," he said to no one.

Deeds squinted at the red numbers as they indicated it was 5:04 a.m. The darkness let him know it was five in the morning, and the exhaustion confirmed. His phone was going off.

He reached over to his nightstand drawer where he kept his phone and opened it. Deeds kept his phone in the drawer, thinking the radioactive properties would not be able to cause him cancer due to the strength of Swedish particle board.

Deeds saw it was Sarah. He inhaled and exhaled and answered, not knowing what to expect.

"Hi," Sarah simply said.

"Hi back." Deeds asked, "Are you OK?"

"Yeah," she said but corrected herself. "I mean, no, I'm not."

Deeds did not blindly offer to do something. He simply asked, "Yeah?"

"Well," Sarah hesitated, meaning she was going to get deep, "you really hurt me today."

Deeds spoke but was quickly interrupted. "Sarah, it wasn't my intention—"

"I'm not finished. You really hurt me today, and it made me realize what I'm feeling."

"What are you feeling?" Deeds asked in a calm tone, yet he possessed strong concern.

"I feel sad. I feel betrayed. I feel angry. I feel like life is a fucking asshole, and I wanna kick its ass. I wanna kick that Little Fucker's ass. I want him to suffer. I want him to feel as bad as I do plus a thousand. I want to know why he took Amanda away from me. I just want to know why, goddamn it!" Her words were spoken very fast, emphasizing the emotional severity of the situation.

Sarah took a deep breath and let it out. "But that's vengeance. That's a vigilante mentality, and I have to remind myself that I—we, as a society, are better than that."

Deeds sensed something in Sarah's words. "What do you want to happen, Sarah?" Deeds asked this question that appeared to be indirect and broad on the surface. It could have been interpreted as a general question with an overall feel to it. However, it was indeed a clear and direct question.

"What I want is for that Little Fucker to get what he deserves."

"OK," Deeds calmly answered. Before she could elaborate and become involved with a possible and potential criminal act, he changed the subject and asked, "Have you talked with your sister recently?"

Deeds just had a vision of Jess's eyes as she climaxed over and over and over again. *I miss her, but it's for the best. I have a feeling I'll be missing Sarah, too.*

"No, why?"

"Just wondering." There was a pause. He decided to mislead her. "Well," Deeds began, "I think we may have to accept the fact that everything rests in the police's hands."

"I know," Sarah said in an irked tone. "It really sucks."

"Yeah, it does."

"Listen," Deeds said, continuing to alter the direction of the conversation in hopes of misleading Sarah and distancing Deeds from any possible outcome, "scumbags that hurt people do not go on to live long lives. They're criminals, and they get caught and go to jail, at some point."

"I hope you're right, Shane."

"He'll get his, one way or another. I promise."

"You promise?"

"Yup. Karma's a bitch."

"And she's in heat." They both chuckled at the old lame joke.

"Exactly."

"I'm just so mad and angry and sad."

"I know. I'm glad you can admit that. Just be patient. What goes around comes around." Deeds was satisfied.

Things were left open to interpretation. No threats were made. No agendas were communicated. Deeds attempted to plant the seed: he was going by the book and asking Sarah to have faith in the system, and perhaps a cosmic force would take care of everything. The ploy appeared to be working.

"Thanks for talking with me, Shane. I appreciate it."

"No worries."

"I was just lying here, seething, you know? Lying here and being angry."

"Yeah, nights can be very hard. Tomorrow night, do your best to be exhausted, and then go to sleep. Trying to sleep during an emotional episode can be difficult."

Sarah chuckled and said, "I mean, I wanted to hire a hit man to take this fucker out. That's what I was lying here thinking about, for Christ's sake."

"Well, make a few calls, get a white envelope full of cash, it can happen." Deeds was using humor to disperse the idea of retribution.

"Yeah, well, I don't have a white envelope and I'm low on cash."

"Well, there goes that plan."

"Damn, so close. Oh well."

Deeds wanted to wrap this up as he felt it was a good point to end things lightheartedly. "Why don't you get some sleep, and we'll talk later."

"OK. What are you up to tomorrow?"

"Don't know. I'm gonna sleep in. I know that much. Maybe I'll call the detective. See if he made any progress. Then I'll hit the gym and go to work. Just another day."

"Yep," Sarah said and reiterated, "just another day."

They both were silent for a moment too long.

"OK, Shane. Thanks so much for everything, and I'm sorry about earlier."

"You don't need to apologize to me. OK?"

"OK. But I am."

"I know."

"Good night, Shane. I love you."

Deeds felt some guilt. "I love you, Sarah. I really do. Please know that." Deeds meant it despite the evening's earlier events pertaining to his neighbor.

CHAPTER FIFTY

"Joe," Susan said with a voice that was marked by fatigue.

Joe heard her and then turned to face her as she looked downward. Her otherworldly aura was beatific.

With the tips of her index finger and thumb at the base of her nose between her closed eyes, Susan said, "Joe," again.

Joe slowly turned away for a moment and then turned back, and Susan was looking at him. She looked angelic.

"Joe, you're so full of shit, your eyes are brown."

Joe was impressed and nodded. "Nice talk for a lady."

Joe took a sip of his beer, tasting the lime wedge and savoring it. "I would have also accepted 'Joe, you're so full of shit, your breath smells like a used diaper.' But yours is good, too."

Susan nodded and said, "Because it's far superior."

Joe took another sip and set the bottle down on the little table that separated their beach chairs. "Jury's still out on that one. But, no, I'm absolutely correct about the other thing."

Susan shook her head again and said, "Joe, there's no way *The Wizard of Oz* is a political satire."

With a closed-lip smile, Joe said, "Yes, it is, Susan."

"How? Explain it to me, Professor Bullshit."

"I can't remember all the examples, but—"

"But you're still an expert, huh?"

With an authoritative look you would give a bratty child, Joe said, "If you want to learn this, I have to be able to speak. Will you listen?"

Susan put up her hands in an acquiescing fashion but in no way was admitting defeat. "Fine."

"As I was saying before I was so rudely interrupted with such insufferable insolence, *The Wizard of Oz* was filled with symbols and metaphors that were advocating the political platform of the late-nineteenth-century Populist Party—"

"Well, I am oh so very eager to hear those references."

"Thank you. You were polite, but you interrupted again."

"No, I did not!"

"And again."

"There was a lull in the statement. I was adding to the conversation."

Joe shook his head. "If I introduce what I'm gonna talk about, wouldn't you think the lecture would continue?"

"Joe," Susan said, and Joe looked away. The waves were now quiet. They weren't breaking as loudly or as frequently.

"Tide must be low," he said.

"Joe—"

He looked at Susan.

"Joe, please come back to me."

"Right." Joe tried to take a sip, but the bottle was empty, and he looked around and saw no one to procure another round. "Anyway, the Populist Party was pro farmer. The farmers at the time were growing too much wheat, and the prices were very low, and they weren't getting enough money—you know, supply and demand—and they were pissed. I think Jefferson wanted America to be a farming nation, but by the 1890s, or whenever, the supply was plentiful and the demand lowered. Anyway, the Populists wanted the dollar to be backed by gold and silver, the bimetallic standard."

Susan raised her hand.

"Mrs. Duran?" Joe said.

"Didn't Nixon do something about that?"

Joe nodded. "We'll get to that. Anyway, the story was filled with references. The movie changed some things from the book, but the themes are evident. 'Follow the yellow brick road' is a reference to gold. Where were they trying to get to? The Emerald City. Emerald is green, which represents cash. Who were they trying to meet? The Great and Powerful Oz. Oz is an abbreviation for ounce, which gold and silver are measured in."

Joe looked around and still could not find anyone to procure another round.

"Joe," Susan said.

Joe continued without looking at Susan this time because he would have been wonderfully distracted, and he had to win this debate.

"The Scarecrow had no brain. The Scarecrow represented the farmers who grew too much wheat and drove down the prices. Not too smart." Joe then sang "If I Only Had a Brain" and then continued. "The Tin Man had no heart. This represented automation, technology, the workforce being replaced by mechanization, the decrease in the dependence on man to manufacture products—the decrease of the human element in production caused men to lose their jobs, which was mean and…heartless."

Susan asked, "What did the Cowardly Lion represent?"

"Not what, but whom. The cowardly lion represented a politician: William Byron…William Jennings… William Bryan…William Jennings Bryan—that's it. He was a great orator and spoke with a loud booming voice, and he solemnly pledged to deliver the party's goals, blah blah blah. He ended up kind of abandoning his positions after the economy improved, which it will always do. So Populists accused him of chickening out, deemed him a coward." Joe looked around again. "Where's that damn waiter?"

Joe saw no one and continued with the lecture. "The flying monkeys represented Asians, and the poppy field—opium. The munchkins represented the working man, the factory worker, the farmer. They were of the 'Lollipop Guild'—suckers. That's where the insult came from. The Wicked Witch was from the East, which represented overpopulation, pollution, big cities with big-city problems, corporations. The wealthy tyrants lived on the East Coast and ran steel mills, factories benefiting from the cruel harm and disfigurement of young kids who should have been in school while millionaires were buying mansions as summer homes. Technology, crime, poor treatment of your fellow man just for profit—that was back East. The house fell on the other witch, which was a metaphor for foreclosures. Farmers lost their homes and farms."

"What about Dorothy's ruby slippers? Blood of the workers? Their blood will take you home? Doesn't that go against their platform?"

"Yes, but in the book, apparently—I've never read it—the slippers were silver. And they would take you home. Another reference to a bimetallic standard.

Silver slippers on the yellow brick road will take to the Emerald City. Silver, gold, and cash."

"Didn't someone kill himself and you can see it, but it was just an urban legend. Just a bird or something?"

"There are two or three versions of the film. In the most recent one, or ones, obviously a bird is quite visible and spreading its wings. In the earlier color version—I haven't seen a black-and-white version—there is clearly a corpse swinging from a noose in the background. You compare the two, and the bird in the later versions is conveniently located where the corpse swung."

"Why, Joe? Why?"

"Uh." Joe was startled. "I don't know. Maybe his wife kept interrupting."

"Joe! Joe!"

"What, Susan? I'm here, hon." But she wasn't there anymore. Joe looked around, and the beach wasn't there anymore. There was nothing.

"Joe!"

"Susan?"

"Joe, you goddamned son of a bitch!"

Joe's eyes opened. Joe saw weird things and felt a lot of pain. He felt like he was being choked. Something was in his mouth, and he tried to cough it up. Hands, lots of hands, and voices prevented that and told him not to.

Joe was groggy and in pain. People were asking him questions, and he tried to answer them but could not speak, so he just nodded. He heard a beep. It was…a medical beep. It was a heart monitor's beep. Christ, it was his heart that was being monitored!

I'm in a hospital? Am I hurt? Was I shot? Wait—I'm alive. That's good. Where's Susan? Did I have a health emergency? What happened? I guess I was dreaming. I thought I was at a beach. Where's Susan? I was going to call someone. Susan? Where am I?

His mind was in a daze. He saw strangers above him. He heard a lot of chatter. Loud talking. A series of adamant conversations were slowly calming down. Orders were being barked. Joe heard his name.

"Joe?"

He nodded.

"Joe, can you hear me OK?"

Joe nodded again.

"OK, Joe, you're all right now. There are tubes in your mouth. Do not reach for them, OK? I know they're uncomfortable, but leave them in."

Joe nodded.

"You're in the hospital, Joe. You understand?"

There was a buzz of activity as people continued to accomplish tasks. The first voice became distant but not too far. Someone spoke to him, but now it was a different voice, a man's voice, obviously from back East.

"Joe, I need you to listen to me, OK? I'm Doctor Spadaccini. You had a heart attack earlier. Do you understand me?"

Joe cried. Tears welled up, and they were shed and ran down the sides of his face.

"You're going to be OK, boss. You suffered a cardiac arrest, but I have confidence that you can make a full recovery. You're gonna be here for a while, and you'll have to make some changes and adjustments, but I have confidence you can live a long life."

Joe continued to cry.

"Joe, we checked and your coworkers called your sons, and I'm told by your Captain Tertel that they'll be here by tonight. They're both away at school?"

This was a good tactic the doctor was utilizing. Keeping Joe involved in the conversation made him focus as they looked to him for confirmation on details. It worked. Joe nodded and tried to remain calm.

"If your condition improves, I'll make sure your sons visit, but only if you're up for it. Your coworkers will have to wait till tomorrow for visits, OK? They're all out there pulling for you. It's a good crew, real good."

Joe nodded and cried and tried to ask a question, but he could not speak with the tubes down his throat. He was getting frustrated, frustrated on top of being scared. A lot was going on, and it was a lot to take in. It was life altering, but at least he still had a life that could be altered. He was overwhelmed, but the doctor now had a little smirk on his face.

"Now, Joe, I needed help. I needed a…a second opinion, if you will. So I asked a colleague of mine.

She's a doctor. Trust me. I saw an ID. She's going to oversee your recovery and report your progress, so we can make sure you're fit to retire, someplace warm, right?"

Doctor Spadaccini looked away and was referring to someone near. Joe, unfortunately, did not have the strength to raise his head. Then he heard high heels walk toward him and felt a familiar and yet new grasp on his hand.

Joe did have some strength to squeeze back. A vision of angelic beauty that made Joe want to live like no other force could appeared over him. He cried again.

"Yes," his beautiful Susan said. "Yes, we were thinking someplace warm, right, Joe?"

Joe cried and nodded.

CHAPTER FIFTY-ONE

Deeds hung up and put the phone back in his drawer. Rather, he tried to put the phone back into the drawer but had forgotten that he'd closed it. Deeds had very carefully put his hand over where the open nightstand drawer should have been and dropped the phone to the floor.

Deeds got up, picked up the phone, put it on top of the nightstand, and went to the bathroom. He walked into the darkened bathroom and closed the door but not the whole way. With his arm outside the door, he felt for the hall light and turned it on. The bathroom light would have made him squint.

Deeds took a long, first-of-the-day, postslumber piss, even though he'd only been asleep for a few hours. He dribbled the last few drops out and flushed.

He ran water over his hands and wet his face a little. He couldn't see himself in the mirror too well.

He took the hand towel and dried his hands and face off. He folded it neatly in the dark but did not return it to the ring. He just set it on the counter.

Deeds leaned out and turned off the hall light as he walked into his living room. The night was just giving way to a dark purple dawn as he looked out the patio glass door to the Devil Mountains due north.

A high-pressure front had come through. This day would be colder than any other recent day. The freezing, crisp, boreal air would purify everything.

The frost and snow would be white, a pristine white. The sky would be a gorgeous and pure darkened blue. Everything would look dreamy. It would look like a living painting. The colors would make every detail a visual gift.

This day should be commemorated. The beauty that would be achieved today should be remembered. These days were rare. Once in a while, a beautiful day like this would occur, and it demanded, from those who were worthy to see it, acknowledgment. It was cold, enthralling, and beautiful.

Deeds turned the heat up, went into the bedroom, and got the comforter from the bed. He threw it on the couch and then fully opened the patio sliding-glass-door blinds, exposing the brilliant, frozen, and crystallized scene outside his window.

He arranged the comforter and wrapped himself up as the heat kicked in. He lay there and viewed the outside world. He saw no one. He heard no one. He was aware of no one.

Light was emerging. A new day was emerging. Deeds felt the dawn. Deeds felt a new beginning. A comforting warmth enshrouded him, and with that comfort he drifted off to the best sleep he had had in a long time.

Sometime later, after a warming sleep provided a vivid dream, Deeds awoke and cried for a while. It was a release of all the emotions he'd felt recently and throughout his whole life.

When the last tear was shed, he lay there in the warmth and reflected on the dream he'd just had. After a while, Deeds got up and went into the bathroom. He looked at himself in the mirror. The details of this dream had not faded as they usually did. Deeds knew what he had to do.

Deeds cleaned up and got dressed. He made a calorically substantial breakfast and brewed coffee. The leftover coffee, he would save for later tonight after dinner.

Deeds grabbed his pocket knife and his large now sheathed fixed serrated-blade survival knife, keys, wallet, hat, and gloves because he knew it was cold out.

Without looking, Deeds knew the sky was a perfect dark blue, the ground was a pristine white, and the horizon was gray, and hopefully fortune would be favorable and allow for crimson.

CHAPTER FIFTY-TWO

"Don't worry; it's my brother's place, and, well, he's out of town for, you know, a year or so. The lawyer said it might be six or seven months, though."

The Elf walked in with his old military-surplus duffel bag but did not set it on the ground. "Ah. Got it." *Sounded like possession.*

The small apartment looked like it had been a nice place at one point. Lots of pictures, lots of colorful things, older yet restored funky pieces of furniture. Yet in the course of her brother's incarceration, she'd apparently fallen off the wagon, started hooking and partying again, and let the once-nice apartment belonging to her brother go to shit.

It smelled of cat piss, cigarette and pot smoke, and rotten food. There was litter all over the place. It was as if she went out of her way to not throw anything in a garbage receptacle. *What is it with the people I know letting their places go to hell? Just a night.*

"Nice place," the Elf remarked.

"Thanks," she said as she walked back to a bedroom.

The Elf, while still holding his bag, moved some empty fast-food bags from the small couch to the coffee table. He put his bag down and sat next to it.

Even though he knew the answer, he wanted a segue for his next course of action. "Hey, uh, what do you do, you know, to pay for your rent while your brother is gone?" The Elf could see into the bedroom as she took her shirt off and put, presumably, one of her brother's T-shirts on.

"My brother set up an account through his lawyer, or whatever, and rent is being paid for six months. That's all he had after all the fees and shit."

The Elf asked, "What if he's inside longer than six months? What'll you do then?" *Please take the bait.*

"Whatever it takes. Why?"

That was precisely what the Elf wanted to hear. "Well, I got some shit. Sell it. Use it. Whatever. It's yours."

"Oh yeah?" she asked as she walked out of the bedroom in a big shirt and an oversized pair of sweat pants while putting her hair into a ponytail. "Let's see it."

With that obvious invitation, the Elf stood up, threw a baggie on the coffee table, undid his zipper, and showed his erection to her. For some reason she turned away and put her hand to her mouth and made a strange sound.

"You OK?" the Elf asked.

"Yeah," she stammered. "I, uh, thought, I had to, uh, I thought I had to sneeze or something."

She ended up going to bed after he came in her mouth a few minutes later. When the Elf came, he accidentally farted a little but was convinced she did not hear it. She did stand up, run to the bathroom, and vomit though, when he finished.

He assumed she could not handle all of him (many girls told him how big he was when they had sex with him when they were partying), and her gag reflex kicked in, at the end.

He heard the toilet flush and heard the electric toothbrush massage her oral features for a few minutes. *Hmm, her dentist must be intimidating.*

He heard a cabinet door open, something get unscrewed, and a liquid get swished around in her mouth, gargled, and then spit into the toilet, which was flushed again. She exited the bathroom and without looking at him went into the bedroom and turned the light off. *Guess I wore her out.*

He had not seen whatever her name was in a while. He knew she was at least eighteen but did not know too much else about her. The Elf had heard she was in court-ordered rehab and was basically going from party girl to county to parole to party girl—the same

Old Falls song and the same Old Falls dance. It was interesting that she did not have kids though.

"Hey, babe?" There was no response. "Babe? Can I light a cigarette inside?" Silence. "Fuck it." The Elf lit up. As he lay there smoking a cigarette, he flicked his ashes in a can he found on the coffee table and turned upright.

He had found and was cuddled underneath a cathair infested blanket, but he had not yet seen a cat. He smelled the cat's litter but did not see a cat. The loveseat was comfortable. If her brother had his sentence lengthened, no doubt she would let his place rot as she did whatever it took to make rent.

Regarding his current situation, the Elf had every right to freak out, but he felt confident there was nothing tying him to Amanda. He was also confident he could take off and successfully disappear forever.

The idea of permanently walking away from Old Falls was appealing. The thought of beginning a new life, an honest life, was tantalizing as he crushed out his cigarette. A weight was lifting from his shoulders. He just had to leave town and start fresh somewhere. Maybe he'd borrow or just take money from the chick or just take what he could find in this apartment and use it for a bus ticket. Or he might just hitchhike.

He needed to leave, and he was going to. He smiled and nodded. "You're gonna make it, bro," he said to no one in the dirty apartment. He heard snoring from the girl and decided to close his eyes and try to sleep.

The apartment was warm, the couch was comfortable, he'd received a blow job, and he was going to survive this whole ordeal. With these optimistic thoughts, the Elf drifted off to sleep.

He woke up a few hours later as it started to become lighter out. The calm and optimism he'd felt as he'd gone to sleep was still with him, but now he needed to move and get the hell out of the area, pronto! *Boom, you're a ghost!*

The Elf slept in the clothes that were now his traveling outfit. He put on his shoes and went to the bathroom to splash some water on his face. After he dried himself off on the shower curtain, he went into the bedroom to tell the chick he was leaving and ask for some money only to find whatever her name was faceup, mouth open, snoring, and in the oversized sweat pants that were now down to her midthighs. She wore no panties.

Seeing all the red and whitehead bumps a dull razor had created did not stop the Elf from becoming hard. He bent down and smelled her crotch, and he shuddered with delight.

He looked around, as if he was going to see someone, and then used his middle finger to play with her. She remained dry, so he licked his finger and played with her a few more moments before entering her. He felt some moisture and thought she was getting horny when he viewed the color of the residue. *Well, at least she's not pregnant.*

He wiped the finger on the sheets and then gently lifted up the big T-shirt to see some nice, moderately sized breasts. He pulled the shirt back down.

"Babe, I gotta split. Thanks again," said the Elf, but she did not move. "Babe?" he said in a raised voice. She stirred a couple of times. An idea occurred to the Elf. *You know, we never agreed on just one blow job.* The Elf gazed upon this young lady. *Do it!*

The Elf unzipped his pants, took out his penis, and started to rub it on her face and near her mouth. There was no reaction. With her mouth still open, he simply dipped his member in there. It felt great. He took it out of her mouth and then quickly took his clothes off.

Naked, except for his socks, he placed his erection back in her open mouth. Her tongue started to move a little, and before he could say, "Yeah, baby," she made a raspberry sound with her mouth and swatted at the invading foreign object.

Luckily for the Elf, she missed his testicles, but the surprise slap hurt and startled him nonetheless. The Elf lost his temper very quickly even though he knew it wasn't personal, and, basically, out of reflex, he open-palm slapped her across the face and yelled, "What the fuck, bitch!" He then grabbed her hair and flipped her over.

The young lady said, "I'm sorry. I'm sorry. Don't hurt me. I didn't know what was going on."

The Elf, feeling empowered, tightened his grip, removed her sweat pants, stared at her ass, and said, "I'm not gonna hurt you, but you owe me. OK? That slap was bullshit. We cool, but can I get some?"

The Elf didn't wait for an answer as he entered her. She was still not too wet, other than the beginning of her "time" at first, but that did change. The young lady acted like she enjoyed it, but lucky for her it was over pretty quickly.

The Elf started to make a high-pitched whisper-squeal sound, and he pulled out and let loose a small-to-moderate sized ejaculation that covered half of her small badly done Tinker Bell tattoo. "Oh shit, baby! Tinker Bell is covered! Ha-ha!"

The young lady exaggerated a pleasurable moan and said, "I can feel it all over, baby."

The Elf drained his remaining semen and spread it on her buttocks and lower back. He then felt a recharge of vigor and entered her again.

To his surprise the Elf was able to maintain his erection and kept going. The Elf was amazed with himself. This had never happened before, and he was completely shocked and surprised.

The young lady asked in a flat tone bereft of thrill or excitement, "Oh, you're going again? Will you be done soon? I can't wait to feel all the cum"—she yawned—"all over me, baby."

The Elf wasn't paying attention as he started to make the same but intensified high-pitched whisper-squeal again.

This time the Elf felt like he'd earned something special, and since she was on her period, he reasoned that she could not get pregnant. The Elf came inside her, and it felt glorious for him.

The warm captivating sensation, the thrill of the second time, the complete release inside her was all magical. The Elf felt invincible. Finally, something wonderful happened to him, and why shouldn't it?

"Oh my God," the Elf breathlessly said as he pulled out and then collapsed face first onto her backside in exhaustion. *Shit, dude, why didn't you wipe up your load?*

With a warm, smelly, and slimy substance on his face, the Elf grabbed a pillow and, as best he could, wiped his face. *Do it quickly, so she doesn't find out.*

"Now you know how we feel."

The Elf could picture her smiling. "Shut the fuck up!"

"Don't worry," she retorted. "It's good for your skin."

The Elf with as much strength as he could muster spanked her right buttock. The Elf realized how tough she was because she giggled.

"Hey," she stated, "quit that shit. We can't go a third time. You know, the odds and all."

Completely spent, the Elf asked, "What odds?"

The young lady flipped over. The lighting in the room was more present than last night's lighting as she was indeed a butter face.

She had a nice body, but her face was a gravelly mess. She had a missing tooth too, and the rest were badly discolored. There was a booger in her left nostril, and she had a unibrow and a noticeable mustache.

The Elf's eyes widened, and he was embarrassed as he looked around the room again but was relieved as no one else was there to witness the glory of what happened but the shame of whom it happened with.

"The odds of catching."

Getting annoyed at all the talking without answering, the Elf angrily asked, "Catching what?"

"Well," she began, "I got the bug, you know."

Hoping she was referring to the flu, the Elf asked, "What bug?"

She looked at him like he was stupid. "I got the HIV."

The Elf did not move. He did not breathe. He was in a daze from all the recent events—the murders, the fear, the panic, the scrounging, the escaping, the blow job, the lack of sleep, the cuming twice, the inadvertent facial—and now he was questioning his hearing and her IQ. The Elf remained as a statue, gaze affixed to her.

The two intimate strangers held their eye contact, one of them not knowing the monstrous weight their statement held as the other received a death sentence. Hollow eyes were staring blindly.

The young lady got off the bed and stretched. Her stomach rumbled. "Whoa," she said and placed a hand above her belly button. "I gotta take a shit."

The bathroom had no fan, and apparently she was not familiar with the concept of the "courtesy flush." As he heard her waste hit the water, the Elf began to breathe and take in the gravity of the situation. *Did I fucking hear her right? No. No way. This bitch has no fucking idea what she just said.*

The Elf picked up his traveling outfit and dressed himself rather quickly as he was eager to find out some information.

The Elf had his bag packed and placed by the door, so he'd be ready to leave quickly. As she was still on the toilet, he walked over to the door and knocked twice.

"Hey," he said causally.

She answered like she was used to this type of conversation but wanted him to make it quick. "Yeah?"

"You said we couldn't go a third time. The odds, right?"

"Yeah, the odds."

Wishing she saw where he was going—rather, trying to get to—he asked, "The odds of what?" The toilet flushed, and he had to wait a moment before it was quiet to ask again. "The odds of what?"

"The odds of catching."

Clenching his fists, he said, "The odds of catching what?"

Now she was annoyed. "The bug."

"The bug?"

"Yeah, the bug. Can you give me a minute? Fuck."

"No, I fucking can't. The bug. What fucking bug?"

She made a disgust-based exhalation noise. "Hhhh. Hang on."

The toilet flushed again. The Elf unclenched his fist and slapped the wall next to the door, startling her.

"Hey! What the fuck was that?"

With a stern tone that dictated he meant business, he said, "What fucking bug? Answer me, now!"

"What do you mean 'what fucking bug'?"

"You're pissing me off, bitch! What fucking bug? Answer the goddamned question! Now!"

"I've answered you like a hundred times. Fuck. The bug. I have the bug, asshole."

The Elf made a fist, punched the fragile door, and yelled, "What fucking bug, bitch?" He punched the door again.

"Watch the door," she said. "My brother will kick your ass."

"What fucking bug? Say it! Fucking say it!"

"Jesus Christ, you fucking asshole, I have the HIV. What the fuck is your problem?"

The Elf did not punch anything. He stood still. "You gave me AIDS."

"No," she stated defiantly. "I don't have AIDS, you idiot. I have HIV, which is not AIDS. Different bugs."

The Elf realized that you can't receive a blow job and have sex twice, once cuming inside her, with an HIV-positive girl and not get it.

All the shit that he'd gone through yesterday, all the shit he'd gone through in his life, all the pain he'd caused, all the pain he'd received, the fact that he was going to turn it around and start a new life—it was all over this morning. He was dead.

"You did it. You finally did it."

"Did what?" she asked.

The Elf answered, "You killed me. You fucking killed me."

"No, I didn't."

She flushed again. After a few moments, she continued. "People with HIV can live for years and years. Normal years."

"That's true." It was as if he was having a friendly discussion. "But you will die from AIDS eventually."

"Oh my God, I have HIV. Not AIDS, goddamn it!"

The Elf took in a deep breath. "HIV leads to AIDS, for which there is no cure. If you're"—the Elf chuckled—"if we're lucky, we'll have five, ten years."

"Then we'll do chemo or something."

"That's for cancer, sweetheart."

"Wait." She was confused. "You have the HIV, too?"

The anger returned. "Yes! Are you fucking kidding me? We just fucked twice. You fucking blew me last night. No fucking rubbers. I fucking got it now. You fucking gave it to me. If I'm real lucky, I have ten fucking years left. Thanks a fucking lot!"

"For real? I thought it was like getting pregnant. Doesn't always happen, but you have to be lucky with the timing."

"No. No, you fucking idiot. Not at all. You just killed me." With a sliver of hope, wishing upon everything that was optimistic, he asked one last question, "How do you know you got it? Did a doctor do a blood test?"

"Yeah. I almost OD'd the other night. It was the ER nurse. It was sooo late. They did a blood test to see what drugs I was on. I was pretty high. They told me I had HIV, or whatever."

"They didn't tell you about not having sex, sharing needles, or getting pregnant 'cause you can pass it to the baby? They didn't go over all that shit?"

"No, some preppie couple got jumped or something, and they had to take care of them. I just grabbed my shit, didn't pay, and came back here and crashed... Wait." She was now starting to comprehend her health emergency. "I can pass it to people?"

"Yes."

"Through sex?"

"Yes."

"Anal? Pussy? Going down?"

"Yes."

"My blood is...is...fucked?"

"Yes."

"If I have a baby, it'll have it, too?"

"Yes."

"I have ten years to live?"

"If you're lucky. Maybe more, probably less."

The Elf heard crying. She was sobbing. He didn't think anyone could be this ignorant on one of the most newsworthy ongoing events of the last few decades, but she was. The ignorant think they are immortal. She was now realizing that she was indeed not.

The Elf said nothing. Her hell was more painful than any he could create. Vengeance was hollow. It filled nothing. His vengeance had caused more problems than it had solved. Fate, karma, or life had a way of making him suffer for the shit he did.

The Elf was defeated and he turned around and went into the bedroom of the incarcerated brother and looked through the dresser and the closet. The Elf found about a hundred bucks in cash and took it. He also grabbed a few shirts, some socks, some boxers, two sweatshirts, and a cold-weather jacket.

On the nightstand, he found a very nice watch. He picked it up and looked at it. He thought about taking it to sell or just to have. On the back was an inscription. It read, "Happy Birthday, Mom and Pop."

The Elf decided to do this guy a favor. He opened the closet and placed the watch in a formal shoe. This was a very nice watch, and for the next special occasion, where he would wear the watch and need some formal shoes, he would find it. Otherwise, some other asshole, in his absence, would take it. Hopefully, her brother would celebrate an early release for good behavior.

The Elf packed the items in his old military-surplus duffel bag. The bag was now a lot heavier. He saw the drugs he'd thrown on the coffee table, picked them up, and put them into his pocket. Maybe he could trade them for a ride to somewhere. He still needed to leave Engel Falls, but the new life he would start would not be a long one.

The Elf went to a front-facing window, looked outside, and saw no one. He saw a cold, desolate, lonely world frozen in time. He decided he would just hitchhike to wherever. He opened the door to a bone-chilling, crisp winter morning.

It was clear, and the day was new. The sun was shining, and the sky was a perfect blue. "Nice day today." The Elf breathed in two very deep and slow breaths and exhaled as his vapor danced in front of him. "Good-bye," he said to no one in particular and walked into the new day.

CHAPTER FIFTY-THREE

There were few colors. It was as if the surroundings were drained of all secondary shades, which focused the attention on the colors that were present and stood out with vivid, majestic beauty. Deeds did not want to wake up.

There was a pure white, a forlorn and unknowing gray, a vibrant dark blue, and a crimson. The sky was a perfect dark blue. The ground was pristine white. The distant horizon was gray. And Deeds dripped crimson.

Deeds was naked, and his hands were on his left side. This was where the wound was, yet he did not dare look at it, out of fear. He was walking on white ground heading toward the horizon. He knew that was where he had to go.

Deeds did not look behind him. He was sure a blood trail was soiling the pristine white, and he felt guilty for having hurt its purity.

There was no sound. There was an echoing reverberation of nothing. The silence was amplified as if in a cave. Deeds walked on. Moments later two feral dogs appeared. They looked bloodthirsty, yet Deeds did not fear the majestic beasts.

Deeds wanted to kneel and display his hand for them to sniff, so they could know he was a friend and not a foe, but alas, he could not do it. He had to keep on the path and move forward, even though he was gravely injured. Deeds was traveling to a desired yet unknown destination.

There was nothing visible except for the colors. All of a sudden, the crimson was not present anymore. An instinct told him there was no more blood being shed. Deeds moved his hands to expose unwounded flesh, which he now viewed without hesitation.

Deeds looked and spanned the entire area around him. There was no more crimson soiling the pristine-white ground. The dogs were now in the distance, seated. They watched him. They did not move toward Deeds. They were just there, viewing Deeds from afar.

Deeds waved to the two dogs. He tried to thank them but was unable to create speech. He was not sure if the two dogs, who must have helped him with the bloodied wound, would ever know how grateful he was to them for healing him and allowing him to keep heading toward his destination.

Their aid was a wonderful gift. He was now able to move forward. Deeds would praise the creatures for saving him and allowing him to carry on toward the horizon, where he would somehow restore the balance of what was owed.

This would all happen somewhere beyond the horizon. That was where Deeds was headed: to the horizon. Deeds was on a path, and the path of Deeds was a struggle.

The End

EPILOGUE

Jess did not date for a very long time after she dumped Erik on the night she shared an eternity with Deeds. Erik had walked up to Jess's apartment. Jess was still tingling and ridiculously wet, and without preamble she simply stated to Erik, "I'm done wasting my time." She turned around, went inside her place, shut the door, locked it, turned out the lights, took off her clothes, and dropped them sporadically on the way to her bedroom.

Erik was loud, vulgar, and abrasive. She barely heard the racket as she put on one of her favorite CDs and began to rub herself. Jess climaxed as she lay naked on top of her covers. During the break she noticed that it had gotten quiet. She did not miss Erik. She missed Shane.

Moments later Jess heard the loud rumble of the exiting silver Corvette and was proud she did not have to hear that sound anymore. In a way it was a tolling bell informing her that indecision, fear of letting go, and bad decisions, in this capacity, were done.

For hours that night, she pleasured herself as the remaining sensual, life-altering, sexually charged orgasmic love made her shudder and parts of her body throb like never before.

Until she was far beyond exhaustion, she did not want to waste a single bit of the powerful energy that Shane had provided for her. If she was a betting woman, she'd place everything on the odds that Shane heard her from his apartment. She was loud.

The next morning, she awoke and was still in a daze from the whole experience. There was no regret as she focused on the positive of what she had been privy to. Jess was happy.

Jess did not hear from Erik for a while. Then the texts and phone calls and e-mails were sent and made but to no avail.

There was no way Erik could ever come close to providing what Deeds had. Jess thought about searching for someone who could maybe make the attempt and with luck come close. Yet at the same time, maybe it would be better to just live her life and not force herself into a situation she would later regret. And besides, she did not think Shane could be bested. *No one, Shane. No one will ever come close.*

With that chapter closed, Jess saw clearer and wondered why it took so long to get rid of Erik. Jess had pretended to but could never honestly forgive him for sleeping with a stripper at his old fraternity brother's bachelor party. Erik's best friend had ratted him out and then subsequently said to her, "I'm here for you…if you ever want to talk about your guy problems."

"Fuck off," she had said to Erik's scummy former best friend as she went back with Erik, not believing what the rat claimed. Jess had replied with the same phrase when Erik's scummy former best friend recently called her after word got around. "Christ, you're all the same, you know that? Fuck off!"

Jess wondered and was amazed at how oblivious and how much in denial she had been. Those days were gone. Her Shane had showed her the way.

She decided to reestablish closeness with her sister—until she found out that Sarah had tried to seduce the mutually sought-after Shane.

They discussed what had occurred with full disclosure, and that caused uneasiness and anger; yet they both realized it was foolish because they both would not end up being with Shane Deeds.

The whole potentially bad situation ended with no jealousy, and they grew closer because of it, often joking that they were close to being "Eskimo sisters."

This closeness became the crucial support they both needed, as they were the only meaningful family they had left after they buried their loving stepdad, Bill McKenna, who passed away from a heart attack.

When the memorial service and the reception had finished, Jess and Sarah took a cab back to Jess's apartment, opened a bottle of wine, and sat on the couch. For a few hours, they sipped wine, discussed fond memories of their beloved stepfather, and cried and laughed at the man who'd taken them in as his own. The tragedy had brought them even closer. Even after the "Shane incident," which they openly talked about without jealousy and in graphic detail of what they would have done with him, they were close, and this just cemented their sisterly bond.

While remembering their stepdad, they both heard someone walk down the hall toward Jess's apartment. Neither one of them particularly wanted company, yet they were curious.

The steps then ceased for just a moment near Jess's front door. They started again, and the sound ended. When the steps were not heard anymore, both Jess and Sarah looked at each other with confused expressions adorning their lovely faces.

Jess and Sarah set their wine glasses down, stood up, and eagerly walked to the door. Jess looked through the peephole and saw nothing. She cautiously opened the door with Sarah behind her.

Sarah saw no one, and Jess acknowledged no one as she stood at her opened door.

"What is it, Jess?" Sarah asked as she came to her sister's side.

They both looked down at what was on Jess's doorstep: two lovely bouquets of thirteen red roses.

I would like to thank my parents for their support and encouragement, my dad having led by example: thank you for all the assistance. I would like to thank Grandpa Wayne for his support as well. I'd like to thank Dave, Kevin, Jeff, and Teo for their invaluable critiquing as well as the editors at CreateSpace. I would also like to thank Teo for all his business guidance and research. Thank you all for your time and effort! And last but not remotely least, I'd like to thank my wife, Chelsea, for her love, support, patience, trust, encouragement, optimism, caring, and devotion.

Jason Worrell

ABOUT THE AUTHOR

Jason Worrell earned his BS in kinesiology. He enjoys lifting weights, playing rhythm guitar, and watching hockey. Worrell and his wife live in San Francisco.